A Mother's Secret

Dilly Court

A Mother's Secret

arrow books

Published by Arrow Books 2010

2 4 6 8 10 9 7 5 3 1

Copyright © Dilly Court 2010

First published in Great Britain in 2010 by
Arrow Books
Random House, 20 Vauxhall Bridge Road,
London SW1V 2SA

www.rbooks.co.uk

Addresses for companies within The Random House Group Limited can be found at:
www.randomhouse.co.uk/offices.htm

The Random House Group Limited Reg. No. 954009

A CIP catalogue record for this book
is available from the British Library

ISBN 9780099538820

The Random House Group Limited supports The Forest Stewardship
Council (FSC), the leading international forest certification organisation. All our
titles that are printed on Greenpeace approved FSC certified paper carry the FSC logo.
Our paper procurement policy can be found at
www.rbooks.co.uk/environment

Mixed Sources
Product group from well-managed
forests and other controlled sources
www.fsc.org Cert no. TT-COC-2139
© 1996 Forest Stewardship Council
FSC

Types   ed,

Printed   25 8TD

In fond memory of Ollie, who did more than most in the short time he had.

Private Oliver Rupert Ellwood,
1st Battalion the Parachute Regiment
1978–2001

Chapter One

Cripplegate, London, 1863

The dense, evil-smelling London particular had all but drowned the city in a greenish yellow morass of fog and smoke. Each breath she took was difficult and painful as the woman walked on, clutching the warm bundle of life in her arms. The baby whimpered but did not cry. She hugged the child closer to her breast as a drunken man lurched out of the gloom, almost knocking her down as he barged past. 'Excuse me, mister. I'm looking for Three Herring Court.'

'Bah.' The man staggered crabwise but was enveloped by the pea-souper before he had gone more than a few feet. The woman, a maidservant more used to the heat and dust of India than the cold and damp of an English winter, shivered and wrapped her shawl more closely around the babe in her arms. The clock in the tower of St Giles, Cripplegate, struck six sonorous chimes, making her turn with a start. The carriage belonging to her mistress had dropped her close to this spot a good half an hour ago, and she realised with a groan that she must have been walking in circles ever since. The coachman had made it clear that he considered it beneath him to visit this impoverished part of the city. He had told her in no uncertain terms that Three Herring Court was inaccessible except by foot, and even then it was approached down a flight of steps.

Holding out her hand she sighed with relief as her fingers came in contact with a low stone wall. She paused for a moment, making a vain attempt to get her bearings. She had been heading north, past the debtors' prison, but the compass points meant nothing to her now and the high prison walls were hidden behind a curtain of fog. She cocked her head on one side, listening for sounds of life, but there were none. She and the baby might as well have been the last living souls on earth for all the company they had on this bleak night. The baby began to whimper in earnest. It was well past the time when at home she would have been fed on bread soaked in warm milk and sweetened with a dusting of sugar.

'Hush, little one, Mahdu will look after you.' Hitching the baby over her shoulder, she continued on her way, her slim fingers feeling the cold slimy stones until they came to a pillar and then there was nothing but a void. Walking like a blind woman with her free hand outstretched, she almost fell over a small body slumped on the pavement. A startled cry was wrenched from her lips as she stopped, thinking she had come across a corpse, which was not unusual in this part of London on a bitterly cold winter's night, but the bundle of rags moved and unfolded its skinny limbs. When the child stood up he reached no higher than her waist.

'Look out, you,' he grumbled. 'You nearly trod on me, you stupid cow.'

'I'm sorry,' Mahdu said, breathlessly. 'I couldn't

see you in this fog. Anyway you should be at home with your family, not lying about on the pavement for anyone to fall over.'

'Foreign ain't yer?' The boy peered up into her face. 'Is that your nipper?'

'I'm trying to find Three Herring Court,' Mahdu said, ignoring his impudent question. 'There's a penny for you if you can lead me there.'

The boy eyed her curiously. She wasn't from round these parts, it was clear. It was too dark to make out her features or the colour of her skin, but her voice was soft and gentle. 'Let's see the colour of yer money then, missis.' He held out his hand, but the woman was obviously wise to the ways of street urchins and she took a penny from her purse, holding it high above his head. He decided against snatching it from her as there was a copper on the beat somewhere in the vicinity and a scream from the old girl would bring him running. 'All right then, missis. Follow me. I can find me way easy as pie.'

'What's your name, boy?' Mahdu had to quicken her pace in order to keep up with him. She did not particularly care for the little creature, and the smell emanating from his scrawny body made her want to retch, but she was curious as to why a boy of seven or eight might be out alone on such a terrible night.

'Nosey bugger ain't yer? Me name's Bailey and I was just resting me body when you come along and trod on me.'

She followed him in silence and to her relief, the baby had stopped crying and had fallen asleep on her

3

shoulder. She would miss the little girl more than she was prepared to admit even to herself. From the moment of her birth, the infant had clasped Mahdu's heart in her tiny hands. Each stage in the baby's development had seemed like a miracle from her first smile to the time when she murmured her first word. It might have been mama, but it could easily have been an attempt to say Mahdu. Now they were to be parted, possibly forever. Mahdu's throat constricted as she faced the fact that she had been trying to ignore ever since they left India. Born out of wedlock with the added stigma of mixed race parentage, there had never been a future for baby Cassandra Phillips. Mahdu knew that she would always feel guilty for aiding and abetting her young mistress in her love affair with the handsome Anglo-Indian officer in her father's regiment. Colonel Phillips would have sent his daughter home on the first ship bound for England had he discovered their liaison earlier, but by the end of that summer which the white women spent in Simla in order to escape the heat in Delhi, it was already too late. Mahdu paused to catch her breath. 'Stop a minute, boy. I can't go as fast as you. I need to rest for a moment.'

'It'll cost yer then,' Bailey muttered. 'Another farthing or I'm on me way.'

Mahdu leaned against the damp brick wall of the debtors' prison. 'All right, just give me a minute or two.' She closed her eyes and tears trickled unbidden down her lined cheeks as she thought of her home-land, and the months spent in the hills where the pine-scented air was touched with a chill from

4

the snow-capped Himalayas, and the sun shone down on the baked red earth scattered with the blossoms of bougainvillea and golden marigolds. She could hear her mistress's musical, soft-toned voice calling to her on the day after their arrival in Simla.

'Mahdu, come quickly, I need my white muslin gown and my satin slippers for the ball at the Residency. Have you unpacked my things, yet? Oh, Mahdu, I can't wait until this evening. I think I will die of excitement.' Belinda lifted her arms and twirled around on her toes. The thin silk of her peignoir floated around her slender figure like the petals of a lotus blossom and her long, corn-gold hair swung around her head and shoulders to form a shimmering halo as it caught the light.

Mahdu had been in the dressing room that led off Belinda's bedchamber in the bungalow high on the hill above the town. She had been shaking the creases out of the muslin ball gown, knowing instinctively which one her young mistress would choose for tonight's entertainment at the Residency. They had arrived last evening on the train from Delhi after a long and hot journey, but Belinda had never once complained. She had been in a fever of anticipation and they both shared the secret knowledge that it was all down to the handsome Captain George Lawson, who had been assigned to escort the ladies to Simla. Colonel Phillips had taken the young officer under his wing, oblivious to the raised eyebrows from those who considered that an officer of mixed blood had no place in the British army. Colonel Phillips was a fair man with few prejudices, preferring to judge an officer by his deeds and actions in battle

5

than to look down on him for something over which he had no control. The Colonel had valued George's father both as a friend and a fellow officer, and although he had counselled Major Edward Lawson against marrying the beautiful high-born Indian lady, he had understood how a man could be entranced by her wit and beauty. Despite his misgivings he had been best man at their wedding, but less than a year later the young bride had died giving birth to her son. Edward Lawson, broken-hearted, had never recovered from his loss and was killed in battle several years later, leaving George to be educated at Harrow and then Sandhurst. Colonel Phillips had been pleased to have the young officer in his battalion even though there were some who voiced their disapproval of such an appointment. Mahdu feared that history was about to repeat itself, but she had raised the motherless Belinda since she was six years old and could deny her nothing.

'I have your gown here, baba. I will hang it outside on the veranda where it will be caressed by the breeze and the creases will have dropped out by this evening.'

Belinda did a pirouette of sheer joy and she hugged Mahdu, ignoring her protests. 'I love you, Mahdu. What would I do without you, larla?'

Mahdu smiled despite her worries for the girl she thought of more as a daughter than a mistress. The term of endearment had slipped so easily from Belinda's lips and it was sincerely meant. Mahdu returned the embrace but drew away quickly in case any of the other servants should happen to pass the window and see them. There was an unwritten code of conduct, and no matter how close the relationship between mistress and servant, Mahdu was only too well aware that there was a line that must never be crossed. 'You would manage, baba. One day soon you will marry and have no need of your ayah.'

Belinda touched Mahdu's cheek with a gentle brush of her fingers. 'I will always need you with me, larla. When I am married you will come with me, of course, and when I have children you will be their ayah as you have been mine. We will never be parted, I swear it on my mother's grave.'

Mahdu felt a shiver run down her spine, as she looked into Belinda's bright eyes. 'You will not do anything rash? The handsome officer is not for you.'

Belinda felt the blood rush to her cheeks and she snatched up her fan, waving it energetically to and fro in front of her face. 'I don't know what you mean.'

'I've seen the way he looks at you, and I think you like him too much for your own good.'

'We like each other. That's not a crime. Papa thinks highly of George.'

'But marriage is another matter entirely.' Mahdu picked up the ball gown and went out onto the veranda to hang it from one of the cast-iron brackets that supported the sloping tin roof.

Belinda slumped down on a chaise longue placed strategically near the window so that she could rest in the heat of the day and enjoy the view of the pine-forested hills. She adored Mahdu, and she knew that what she said was true, but she had fallen in love with George at first sight and he with her. It seemed like a miracle that two people should connect so deeply on such a short acquaintance, but she knew instinctively that he was her soul mate, her other half; the one man in the world who made her feel complete. They had met at a ball in Delhi just three months ago but it seemed from the start as though she had known him all her life. When Papa had announced that she was to leave for Simla in the company of Mrs Arbuthnot and Miss Minchin and a group of officers' wives, she had been devastated at the thought of parting from George. But it seemed as though the heavens had smiled on them. It was only five years since the uprising that had seen so much carnage on both sides and the scars were still in evidence. In view of this, Colonel Phillips had decided at the last moment to allow George to command the small party of soldiers who were to provide security for the ladies on their journey.

Belinda sighed and closed her eyes, shutting out the view of the sloping garden filled with roses and the feathery green leaves of cosmos that grew wild amongst the deodar and rhododendron that clambered up the foothills to merge with the dark jagged pine trees. She allowed herself to dream of being held in George's arms as they danced the night away at the Peterhof, the official residence of the Viceroy.

She was awakened by a soft rustling of the chik, the split cane sunblind that Mahdu must have lowered to keep the room cool before she left to carry out her household duties. Belinda opened her eyes and her heart leapt in her breast as she saw the shadow of a man standing outside on the veranda. She knew instantly that it was

George and she rose to her feet, quite forgetting that she was naked beneath her silk peignoir. She glided over the polished wooden floorboards, her feet barely touching the ground, and the sunshine flooded in as she opened the half-glassed door. George crossed the threshold in two strides and took her in his arms, claiming her mouth in a kiss that made her weak with desire. When he drew away to look deep into her eyes she clung to him dazed and deliriously happy. She could still taste him and her body seemed to melt into his, fitting each curve of his finely honed physique as if they had been created to form a single entity. 'George,' she whispered, savouring his name with delight. 'Are you mad? You shouldn't be here.'

His hazel eyes glowed with flecks of gold like dust motes in the sunshine, and his lips brushed hers with small, tantalising kisses that made her long for more. 'I think I must be out of my head with love for you, my darling,' he murmured, resting his cheek against her tumbled hair. 'I couldn't wait until this evening at the Peterhof. I wanted to hold you in my arms and have you all to myself, even if it was only for a few moments.'

She uttered a sigh of ecstasy as the scent of him made her dizzy with longing. 'I wish this moment would never end, George.'

His eyes darkened with desire as his hand slid down her neck, stroking her flesh until she shivered with delight. He had not planned this clandestine meeting and he was here on official business, but when he had seen her through the window he had forgotten everything but his love for her. The small voice in his head advocating restraint and insisting on retreat was ignored as he drank in her beauty like a man dying of thirst. Her peignoir had slipped off one shoulder and he cupped her breast in his hand, uttering a low moan of pleasure. He bent his head to kiss the nipple that had hardened with desire, but he drew away almost instantly, covering her nakedness with a swift movement. Conscience had won over animal instinct and he was bitterly ashamed of his behaviour. 'I'm sorry, my love. I shouldn't have done that. It was unforgivable.'

Belinda's breath hitched in her throat. Sensations that she could never have imagined raked through her body and she slid her arms around his neck. 'Don't stop, George. I love you so much.'

His kiss was passionate, but George had himself well under control despite the lapse that had just occurred. He had come to the bungalow with a message for the Colonel's wife but he had allowed his love for Belinda to override everything. He knew he was behaving like the worst possible bounder, but his feelings for her were genuine and overpowering. She was like a beautiful and delicate flower that had been plucked from its homeland to struggle for existence in a hot and sometimes alien environment. All his instincts were to love and cherish her, and to have her for his own, even though that seemed an impossible goal for a man of his lineage. Colonel Phillips might treat him like a son, but George was no fool. He was only too well aware that this would change in an instant the moment he asked for Belinda's hand in marriage. He stroked the golden curls back from her forehead. She was smiling at him as trusting as a child and almost as helpless. He could take her here and now as his body demanded and she would gladly give herself to him, but he loved her too much to take advantage of her innocence. He held her at arm's length, fighting the need to comfort her and wipe the stricken look from her eyes. 'I must go now, sweetheart. I have business with the Colonel but I couldn't resist the temptation to spend a few precious moments with you.' The words came out pat, and to his surprise George realised that he meant them. Before he met Belinda he had conquered many fluttering hearts, but she was different.

She smiled but her eyes were bright with unshed tears. 'I understand, George.'

If she had railed at him it would have hurt less. He felt guilty and ashamed to have taken advantage of her, exciting her desire and then leaving her unsatisfied and wondering what she had done to deserve such cavalier treatment. He raised her hand to his lips and kissed it. 'Until tonight, my love.' He strode out of the room before he had a chance to weaken in his resolve. He had come close to dishonouring the girl he adored and he was shaken to the core by the intensity of his passion for her. As he made his way round to the front door of the bungalow, George Lawson knew that his heart was lost forever.

That evening they met again in the formal atmosphere of the Residency. George had intended to keep a cool head on his shoulders and behave like an officer and a gentleman, paying attention to all the unattached young ladies so that he did not give fuel to the matrons who sat around watching the dancers like hawks, ready to exercise their gossiping tongues. But when Belinda walked into the ballroom on her father's arm, all George's good intentions flew out of the window. One look at his beloved and he was like a man in a trance. He crossed the floor, pushing past other young hopefuls who wished to have their name written on Belinda's dance card. He snapped his heels together and bowed from the waist, requesting the first waltz. After that he would have gladly floored any man who dared to claim her as a partner. They whirled around the floor to the strains of a Viennese waltz, a gavotte and a lively polka.

Belinda did not care that they were flouting the unwritten rules of the ballroom. She was happier than she had thought possible. The floor might have been empty of other couples for all she knew or cared. There were only two people in the whole world, herself and the handsome young officer who held her in his arms. The scent of his pomade and the faint musky smell of his body filled her nostrils, and the touch of his hand on her waist kindled a fire in her blood. Belinda could have cried when her father tapped George on the shoulder and claimed her for the schottische, but she made a brave attempt at a smile as he somewhat awkwardly steered her round the room.

'You're making a show of yourself, Belle,' he said gruffly. 'I'll have words with young Lawson in the

morning. Not that I blame him for wanting to monop-
olise the most beautiful girl in Simla, but it won't do,
my pet. It just won't do.'

For the rest of the evening Belinda tried not to catch
George's eyes, and when a young subaltern shyly asked
permission to lead her in to supper she wanted to tell
him to go to hell, but a stern glance from her father
warned her not to do anything so rash. She allowed
him to lead her into the dining room ablaze with
candles, and the table set with all manner of tempting
delicacies, but she had no appetite. She was constantly
aware that George was glaring at her escort with a
jealous frown, and although it thrilled and excited her,
she was anxious for his sake. She managed to move
close enough to talk to him having sent her escort to
get her a glass of wine. 'We must be careful, George,'
she whispered. 'Papa is suspicious.'

'I can't bear to see you with that young puppy.'
George covered her hand with his. 'Every time he looks
at you I want to kill him.'

Unfurling her fan, Belinda covered the lower part of
her face so that she could answer without being
observed. 'I think that might make Papa very cross,
dearest.'

A reluctant smile curved his lips, and his heart
swelled with love for her. He wanted to take her in his
arms there and then, but he managed to restrain
himself. 'Tomorrow, my darling. I'll see you at the club.
I'm playing in the polo match.'

'Miss Phillips, I've brought you a glass of bubbly.'

Flashing George a brilliant smile behind her fan,

Belinda snapped it shut as she turned to the subaltern. 'Thank you, Bertie. That's very kind of you.' She could feel George's eyes willing her to look round, but she accepted the glass of champagne and took a sip. Bertie was watching her with the eagerness of a young puppy waiting for his master to throw him a ball, and she felt dizzy with power and also slightly ashamed of herself for enjoying the sensation.

Next day at the polo match, Belinda sat between Mrs Arbuthnot, wife of General Sir William Arbuthnot, and her companion Miss Minchin, a scrawny spinster schoolteacher whose father had been an army padre, but was long since deceased. The two ladies were chatting across her but Belinda's attention was devoted to watching George as he manoeuvred his spirited mount with superb control. It was hot, even though they were fanned by a cool breeze from the mountains, and despite the shade of her parasol Belinda could feel her chemise sticking to her flesh beneath the tight confines of her stays. She wished that she had not urged Mahdu to pull them in quite so tightly, even though her waist was reduced to a minute eighteen inches. There was a shout of approval from someone in the ranks as George scored, and the game ended with his team having triumphed. Until now Belinda had had little interest in polo and she was hazy as to the rules, but she understood winning and she could barely contain her delight when he leapt off his horse and came striding over to them. He doffed his topee to the two older ladies, his teeth flashing white against his dark skin. 'I hope you enjoyed the game, Mrs Arbuthnot, Miss Minchin.'

Mrs Arbuthnot inclined her head with a tight little smile. 'Well played, Captain Lawson.'

'Well done, sir,' Miss Minchin echoed, eyeing George with distaste. He really was a forward young man, but then what would one expect from a person of mixed blood? She turned to her friend, pursing her lips and raising an eyebrow to show that she was being magnanimous and behaving like a true Christian, as her papa would have urged, even though she disapproved strongly of miscegenation.

Mrs Arbuthnot received the glance with the barest of nods, but she knew what Eulalie Minchin was thinking; it was written all too plainly on her extremely plain face. Mrs Arbuthnot twisted her lips into what she hoped was a convincing smile; after all Captain Lawson was an officer under her husband's command and despite the shortcomings of his birth, she was well aware of her duty to the regiment.

George had seen that look many times before and whereas once it would have cut him to the quick, it now simply amused him. Having done his duty by the ladies, he turned to Belinda. 'Will I see you in the club, Miss Phillips?'

She had risen from her seat and she twirled the parasol so that her face was hidden from the two older women. 'Yes, I think so, Captain. I would dearly love a glass of iced lemonade.' She pursed her lips to mime a kiss, putting her heart into a smile which was for him alone.

The urge to take her in his arms there and then and part her cherry lips with his tongue, kissing her until she swooned with delight, was almost overwhelming, but George merely inclined his head, tucked his topee beneath his arm and strode off to the changing rooms in the clubhouse.

'My dear, you ought to be wary of that young man,' Mrs Arbuthnot said sharply. 'You know that your papa would disapprove strongly if you were to allow any intimacy to develop between you.'

The bubble of happiness that welled up in Belinda's breast was burst in an instant. Last night she had been oblivious to everything and everyone while George held her in his arms, but Mrs Arbuthnot's caustic remark brought her abruptly down to earth. She flinched, staring at the florid face of the Colonel's wife. Perspiration trickled down the woman's forehead, running into her pale grey eyes, watery like a sheep's, Belinda thought angrily. She took a deep breath and forced her lips into a smile. 'I'm sure I don't know what you mean, ma'am. Captain Lawson is nothing to me, I assure you.'

Miss Minchin sniffed derisively. 'That's not what I heard, young lady. You and he made quite a show of yourselves at the Residency last evening. I was quite embarrassed for you.'

Mrs Arbuthnot heaved herself from her chair, fanning herself energetically. 'What Eulalie says is quite true, Belinda. You are very young and impressionable, and he's a handsome devil, but he's not for you. Your poor mother would turn in her grave if her only child became involved with a half-caste.'

Belinda wanted to slap them both, but she had been well schooled in manners and she knew they were voicing the views held by many people, including her own father. She drew herself up to her full height. 'I may only be seventeen, ma'am, but I am quite well aware of my duty to my father and to the regiment. Now, if you'll excuse me, I would really like to go into the clubhouse where I am to meet Papa for tiffin.'

Without waiting for a response, Belinda picked up her skirts and made her way across the grass to the clubhouse. Glancing over her shoulder to make sure she was not being watched she changed course, avoiding the main entrance as she hurried to the rear of the building where the changing rooms were situated. It was, of course, out of bounds to ladies but she was desperate to spend a few moments alone with George, and she needed to tell him that Mrs Arbuthnot was suspicious and that they must be extra careful. She hid in the shadows, praying that he would be one of the first to emerge; it would be dreadfully embarrassing if she were to be spotted by his fellow officers. Two of the opposing team strolled out first but they were too busy chatting about the match to notice Belinda, and she heaved a sigh of relief as they walked off towards the main entrance. To her intense relief it was George who appeared next and she called his name softly. He stopped, turning to her in surprise. 'Belinda?'

She rushed towards him, throwing herself into his arms. 'I couldn't wait another second, George. They know about us. The old tabbies warned me against you.'

He held her briefly, and then gently pushed her away, glancing over his shoulder to make certain they had not been observed. 'We need to talk, my love,' he said urgently. 'I have something to tell you.'

'What? What is it, George? Oh, you must tell me now; I can't go in there and behave normally if you won't tell me what's wrong.'

He tucked her hand into the crook of his arm. 'Will you come with me now, or are you supposed to meet Mrs Arbuthnot in the clubhouse?'

'No, I said I was having tiffin with Papa, but that was a ruse to get away from them.'

'Do you dare come to my quarters, Belle? The chaps are out on manoeuvres and we'll be quite alone. Would you risk your reputation just this once, my love?'

'Of course I will, George. I'd do anything for you.'

He brushed her lips with a kiss. 'Come on then. It's quiet at this time of day and we should be able to get there without being seen.'

Inside the wooden bungalow that George shared with two other officers, Belinda looked round the untidy room with a critical eye. 'It's not exactly luxurious, George. I thought you would be housed a little better than this.'

'They don't pander to us bachelors,' George said, grinning. 'Married quarters are much better.'

She turned to him, hands clasped over her breasts as her heartbeats quickened to an alarming rate. 'Are you proposing to me, Captain Lawson?'

He took her in his arms. 'Of course I am, my darling. I want to hold you and keep you safe from harm for the rest of my life. Will you marry me, Belle?'

'I will.' She raised her face, closing her eyes ready to receive the kiss that would seal their pledge, but although she could feel his breath on her cheek and the scent of him made her go weak at the knees, nothing happened. She opened her eyes, and found him looking at her with an expression of deep concern. 'What's the matter, George? What haven't you told me?'

'I only found out this morning, sweetheart. I'm to leave tomorrow for the North-West Frontier, and I don't know how long I'll be gone. It's just possible that I might never . . .'

She covered his mouth with hers, kissing him until he responded with equal fervour. Her bonnet fell to the floor as he raked his hand through her hair, releasing her curls so that the pins flew in all directions. There was desperation in their embrace and unbridled passion that would not be denied. He picked her up in his arms and carried her across the living room. Kicking open the door to his bedchamber, he laid her on the unmade bed. He leaned over her without touching her trembling body as he looked deeply into her eyes. 'I want you, my darling. We may never have this chance again, but if you tell me no, then I respect your wishes. We can be engaged in secret and I'll carry the memory of you in my heart.'

Belinda knew little of physical love but she was unafraid and ready to sacrifice her virginity and her reputation for the man who already owned her heart and soul. She reached up to touch his cheek, tracing the outline of his jaw with her finger. All the pent-up emotion of the past months, the denial and desire, had come to a peak and she knew now that there was no turning back. She knotted her hands behind his head, pulling him down so that their lips almost touched. 'I will marry you in spirit and with my body, my dearest George. I love you and I'll always be yours.'

The news that Captain George Lawson had been killed in a skirmish with the Afghans on the Khyber Pass came three months later. Prostrate with grief Belinda lay on the chaise longue in her bedchamber, but her eyes were blind to the striking beauty of the magnificent vista outside. Her heart was shattered into tiny shards and she knew she would never love again, but her eyes were dry and there were no more tears to shed. She had sobbed for two days, refusing food and only taking sips of tea.

She heard footsteps but she did not look round.

Mahdu knelt beside her, placing a tray of food on the brass-topped table at Belinda's side. 'You must eat something, baba. If not for yourself then for his sake. The Captain would not want to see you suffering so.'

Belinda barely heard the words as the strangest of sensations inside her belly made her snap upright. 'I felt it move, Mahdu. My baby, his baby, it moved. My darling George isn't completely dead. Now I know for certain that I have his child to live for and love.'

Mahdu attempted to smile but she was afraid. She took Belinda's hand in hers, holding it as she had when her baba was a little girl and terrified of the dark. 'You will have to tell the Colonel. He has to know soon, before you begin to show and the gossips begin to talk.'

Belinda closed her eyes, sinking back against the cushions. 'I daren't tell Papa. I'm afraid it will be the end of his career in the army. I can't do that to him, Mahdu. What shall I do? Help me, Iarla. I'm scared.'

Chapter Two

Cripplegate, London, December 1872

The undertaker's parlour was dark even at midday. The pale winter sun reflected off the snow outside, but the feeble rays barely managed to penetrate the grime-encrusted windowpanes. Cassy stood in the doorway clutching the tiny bundle wrapped in a tattered piece of old sheeting. She had made the short walk from Three Herring Court to Elias Crabbe's funeral parlour on many occasions in the past but the onerous task of bringing the dead babies to their last resting place never grew any easier. She swallowed hard, biting back the tears that threatened to spill from her eyes as she cradled the infant's body in her arms.

'Not another one so soon?' Elias eyed her with a sardonic curl of his thin lips. 'What does the old soak do to them poor little mites?' Despite his caustic words, he stepped forward to relieve Cassy of her burden. 'That's the third one this month and it ain't Christmas yet.'

'He was sick when he come,' Cassy said, wiping her eyes on her sleeve. 'Biddy said he was an eight-month baby and never stood a chance.'

Elias shook his head as he laid the pathetic corpse on the top of a gleaming mahogany coffin. 'How old are you, Cassy?'

'It's me tenth birthday today,' Cassy said proudly,

although she knew it would be no cause for celebration in Three Herring Court; Biddy didn't hold with birthdays and such.

Elias shook his head, tut-tutting. 'It ain't right that she sends you to do her dirty work.'

'I tried to look after him,' Cassy said, feeling that she was in some way to blame for the baby's demise. 'I sat up nights with him, mister. Honest I did, but he just seemed to fade away like he had no wish to live. Poor little chap never even cried, not like some of 'em that come to us; they never stop bawling for their mas, especially the older ones. It's enough to break a person's heart.'

Elias peeled back the none-too-clean sheet and his harsh features softened just a little as he stared down at the tiny child, who looked perfect in death like one of the marble cherubs Cassy had seen in the graveyard. 'Any known parents for this 'un, Cassy?'

She shook her head. 'Biddy never said there was. No parents and no money for the funeral. She said do the usual, Mr Crabbe.'

'As it happens there's a young woman died in childbed, her infant too, so this little fellow needn't be on his own.' He held out his hand. 'Money in advance, as usual.'

Cassy put her hand in her pocket and took out a silver shilling. 'There might be another before the day's out, guv. Little Freddie has the whooping cough something awful. I tried blowing flowers of sulphur down his throat but it made him sick. I dunno what else to do for him and that's the truth.'

'It ain't right. Old Biddy Henchard should be strung

up by the thumbs for the way she treats the nippers in her care and that includes you, young Cassy.' Elias lifted the small body, holding it in the crook of his arm. 'I'll just settle this young fellah in with his new ma and sister. I don't doubt he'll be better off underground with them than raised in that rat-infested hovel. You should get away from there, girl. Take my advice and grab the first opportunity to escape from that old besom's clutches.'

Cassy shrugged her thin shoulders. 'You may be right, Mr Crabbe, but I got nowhere else to go, and if I left who would look after them poor children?'

'You're a good girl, Cassy. It's a crying shame you ain't got no one to look out for you.'

'Oh, but I have, Mr Crabbe. There's Bailey, he's like the best brother a girl could have, and I ain't no orphan. I got a ma but she's an Indian lady, so Biddy says. I think she's in service somewhere in London, and she comes once a year on me birthday to give Biddy the money for me keep. She comes in the dead of night so I ain't seen her yet.'

Elias slammed his hand down on the coffin lid. 'You earn your keep and more. It's a disgrace that's what it is, and if I ever sees your ma I'll give her a piece of me mind.'

'She can't help it,' Cassy cried passionately. 'I'm sure she loves me but she has to earn her living and she can't keep me, but one day I know she'll come for me and take me home to India where it's hot and sunny all the time.'

'It would explain your looks,' Elias said, squinting at her as if seeing her clearly for the first time. 'It's

24

obvious you don't come from round here, and with that black hair and them big dark eyes you'll either end up on the stage or on the streets. It's a crying shame but there's not much chance for anyone raised round here.' He opened a plain pine coffin and laid the tiny body carefully inside.

Cassy backed towards the door. The smell from inside the box was worse than the combined stench of the sewers and the horse muck, which was almost knee-deep on the streets beneath a frosting of snow. 'Got to go, Mr Crabbe.' She opened the door and stepped outside into the bitter cold. She shivered as she felt shards of ice piercing the thin soles of her boots, and snow melt seeped through the gaps in the worn leather uppers. She wrapped her shawl tightly around her head and shoulders as she started towards Three Herring Court and the only home she had ever known.

'Ho, wait for me, Cassy.'

She stopped, turning her head with a ready smile. 'Bailey. I thought you was sent on an errand.'

He caught up with her in long strides, his muffler flying out behind him like a pennant and his cap askew on his head. His cheeks were flushed and his eyes sparkled like chips of sapphire in his tanned face. Despite the fact that his jacket was a size too small, frayed at the cuffs and clumsily patched at the elbows, and his trousers barely came to the tops of his boots, he exuded warmth and vitality. 'I had to put some money on a fight for Biddy, and I went to the market and got something for you. It ain't your birthday every day of the week and you're into double numbers now.'

Cassy puffed out her chest. 'I'm almost a woman, ain't I, Bailey?'

Hooking his arm around her shoulders, he leaned down to plant a kiss on the tip of her nose. 'You're still my little sister, Cassy. Don't grow up too soon.'

She smiled up at him but she could not quite shake off the sadness that had enveloped her since the unnamed baby boy had died in her arms. 'I wouldn't be here at all if it wasn't for you,' she murmured. 'If it had been left to Biddy I'd have been dead long ago, just like them other poor little mites.'

He gave her a hug. 'Don't talk like that. We look out for each other and that's the truth.' He thrust his hand in his pocket and pulled out a bulging paper poke. 'Your favourite,' he said, grinning. 'Peppermint creams.'

Cassy tried not to snatch but her mouth was already watering as she anticipated the sweet minty taste. She popped one in her mouth, closing her eyes in ecstasy. 'Mmm,' she breathed. 'That's so lovely. I could eat peppermint creams all day.'

Her shawl had slipped off her head and Bailey ruffled her hair. 'Don't make yourself sick, little 'un.'

Stuffing another sweet in her mouth, Cassy grinned as she offered him the bag. 'Go on, take one. It's no fun enjoying meself all alone and you did buy them with your own money.' She hesitated, eyes widening as she watched him take one. 'You didn't use hers, did you?'

Bailey tapped the side of his nose, winking. 'Ask no questions and you'll be told no lies, young 'un.'

Cassy reached up to cuff him gently round the ear.

Her hand was too small to inflict pain and she did not intend to cause him harm, but she faced him like a small tiger. 'Call me that again and you'll get what for, Bailey Moon.'

He responded by lifting her off the ground and setting her on his shoulders. 'Let's get you home afore you catch a chill and end up in old Crabbe's parlour.'

She wrapped her arms around his neck as he jogged along the slippery pavement. His hands were warm on the bare skin of her calves as he held her in a firm grasp, but she felt safe with Bailey. He had been there for her as long as she could remember. He had protected her from Biddy's volatile tempers and drunken rages. It was Bailey who had looked after her when she almost died of measles, the dreaded childhood disease that had taken the lives of three of Biddy's youngest charges. He had wiped her nose when she cried and bathed her knees when she took a tumble. Bailey might not be her blood brother but he was something more to her; he was her whole family and she loved him dearly.

He set her down at the top of the steps leading into Three Herring Court. 'Best not look too happy when we go inside,' he said, setting his cap straight. 'Hide them sweets too, or she'll have 'em off you quicker than you can blink.'

'I'm ten, I ain't daft,' Cassy said, tucking what was left of her treat inside her ragged blouse. 'Let's hope she's dead drunk by now and we'll get a bit of peace.'

Bailey took her by the hand as they negotiated the slippery stone steps that were treacherous even in summer, worn down in the middle by the passage of feet over two hundred years or more. Three Herring Court was a narrow street lined with run-down buildings that had had many uses over the centuries but now housed small businesses: a printer of religious tracts, a walking stick maker, a milliner who eked out a meagre living by taking in gentlemen lodgers, a pie maker of dubious repute, a candle maker whose small shop filled the street with the smell of hot wax and tallow, and an oriental gentleman who professed to practise Chinese herbal medicine but everyone knew he ran an illicit opium den. The rest of the dilapidated buildings were crammed with tenants, twenty to a room in some cases, and at the very end was Biddy Henchard's tall and narrow house which she advertised as a nursery and board school, but Cassy knew that the locals referred to it as a baby farm.

The front door groaned on rusty hinges as Bailey thrust it open. The stench outside was as nothing compared to the smell that assailed Cassy's nostrils as she followed him into the narrow hallway. Festoons of cobwebs hung from the ceiling and the walls had shed flakes of limewash to cover the bare boards like a powdering of snow. The mixed odours of dry rot, baby sick and the rancid stench of cheap tallow candles were almost overpowered by the fumes of jigger gin and tobacco smoke, which made the whole house reek like the taproom of a dockyard pub. Echoing throughout the building the wailing of infants came to a sudden halt, drowned out by a roar from Biddy's gin-soaked throat. 'Shut up you little buggers or I'll beat your brains out.'

Not for the first time, Cassy wanted to turn and run away from this nightmare place, but the sound of a child coughing and whooping put all thoughts of flight from her head. She hurried along the narrow passage that led into the one large room which served as a kitchen, living room and nursery for some of the youngest children. The bare floorboards were littered with scraps of half-eaten crusts, potato peelings and balls of fluff which might have been dead mice or simply an accumulation of dust and fibres. The furthest part of the room was in semi-darkness with a tattered curtain drawn across the window which overlooked the court, and it was here that the children were stacked in boxes and crates like goods in a warehouse. The smell of ammonia from urine-soaked bedding was enough to floor an ox, let alone a ten-year-old child. Cassy covered her nose and mouth with her hand, shocked by the noxious fumes even though she was used to living in such conditions. The air outside had seemed sweet in comparison to the rank odour in the nursery. She made a move to snatch Freddie from the wooden crate where he spent most of his time but Biddy, who had obviously been asleep in a high-backed Windsor chair by the range, rose to her feet clutching a gin bottle in her hand and she advanced on him with a ferocious snarl.

Cassy snatched the infant up in her arms as a paroxysm of coughing racked his tiny body. 'Leave him alone, missis.'

Biddy squinted at her through half-closed eyes. 'Where've you been?' She took a swipe at Cassy's head but her aim fell far short. She staggered drunkenly and would have fallen if Bailey had not caught her. He pushed her unceremoniously back onto her seat.

'I think you've had plenty, missis. The drink will be the death of you if you ain't careful.'

With the bottle still clutched in her hand, Biddy pulled the cork out with her teeth and took a swig. 'I ain't drunk enough. When I can't see or hear them horrible brats, that's when I stop.' She closed her eyes, holding the bottle to her lips and tipping its contents down her throat as if it were water.

Cassy hitched baby Freddie over her shoulder, patting his back in a vain effort to help him breathe. 'He ought to see the doctor,' she whispered. 'I dunno what else to do, Bailey.'

He angled his head, glancing from the suffering infant to the shapeless form of Biddy slumped in her chair. 'He don't look too good. I think it's the hospital for young Freddie, if we ain't too late already.'

'Don't say that,' Cassy cried, hugging Freddie closer to her thin chest. 'I won't let him die. I won't.'

'Well, she's dead to the world,' Bailey remarked, jerking his head in Biddy's direction. 'C'mon, we'll take him to Bart's. They'll see him for free, only it might be a long wait.'

Cassy bit her lip. She knew that Bailey was right, but it would mean leaving the other young children to Biddy's tender care, and that was worse than nothing. She was torn between love and duty. She had formed a bond with little Freddie and he was clinging to her now as if his life depended upon it, which of course it did. 'I'll take him if you'll stay here and look after the others.'

Bailey shook his head. 'I ain't no nursemaid, Cassy.'

'Oh, please, Bailey.' Her bottom lip trembled as she fought to hold back tears. 'He needs me to hold him. He'll be scared stiff of them men in white coats.'

'Then I'm the best one to take him,' Bailey said, gently prising Freddie from her arms. 'I won't stand no nonsense from them doctors and nurses. You stay here and tend to the babes; they need you more than he does just now.'

Cassy knew that he was talking sense but the sight of Freddie's stricken face and the way he held his arms out to her almost broke her heart. 'Take him then, and hurry.'

'I'll be quick as I can.' Holding Freddie as tenderly as any woman, Bailey strode out of the room.

Tending to the remaining infants kept Cassy fully occupied, but her thoughts were with Freddie. She knew that doctors were clever coves who had spent years at school studying books, and that made them able to cure even the sickest person. Bailey had told her all manner of interesting things that he had learned at the ragged school. Biddy had sent him there, he said, because she could neither read nor write and she needed someone to answer letters from anxious mothers who had put their children in her care. Then there was the matter of sending out bills to those tardy in paying the cost of care for their offspring, although Cassy was painfully aware that Biddy accepted payment for infants long dead, and only admitted their demise if threatened with a visit from the parent or if they were in a position to reclaim their fostered child.

Cassy sat on a low stool with baby Anna in her arms, feeding her cow's milk from a spoon. Head lice crawled through the infant's thin blonde hair and Cassy's scalp itched at the sight of them. They were all infested with parasites, including fleas and roundworms, but so were all the other children who lived in Three Herring Court. Cleanliness came a poor third to having enough to eat and keeping warm in winter. There was a pump on the corner of the court but the water was often contaminated with sewage, causing outbreaks of cholera and dysentery, and in summer Biddy forbade them to drink it. She provided small beer for the older children and milk for the infants, but both were in short supply and Cassy had to ration out their meagre allowance each day.

Milk dribbled out of the corners of Anna's mouth and she closed her eyes with the barest breath of a sigh. Cassy laid the baby in the wooden orange box that served as her crib. Anna was probably six months old, although like the others she had not come with a birth certificate and her exact age was a matter of conjecture. She had been frail and puny right from the start and she would, Cassy thought sadly, be unlikely to see her first birthday whenever that might be. She changed the baby's soiled rags and put her down in her box on a bed of straw covered by a thin piece of blanket. Anna looked like a wax doll, and it seemed to Cassy as though she was already laid out in her coffin. A cold shiver ran down her spine, and she turned her attention to Samuel who was bawling his head off.

At nine months old he was already displaying the qualities of a fighter. She knew instinctively that he would survive against all odds, and she gave him a cuddle as she lifted him from the tea chest where Biddy insisted that he must be kept since he was trying to crawl and might otherwise come to harm.

Samuel stopped crying and tugged at her hair with surprising strength. She set him on her knee and fed him on tiny morsels of stale bread soaked in the milk that Anna had not managed to drink. When he had eaten his fill, Cassy changed his rags for clean ones and allowed him to crawl around the flagstone floor for a while, although when he tried to put a dead cockroach in his mouth she decided it was time to put him back in the tea chest. He protested loudly, but with his belly full he soon fell asleep. There were two more tiny tots, twin girls who had been brought to the house a few months ago by a young woman with a painted face and tragic eyes. She had sobbed brokenheartedly, begging Biddy to be kind to her newborn babies and promising to return once a month with money for their keep. Biddy had nodded and made the appropriate noises but as soon as the door closed on the unhappy mother, she had thrust the infants into Bailey's arms. 'That's the last we'll see of her,' she had said grimly. 'Stow them in a box and give them enough just enough to keep the little buggers quiet. If they should take sick and pass away, no one will be the wiser.'

This callous remark had upset Cassy more than she had words to express, and Bailey protested loudly but was silenced by a clout round the head from Biddy that sent him reeling backwards against the kitchen wall. He had clenched his fists and threatened to retaliate but on seeing Cassy's stricken face he had seemingly changed his mind, and had put the twin girls to bed in a herring box filled with fresh straw. He had waited until late that night when Biddy staggered back from the pub and had fallen into a drunken stupor, and Cassy had helped him feed the infants with warm milk. They continued to succour them in secret and the twins clung stubbornly to life, much to the delight of their mother who confounded Biddy's fears by turning up regularly once a month with money for their keep. Cassy watched the young prostitute cradle her babies in her arms, crooning to them and kissing their tiny wrinkled faces as if they were the most precious things in the world.

'They ain't got no names,' Cassy said shyly. 'What shall you call 'em, missis?'

The light dimmed in the young woman's eyes. 'I doubt if I'll be here to see my babies grow up, but they should have good names. Heaven knows I'm a sinner, but what choice did I have?' She fixed Cassy with a questioning stare as if expecting her to offer a benediction.

'I dunno, missis,' Cassy murmured, shuffling her bare feet on the cold flagstones.

'None, I tells you, little girl. I was sold to an evil man when I were not much older than you. Now I makes me living the only way I knows how, and it ain't what I wants for me girls.'

Cassy looked up into the raddled face of the woman,

who might have been any age from sixteen to thirty. Tears had made runnels in the paint on her face and her eyes were red-rimmed. Cassy said nothing and the woman clutched her babies to her breast.

'Charity and Mercy,' she murmured, closing her eyes. 'I ain't seen much of either, so I hope they fare better than their ma.' She kissed each one on the forehead and laid them back in their box. 'Goodbye, my little dears.'

The words sounded final even to Cassy's ears and she was alarmed. 'But you'll be back to see them soon, won't you?'

'I'm sick, dearie. Something you wouldn't know nothing about. I'll come if and when I can, but I want you to promise to look after me babes.' She reached out to grasp Cassy's hand. 'Promise.'

'I'll do me best.'

The mother had returned one more time, and Cassy could see a startling change in her appearance. Without the paint, her face was white as the snow outside except for livid bruises around both eyes and a split lip that could not disguise the gap where two of her front teeth were missing. She was even thinner than before and her eyes were sunken. She looked old, Cassy thought; older even than Biddy. The poor creature had wept when she said goodbye to her babies and her sobs had echoed round the court as she limped away.

'We won't see her again,' Biddy said, pocketing the handful of coins. 'Half measures for them little bastards from now on. I ain't a bloody charity.'

Brought painfully back to the present by the mewling

35

of the twins, and with concern for Freddie pressing down on her like a black cloud, Cassy made a pot of tea using tea leaves that had already been brewed several times and left out to dry. The resultant liquid was pale, straw-coloured and tasted more like hot water than a refreshing beverage, but it warmed her stomach and made it easier to swallow the stale bread which was all she had to eat. When all the babies finally slept, she set about tidying the room although it would have been a daunting task for someone twice her size. She swept the floor and emptied the dustpan out of the window into the yard, sending a shower of dead cockroaches to feed the crows and sparrows. A gust of ice-cold air filled the room and Biddy stirred, snorted loudly and then fell back into a drunken stupor.

Cassy went outside to the pump but found it frozen solid. She filled a bucket with snow and took it indoors to melt on the range. The fire was burning low and there was very little coal left in the sack. She could do nothing about it until Bailey returned and she sat down to wait. The infants might be asleep but the house was filled with sound of movement and people talking, shouting and the occasional slamming of doors. In the room directly above her she could hear the deep rumble of a man's voice followed by shrieks of female laughter. There was a brief silence followed by the rhythmic creak of the bedsprings, suggesting that Wall-eyed Betty was at it again with one of her gentlemen. Well, a girl had to live as Betty often said with a wink of her pale blue eye; the other was brown, hence her nickname. She shared the room with Edna, a fresh-faced girl from the country who had come to London to seek her fortune and in less than a year had changed into a shrill she-cat with a voice that could shatter glass, and a vocabulary of swear words that even made Bailey blush.

Thinking of Bailey, Cassy went to the front door to peer out into the snow, hoping to see him coming down the steps with Freddie in his arms, all well and smiling, but there were only the birds scavenging for food. A door opened and the crippled boot maker limped out with a pair of shiny new boots tied together by the laces and hung about his neck like the decoration on a Christmas tree. He acknowledged Cassy with a nod of his head, and leaning heavily on his crutches he moved across the snow like a bluebottle skating on a bowl of melted fat.

She was about to close the door when she noticed a stranger standing at the top of the steps. It was more than curiosity that made Cassy stare at the woman who had stopped to speak to the boot maker. Her breath hitched in her throat and she started forward, breaking into a run. 'Mama,' she screamed. 'Mama, you've come for me.' Slipping and sliding, oblivious to the cold that gnawed at her bones, Cassy hurled herself into the dark-skinned woman's arms.

Mahdu was almost bowled over by the force of the small child who clung to her and gazed up into her face with an expression of sheer delight. 'Cassandra?' she whispered. 'Is it really you?'

'I'm Cassy and you are my ma. I knew you'd come for me on my birthday. Are we going back to India now?'

'Best take her indoors,' the boot maker said as he

negotiated the steps, swinging himself up on his wooden crutches. 'But be careful of the old cow. She'll have that fine cloak off you, missis. It'll be sold at the Rag Fair in Rosemary Lane afore you can blink.'

Mahdu took Cassy by the hand. 'Let's go indoors, larla. It is too cold out here for you.'

Cassy could hardly bear to take her eyes from the dark-skinned lady's face. She wanted to drink in every detail of the fine eyes, almond-shaped and the deepest darkest brown so that they appeared black, and the silky hair shining like coal in the bright light with just a touch of silver at the temples. She felt the material of the woman's cloak, fingering it in wonder that anyone could wear anything so fine. There was not a moth hole or a patch in sight and the lady smelt nice, like a bunch of exotic flowers. 'You are my ma, aren't you?' Cassy whispered eagerly, and yet she was afraid to hear the truth.

Mahdu nodded her head. 'We will agree on that, little one. But now I must see your guardian.'

'Me what?' Cassy stopped in her tracks. 'What's a guardian?'

'Biddy Henchard, the woman who takes care of you.' Mahdu angled her head, staring at Cassy's ragged blouse and skirt. 'Although looking at you, I don't think she does her job very well.'

'You're right there, Ma. Biddy only takes care of herself, but you should know that. You come every year when I'm asleep, she told me so.'

'Yes,' Mahdu said with a sigh. 'I should have insisted on seeing you in the daylight, but I had my reasons.'

38

'Never mind that,' Cassy said, taking her by the hand. 'Come inside, Ma. You'll freeze to death out here and I can see that you're a lady and used to fine things.' She led Mahdu through the snow that was rapidly turning to slush, its pristine whiteness violated and sullied by footprints turning black as the filth below was brought to the light.

Mahdu gave an involuntary gasp of dismay as Cassy showed her into the house. 'I've only been here in the dark,' she murmured. 'It was different then.'

'It could be worse,' Cassy said cheerfully. 'Come into the kitchen. I cleaned it up so it ain't looking too bad.' She thrust the door open with a grand gesture. 'See how well I done, Ma. I earns me keep. She can't deny that.'

'My poor child. I don't know what to say.' Mahdu looked about her in horror. 'This is even worse than I remembered.'

Cassy held her finger to her lips. 'Shush, Ma. Don't wake Biddy yet. There's so much I want to ask you.' She pulled up a chair, dusting the seat with the hem of her skirt. 'Sit down, and I'll make you a cup of tea.'

Mahdu sank down onto the hard wooden seat. She picked up her skirts as a rat scuttled across the floor to disappear into a hole in the skirting board, and she shuddered. 'This is wrong, Cassandra. We cannot allow this to go on.'

Cassy had been draining the tea leaves and was about to refresh them with water from the kettle but she paused, staring at Mahdu and hardly daring to hope. 'You're going to take me with you?'

'Not today, larla. You must understand that it is not up to me. I must speak to my mistress and then perhaps we can come to some arrangement.'

'I don't understand.' Cassy swallowed hard. She must not cry. Only babies cried.

'I work for a kind lady,' Mahdu said gently. 'She is very concerned about you but there are difficulties which you would not understand.'

'If she's so kind then why won't she let you take me home with you?'

'There are reasons, larla.'

Cassy sniffed and wiped her nose on her sleeve. 'Me name's Cassy, not larla.'

'You must trust me, Cassy.' Mahdu produced a reticule from beneath her cloak and from it she took a small silk purse, placing it on the table.

The clink of the coins brought an instant reaction from Biddy, who opened one eye and then the other. She snatched the purse, weighing it in her hand. 'What d'you mean coming here in the daytime? Ain't I told you to come after dark?'

'You did, but I'm here now and I'm not happy with what I see.' Mahdu rose to her feet, towering over Biddy with an air of superiority that impressed Cassy and seemed to make Biddy shrink in size.

'Let's see the colour of your money afore I throw you out on the street,' Biddy said, tipping the coins from the purse. Golden sovereigns gleamed in the firelight and she picked one up to bite it between her remaining two teeth. 'You've paid your dues, now get out.'

'No,' Cassy cried, rushing across the floor to fling her arms around Mahdu. 'Don't leave me, Ma.'

Biddy heaved her bulk from the chair, her mobcap awry. 'Very touching. I won't say a word if you get out of that door this minute.'

Cassy felt Mahdu stiffen and she was frightened. 'Don't take no notice of her, Ma. Take me with you now.'

'I cannot, little one. But I will return, I promise you.' Mahdu extricated herself from Cassy's frantic grasp. 'Be brave, larla. This cannot go on.' She made for the door but Cassy ran after her, clinging to her skirts.

'No, don't leave me again, Ma. Not now you've found me. I'll work for your lady. I'll do anything if you'll take me with you.'

Biddy's hand shot out and she grabbed Cassy by the hair, jerking her roughly away from Mahdu. She glared at her, twisting Cassy's long dark hair until she cried out in pain. 'Keep your trap shut, woman,' Biddy hissed. 'I could set the paving stones on fire if I told what I know, so be warned.'

Mahdu hesitated in the doorway, her expression bleak. 'We shall see.' She left the room and at the sound of the front door opening and then closing again, Biddy released Cassy, throwing her across the room.

'One word from you and I'll slit your throat, you little bastard. We'll see who has the upper hand.'

Chapter Three

Belinda sat in front of her dressing table, staring at her reflection in the mirror. The eyes that looked back at her were the same as they had always been, large and blue, fringed with long corn-coloured lashes, but the expression in them was not that of the young girl desperately in love. These were the eyes of a woman ten years older and wiser in the ways of the world but far from happy. In the room behind her she could see the reflected trappings of wealth and luxury that marriage to Sir Geoffrey Davenport had brought her. The elegant Louis Quinze furniture had been imported especially from France in order to please a young bride. The luxurious Chinese carpet in pastel shades of pink and blue complemented the swags and curtains at the tall Georgian windows of their town house in South Audley Street, and exactly matched the hangings on the four-poster bed. The cut-glass jars and perfume bottles and the silver-backed hairbrushes and mirror set neatly on the table in front of her went unnoticed and were taken for granted. The diamond rings on her fingers and the earrings that sparkled with each movement of her head meant nothing when compared to the hollow where once her heart had beaten for joy at the sound of a man's voice and the touch of his hand.

Belinda studied the looking-glass and Lady Davenport stared back at her, still young and beautiful at the age of twenty-seven, but a pale shadow of her former self. She sighed and her lips curved into a wry smile. She might be known as an accomplished and charming hostess and the wife of an eminent diplomat, but only she and Mahdu knew that the woman who moved about London society with such grace and apparent ease was a living ghost, a polished gem with no feelings or desires other than to sparkle and be admired. Belinda's heart was buried with the love of her life in a far distant grave, and the child whom she adored had been wrested from her arms the moment their ship had docked in London. Tears welled in her eyes as she remembered that foggy day in February when her three-month-old baby had been taken from her. She could still feel the tug of that tiny but insistent mouth on her nipples as she had given Cassandra her last feed, and the pain of her breasts engorged with milk that continued to flow for days after the baby was spirited away. Only Mahdu knew of her suffering, and it was she who had found a woman to care for the innocent love-child, whose only crime was to be born out of wedlock. Belinda dashed away the tears that trickled down her cheeks. Today was her daughter's tenth birthday, but there was little likelihood that she would ever see her child again.

She rested her forehead on her hand, trying hard to suppress the bitterness she still felt for her father, who had died not in battle but from an attack of cholera three years previously in the military hospital in Delhi.

He had been the one who engineered her marriage to Sir Geoffrey, who at the time was a widowed district officer who had elected to return to London, having accepted a prestigious position in the Foreign Office. Their courtship had of necessity been brief, fitted in between Sir Geoffrey's return to Delhi from Peshawar and his passage back to England. There had been the formal introduction, followed by well-chaperoned meetings that culminated in a rather stilted proposal of marriage in the grounds of the Red Fort. Schooled by her father and caring little what happened to her, she had accepted politely but with little enthusiasm. If Sir Geoffrey had been disappointed by her lukewarm response he did not show it; in fact he seemed relieved to have brought the matter to a satisfactory conclusion. It was, as Belinda told Mahdu later, as if he had negotiated a truce between warring factions and could retire from the battlefield with honours. He had kissed her hand and then, strangest of all, had blurted out the fact that he had a five-year-old son living in England and did not want to go through all that wretched business of having another child. He must, he had said gruffly, make that plain from the start so that she understood the situation and accepted the fact that there would be no issue from their union. He might have expanded on this further, but Colonel Phillips and the rest of the party emerged from the Red Fort ready it seemed to offer their congratulations even before the engagement had been announced. Belinda was to discover later that Sir Geoffrey's first wife, again a much younger woman, had died in childbirth, for which he blamed his son and heir. Young Oliver had been left at home in the care of a nanny and under the aegis of Sir Geoffrey's eccentric aunt, Mrs Flora Fulford-Browne.

Belinda laid her hand on her flat stomach, remembering how she had been kept out of sight as soon as the pregnancy began to show. What stories her father had invented to cover her non-appearance at functions she had never bothered to ask, but she and Mahdu had been sent to Bombay at the earliest opportunity. They stayed in the home of a retired army captain and his Indian wife, and it was there in a small room at the back of the house that Cassandra Phillips had been born. The labour had been long and difficult and Belinda had been certain she was dying, but the Scottish doctor who attended her had been brusque and to the point, never allowing sympathy to cloud his professional judgement. Mahdu had been at her side the whole time, bathing her forehead with cool water fragranced with rose petals and giving her sips of sweet coconut milk in an attempt to keep up her strength. When it was all over, Belinda had held her baby in her arms and for the first time since she heard of George's death, she felt something other than grief. She fell in love all over again but this time it was with their daughter. She was the most perfect and beautiful thing that Belinda had ever seen, but reality was soon to overshadow her joy and a week later they were on a ship bound for England.

'My lady, I am come.'

Belinda turned with a start at the sound of Mahdu's

45

voice. 'You've seen her? Did you speak to her? How is she? Is she well and happy?' The words tumbled from her lips, culminating in a sob.

'I saw her and I spoke to her, larla. But all is not well.'

'What do you mean? Is she sick?' Belinda's hand flew to her throat. She could feel her heart beating at twice its normal rate and she could hardly breathe. 'Tell me, Mahdu.'

'We knew that the place was not ideal, but until now I had only seen it at night, and the woman we trusted with our precious pearl was drunk today. She was dead to the world and stinking. It was all I could do to keep from snatching the little one up in my arms and bringing her home.'

'This is terrible news.' Belinda stared at her maid-servant, barely able to imagine the conditions in which her only child was living. 'Why didn't you notice this before? How could you have visited there every year on her birthday and not seen that she was living in squalor?'

Mahdu clasped her hands together, tears rolling down her cheeks. 'You have led a sheltered life, larla. You know nothing of how poor people live either in India or in London. If there was to be secrecy then this was the only way. Believe me, it hurt my heart to leave the baby in a slum with that woman, but she was supposed to be one of the best, and your gold was the insurance needed to keep your child alive. Others in similar circumstances are not so fortunate.'

Belinda stared at her in astonishment. This was the

longest speech she had ever heard coming from Mahdu's lips, and she realised that it was the plain and simple truth. A shaft of pain made her clutch her chest as if a dagger had pierced her heart. She had brought this terrible plight on the one person in the world who truly belonged to her: the child born out of the love she had shared with George. If only she had been honest with Geoffrey from the outset, but she had been very young and controlled by a domineering father as well as the mores of the times. But surely, she thought desperately, it would have been better to suffer disgrace and public ostracism than to bear the loss of her baby and to put her child's life in jeopardy. She raised her eyes to Mahdu's face and saw her pain mirrored in her trusted servant's eyes. 'What is she like, my baby girl?'

'She is brave and good. She looks like you but she has her father's dark hair and the eyes of a young doe, big and trusting yet fearful. She looks after tiny babies as if she were their mother. They call her Cassy.'

'Cassy.' Belinda savoured the name, repeating it over and over again. 'What have I done, Mahdu? How can I atone for my sins?'

'You are not the wicked one, Iarla. You were forced to give up your child by others. It is they who are to blame.'

Mahdu's loyalty brought a smile to Belinda's lips but her words were small comfort. 'I gave my baby up for all this.' She dismissed the opulence and luxury of her surroundings with a wave of her hand. 'I allowed myself to be bought and sold like a commodity, and

47

in doing so I lost my soul. I must do something for her and I want to see her for myself. I can't live a lie any longer, Mahdu.' She bowed her head and her slender body was wracked by sobs.

'There must be a way. We will think of one.' Kneeling at Belinda's side, Mahdu wrapped her arms around her, rocking and comforting her as she had done years ago when her mistress was a small child, but startled by a sudden rapping on the door she clambered to her feet.

'Wh-who is it?' Belinda asked, taking a handkerchief from one of the dressing table drawers.

'It is I, my dear.' Sir Geoffrey's voice sounded tentative and almost apologetic, as if he were overstepping his conjugal rights by visiting his wife in the afternoon.

'Tell him I'm asleep,' Belinda said, mopping her eyes with the scrap of fine cambric and lace.

Mahdu went to open the door. 'Her ladyship is resting, Sir Geoffrey.' She held the door slightly ajar making it impossible for him to see into the room.

'I'm afraid this won't wait.'

Taking a powder puff from a glass bowl, Belinda dabbed at her red nose and rising hastily she moved to the chaise longue by the fireplace. 'Come in, Geoffrey.'

Mahdu left the room as Sir Geoffrey entered. He regarded his wife with an anxious frown. 'Are you feeling unwell, my dear?'

The winter sun had already set and the shadows in the room were lengthening. Belinda had her back to the fire and she welcomed the half-light. 'I'm a little tired, Geoffrey.'

He nodded his head. 'You had a luncheon appoint-ment with Adele Pettifer, I believe.'

'It was in aid of the Houseless Poor. We serve together on the charity committee with several others.'

A glimmer of a smile flickered in Sir Geoffrey's grey eyes. 'No wonder you are exhausted, my dear. You must conserve your strength, you know.'

It was on the tip of her tongue to ask what for, but not wanting to hurt his feelings she held her tongue. Geoffrey was undemanding when it came to wifely duties in the bedchamber, and although that in itself was a relief she would have welcomed an occasional show of genuine affection. They had had separate bedrooms from the beginning, and their union had not been consummated for several weeks after the wedding. Even then it had been a brief encounter, repeated infrequently since that time. Sir Geoffrey was a polite lover, considerate but embarrassed as if the act was slightly distasteful and warranted an apology after-wards. If Belinda had not known love with George she might have gone through her married life completely oblivious to passion and ecstasy. 'Did you want some-thing, Geoffrey?'

'I'm afraid I have received rather disturbing news.' He paced the room with his hands clasped behind his back. 'My son, Oliver, has been expelled from Eton.'

His expression was so tragic that Belinda had an almost irrepressible desire to laugh. 'Oh, dear. I'm so sorry,' she murmured, holding her handkerchief to her lips. For a moment she had thought it was something terrible that he was about to tell her, but knowing Olly's ebullient nature he should have been prepared for something of the sort.

'It's such a dreadful thing to happen.' Sir Geoffrey continued pacing. 'Such a disgrace. Nothing like this has ever occurred in the Davenport family during the last five hundred years.'

'Perhaps it wasn't his fault?'

He stopped in front of her, his eyes bleak even as his lips made an attempt at a smile. 'You are too kind, Belinda. You have a generous nature, my dear. But Oliver is fifteen, almost a man, and he ought to know better.'

'What did he do?' Intrigued, Belinda forgot her own problems for a moment.

'He got drunk. I can't bear to repeat what he did when inebriated but it led to his expulsion. He's downstairs in the morning parlour as we speak.'

Concern for the boy brought Belinda to her feet. 'You haven't left him there all on his own, have you, Geoffrey? Is he all right? Has he eaten?'

He shook his head. 'I didn't ask.'

Belinda signalled to Mahdu. 'Go and see if Master Oliver wants for anything, please. Tell him I'll be down as soon as I've dressed.'

'Yes, my lady.'

Mahdu hurried from the room, leaving husband and wife facing each other. Sir Geoffrey glanced down at Belinda's breasts which were revealed as her peignoir had slipped from her shoulders, and he averted his eyes, a faint flush colouring his pale cheeks. 'Thank you, my dear. I'm afraid I'm not good at these things.

I have a meeting with the Secretary of State in half an hour and I mustn't be late.'

Belinda clutched the soft folds of silk and Brussels lace to cover her exposed flesh. 'I understand. Don't worry about Oliver, I'll look after him.'

'Don't spoil the boy, Belinda. I'll have stern words to say to him on my return.' Sir Geoffrey made to leave the room but hesitated, glancing back at her over his shoulder. 'I'll send your maid to help you get dressed. You'll embarrass the boy if sees you en déshabillé.' He stalked from the room clearing his throat as if he had just said something shocking.

Belinda's former languor was forgotten in her concern for young Oliver. Slipping off her peignoir she went over to her bed where Mahdu had laid out her afternoon gown. The dove-grey silk floated about her in a swirling mass, but as she attempted to fasten the tiny mother-of-pearl buttons at the back she found herself struggling. It was a relief when Mahdu returned to help her.

'You should have waited,' Mahdu scolded. 'I came as quickly as I could.'

Ignoring the implication that she was as helpless as a baby, Belinda was more concerned with Oliver than for herself. 'How is the boy? Is he very upset?'

Mahdu shook her head. 'He's full of bravado, but I think he's a little scared of his father.'

'I must see him right away.' Belinda fidgeted and received a sharp reprimand from Mahdu, but eventually she was ready to go downstairs to the morning parlour, and as she entered the room Oliver Davenport sprang to his feet. His anxious expression melted into a wide grin when he saw her.

'Have you come to nag me, Stepmother?'

Belinda held out her arms. 'Are you too big to give me a hug, Ollie?'

'Never. At least I don't mind in private. If the chaps at school could see me they'd think I'd gone soft in the head.' He crossed the floor to wrap his arms around her, lifting her off the ground in the process. She realised with a pang of regret that the little boy she had come to love was almost grown to manhood and would soon set female hearts aflutter. He was now tall and slim, and the once pretty child was maturing into a handsome young man who would no longer need his stepmother to comfort and cosset him.

'Put me down,' she said, chuckling. 'I want an explanation from you, my boy. What have you done this time?'

Oliver set her back on her feet. He ran his hand through his already tousled fair hair causing it to stand on end, and the contrite look on his face made him look young and vulnerable. 'Got drunk with the fellows and had a bout of fisticuffs with some of the local chaps. It was all good-natured at the start, but it got a bit out of hand and I knocked a bobby's helmet off. It didn't go down too well, I'm afraid.'

Belinda's lips twitched. 'You naughty boy. I don't know what your papa will say.'

'I do. He'll probably give me a good wigging and bundle me off into the army or worse.'

'He'll be angry, of course, but he wouldn't do that.'

Oliver's air of insouciance vanished and his face crumpled. 'He hates me, Belle.'

Shocked and alarmed by his obvious sincerity, Belinda laid her hand on his arm. 'No, Ollie. Of course he doesn't hate you.'

'He's every right to. I killed my mama.' Oliver's voice broke and he turned away from her, wiping his eyes on the back of his hand. 'If it hadn't have been for me, she'd be alive now.'

Belinda slipped her arm around his shoulders. 'That's nonsense, Ollie. Your mother died in childbirth. It's tragic but it's not uncommon. It wasn't your fault and no one, least of all your father, thinks any differently.'

He turned to look into her eyes. 'You're wrong, Belle. He can't abide me. That's why he left me in England while he went off to India. You wouldn't have abandoned your child, would you?'

His words struck her like barbs and she held him close, unable to look him in the eyes. Hadn't she done exactly the same thing, although for very different reasons? She could feel his pain and her heart ached for him. 'Now listen to me, Oliver,' she said softly. 'Your father left you in England because it was better for you, and not because he didn't want you with him. Have you any idea how many infants and young children die from disease in that country?'

He shook his head.

'It would have been a terrible risk,' Belinda continued without giving him time to voice further concerns. 'Your father knew that you would be safe here in London, and that your Aunt Flora would look after you.'

Oliver made a sound between a snort and a sob. He drew away from her and went to stand with his back to the fire, in a seemingly unconscious copy of the stance that his father often took. 'Aunt Flo is mad as a hatter, Belle. You wouldn't believe the things I saw and heard living with her. By the time I was five I'd had my first glass of port and puffed away on several cigars. I'd seen exotic dancers and men dressed like women. I'd stayed up until the early hours at some of her parties, falling asleep in a corner unnoticed until the tweeny came to clear the grate next morning.'

Belinda shrugged her shoulders. Flora Fulford-Browne's reputation for partying and eccentricity was almost legendary, but she had a good heart and her house in Duke Street was always filled with people, even if most of them were down on their luck and living on their hostess's generosity. 'That's as maybe, Ollie. But don't judge your father too harshly. He's a good man and he does what he thinks is right. No one can do better.'

'And do you love him, Belle? Does he make you happy?'

'Of course I'm happy. Why wouldn't I be?'

'Something makes you sad. I've heard it in your voice and seen it in your eyes. Sometimes I think it's because of me. I've always been a trial to you, I know that.'

Belinda met his troubled gaze with a straight look. 'Don't ever say that, Ollie. Yes, you've been a handful, and no you don't make me sad. In fact, I think having you to love and care for has made my life happier than

I could have hoped for, so don't let me hear you talking like that again.'

A reluctant smile lit his blue eyes. 'You're a fierce little thing when roused, aren't you, Belle? I love you, you can be sure of that.'

She went to him and had to raise herself on tiptoe to kiss his cheek. 'And I love you, you silly boy. So let's put all this behind us and think how we're going to set matters right with your papa.'

A knock on the door put a stop to the conversation and Hartley, the ageing butler, entered bearing a tray of cold pie and small beer. 'Cook sent this for Master Oliver,' he said stiffly as he placed the tray on a sofa table.

'Thank you, Hartley. That will be all.' Belinda waited until he had left the room. She turned to Oliver but he was already attacking the food with the appetite of a hungry schoolboy. 'Eat up,' she said, smiling, 'and then we'll decide what we're going to do with you.'

He swallowed convulsively, washing the mouthful down with a draught of ale. 'Good pie. The tuck at school is pigswill compared to Cook's food.'

'It's nice to see you haven't lost your appetite,' Belinda said wryly.

Oliver wiped his lips on a linen table napkin. 'I think it might be best if I go and stay with Aunt Flo for a few days, Belle. All things considered, it might give Pater a chance to cool down.'

'I think that's a very good idea.' Belinda tugged at the embroidered bell pull by the fireplace. 'I'll send for the carriage.'

'Are you coming with me then?' Oliver glanced up from his plate.

Belinda nodded her head. An idea had come to her and she wondered why she had not thought of it before.

Flora Fulford-Browne sat in a wingback chair by the fire, smoking a small black cheroot, and taking sips from a cut-crystal brandy glass. She eyed her nephew with unconcealed amusement. 'So you've been expelled from Eton, Ollie. I'm not surprised you've come to seek sanctuary in my house.'

'I knew you'd understand,' Oliver said happily. 'The pater ain't at all happy about it.'

'He'll get over it.' Flora held her glass out to him. 'Make yourself useful then, my boy. Pour me another snifter and then Poulton will find you a room. If there isn't one free then I'm afraid you'll have to share with someone.'

Belinda shifted on her seat, suddenly uncomfortable. 'What sort of person would he share with, Flora? I mean, Geoffrey would be very angry with me if I allowed him to put you out in any way.'

'Or if he were to share a room with one of my protégés,' Flora said, smiling. 'I know exactly what Geoffrey thinks of me and my household, although it didn't seem to worry him when he left Ollie with me and toddled off to India.'

Oliver had been attempting to pour a measure of brandy into the glass but his concentration faltered and he spilled some on the silver salver. 'I don't want to put you out, Aunt Flo.'

'Don't waste good cognac. That's one of the first lessons you'll have to learn if you're to stay here for any length of time.' Flora held out her hand to take the glass from him. 'You'll be fine here, Ollie. I'm sure we can squeeze you in somewhere, even if you have to share with the boot boy.' She tossed the butt of her cheroot into the fire. 'I'm teasing you, silly. Now go along and find Poulton, he'll look after you.'

As the door closed on Oliver, Belinda was still anxious. 'He's very young,' she said carefully. 'And some of your acquaintances are rather . . . er . . .'

'Bohemian?' Flora raised an eyebrow. 'Stop worrying about him and tell me why you came here today, Belinda.'

'Is it so obvious?'

'My dear girl, it's too late in the afternoon for a social call, and you could have sent Ollie on his own. After all he lived here for the first five years of his life, so it's not like sending him to the Antipodes. And you are troubled. I can see it in your eyes. Is it my brother? Does he beat you or is he having an illicit liaison with Adele Pettifer?'

The ridiculousness of this question wrought an involuntary giggle from Belinda. It was common knowledge amongst his family and close friends that Sir Geoffrey loathed Adele, and that the feeling was mutual. 'No, of course not, Flora,' she said hastily. 'Geoffrey wouldn't think of such a thing.'

Flora took another cheroot from a silver box on the table beside her chair and lit it with a spill from the fire. She inhaled and then exhaled with a satisfied sigh.

57

'You don't smoke, do you? No, I thought not, but maybe you should try it. Very good for the nerves and yours are apparently on edge. Now tell me what's bothering you, child.'

'I'm twenty-seven,' Belinda protested.

'And I'm sixty-two, six years Geoffrey's senior and more than twice your age, and I know a thing or two about life and love. Heaven knows I've had three husbands and outlived the lot of them, so I am an expert in my field.' She leaned forward, fixing Belinda with a gimlet eye. 'Geoffrey's not very good in the bedroom department, eh?'

Belinda's hands flew to her cheeks as she felt the blood rush to her face.

'There's no need to blush and look sheepish, Belle. I can imagine what my dear brother is like in bed and I wouldn't want to be on the receiving end of his polite prodding. Lord knows how he managed to father a child on poor young Emily, or why he left it until he was forty to get married in the first place. What he must have been like by the time he got to you, I shudder to think.'

Belinda could stand it no longer. 'Please, Flora, I didn't come to discuss my private life.'

'Then what did you come for?'

Struggling to regain her composure after this frank and embarrassingly shrewd assessment of her married life, Belinda took a deep breath and began slowly. 'As it happens, I had lunch with Adele and her friends today. We're on several charity committees and there's one particular case that's come to my notice.'

'It must be something close to your heart to bring you out when you should be at home dressing for dinner. I suppose Geoffrey demands it on the dot of eight and not a minute sooner nor a second later?'

'Yes, but that's not important compared to the fate of this poor child.' Belinda dropped her hands to her lap, clasping them tightly and digging her fingernails into her palms. 'A ten-year-old girl needs a good home. She's used to hard work, so I've been told, and is well-mannered and personable.'

'London is full of such children. Why would this one be any different from the rest? And what could I do for her that you could not?'

Belinda swallowed hard. This was going to be much more difficult than she had imagined. Now that she was putting her thoughts into words the whole matter must sound trivial and unimportant to one who was uninvolved. 'You know how strict Geoffrey is with the household budget.'

'Parsimonious, you mean.'

'Don't put words in my mouth, Flora. He's just careful and encourages me to run the house without undue extravagance.'

'Oh, save me from hearing any more of my brother's admirable qualities. So you want me to take this child into my house as a servant. Is that it?'

'I thought perhaps you could start her on light duties, perhaps a little dusting or helping in the kitchen, bearing in mind her tender years. And then, when she is a little older perhaps she could train as a lady's maid? You would hardly notice one more mouth to feed in such a large household, and the situation she is in now is quite intolerable, I assure you.'

'So where is this child now? What makes her life more precious than any other orphan or street urchin in London?'

Belinda winced as her fingernails cut into her flesh. She must keep calm and not appear too much involved or Flora, who was no fool, would see through her pretence of being a mere patron of a charity. 'It's been drawn to my attention,' she said, making an effort to remember recent newspaper reports on a similar case, 'that this little girl came from a good family but had the misfortune to be born on the wrong side of the blanket, as they say. She was left with a woman who purported to be respectable and agreed to care for her, but it appears this creature runs what they call a baby farm. She takes infants from their desperate parents for a sum of money and then neglects them grievously. Many of them die but the ones who survive are sold into virtual slavery or prostitution.' Belinda heard her voice break on a sob, but she could no longer control her emotions. 'I know you think I am a soft fool, but if I could just save this one poor child . . .'

Chapter Four

The beating that Cassy had received at Biddy's hands left her bruised and bleeding. Her calico blouse was ripped to shreds and the babies, who had been awakened by her screams of pain, were bawling their heads off, which further infuriated an already maddened Biddy. She tossed the cane across the room, snatched up the bag of coins that Mahdu had left to pay for Cassy's keep, and stamped out of the house slamming the door so hard that the windows rattled.

Despite her pain, Cassy's first instinct was to calm the terrified infants, but when they had settled down to sleep she found that she was shaking uncontrollably, and she finally gave way to tears. She collapsed onto a chair at the table, burying her face in her hands, and it was in this state that Bailey found her. He ministered to her injuries as tenderly as any woman, listening attentively to her tearful account of what had occurred earlier. He said little but she sensed that he was inwardly seething with rage.

'This can't go on,' he said as he finished bathing her wounds. 'It's happened afore, and I'm afraid she'll kill you if she ain't stopped.'

'Don't do nothing stupid, Bailey,' Cassy pleaded. 'You'll only make things worse.' She reached for the tattered blouse which he had peeled carefully from her raw flesh, but it was beyond repair and stiff with dried blood.

Bailey took it from her hand. 'You can't wear that, it's ruined.' He went to the corner of the room where his palliasse was rolled up against the wall and pulled out a bundle of clothes. He selected a shirt and wrapped it around her shoulders. 'There, that's me only good 'un. Your need is greater than mine, nipper.'

She slipped her arms into the garment which was far too big for her and the coarse material chafed against her sore back, but she managed a smile. 'Ta, Bailey, you're a toff. But now you ain't got a spare.'

'It don't matter,' he said, shrugging his shoulders. 'I'll take some of the old bitch's money and get us both new duds at the Rag Fair, but until then you're going to have to look like a scarecrow.'

This made her giggle despite her pain and then she remembered Freddie. Her bottom lip quivered. 'Where's me boy? What happened at the hospital?'

'Don't upset yourself again; he's in good hands. They took him in and put him on the children's ward where he'll be looked after proper.'

'He will get better, won't he, Bailey?'

He looked away as if afraid to meet her anxious gaze. 'I dunno, ducks.' He moved swiftly to the range and poked the embers into life. 'I'll make us a pot of tea. That'll be the ticket.'

Cassy wiped her eyes on the dangling shirtsleeve which was twice as long as her small arm. Her back felt as though it was on fire and every inch of her body ached, but she was still concerned for the babies left in her care. She went to check on them again, but Anna, Samuel and the twins lay asleep in their boxes, pale and silent like small wax effigies. She had to bend close to make certain they were still breathing. Despite all Cassy's best efforts, only the strong survived Biddy's regime of cruel neglect, but thankfully these little lives had been spared for another day.

'Come and get your tea, Cass,' Bailey said in a stage whisper.

She joined him at the table where to her delight she discovered that he had bought a pork pie for their supper. 'How did you afford it?' she murmured, licking her lips in anticipation of such a treat.

'Never you mind,' he said, tapping the side of his nose. 'Eat up and enjoy it. I don't want to see a crumb left or the old besom will know I've fiddled her out of tuppence, that is if she ever sobers up long enough to count her change.'

Cassy munched the pie, savouring each mouthful and making it last as long as she could. Good food was a rarity in Three Herring Court and their diet consisted mostly of bread and scrape, with the occasional smear of dripping if Biddy was feeling generous, or if Bailey managed to smuggle extra rations into the house. Having demolished the last crumb of pastry and licked her fingers one by one, Cassy sipped her tea, eyeing him curiously over the rim of the tin cup. 'Why do you stay here, Bailey? You could get a proper job and have a decent life away from this place.'

He scrunched up the piece of newspaper that had

been wrapped around the pie and tossed it onto the fire. 'I remember the day that Indian woman brought you here. The fog was so thick you couldn't see your hand in front of your face, let alone where you was stepping, and she almost tripped over me. She was looking for Biddy and I led her here, although God help me I don't think I done you any great service. In fact if I'd known what you was going to suffer all these years I'd have run away and left her to take you back home, wherever that was.'

'But I'd never have known you,' Cassy said, smiling despite her pain. 'And you're me bestest friend in the whole world.'

He reached across the table to pat her hand, but his eyes were bleak. 'You might not think that when I tell you me news, Cass.'

He did not seem to be able to look her in the eyes, and suddenly Cassy was afraid. 'You've found work somewhere and you're going to leave me here with her.'

'I got to go, Cass. I'm seventeen and I want to make me way in the world. If I can earn good money I'll make a home for you and me. I'll come back for you, I promise.'

A wail of despair rose in Cassy's throat and she struggled to contain it, clenching her teeth and hands in an attempt to prevent the scream from escaping her lips.

'Don't take on, little 'un. It ain't settled yet; I only met the recruiting sergeant today. He were looking for blokes like me, he said, and he made life in the army sound just the job. When I got enough money together

I'll rent a house and you can keep it for me. We might even be able to take young Freddie with us.'

A glimmer of hope punctured the black cloud that had descended upon Cassy. 'And Sammy too, and Anna and the twins?'

'Hold on, nipper. I ain't starting up in competition to old Biddy. I said maybe we could take Freddie, but that's just supposing everything goes well. What do you say, Cassy? Should I enlist in the army? It would mean I'd have to leave you for a while, but it wouldn't be forever, and we can't go on like this.'

Forever was a word that held little meaning for Cassy. She lived minute by minute, never knowing when the next blow was going to fall or where the next meal was going to come from. For a few brief moments she had dared to hope that her ma would take her away from this place, but Biddy had sent Mahdu off with a flea in her ear and Cassy's dream of being permanently reunited with her mother had disappeared like a puff of smoke from Biddy's clay pipe. Now she was in imminent danger of losing the one person who meant everything to her. She knew what he said made sense, but that did nothing to ease the agony of fear that threatened to overwhelm her. She said nothing, staring at Bailey as if she had been struck dumb. His face creased into lines of worry. 'Say something, Cassy. Tell me you understand.'

She shook her head and the tears that she had been struggling to hold back spilled from her eyes in an unstoppable bout of sobbing that wracked her small body. Bailey leapt to his feet and moved swiftly to her side, rocking her in his arms. 'Don't cry, nipper. Nothing's settled yet.'

'D-don't leave m-me. I'll d-die if you goes away.' Cassy had tried to be grown-up and brave, but the fear of living without Bailey was too great to bear. 'S-stay with me, p-please.'

He stroked her hair back from her forehead. 'Yes, yes, little 'un. Don't fret, I'll not desert you. The army can wait a bit. I daresay they can manage without Bailey Moon for another year or maybe two.'

Cassy rose from her palliasse early next morning. She had slept on her stomach to avoid hurting her back but the pain had awakened her several times in the night. She had lain petrified in the small hours when she had heard Biddy come crashing into the house, stumbling drunkenly into a chair and knocking it over. The babies had stirred in their sleep and Cassy had held her breath, praying that they would not cry. She knew only too well what Biddy was capable of when roused to a rage fuelled by drink. Cassy had once witnessed a horrific episode when a crying infant had been smashed against the wall by a drunken Biddy, who apparently remembered nothing when she sobered up next day. The baby had died, but if Elias Crabbe had suspected foul play he had said nothing, and the tiny corpse had been interred with a stranger. Cassy had lain there, stiff and silent, until Biddy had collapsed onto her iron bedstead and succumbed to the combined effects of alcohol and opium.

The babies began to whimper, but when Cassy went

to the larder to fetch the milk she found that it had turned sour and she would have to go to the dairy for a fresh supply. She did not want the infants to wake Biddy, and to keep them pacified if only for a short while she dissolved a spoonful of sugar in tepid water from the kettle. The air in the room was rank with the smell of sweat and stale alcohol, and Cassy felt her stomach heave as she crept past Biddy's bed. She paused as she saw a trail of vomit that had spewed from Biddy's mouth and pooled on the floor. There was something unnatural about Biddy's prostrate form. A cockroach crawled out of her open mouth and Cassy dropped the cup with a cry of horror.

'What's up?' Bailey raised himself on his elbow, gazing blearily around the room. 'What's wrong, Cass?'

She could not speak, only point. He leapt out of bed and hurried to her side. 'Oh, my God!' He leaned over to feel for the pulse in Biddy's fat neck. 'She's dead. Choked on her own vomit by the looks of things.' He pulled the filthy scrap of sheeting up to cover her head. 'She won't ever hurt you again, Cass. She's gone for good.'

The room began to spin around Cassy and she felt herself falling into a dark pit, but then she opened her eyes and found herself sitting on a chair and bent double so that her head was between her knees.

'Sorry, ducks,' Bailey said, helping her to sit upright. 'I couldn't lie you down because of your poor back.' He held a cup of water to her lips. 'Take small sips and you'll feel better in a moment.'

'Sh-she's really dead?'

'As a doornail. I'll go for the doctor if you're feeling well enough to be left. The nippers are all yelling their heads off so I'll get some milk first, if you can cope with them.'

The dizziness was passing and the water, although stale and tepid, was refreshing. 'It's what I do every day. Biddy never touches them unless it's to slap their poor little bums and legs.'

'Well she won't do that no more,' Bailey said wryly. 'She's gone straight to hell or there's no justice in the other world.' He ruffled Cassy's hair. 'Sit tight, little 'un. We'll sort things out, so don't fret.'

'But what will we do? How will we manage?' Cassy stared at him helplessly. Biddy might have been a monster but she had ruled their lives so completely that the thought of being without her was alarming.

'Before I do anything else I'm going to see if she had any of your ma's money left. I can't believe she could have spent it all in one night.' He went over to the bed and felt around beneath the sheet, turning his head away and screwing up his face as his hands searched for the purse. He uttered a sigh of relief as he found it, but his face fell as he examined its contents. 'There's enough to pay the doctor and bury the old besom,' he said grimly. 'She must have gambled the rest. I'm sorry, nipper, because it was your money.'

'I don't care,' Cassy murmured, turning her head away from the gruesome sight on the bed. 'Just get the milk, please, Bailey. The babies don't care whether she's alive or dead, they just want feeding.'

'There's enough for milk and fresh bread too. She

68

can have a pauper's funeral but we'll have a proper breakfast for once.'

The doctor came, and after a cursory examination he exhibited no surprise at Biddy's sudden demise. He signed a death certificate and advised Bailey to make arrangements with Elias Crabbe. He left holding a clean white handkerchief to his nose.

'I'll get her moved as soon as possible,' Bailey said, patting Cassy on the shoulder. 'We'll be all right, nipper. We'll find the rent money somehow, even if I have to go begging on the streets.'

Cassy gulped and nodded. They might be free of Biddy but she had a feeling that the nightmare was far from over.

Biddy's remains had been carted off to the funeral parlour with the help of Eddie, the rag and bone man who lived at the far end of the court, and his son Bob, who was a bit simple but what he lacked in brains he made up for in brawn. Bailey had bought them a pint or two in the pub by way of thanks, and he arrived back at the house in time to share a pie and mash supper with Cassy.

'We're living like kings,' she said happily. The babies were well fed for once, and clean. Cassy had been able to boil as much water as she pleased without having Biddy grumbling about the cost of the coal or telling her that too much washing was dangerous, particularly in winter. But Cassy instinctively knew that babies should be bathed at least once a day, and that their rags ought to be changed regularly to prevent the rash that tormented their tender skins. Bailey had fetched a large bag of coal from the merchants in Cripplegate, and an ample supplying of kindling. There were candles burning on the mantelshelf and on the table, and they were fragrant beeswax as opposed to the cheaper and smellier tallow. The floor had been swept and scrubbed and Cassy had consigned Biddy's urine-soaked mattress to the dust heap. Their surroundings might not have improved greatly in so short a time, but the room was clean and tidy and the worst of the smells had been eradicated.

Bailey sat back in his chair, grinning and patting his belly. 'That was good. The old bitch would be mad as fire if she could see us now.'

Cassy giggled as she ran her finger round her plate, licking up the last of the lovely thick gravy. 'We're all right, ain't we, Bailey? You don't have to go away now.'

His smile faded. 'I dunno about that, Cass. The money's almost gone and we've got all these mouths to feed. Biddy was going to take in a couple more kids, so I believe, and she used to make a bit extra by laying out corpses.'

Cassy pushed her plate away with shudder. 'I never knew that.'

'She were up to all sorts,' Bailey said, shaking his head. 'I'm certain she used to pilfer things from the dead people and sell the stuff to a fence in Blackfriars. She used to send me there with things although she never let on where they come from.'

'What sort of things?'

'Pocket watches, bits of jewellery, gold chains, silk scarves. All manner of small items that wouldn't at first be missed, and by the time they was she'd have cut and run.'

Cassy digested this in silence. Learning about Biddy's sordid world of petty crime was shocking, but even worse was the fact that Bailey seemed to have been a part of it. She met his frank gaze with a question in her eyes.

'I never stole a thing,' he said as if reading her thoughts. 'I was tempted at times, but I wouldn't want to go down that path. I don't want to spend the rest of me days languishing in a filthy prison cell.'

'What will we do, then? How will we manage?'

Bailey rested his elbows on the table, clasping his hands together with a thoughtful frown. 'Them nippers will have to go to the orphanage, Cass. No, don't look at me like that. It's for the best, because we can't raise babies. You're not much more than a baby yourself and I've got to earn money somehow. They need to go where they'll be looked after proper and nursed when they're sick.'

Cassy bowed her head. She knew what he said made sense, but to lose all her little charges in one go would tear at her heartstrings. 'But they ain't orphans,' she protested. 'Supposing their real mas come for them.'

'Cass, they've been abandoned by their mothers. Do you ever remember anyone coming to take their nipper home?'

'My ma came.'

'And she left again, ducks. I don't want to be cruel

71

but she can't have you with her any more than the unfortunate women who left their nippers with Biddy. They might as well have tossed their babies in the Thames as leave them to her tender mercies.'

'Ma will come back for me,' Cassy said firmly. 'She loves me, I could tell.'

'Of course she does, but don't set too much store by her coming to take you away, that's all I can say.'

Cassy rose to her feet and collected up their tin plates and mugs. 'She'll come back, I know she will. Everything will be all right.'

Bailey reached out to grasp her thin wrist. 'Don't be scared, Cass. I'll look after you, but we must find homes for the little 'uns.'

'And Freddie?'

'Him too.'

Bailey went out early next morning to seek out an orphanage that would take all four infants and Freddie, should he be well enough to leave hospital. Cassy was left alone with the babies and she took extra time with each one, washing and changing them before giving them their milk. If Ma comes back soon, she thought dreamily, perhaps she could take all of them. Maybe the kind lady who Ma works for would like to adopt a ready-made family, and then they could all live together in a big house up West, or perhaps Ma would take them to India. Cassy's imagination was working overtime. Closing her eyes she had visions of eternal sunshine, exotic flowers and beautiful ladies with black hair and dark brown eyes. Bailey had once given her a picture book that had fallen off a stall in Petticoat Lane, or so he said. It had been illustrated in rich bold colours depicting women swathed in bright silk saris and handsome men in strange costumes far different to the way men dressed in London. There had been elephants and tigers, monkeys and mongooses. The whole rich tapestry had filled her head with wonder and longing to see her native land.

Cassy jumped at the sound of someone hammering on the front door. She sat very still, waiting to see if any of the other tenants answered the urgent summons. She had heard Wall-eyed Betty and Edna screeching at each other earlier in the day. They often fought like wildcats and earlier in the morning they had fallen out over one thing or another, and one of them had slammed out of the house leaving the other to retire to bed. Cassy knew that for certain as the groaning bedsprings were an instant giveaway. She held her breath, listening intently, but there was no sign of life in the rest of the house, and if the din continued it would wake the babies and they would start bawling again. Reluctantly, Cassy went to open the door. 'Who's there?'

A booted foot was thrust over the threshold and Nogger Hayes, the rent collector, barged his way in. 'Where is she?' he demanded. 'Where's the old cow? She owes me a month's rent and I ain't going nowhere until I'm paid.'

Cassy backed away from him. Nogger was notoriously short-tempered and not above cuffing a person round the ear if he felt so inclined. 'She's dead,' Cassy whispered.

'Dead.' Nogger slapped his thighs and let out a roar of laughter that echoed throughout the house. 'That's the best excuse I've heard this week.'

'No, really,' Cassy insisted. 'She passed away yesterday. If you don't believe me you can go to Mr Crabbe's funeral parlour and see her laid out in her coffin.'

He scowled at her. 'If you're lying, it'll be the worse for you.'

'I'm telling you the truth.'

He pushed past her and barged into the room, peering into every dark nook and cranny as if he expected to find Biddy crouched in the smallest of spaces. He came to a halt, pushing his battered and greasy top hat to the back of his head. 'Well, she ain't here, that's obvious.'

'She's stone cold dead, I tell you.'

He grabbed Cassy by the scruff of her neck. 'I'll soon find out whether you're lying or not, but in any case, I want you and them brats out of here by tomorrow morning.'

Cassy wriggled free from his grasp. She stared at him with a shiver of disgust. He reminded her of a big black spider with his tight trousers and ill-fitting frock coat that must have belonged to a much smaller man. 'You can't turn us out on the street for nothing.'

He leaned towards her, his breath smelling of rotten fish and carious teeth. 'No rent money, no lodgings. Pay up a month's back rent and a month in advance and I might change me mind.' He strode out of the room and made for the staircase. 'Now this is part of my job I don't mind. I'm going to collect me rent one way or another from Wall-eyed Betty and Edna.' He disappeared around the bend in the stairs.

Cassy closed the door of the big room and leaned against it trembling. She wished that Bailey would come home. She needed to talk to him urgently. Was there enough money to give Nogger what he demanded? She simply did not know, and there was nothing she could do but sit and wait for Bailey to return.

'We haven't got anything like that amount,' Bailey said when she told him of Nogger's demands. 'I thought she might have owed a week, but the old bitch must have been spending the lot on drink and opium. There's no way we can pay him, Cass.'

'What will we do?'

'I dunno.' He took off his cap and threw it across the room. 'I've had no luck with them bloody orphan asylums. They ain't interested in abandoned babies; all they want is nippers from wealthy families who can afford to donate money to their cause. I've worn holes in me boots tramping from one place to the other. No one wants the poor little mites, and that's a fact.'

'Have you paid Mr Crabbe?' Cassy asked as an idea occurred to her. 'Leave Biddy to have a pauper's funeral and we can use the money for rent and stay on here. I'll look after the babies and you can find work somewhere. You can read and write, you're clever, Bailey.'

'It's no use, nipper. Old Crabbe's no fool. He wanted the money up front or he wouldn't take her. I could hardly leave her on the pavement; although it was tempting, believe you me.'

'Then we've no money and no one wants the babies, and tomorrow we're going to be thrown out on the street.'

He ruffled her hair. 'That's it in a nutshell, Cass. But we ain't beaten yet, and the first thing to do is to find the little 'uns a home. If the orphanages won't take them in then there's only one place left.'

'Not the workhouse, Bailey. Oh, you can't mean to leave them poor little mites in that awful place.'

'At last they'll get three meals a day, and a smattering of education. They'll have a chance in life, which is more than they had with Biddy.'

'But the workhouse,' Cassy's breath hitched on a sob. 'I can't bear to think of it.'

Next morning before daybreak, Cassy had fed and changed the babies and they were tucked up in two herring boxes like little fish, protected from the bitter cold by the coverlet from Biddy's bed. Bailey had borrowed Eddie's barrow, promising to return it in time for him to begin his daily round. The steel-rimmed wooden wheels made grinding noises as the cart rumbled over the frosty cobblestones. St Luke's workhouse was less than a mile away, but they had to push the heavy cart through narrow streets choked with horse-drawn vehicles and costermongers' barrows. The workhouse was situated in Shepherdess Walk, not more than a stone's throw from the Grecian Theatre and the Eagle Tavern, but these landmarks held no interest for Cassy.

76

She tried to be brave but leaving the little ones outside the huge iron gates was the hardest thing she had ever done. If it had not been for Bailey's determined cheerfulness and optimism, she would have turned round and taken them back to the only home they had ever known. But the infants slept even as Bailey laid their boxes on the ice-cold paving stones, and he lifted Cassy onto the cart in their place. 'We'll get back twice as quick this way,' he said with a grim smile. 'Hold tight, Cass.'

The first grey light of dawn had begun to filter between the tightly packed buildings in Three Herring Court. They left the cart outside the house where Eddie and his son lived in a damp basement surrounded by piles of objects that had been discarded by some, but might have a small street value to others. Cassy slipped her hand into Bailey's as they walked the last few yards to the home that they were in danger of losing. 'What will we do now?' she murmured nervously. 'Nogger will be back to collect his money and if we can't pay we'll be out on the street.'

Bailey squeezed her fingers. 'I got a job, ducks. I was waiting for the right moment to tell you, but perhaps Nogger will give us a bit more time to pay in the circumstances, and . . .' He broke off as a man in uniform stepped out of the shadows.

'Where was you last evening, Private Moon? You was supposed to report for duty but you didn't turn up. You're on a charge, Private. Absent without leave and you ain't even been in the army one day. Now that's a record in my book. You're in trouble, my son.'

Chapter Five

Cassy sat on the front step with her pitifully few belongings tied up in a scrap of cloth. Dazed and too heartbroken to cry, she huddled against the door that was closed on her forever. Bailey had been dragged off by the recruiting sergeant, who had refused to listen to his protests, insisting that no one was exempt from the rules no matter what their personal situation. Bailey, it seemed, had enlisted in the army thinking he had a day or two in which to sort out his affairs, but the army had other ideas. Now he was gone and the babies would have been taken into the workhouse to endure the fate of the sick and destitute. Then there was poor little Freddie, left in the hospital with no one other than herself to care if he lived or died. She could only hope that some charitable person would take him under their wing and see to it that he had a decent upbringing. Perhaps he would have a better chance now than if he had remained with Biddy.

Cassy made an effort to put him and the other infants out of her mind as she struggled to come to terms with her greatest loss. How she would face the world without Bailey she could not begin to imagine. His was the first voice she remembered hearing and the only person who had shown her kindness and affection. He was her family and she could not envisage a future without him. And then, as if matters could get any worse, Nogger had turned up soon after Bailey's sudden departure and he had been less than sympathetic.

Now she was alone and although Bailey had turned out his pockets and given her everything he had in the whole world, she only had tuppence three farthings and that would not go far. A sleety rain had begun to fall, and she had only a thin woollen shawl to protect her from the cold and damp. The walk to the workhouse had all but done for her boots and the uppers flapped open, exposing her bare toes, while the rainwater seeped through holes the size of pennies in the soles. If only she knew where her mother worked she could make her way there and throw herself on the rich lady's mercy. Ma would look after her, but she had no idea where to find her. For the first time in her life, Cassy was utterly alone and there was no one to whom she could turn. There was only one place to go and she had already been there once that day. She struggled to her feet. She had a simple choice: the workhouse or a slow painful death from starvation and exposure on the streets.

She struggled to her feet, and clutching the bundle beneath her arm she made her way out of the court into Redcross Street. With her shawl wrapped tightly around her head and half blinded by the rain beating on her face, she stepped off the pavement and was almost run down by a carriage and pair. The coachman drew the horses to a sudden halt and Cassy collapsed in the gutter, unhurt but in a state of shock. All round her there was noise. The terrified horses whinnied and snorted, pounding their hooves on the cobbles in their distress. The coachman was roaring expletives and from the carriage came the sound of a woman's voice.

'What's wrong, Smith?'

Someone was lifting her from the mud and dung that clogged the gutter and a voice was demanding to know if she was hurt, but Cassy shook free of the helping hands. If an angel had flown down from heaven and spoken to her she could not have been happier. She staggered to the door of the carriage, peering up at the anxious face of the occupant. 'Ma, is it really you?'

'Heaven preserve us. Cassy.' The door swung open almost knocking Cassy off her feet, but the groom, who had been the one to lift her from the mud, caught her before she fell to the ground.

'Steady on there, nipper.' The voice was gruff but kindly.

'Is she all right, Smith?' Mahdu alighted from the carriage, landing in a filthy puddle but seemingly oblivious to the fact that her shoes were muddied and her stockings ruined. 'Are you hurt, child?'

'It's a miracle,' Cassy breathed. 'You found me, Ma.'

Mahdu cast an anxious glance at the groom. 'Lift her into the carriage, Smith. The poor child must be delirious if she thinks I am her mother.'

Smith looked doubtful. 'But she's a guttersnipe. She must live round here and her folks will be looking for her.'

'This is the child I came for,' Mahdu said firmly. 'I

don't know why she is in this state, but I am instructed to take her to Mrs Fulford-Browne's establishment in Duke Street. Those are Lady Davenport's orders.'

Reluctantly, Smith lifted Cassy into the carriage, and Mahdu climbed in after her. 'Tell Watkins to drive on. Mrs Fulford-Browne is expecting us.' She slammed the carriage door as if to emphasise her words and the groom disappeared from view. Moments later the carriage began to move forward and Mahdu turned to Cassy with an anxious expression on her normally serene countenance. 'Are you hurt in any way, child?'

'Mama, you came for me,' Cassy sobbed, throwing herself into Mahdu's arms. 'I knew you would.'

Gently Mahdu freed herself from Cassy's frantic grasp. 'I could not leave you with that dreadful woman, larla. But there is something you must understand.'

Cassy stared into the handsome face of the woman she believed to be her mother, and she knew that she would do anything to please her. 'Tell me, Ma. I'll be a good girl, I promise.'

'I have no doubt about that, but you must never refer to me as your mother. Never. Do you understand?'

'Why mustn't I?'

'There are good reasons, larla. You must trust me, and do exactly as I say. I am taking you to the home of a kind but slightly eccentric lady, called Mrs Fulford-Browne. She is related by marriage to my mistress, Lady Davenport, who has your best interests at heart. Our relationship will be a big secret, and one you must keep.'

'A secret,' Cassy repeated slowly. 'Are you ashamed of me, Ma?'

'Mahdu. You must call me that.'

'I don't understand.' Cassy's eyes filled with tears and her bottom lip quivered. She was trying hard to be brave and grown-up but it was all too much for her.

Mahdu slipped her arm around Cassy's shoulders. 'There, there. Don't upset yourself, little one. All I am allowed to tell you is that you will be well looked after by Mrs Fulford-Browne, and I will be able to see you from time to time. One day, when the time is right, the secret of your birth will be revealed, but until then you must be a good girl and do as you are told. Will you make me that promise, larla?'

Cassy's head was whirling. Everything had happened so fast that it seemed as though the world was spinning at a different rate. She was emotionally exhausted, tired and very hungry. She nodded her head, unable to speak.

'I think we understand each other,' Mahdu said gently. 'You will be well looked after, little one. Don't be afraid.'

But Cassy was afraid when Smith lifted her from the carriage and set her down on the pavement outside the elegant Georgian townhouse in Duke Street. She gazed up at the imposing façade thinking that no lesser personage than a duke must live in such a grand mansion, and he had the street named after him too. Perhaps Mrs Fulford-Browne was his housekeeper, a bit like Biddy, because it would be impossible for a mere woman to own such an establishment. Cassy knew nothing about houses belonging to the gentry, but she was certain that poor children were not normally allowed to enter by the front door, especially when it was opened by a man in a black tailcoat who looked as though he had swallowed a poker.

'Good morning, Poulton,' Mahdu said calmly. 'Mrs Fulford-Browne is expecting us.'

Poulton's sallow skin flushed brick-red as though, Cassy thought, the fire iron he had apparently swallowed had been white hot. She eyed him warily. He was looking down his nose as if she were a nasty smell and she hid behind Mahdu, clutching her skirts as she stepped over the threshold forcing Poulton to move aside.

'Really, miss. This won't do,' he said stiffly. 'The tradesmen's entrance is more suitable for her sort.'

Mahdu fixed him with a stony stare. 'Please inform Madam that we are here.'

This was a side of Mahdu that Cassy had not seen before, and it was obvious that Ma could hold her own when confronted with a bag of wind like the pompous butler. Cassy's heart swelled with pride. She did not understand what was going on, but she could see that the man was annoyed.

Poulton's shoulders twitched and his lips disappeared into a thin line of disapproval but he stalked off, leaving them standing in the vestibule while he mounted the staircase, which curved in a great sweep to the first floor. Moments later he reappeared at the top of the stairs, beckoning to them with a set expression on his face.

'There's no need to be scared,' Mahdu said, taking Cassy by the hand. 'Speak only when you're spoken too and leave the rest to me.'

If Cassy had thought that the entrance hall, stairs and first floor landing were grand, she was almost overwhelmed by the spacious drawing room. It might be raining outside but the gasoliers filled the room with light, making it seem as if the sun was shining through the tall windows. A fire burned brightly in the grate and the groups of spindly gilded chairs and sofas were upholstered in rich blue velvet. Matching curtains and swags framed the windows and the deep colour contrasted with the pale cream carpet. There were mirrors everywhere and gilt candle sconces on either side of a white marble fireplace. Cassy's eyes almost popped out of her head as she gazed around the luxurious room. Never in all her born days had she imagined that anyone could live like this. She jumped as she realised that Mahdu was speaking to her.

'Curtsey,' Mahdu hissed. 'Show some respect, Cassy.'

'What's curtsey when it's at home?' Cassy whispered.

'Come closer so that I can see you.'

The strident voice emanating from the depths of a wingback chair close to the fireplace made Cassy turn to Mahdu in sudden panic. 'I want to go home.'

'Nonsense,' Flora said, leaning forward and raising a lorgnette to peer at Cassy. 'Come here, child. I won't eat you.'

Mahdu nodded her head, and Cassy approached the lady, clasping her hands tightly behind her back. 'You ain't going to clout me round the lughole, are you, lady?'

Flora recoiled slightly and then her lips quivered and she chuckled. 'No, I'm not going to do anything of the sort. Come here, and let me look at you.' She angled her head, surveying Cassy from head to foot. 'Great heavens, child. What a state you're in.' She beckoned to Mahdu. 'Take her to Mrs Middleton, and tell her to make certain the child is bathed and deloused before I see her again. Just looking at her is making me itch.'

Cassy found herself dismissed with a wave of a hand laden with gold rings. The old lady was wearing more jewellery than the Queen, although Cassy had only seen pictures of that royal personage. If Mrs Fulford-Browne had a crown or two tucked away in her room, Cassy would not have been surprised. She was so taken with her new employer's clothes and jewels that she forgot to be scared. 'Are you very rich, missis?'

Mahdu's gasp of horror was accompanied by a slap. 'Mind your manners, Cassy. Apologise to Mrs Fulford-Browne for your impudence.'

'Don't scold her,' Flora said, smiling. 'She says whatever comes into her head, and I find that refreshing. Too many people say what they think I want to hear. That's the penalty wealthy widows have to pay for inheriting the estates of three husbands. Yes, Cassy. I am very rich and I'm not ashamed to say so.' She leaned forward, abandoning her lorgnette. 'And I think beneath that veneer of grime you have the promise of great beauty. I don't doubt that one day your face will be your fortune. Now go away and get cleaned up. I don't want to see you again until you smell like a rose and look like a human being rather than something dragged out of the gutter.'

Mahdu was still scolding Cassy when they arrived below stairs in the servants' hall. 'You must not ever speak to the lady of the house in that impertinent way again.'

'No, Ma.'

'What did I tell you about that?' Mahdu leaned down so that her lips were close to Cassy's ear. 'I am not your mother, larla. Remember that always.'

Before Cassy had a chance to reply they were interrupted by the entrance of a woman almost as grand as Mrs Fulford-Browne, although this person was dressed in sombre black bombazine and not fine silks. The only embellishment to her high-necked gown was a chatelaine at her waist laden with keys of all shapes and sizes.

'Say how do you do to Mrs Middleton,' Mahdu urged. 'She is Mrs Fulford-Browne's housekeeper and from now on you will do as she tells you.'

'So this is Lady Davenport's protégée.' Mrs Middleton looked Cassy up and down with apparent distaste. 'She's small and puny. I doubt if she will be much use to me.'

'She will grow,' Mahdu said defensively. 'The poor child has not had the best start in life. Good food and warm clothes will make all the difference. She is bright and she will learn quickly.'

'She's filthy.' Mrs Middleton moved to the doorway which led into the kitchen. 'Nancy, come here.'

A girl of fourteen or fifteen bounced into the room, wiping her hands on her apron. 'Yes, Mrs Middleton.'

'Take Cassy to the scullery and clean her up. Wash her hair and give it a thorough rinse with vinegar. Take all her clothes and burn them. I'll see if I can find her a dress in my linen cupboard, although I doubt if there are any small enough.'

'I can sew, missis,' Cassy said, braving the stern woman's scorn. 'I used to make nightgowns out of old sheets for the little 'uns.' Her eyes filled with tears yet again at the memory of the babies they had abandoned at the workhouse gates.

'I've no wish to hear that. Take her away, Nancy. I don't want to see her again until she's decent.' Mrs Middleton turned to Mahdu, dismissing Cassy with a wave of her hand. 'You can tell your mistress that the child will be well cared for here.'

'C'mon, you.' Nancy prodded Cassy in the back. 'Go through the kitchen into the scullery. I hope there's plenty of hot water 'cos it looks like you'll need a good soak and a scrub with carbolic to get you white again.'

Cassy shot a helpless glance in Mahdu's direction but she seemed deep in conversation with the woman in black. Cassy knew then that she was well and truly on her own. She stopped in the doorway, turning on Nancy with a determined lift of her chin. 'It ain't all dirt. I was born in India and I can't help the colour of me skin.'

Nancy grinned. 'Well, I'm half Irish. I suppose that makes us both foreigners.'

An hour later Cassy was wrapped in a towel and

seated at the long table in the servants' hall eating boiled mutton and caper sauce, a delicacy that she had never even heard of, let alone tasted. Her scalp was sore where Nancy had dragged a fine-toothed comb through it again and again to remove the head lice and nits, and her eyes still smarted from the vinegar rinse that had found its way into them even though she had kept them shut tight. Her whole body glowed after being rubbed with lye soap and scrubbed with a loofah. She was licking the gravy from her plate when Nancy entered the room carrying a bowl of something that smelt sweet and delicious.

'Strewth, girl. You'll bust a gut if you keep stuffing your face like that.' Nancy whisked away the plate. 'And don't let Mrs M catch you doing that. It ain't done.' She set the bowl on the table in front of Cassy. 'Try that. I bet you ain't never tasted nothing like Cook's treacle pudding and custard. I reckon we're the best fed servants in the whole of London. We has to work hard for our vittles, but at least Mrs Middleton sees we gets fed proper. I never saw such food until I come here. Bread and scrape is what we gets at home in Clapton, with Clare Market duck on high days and holidays.'

Cassy paused with a spoonful of golden pudding and creamy custard halfway to her lips. 'What's Clare Market duck when it's at home?'

'Boiled bullock's head stuffed with sage and onions. Very tasty, but Cook wouldn't be seen dead serving suchlike to her upstairs. Very particular is Mrs Fulford-Browne.' Nancy pulled out a chair and sat down next to Cassy. 'We calls her Flo in private, that's the nick-name given her by her toff friends, but be careful not to say it in front of Mrs M or Cook. They'd tan your backside if they heard such disrespect.' Nancy tapped the side of her nose, but her smile faded as Mrs Middleton entered the room.

'Haven't you any work to do, Nancy?'

'Yes'm.' Nancy bobbed a curtsey and hurried into the kitchen.

Cassy eyed Mrs Middleton warily, gulping down her food as fast as she could in case her plate was snatched away from her before she had scraped out the last deli-cious drop of custard.

'I've found a dress that fitted the scullery maid when she first started working here,' Mrs Middleton said, holding up a garment that was far prettier than anything Cassy had ever possessed in her whole life. She dropped her spoon on the plate with a clatter.

'Is that for me, missis?'

'You must address me as Mrs Middleton. Stand up and drop the towel. There's no one to see you but me, and I've had five children of my own, so the sight of a naked girl is nothing new to me.'

Cassy stood up and allowed the towel to fall to the floor, holding her arms above her head and shivering as the cool cotton print slid over her skinny frame. Mrs Middleton made tut-tutting noises as she fastened the buttons at the back. The dress was at least two sizes too large, but with a few judicious tucks and by dint of tying the sash tightly round Cassy's slender waist, the resultant fit was reasonable.

'Passable,' Mrs Middleton said, pursing her lips. 'But you'll soon grow into it. Now we must find you some boots. Your old ones have been consigned to the dustcart.'

Cassy fingered the material with a thrill of delight. 'I ain't never had nothing so fine.'

'Undoubtedly. Now what on earth am I to do with a girl your age?' Mrs Middleton eyed Cassy as though she were a firework about to explode. 'What can you do, child?'

'I can sweep floors and look after babies,' Cassy said earnestly. 'I'm good with nippers.'

'There are no nippers, as you call them, in this house. You are the youngest person here and I intend it to remain that way.'

'But where are your nippers?' Cassy asked shyly. 'Don't they live with you now?'

'My children are grown up and married with families of their own. Not that it's any of your business, Cassy. You must learn to be seen and not heard. You are not only a child, but you are in service now. You will share an attic room with Nancy and Clara, and you will do as you are told at all times. Do you under-stand me?'

Cassy understood only too well. She had spent her short life under Biddy's strict rule where even the slightest mistake was rewarded by a thrashing or a cuff round the head. She expected nothing less here. The house might be a palace and she might be dressed like a little princess, but she had few illusions as to her position in the scheme of things. She was at the bottom of the pile, but even so a small flame of optimism burned in her soul. From the bottom there was only one way to go and that was up.

Mrs Middleton tweaked Cassy's ear just hard enough to make her look up with a start. 'You were day-dreaming. I don't believe you heard a single word I said.'

Cassy bit her lip. The accusation was true; she had not even been aware that Mrs Middleton was speaking. She said nothing, which had been the safest course when she was being berated by Biddy. Mrs Middleton sighed heavily. 'I can see that this is going to be very difficult. Come with me.'

Cassy followed her out of the servants' hall and down a winding passage with doors leading off on either side. There was lettering on them but as Cassy could not read the words meant nothing to her. Mrs Middleton stopped and selected a key from the bunch hanging at her waist. She unlocked a door and went into the room, beckoning Cassy to follow her. 'This is the sewing room,' she said, pointing to a chair. 'Sit down and you can show me how competent you are with a needle and thread.' She selected a torn sheet from a pile on the table and held it up. 'This sheet has been turned sides to middle, but is now past repair, and I want it made into dusting cloths.' With one swift movement she ripped it in half, repeating the action until she had six raw-edged pieces of material. 'I want these hemmed neatly.' She took a wicker sewing basket from a shelf and put it down on the table in front of Cassy. 'You'll find needles, thread and scissors inside.

91

I'll leave you to get on with it and I'll come back in an hour to see how you're getting on.' She whisked out of the room without giving Cassy a chance to speak.

Cassy was eager to please but she was also curious. She sat for a moment taking in the details of the small room, from the red Turkey carpet on the floor to the whitewashed walls lined with shelves. The dark wood mantelshelf was bare of ornaments except for a small brass clock, but as Cassy could not tell the time it was pointless trying to work out the passing of the hour. The furnishings were minimal: a table covered with a chenille cloth; two wooden chairs with rush seats; and a strange-looking contraption set against the far wall. Cassy rose to her feet to examine the sewing machine but a tentative touch of her foot on the treadle made the thing whirr into life, causing her to leap away from it in fear. She had no idea what it did, but she was not going to touch it again in case it did something even more alarming. She had visions of her fingers being trapped beneath the fierce-looking needle, or her hair being caught up in the wheel. She went instead to the window and peered out, but all she could see was a narrow passage and a high wall topped with iron railings. She went back to the table and opened the basket to search for a needle and thread. She had never been taught how to sew but had picked up the rudiments by studying seams on ready-made clothes. She had also taught herself to darn after a fashion, and sewing a straight seam was reasonably easy.

She set to work, eager to please Mrs Middleton and to demonstrate that she was capable of earning her keep. But as she plied her needle her mind was free to wander and her thoughts inevitably turned to Bailey and the children she had been forced to abandon. She hoped and prayed that he would not be in too much trouble with the angry sergeant, and that they would not punish him for trying to do the right thing by her and the nippers. A lump of sheer misery settled in her stomach with the thought that she might never see her friend again. Even if he was allowed leave from the army, he would not know where to begin looking for her, and she had no idea where to find him. As to the babies, she could only hope that they stood a chance of survival in the workhouse. She tried not to think of the young girl who was mother to the twins; the poor thing would be heartbroken if she tried to find them in Three Herring Court and discovered that her babies had been spirited away. It would be enough to kill her, Cassy thought sadly. Then there was Freddie, left in the children's ward at Bart's hospital. As she plied her needle, Cassy made a firm resolve, a promise to herself that she would find a way to visit him there, come what may.

She had been so intent on her task that she had not noticed that it was getting dark, and the room was cold as no one had thought to light a fire to keep Cassy warm while she worked. She had no means of lighting the work candles and she was having difficulty in seeing her stitches. She looked up with a start as the door opened and light flooded into the room.

'Good heavens, child. Why are you sitting in the dark?' Mrs Middleton sailed into the room carrying a lighted oil lamp which she placed on the table. She glanced at the empty grate and shivered. 'I told that dratted girl to light the fire in here.' She snatched the piece of material from Cassy's numb fingers. 'You're blue with cold, child. Have you no commonsense? Why didn't you come and ask for candles and someone to light the fire?'

Cassy shook her head. 'I didn't like to.' She thought for a moment that Mrs Middleton was going to tell her off, but she turned away to examine the tiny stitches that Cassy had laboriously worked on the worn cloth.

'I'm surprised,' Mrs Middleton said, picking over the small pile of dusting cloths. 'You've worked hard and these are quite passable for their intended purpose. I think with some tuition you might become a good needlewoman, Cassy. Maybe you will be of some use to us after all.'

Cassy's heart swelled with pride. This was the first compliment she had ever received and she did not quite know how to respond. She said nothing, but she could not help smiling.

'I'd quite forgotten you,' Mrs Middleton said, folding the cloths and replacing them on the table. 'We've had supper but I'll get Cook to make up a tray for you, and as a special treat you can have it in my private room. I don't want you going down with a chill on your first day in Duke Street. Come with me.' She bustled out of the room with Cassy stumbling after her.

Later, after a supper of vegetable soup and a plate of bread thickly spread with butter, followed by a slice of seed cake and a cup of cocoa, Cassy was taken up to the top of the house where she was to share a room with Nancy and Clara. It was chilly in the room beneath the eaves, but for the first time in her life she had a proper bed with a wool mattress, a pillow, clean sheets and a patchwork coverlet. Clara, the scullery maid who had outgrown the frock that Cassy now wore, had been delegated to show her where she slept. She was a lumpy East End girl of fourteen, with a spotty complexion and a wide mouth that never seemed to be closed. Words spilled from her mouth in a constant stream, and if she was not complaining about one thing or another she was passing on titbits of gossip. She had made it plain that she thought the task in hand was beneath her, but she rather grudgingly emptied a drawer in the pine chest for Cassy's use.

'Is that all you got?' Clara said, eyeing Cassy's possessions with a curl of her lip. 'I'll be keeping an eye on you, young 'un, so don't think you can borrow any of my things, because if you touch anything of mine I'll chop your fingers off.' She whisked a large white china chamber pot from beneath her bed. 'If you have to go in the night you piss in this, not on your mattress. The last kitchen maid we had was a regular bed-wetter. Mrs M got rid of her pretty damn quick I can tell you. You don't do that, I hope.'

Cassy shook her head. She was still eyeing the chamber pot in awe. All they had in Three Herring Court was a zinc bucket, which was put out in the morning for the night soil collectors. She was learning how the rich folk up West lived and it was quite a revelation.

'It won't bite you, silly,' Clara said impatiently. 'Anyway, you'd best get into bed afore Nancy and me comes up. We're slipping out for a few minutes. Nancy has her eye on the boot boy next door, and I fancy the butcher's lad, but he can't always get off in time so we might be out after lock-up.'

'But how will you get in if the door's locked?' Cassy stared at her wide-eyed.

'We got our ways of getting in after old Poulton's gone to bed, but if you split on us it'll be the worse for you, nipper. I'll cut your tongue out with Cook's sharpest chiv. D'you understand me, Cassy?'

She might not be able to read and write but Cassy knew that a chiv was a blade, and she had learned long ago that you did not argue with someone wielding a knife. She was not sure that Clara would carry out such a threat, but she was not going to take any chances. 'I won't say nothing, Clara. Cross me heart and hope to die.'

'You will if you peach on me,' Clara said grimly. 'Now pipe down and go to bed. I ain't paid to be a nursery maid, and get this into your head, nipper. If you tells on us I'll have your guts for garters and you'll not live to see your next birthday.'

Chapter Six

The next few days were a steep learning curve for Cassy. Everything she said or did was under close scrutiny not only from Mrs Middleton but the whole of the staff in Duke Street, from the hall boy to Cook. Every time she opened her mouth she seemed to say the wrong thing or else her grammar was incorrect. Her table manners came in for criticism from Poulton, the butler, who seemed to be in charge of everything and everyone below stairs and was treated like a demigod. She had to learn who was who and who did what in a very short space of time. The servants, she discovered, were very touchy about their place in the hierarchy and it was easy to offend someone albeit unintentionally. She tried hard to remember their names and what position they held, and which of them was more senior than the other, but she often got it wrong and was subjected to stern reprimands. But these were as nothing compared to the beatings she had received at Biddy's hands and she began, very gradually, to settle into the daily routine.

Her first proper assignment after merely observing the workings of the big house was to help Clara in the scullery, but being small in stature Cassy found it necessary to stand on an upturned bucket in order to wash the vast mountain of dishes, pots and pans. She managed for a while but when Clara poured a kettle of extremely hot water into the sink Cassy lost her balance, falling backwards onto the quarry tiles, cracking her head and even worse breaking a valuable cut-glass bowl in the process. Cook marched into the room, but her angry tirade ceased when she realised that Cassy had been scalded and that blood was flowing freely from a cut on her hand. When she had been cleaned up and had salve put on her burns and a bandage applied to the afflicted hand, Cassy was set to work with the tweeny. She was dusting ornaments in the dining room, but her injured hand made her clumsy and she dropped a Dresden shepherdess on the hearth, watching in horror as the smiling porcelain head rolled across the tiles. This time she was marched off to stand before her new employer with Mrs Middleton protesting volubly as to the seemingly impossible task of supervising a clumsy ten-year-old.

Flora was dressed for going out in an emerald-green velvet mantle over a pale grey silk gown. The skirts were draped at the front and gathered up at the back to form a low-placed bustle, and a small hat trimmed with iridescent blue-green feathers was perched at a jaunty angle on her head. Cassy had never seen anyone looking so fine and she could barely take her eyes off her benefactor.

'Find her something less taxing,' Flora said, slipping her bony hands into grey kid gloves. 'There must be work that the child can do which will not wreck the house.'

Cassy hung her head. 'I'm sorry, missis.'

'Ma'am,' Mrs Middleton hissed. 'Can't you remember the simplest things, Cassy?'

'Ma'am,' Cassy repeated.

'I'm late for my luncheon appointment,' Flora said irritably. 'You'll have to deal with this, Middleton.' She swept along the hallway, and the footman leapt to attention, bowing from the waist as he opened the street door.

Mrs Middleton turned to Cassy with a frown. 'What am I to do with you?

Cassy stared at the black and white marble floor tiles, hardly daring to breathe. Surely Ma had not meant her to suffer like this? Why had she brought her to such a place?

'Perhaps you could run an errand for me,' Mrs Middleton said thoughtfully. 'You can't do much indoors until your hand heals, and I haven't the time to supervise you.' She beckoned to the footman. 'Harris, find a cab to take Cassy to Bull and Mouth Street. I want her to fetch one of Madam's gowns from the dressmaker. She needs it for the charity ball tonight, and I can't spare any of the other servants. Tell the cabby to wait for her and bring her back here when he will be paid in full.' She turned to Cassy. 'You are to go to number six Bull and Mouth Street off St Martin's Le Grand, and collect the gown from Mrs Hawthorn.' She handed Cassy a purse. 'You must give this to the seamstress. 'I hope you won't let me down.'

'I won't,' Cassy promised. 'I'll do it right this time.'

The hansom cab tooled through the West End streets giving Cassy a good view of the part of London she had never thought to see. She felt like a real lady as she sat back against the leather squabs. The shops and buildings flashed past her and she leaned forward to get a better view of the toffs as they strolled along Piccadilly and the Strand. Progress slowed down as they reached the busy thoroughfare of Fleet Street and then they were in the crowded heart of the City. Her head was filled with the sights and sounds she had seen but the journey was over all too quickly. She could have ridden round London all day and never tired of staring out at the polyglot crowds and the bustling life of the metropolis.

'We're here,' the cabby said, drawing the horse to a halt. 'Be quick, missy. Don't want to hang around all day. I got a living to earn.'

Cassy carried out her instructions to the letter. She found the right house and collected the gown wrapped in butter muslin from a small, wrinkled woman with gnarled fingers and weak, watery eyes. Cassy handed over the purse which was suspiciously light, confirming her suspicion that the seamstress earned very little for her labours, and then it was time to get back in the cab. It was impossible to turn the equipage in such a narrow street and Cassy realised with a sudden jolt that she was vaguely familiar with the area. Although she could not read the name emblazoned on the sign, she recognised Bart's hospital. She had accompanied Biddy there on the rare occasions when sick infants needed urgent medical attention, and regular payments from their parents made it worth Biddy's while keeping the poor mites alive.

'Please stop, cabby.' She reached up to bang on the ceiling. 'I want to get out here.'

The cab drew to a halt outside the hospital. 'What's up?' the cabby demanded. 'Are you sick?'

'Please wait for me; I won't be long. They'll settle up at the big house.' Cassy had no way of knowing whether this was true, but she was not going to pass up the opportunity of finding out what had happened to Freddie. She leapt from the cab, leaving the ball gown on the seat, and she raced into the hospital receiving room, arriving at the nurse's station breathless and desperate for news. After searching through the pages of a leather-bound register, the nurse on duty sent Cassy to the children's ward. She hurried there with renewed hope. If Freddie was still on the ward then he must have survived the dreadful disease that might easily have claimed his young life. She was stopped at the door by a young nurse probationer, who directed her to the sister's desk.

'Are you related to Freddie?' The sister's face was lined and there were dark shadows beneath her eyes as if she had been on duty for many hours and was bone tired, but her expression was kindly and her voice gentle.

'I'm his sister, miss,' Cassy lied. 'Can I see him?'

'Well, you're just in time, my dear. He has made a remarkable recovery but as no one has claimed him, we were just about to discharge him to the care of the orphan asylum. Why didn't you come before?'

Cassy thought quickly. 'We was all took sick, miss. Ma, me and me other brothers and sisters, all went down with the fever. Ma said it would kill poor Freddie if we brought him home then.'

'Have you any proof of your identity, my dear? How do I know that you are who you say you are?'

Cassy gave the sister her best smile. 'Freddie will know me, miss. Leave it to me little brother.'

Freddie was sitting in a high-sided cot. He looked cleaner and healthier than he had ever been in the past. His fair hair was washed and brushed to the side, making him look oddly grown-up, but his baby features were the same and his mouth stretched into a wide grin when he spotted Cassy. He held out his arms, shrieking with delight and she scooped him up, cuddling him and dropping kisses on his chubby cheeks. 'My my, you look just the thing, Freddie. I've missed you so much.'

Freddie reached up to grab Cassy's hair, tugging a strand loose from beneath the bonnet that Mrs Middleton had found at the back of a cupboard. The straw was battered and the ribbons faded, but Cassy loved it and hoped that she might be allowed to keep it for her own. She loosened Freddie's starfish fingers from the ribbon as he tried to put it in his mouth. 'Bad boy,' she crooned. 'You ain't changed a bit, you little monkey.'

'I see that he knows you,' the sister said, smiling. 'If you will just sign the discharge book I see no reason why you cannot take Freddie home. We are in desperate need of his bed.'

Cassy hitched Freddie onto her hip and followed the nurse back to her desk. 'I can't read nor write, miss.'

'Just put your mark here then, and I'll print your name above it. What shall I write, dear?'

'Cassy.' She hesitated. Biddy had never seen the need to give her a surname and Cassy said the first thing that came into her head. 'Cassy Moon.'

'And your address, just for the record.'

'I'm working for a toff in Duke Street,' Cassy said, hoping this would be enough information. She was eager to get away and she prayed that the cabby would still be waiting.

'In Duke Street, Mayfair?' The sister's eyebrows shot up to her hairline.

'I've just been taken on as scullery maid,' Cassy improvised. 'Me ma's going to pick Freddie up later when she finishes work.'

'What number Duke Street?'

'I forget, but the mistress is called Mrs Fulford-Browne. Maybe you've heard of her?'

The sister recoiled slightly and her eyes widened in surprise. 'As a matter of fact I have. I believe she does quite a lot for charity. You are a very lucky girl, Cassy Moon.'

'You don't know the half of it,' Cassy said with feeling. She hoisted Freddie onto her back. 'Ta-ta then, miss. Ta for looking after Freddie and making him well. One day maybe I'll be on one of them charity committees and do good things for the hospital.'

The sister's chuckles followed her down the corridor.

If the cabby was surprised to see Cassy climb into his cab holding a year-old baby boy, he said nothing but simply flicked the whip and urged his horse to a trot. Dandling Freddie on her knee Cassy was happier than she had been since parting with Bailey. She was delighted to see Freddie looking so well and when he smiled she realised with a feeling of pride that he had two new teeth. She cuddled him and told him all about the house in Duke Street, even though she knew he could not understand a word of what she said. It was only as they drew closer to home that Cassy began to realise the enormity of what she had done, and to wonder how she was going to explain Freddie's presence in the grand house. She had not thought it through, and as the cab pulled up outside the mansion, she was terrified that they would take Freddie away from her. Luckily he had fallen asleep in her arms, and as Harris strode down the steps to pay the cabby she hitched Freddie over her shoulder and concealed him beneath the bundle of butter muslin containing Mrs Fulford-Browne's gown. She managed to get into the house without anyone being the wiser, but her heart sank when she spotted Mrs Middleton standing in the middle of the entrance hall with the woman who came to fill the many urns and vases with hothouse flowers. Cassy was about to sidle past them, praying silently that Freddie would not wake up and give the game away, but Mrs Middleton stopped talking and turned her head to glare at her. For a moment Cassy thought that all was lost, but she found herself dismissed with a wave of a hand. 'Take the gown up to Madam's room,' Mrs Middleton said imperiously. 'Lay it carefully on the bed. If you crease it there'll be trouble.'

Cassy escaped with a sigh of relief, but although she had smuggled Freddie into the house, she knew that this was only the beginning. She ascended the stairs carefully, praying that he would stay asleep until she had deposited Mrs Fulford-Browne's ball gown in her bedchamber. As luck would have it the tweeny had finished her work and Cassy did not encounter anyone on her way upstairs, but as she entered the bedroom she came face to face with Miss Perkins, the lady's maid. Cassy stopped short, not knowing what to say or do as the straight-faced woman advanced on her with a purposeful step. 'You've brought Madam's gown. Thank goodness for that, but if you've creased it I'll be very angry.'

Cassy backed away from her. 'I'll see to it, miss. There's no need to trouble yourself.'

'What are you talking about, you stupid child? Give it to me this instant.' Miss Perkins made a grab for the bundle but Cassy managed to dodge her.

'No, really. I can look after it, miss.'

'Are you mad? That gown cost a fortune and I need to check the needlewoman's work.' Moving swift as a tiger pouncing on a lamb, Miss Perkins snatched the bundle of butter muslin and expensive silk from Cassy. She recoiled with an exclamation of horror at the sight of Freddie, who had been rudely awakened and had begun to whimper. 'What on earth is that?'

'It's me baby brother,' Cassy murmured. 'Please

don't tell on me, miss. He's just come out of hospital and . . .'

'Hospital?' Miss Perkins took a step backwards, staring at Freddie as if he were a plague victim. 'What's the matter with him? How dare you bring a diseased child into this house?'

'He's not sick now,' Cassy protested. 'He's better and I got nowhere else to take him. Please let me keep him, miss. I'll look after him like I always done and he won't be no bother.'

Miss Perkins threw the ball gown onto the bed, twirling round to catch Cassy by the ear. 'You're coming with me, you little monster. We'll see what Mrs Middleton has to say about this.'

'No, miss. Please don't tell on me.'

Ignoring all Cassy's heartfelt pleas, Miss Perkins dragged her from the room and down the stairs to the entrance hall where Mrs Middleton was admiring the florist's latest creation. She turned with a start at the sound of Freddie's terrified sobs. 'What the devil?'

'I caught this ragamuffin trying to smuggle a baby into the house,' Miss Perkins said, giving Cassy a spiteful shove in the back which sent her stumbling into Mrs Middleton's path.

'I only just found Freddie, Mrs Middleton,' Cassy cried passionately. 'He nearly died of the whooping cough but they made him better in the hospital. Please don't send him away.'

Mrs Middleton pursed her lips and her eyes narrowed to slits. 'I knew you would be a trial, Cassandra. You were rightly named after the prophetess of doom. You've caused nothing but trouble since the first moment you arrived. What have you to say for yourself?'

'Please let me keep Freddie. He don't eat much and I'll look after him. He's a good little boy and he don't have no one else.'

'I'll leave her in your hands, Mrs Middleton,' Miss Perkins said with a note of satisfaction in her high-pitched voice. 'I dread to think what Madam will say when she finds out about this example of gross incompetence on your part.' She whisked away with the swish of starched tarlatan petticoats, leaving a faint whiff of lavender oil in her wake.

'Where did you get that child?' Mrs Middleton demanded, eyeing Freddie as if he had grown two heads and a forked tongue.

'I took him from the hospital,' Cassy said truthfully. 'He was one of the babies left in Biddy's care but he took sick with the whooping cough, and Bailey left him in the hospital to get better. He's like me brother, miss. I couldn't just leave him to be sent to the orphanage or the workhouse.'

'It's not your decision, child. You had no right to bring him here and now I'll have to sort this mess out. Go to your room, Cassy.'

As if on cue, Freddie began to howl.

'But he's hungry, miss. He needs feeding.'

'Then take him to the kitchen and tell Cook to do anything that will keep him quiet. Lord knows what Madam will say when she finds out what you've done, you wretched child.'

*   *   *

'What's the world coming to?' Cook demanded crossly. She wagged a floury finger at Cassy. 'You're trouble with a capital T; that's what you are.'

'He's hungry,' Cassy muttered. Freddie was wriggling in her arms like a bag of eels, and he seemed to have put on weight during his stay in hospital. His protests grew louder and louder and she knew that food was the only thing that would pacify him, but Cook seemed reluctant to cooperate. Nancy and Clara were openly enjoying the spectacle, and then to make matters worse the door leading into the butler's pantry opened and Poulton marched into the kitchen.

'What's going on, Mrs Hudson?' His angry gaze lit on Cassy and Freddie. 'What is that?'

'You may well ask, Mr Poulton.' Cook assumed an air of martyrdom. 'Heaven knows I'm a patient woman, but this is beyond a joke. That child has foisted a baby on us. Next thing you know we'll be overrun with street Arabs like a plague of rats.'

Poulton looked down his beaky nose and sniffed. From her low vantage point Cassy could see the hairs in his nostrils wafting in and out with every breath he took. She jiggled Freddie up and down in the hope of soothing him, but his shrill cries grew even louder.

'Put a sock in it, nipper,' Clara said with feeling. 'He'll split me eardrums if he don't shut up.'

Mrs Hudson moved swiftly round the table where she had been making pastry and she snatched Freddie from Cassy only to thrust him into Nancy's arms. 'Here, you've got younger brothers and sisters. Feed the little brute with some bread and milk and then take him up

to the attic. Put him to bed and tie him down if necessary, but keep him out of my sight.'

'No,' Cassy cried, leaping forward in an attempt to
rescue Freddie, but Poulton caught her by the scruff
of her neck.

'No you don't, young lady. It's the broom cupboard
for you. There you'll go and there you'll stay until Mrs
Fulford-Browne says otherwise.'

'But Freddie's a baby,' Cassy sobbed. 'Please let me
look after him. He's been poorly and he'll be frightened upstairs on his own.'

Nancy held Freddie at arm's length, eyeing him with
distaste. 'Don't worry, Cassy. He'll have plenty of
company up there with the rats and spiders. That'll
shut him up, and if he does cry we won't hear him.'

'I hope you don't expect us to look after him at night,'
Clara muttered, scowling. 'I ain't a bloody nanny.'

'Language, Clara,' Poulton snapped. 'One more word
like that and Mrs Hudson will wash your mouth out
with soap.' With a swift movement and an amazingly
supple action for someone who appeared to be stiff
and unbending, Poulton whipped Cassy under his arm
and carried her kicking and protesting from the kitchen.
He deposited her in the broom cupboard and slammed
the door. She heard the key turn in the lock and she
was enveloped by darkness. Cowering in a corner,
she buried her head in her arms and sobbed.

How long she remained there she did not know,
but it seemed like an eternity. She was cold, cramped
and hungry. She began to think that the rest of the
household had forgotten her and that she would be

left to starve to death in her dark prison. Adding to her own woes, she was worried sick about Freddie. Left alone in the cold attic and probably tied to the bed by an unsympathetic Nancy, he might die of fright. And he had been ill. It was not fair. If only she had some way of contacting Ma. She would put a stop to this torture, of that Cassy was certain. She curled up with her arms wrapped around her knees and closed her eyes.

She awakened with a start, blinking in the bright beam of light from an oil lamp held by Miss Perkins. Drugged with sleep, Cassy stared dumbly at the grim-faced lady's maid.

'Get up and come with me.' She did not wait to see if Cassy had followed her curt order. She strode off leaving Cassy to scramble stiffly to her feet and hobble after her.

The kitchen was empty and it was dark outside. Cassy could only guess that the rest of the staff were in the servants' hall enjoying their evening meal. It did not look as though she was going to be offered food and her belly ached with hunger. Her mouth was dry and she was so thirsty that her tongue felt as though it was wearing a fur coat. This must, she thought wearily, be part of her punishment.

'Keep up,' Miss Perkins snapped. 'I've better things to do than act as messenger for the likes of you.'

'What's happening?' Cassy asked nervously. 'Where's Freddie?'

Miss Perkins remained in stony silence as she led the way upstairs to the drawing room. She opened the double doors and thrust Cassy inside, leaving without a word and closing them firmly behind her.

After the dark and cold of the broom cupboard, the luxurious drawing room seemed like a different world. The warmth enveloped Cassy like a hug and the fragrant air was heavy with the scent of hothouse flowers and expensive perfume. It took a moment for her eyes to become accustomed to the gaslight but she realised that there were three other people in the room. Mrs Fulford-Browne was seated at a small table with two other women and Cassy's heart leapt for joy when she realised that one of them was Ma. She had to restrain the impulse to rush forward and fling herself into her mother's arms, but then she realised that Ma was sitting a little apart as her lowly status demanded, and she was staring down at the carpet as if studying deep cream pile. The other lady was young and had the face of an angel. Cassy was drawn to her like a moth to a candle flame, but Mrs Fulford-Browne was speaking and beckoning to her. 'Come here, child.'

Cassy approached slowly with her hands clasped tightly behind her back, as she did when she was nervous or wary.

'This is your protégée, Belinda. I hope you're proud of her.' Flora's tone was calm, even slightly amused, which made Cassy look up into her face in astonishment. She had expected to receive a beating at the very least, but Madam seemed to think her predicament was funny.

'Where's Freddie?' she demanded, suddenly feeling

111

brave. 'They was going to tie him to the bed. He'll die of fright or get lung fever shut up in that cold attic.'

'Good heavens, Flora. The poor child is covered with cobwebs.' The beautiful lady spoke for the first time and there was a break in her soft voice. 'What on earth have they done to her?'

'Heaven knows. It's none of my doing I can assure you, Belle. But it's a damned nuisance. I should be upstairs in my boudoir changing for the charity ball, not sitting here in judgement on a junior miscreant as if I were a magistrate.'

Belinda held her hands out to Cassy and her eyes were magnified by tears. 'What have you to say for yourself, Cassy?'

'I dunno who you are,' Cassy mumbled. The lady's obvious concern for her was confusing and she could not understand why someone like her would care what happened to a street girl. She wished that Ma would say something, but she still refused to meet her anxious gaze. The world seemed to have gone mad, Cassy thought tiredly. Her stomach rumbled and she felt herself blushing. They must all have heard the dreadful internal growl. She swayed on her feet as a feeling of faintness overcame her.

The lovely lady jumped up and guided Cassy to a chair. 'You are unwell. Sit down, my dear.'

'I'm just hungry, missis,' Cassy murmured. 'Just felt a bit dizzy, but I'm fine now, ta.' The lady stroked her cheek with the soft touch of an angel's wing, Cassy thought, as the lovely face hovered anxiously above her. 'I'm sorry, missis. I didn't think.'

Flora rose to her feet. 'No, you certainly did not, you bad girl. I should cast you back on the street where you belong.'

'No,' Belinda cried passionately. 'Don't say such things, Flora. The poor little thing was acting out of the kindness of her heart.'

'I shouldn't have listened to you,' Flora continued calmly. 'I allowed myself to be persuaded into taking in a child from the gutter and now there are two of them. Next week they might have doubled their numbers again. I don't mind giving to charity and attending their boring soirées and balls, but I am not turning my beautiful home into an orphanage.'

Belinda laid her hands on Cassy's shoulders. 'What will you do?'

Cassy looked up into the lady's troubled face and was surprised to see teardrops glistening on her eyelashes. One of them fell onto Cassy's hand and lay there glistening like a tiny diamond. 'Don't cry, missis. Let me come and live with my ma and you. I'll be a good girl, I promise.'

'You heard her,' Flora said with a wry smile. 'What have you got to say to that, Belle?'

'You know that it's impossible.' Belinda's voice was small and tight as though she was trying hard not to cry. She brushed her hand across her face and lifted her chin to stare at Flora. 'You took the child in as an act of charity. Are you going to give her up because of a small mistake?'

Flora glanced at the clock on the mantelshelf. 'I must go and change, Belle. This conversation will have to take place another time.'

113

'You can't just leave the child to the mercy of your servants.' Belinda barred her way as Flora made for the door.

'You're making a great deal of fuss over a little bastard, Belle. Anyone would think she was yours.'

Cassy held her breath as she saw the lovely lady pale visibly. She must, Cassy thought, be a very kind person to care so much for a complete stranger. Her distress was obvious and Mahdu had risen and moved swiftly to her side.

'Are you all right, larla?' She slipped her arm around Belinda's shoulders. 'Would you like me to send for the carriage?'

'Not yet, Mahdu. Give me time to think.' Belinda went to stand by the window. The curtains had not yet been drawn and she stared out into the gaslit street. Cassy watched her closely, noting the way in which the lady's delicate white fingers plucked at the skirts of her gown. It seemed as though she was struggling with some inner conflict and for a moment Cassy forgot her own troubles as a wave of sympathy washed over her. She shot a covert glance at Mahdu and she could tell by her worried expression that Ma's concern for her mistress was deep and heartfelt.

After a moment, Belinda turned to face Flora and she appeared to be somewhat calmer and more resolute. 'I will find a home for the baby boy, but I beg you to give Cassy another chance.'

The soft glow emanating from the street lamps outlined Belinda's slender figure, and Cassy was convinced that she could see a halo of light shimmering around the lady's head. She was certain now that this was a heavenly being who had come to save her.

'Give me one good reason why I should put myself and my household to such trouble, Belle?' Flora said curtly. 'I don't like children and I never wanted any of my own, so why should I be burdened with this one who has proved to be nothing but a nuisance?'

'Because you are a kind woman at heart, and you could save a young person from a life of hell on the streets, or an unloving home in an orphanage.' Belinda held her hands out in a gesture of supplication. 'Please let her stay with you, Flora. Please.'

Chapter Seven

There was a deathly hush in the room. Cassy hardly dared to breathe. She did not know what to think and there was nothing she could do other than wait in silence for Mrs Fulford-Browne to make her decision. Mahdu was standing with her hands clasped together as if in prayer and Belinda was trembling visibly.

'For heaven's sake, Belle,' Flora said irritably. 'Is it necessary to work yourself up over some fellow's by-blow?'

Belinda dashed her hand across her eyes. 'I'm sorry, but I feel strongly about this child. I would take her in myself but you know Geoffrey's attitude to children, which is much the same as your own.'

Flora made a sound between a snort and a cackle of laughter. 'Yes, of course. It's a wonder that young Ollie was conceived at all. If it were left to mine and my brother's inclinations the family tree would have ended abruptly – sawn down in its prime, you might say.'

Cassy stared from one to the other. She wondered how trees had suddenly crept into the conversation. She shot a glance at Ma and received a shadow of a smile in return. Cassy grinned. She must keep Ma's secret but it was hard when all she wanted to do was to give her a cuddle and tell everyone that this was her real mother, and she wanted to be with her always. The lovely lady was talking again and Cassy dragged her thoughts back to the present.

'Don't send her away, Flora. Give her one more chance. Just one, I beg of you.'

'All right, but on my terms this time, Belle. I'll support the child but I'll not have her disrupting my life. She will go to a reputable boarding school where she will receive an education which will enable her to go out into the world and make her own living as a governess, or a flower seller. It doesn't matter what she chooses to do, but at least she will be safe from a life of deprivation and vice. As to the infant, well, if you can find a foster mother for him, all the better. Now I'm desperately late, and although I always plan to make a grand entrance, I fear I might be so tardy that my appearance will go unnoticed.' She swept out of the room without giving Belinda a chance to thank her.

'We should go now, my lady,' Mahdu said in a low voice. 'You can rest assured that the child will be well cared for, and her future will be secure.'

'But I want to come with you, Ma,' Cassy cried, flinging her arms around Mahdu. 'I don't want to go to school. I'd rather be a lady's maid like you.'

Mahdu's self control seemed to slip a little as she disentangled herself from Cassy's frantic grasp. 'That isn't possible, larla. You must do as the memsahib says and all will be well. You cannot come with me. That is just the way it is.'

'You will see us often,' Belinda said gently. 'You are

a brave and beautiful little girl, Cassy. I am so proud of you.'

Cassy angled her head, staring into the bluest eyes she had ever seen. 'Why do you care what happens to me, missis? I ain't your girl.'

With an impulsive sweep of her arms, Belinda embraced Cassy, clasping her to her bosom but she released her almost immediately with a tremulous smile. 'I would be proud to have a daughter like you, Cassy. What you did today may not have been wise, but it was wonderfully brave. I will find a good home for Freddie, and I promise that you'll be able to visit him as often as you please. Mahdu and I will always be there if you need us.' She kissed Cassy on both cheeks. 'I must go now, dear. Be a brave girl.' She stroked Cassy's hair, allowing the silky strands to run between her fingers with a sigh of what might have been delight or regret. 'Ring for a servant, Mahdu. I want to make certain that they understand exactly how to treat Cassy, and someone must fetch the baby. We'll take him with us now.'

'Is that wise, larla?' Mahdu's face crumpled with concern. 'What will Sir Geoffrey say?'

'He need never know,' Belinda said with a tinkle of laughter that sounded to Cassy like fairy bells.

'But a child that age will cry and make his presence felt.' Mahdu had her hand poised to ring the bell for a servant, but she hesitated. 'Perhaps it would be best to collect him tomorrow when you have made the necessary arrangements.'

'No, Mahdu. My mind is quite made up. We will

take little Freddie now, and he will sleep in my bedchamber tonight.' Belinda's eyes twinkled irrepressibly. 'It's the last place Geoffrey will think of looking.'

'But what will happen to Freddie?' Cassy asked urgently. 'He's been ill and he needs looking after. He'll miss me something chronic.'

Belinda sat down on one of the velvet-covered sofas that graced the drawing room. She patted the seat next to her. 'Come and sit by me, Cassy.'

Her shyness forgotten, Cassy went to sit next to the lovely lady. 'What about Freddie, missis? I've looked after him ever since he was left at Biddy's.'

'And you mustn't worry about him, dear. There is a good woman I know whose husband was in my father's regiment. She was recently widowed and she lives in Whitechapel on a small army pension which she supplements by taking in sewing. Her children are all grown up now and she is a very motherly person. I'm certain that she would love to care for Freddie, and I will see to it that she is reimbursed for her trouble. I've no doubt he'll be much loved and well cared for with Mrs Wilkins.'

'But can I see him sometimes, missis?'

'Of course you may, Cassy. Although Whitechapel is quite a long way from here, I'm sure Mrs Wilkins would make you most welcome.'

'I don't want to go to boarding school,' Cassy whispered. 'Can I come home with you and Ma?'

Belinda's lips trembled into a smile but the sad expression in her eyes brought a lump to Cassy's throat.

'That's not possible,' Mahdu said, tugging viciously at the bell pull. 'We must go, my lady. It's getting late.'

Taking Cassy's hand in hers Belinda leaned closer. 'There is nothing I would like more than to take you home with me. But I'm afraid it's out of the question.'

'I'd be good,' Cassy murmured, fighting tears. 'I'm a hard worker and I wouldn't have broken that china thing if I hadn't had a bandage on me hand.'

'It's not that,' Belinda said, stroking Cassy's hair back from her forehead. 'Listen to me, my dear. I'll make you a promise that when you are older, and after you've had a decent education, you will come to live with Mahdu and me. Do you understand?'

Cassy nodded her head although the logic of the lady's words meant nothing to her. What difference did it make if she could read and write, or if she were a year or two older? She was about to ask that question but they were interrupted by the appearance of Molly, the parlour maid. 'You rang, madam?'

'Her ladyship wants you to fetch the baby boy,' Mahdu said firmly. 'Wrap him up well. We're taking him with us.'

Molly's eyes widened. 'Will that be all, ma'am?'

'No,' Belinda said firmly. 'I want to see the house-keeper.'

Molly hesitated, eyeing Cassy with ill-concealed disdain. 'You must come with me. Mrs Middleton's orders.'

Cassy half rose to her feet but Belinda caught her by the sleeve and drew her back onto the sofa. 'No.

Cassy remains where she is until I have seen the house-keeper.'

'You heard her ladyship,' Mahdu said, scowling ominously. 'Go about your business, girl.'

Molly's lips tightened and her eyes narrowed, but she beat a hasty retreat.

'I'll get it in the neck,' Cassy observed nervously. 'Maybe I should go after her, missis.'

'Certainly not.' Belinda patted Cassy's hand. 'I want you to hear what I have to say to Mrs Middleton.'

'Be careful, larla,' Mahdu murmured. 'Servants gossip.'

Belinda tossed her head. 'It's time someone told them how to treat a child who has already suffered greatly at the hands of others. I intend to make certain that Cassy's life is much more bearable in future. Heaven knows, I wish I could do more.' She slipped her arm around Cassy's shoulders and gave her a hug. 'Whatever happens, my dear, just remember that you are no longer alone in the world. There are people who love you dearly, and . . .' She was interrupted by a knock on the door.

Mrs Middleton sailed into the room with an aloof expression on her face. 'You wanted to speak to me, my lady?'

'Yes, I do. I have Mrs Fulford-Browne's permission to tell you that Cassy is no longer to be treated like a menial. She will be attending school soon, but until that time she is to be given a room of her own and made comfortable. She can make herself useful by performing light duties such as sewing, or running errands for your mistress, but that is all. She will take

121

her meals in the morning parlour or in the dining room should Mrs Fulford-Browne request her company. Do I make myself clear?'

Mrs Middleton gulped as if she was attempting to swallow a whole potato and a hot one too, Cassy observed with a degree of satisfaction, but despite her obvious chagrin she managed to nod her head. 'Yes, my lady.'

'You may go,' Belinda said graciously. 'Cassy will remain here to say goodbye to the baby, and then she should have a nourishing supper before going to bed in her own room. I know I can rely on you to see that the fire is lit and the bed aired.'

'Yes, your ladyship.' Pursing her lips so that they resembled a dried prune, Mrs Middleton backed towards the door.

'And I would be grateful if you would send for my carriage,' Belinda added, smiling. 'Thank you, Mrs Middleton. I'm certain that I can rely on your complete cooperation.'

The door had barely closed on Mrs Middleton when Molly arrived with Freddie asleep in her arms. Cassy leapt to her feet and took him from her gently. He stirred but he did not awaken, and she dropped a kiss on his tearstained cheek. 'He must have cried hisself to sleep,' she murmured sadly. 'Poor little Freddie.' She turned to Mahdu with a tremulous sigh. 'You will make sure he's looked after, won't you, Ma?'

'He will be well cared for, little one.' Mahdu held her arms out. 'Give him to me, larla. I will treat him like my own.'

Reluctantly, Cassy allowed Mahdu to hold him. If anyone had to take him it hurt less to give him into Ma's care, although the thought of losing him tugged painfully at Cassy's heartstrings. She was exhausted mentally and physically and weak from lack of food. Her knees buckled and she slumped down on the nearest chair, but a gentle touch on the shoulder made her look up.

'Be brave, Cassy,' Belinda whispered. She placed a small, gilt-edged card in Cassy's hand, closing her small fingers over it. 'That is my visiting card, dear. If you are ever in desperate need that is the address where you will find me.'

Cassy glanced at the black squiggles on a white background. 'It don't mean nothing to me, missis. I can't read.'

'That is why you are going to school, Cassy. Learn to read and write and you'll be able to send me letters telling me how you are getting on.' Belinda turned away, apparently overcome by some emotion that Cassy did not understand.

'Will you come and see me on me birthday, Ma?' Cassy asked, turning to Mahdu. 'Like you done when I was with Biddy?'

'I will come as usual, larla. I promise.'

Cassy's new position in the household did little to improve her lot. She was more comfortable in the small bedroom at the back of the house, but the servants made it plain they resented her new status in small but upsetting ways. Her fire was left unlit on the coldest days and her laundry unwashed. She ate in solitary state in the morning parlour but the food was often cold and the meals scanty. Sometimes she was forgotten completely and went hungry. She did not dare complain to Mrs Middleton and she hardly ever saw Mrs Fulford-Browne, who had acquired a new gentleman friend and was rarely at home. Ignored, lonely and utterly miserable Cassy was left to her own devices. She would have worked willingly but Mrs Middleton had made it plain that she was a clumsy nuisance and not to be trusted with even the simplest of tasks.

The winter days were long and Cassy roamed the house like a pale spirit, spending much of her time in her room staring out of the window at the small town gardens, but the trees were bare of leaves and those that were evergreen were coated with soot. When the tweeny forgot to bring coal for the fire or neglected to clean out the grate, the temperature in the room was low enough for Cassy's breath to turn to frost on the windowpanes, and the only way to keep warm was to climb back into bed and pull the coverlet up to her chin. She lay there shivering until sleep released her, albeit temporarily, from her miserable existence to dream of a life quite different from her own. Bailey was always there and Freddie too. The sun was always shining and they were free to roam the fields and woods of a pastoral idyll far away from the city filth. Awakening to reality was the hardest part, and the only comfort Cassy had was to take Lady Davenport's calling card from its hiding place beneath her mattress and clasp it in her hand. If she closed her eyes she could hear the lady's gentle voice and smell the delicate floral perfume that wafted about her person. Although the thought of attending boarding school terrified Cassy, she was determined to take advantage of an education. She would be able to read the address on the card and then she could go in search of Ma and the golden-haired lady with the blue eyes. It was the hope she clung to and the last thing she thought of each night before she fell asleep.

Three seemingly interminable weeks dragged by without any word as to when Cassy might expect to start school. A wet February had given way to blustery March with winds that whipped dead leaves and bits of straw into whirling eddies in the street and tore at the bonnets of ladies out for an afternoon walk. Like a mischievous child it tipped the hats off their gentlemen companions' heads, sending them bowling over the cobblestones and bouncing into the gutter. Cassy had begun to think that Mrs Fulford-Browne had changed her mind about her school, until one morning soon after breakfast she was standing at the window in the morning room, idly watching the raindrops trickling down the glass panes, when Mrs Middleton sailed into the room announcing that she was to accompany her to an emporium in Oxford Street to be fitted out with her school uniform. It was not the happiest of excursion as Mrs Middleton made it plain that she considered that such a task was an imposition on her good nature, and she left Cassy to be measured, prodded and squeezed into the garments on a lengthy list.

Two days later Cassy sat on the box containing all her worldly possessions as she waited for the carriage to be brought round to the main entrance of the house in Duke Street. The navy-blue serge skirt was scratchy and the starched collar of the white blouse threatened to decapitate her if she turned her head too quickly, but the merino cape was thick and warmly lined with scarlet flannel which was a comfort. Harris stepped forward to open the front door and a blast of cold damp air blew in from the street. Cassy leapt to her feet as Mrs Fulford-Browne entered on the arm of a mustachioed gentleman resplendent in a silk top hat and a cashmere overcoat with a fur collar.

Flora was laughing and flirting outrageously but she stopped short when she saw Cassy and a frown creased her brow. 'Good heavens, it's you, child. I hardly recognised you.'

'Who is this, cara mia?' the gentleman asked in a musical voice with a strong foreign accent as rich and silky in tone as one of the street singers Cassy had heard busking in Oxford Street. 'This is your little daughter, yes?'

Flora slapped him gently on the wrist. 'You know that I have no children, Leonardo. The child is one of my charity cases. I am sending her off to boarding school to be educated.'

'You are a saint, cara,' Leonardo said smoothly. 'Santa Flora.'

'And you are anything but a saint, you wicked man.' Flora's smile faded as she turned her attention to Cassy. 'Well, child. This is where we part company. Be good, work hard, and I expect to have nothing but good reports from Miss North.'

'Yes, ma'am.' Cassy bobbed a curtsey. She had watched the servants perform this punctilious act and she had been practising in her room. She managed it without tripping over her feet and she felt a faint flush of pride. She would prove that she was not as stupid and clumsy as they said. She would learn her lessons. She would show them all.

Miss North's Academy for Young Ladies was situated on Highbury Hill. A detached Georgian house with an imposing façade and wide steps leading up to a portico, it was a daunting prospect for a girl brought up in Three Herring Court. Set in its own tree-lined grounds, it seemed even grander to Cassy than the house in Duke Street. The door was opened by a prim maid-servant wearing a severe black dress with a starched white pinafore and cuffs, and an expression that was equally stiff and unwelcoming. The large entrance hall was sparsely furnished with a hat stand on which navy-blue bonnets were ranged in serried ranks with their owners' capes hanging on the pegs beneath. Cassy's footsteps echoed off the encaustic-tiled floor as she followed the dour maid along a wide corridor to the principal's office.

Having been announced and shown into the room by the maid, Cassy stood in front of the kneehole desk and was forced to wait while Miss North finished writing in a leather-bound ledger. The oppressive silence was broken only by the tick-tock of the long-case clock in one corner of the room, and the tinkle of the metal on glass as Miss North dipped her pen into the inkwell. Cassy had plenty of time to observe the bookshelves that lined the walls, and she wondered what it would be like to open one and be able to read its contents. The only book she had ever possessed had been the one that Bailey had bought for her in Petticoat Lane, and that had pretty pictures on every page. She doubted whether there were many such illustrations in the tomes on Miss North's shelves. Cassy sidled closer to the hearth where a few lumps of coal made a feeble attempt at being a fire, but it gave only a modicum of warmth and she shivered both from cold and from nerves. She wished that the lady would look up and speak to her and she cleared her throat, but the sound was lost in the sonorous chimes of the grandfather clock.

Miss North raised her head and stared at Cassy as though she had no right to be there. 'Who are you, child?'

'Cassy, ma'am. Mrs Fulford-Browne sent me to you.'

Miss North flipped through the ledger and ran her finger down the page. She looked up, unsmiling. 'Cassandra Lawson.'

Cassy shook her head. 'That's not me, miss. I'm Cassy, commonly known as Cassy.'

'That's not what I have written here. Mrs Fulford-Browne enclosed a note from your anonymous patron stating that your name is Cassandra Lawson. That is how you will be addressed from now on. Do you understand?'

'Yes'm.'

'Yes, Miss North.'

Cassy obliged her by repeating her words, parrot fashion.

'You have an execrable cockney accent, my girl. We will soon put a stop to that.' Miss North reached behind her to tug at a bell pull. 'Moss will show you to your dormitory.' Taking a sheet of paper from a neat pile on her desk she handed it to Cassy. 'These are the rules. You will read and inwardly digest them.'

'You mean I got to eat them?' Cassy cried in horror.

'No, you stupid girl. Don't you understand the Queen's English?'

'I think I do, but I didn't know it belonged to her majesty,' Cassy murmured anxiously. 'Will she mind me using her words?'

Miss North's green eyes narrowed like a cat's and her jaw tightened as she leaned forward to glare at Cassy. 'You may think you're very clever, Cassandra, but you will soon learn that I don't take kindly to little girls who think they are smarter than me. Hold out your hands.'

Cassy had no idea what she had said that could have caused so much irritation to her teacher. Obediently, she held out her hands expecting to be given the sheet of paper, but to her astonishment Miss North snatched a wooden ruler from a drawer and brought it down hard across her palms. She cried out in pain and would have snatched her hands away but Miss North was too quick for her and she grabbed the tips of Cassy's fingers, bringing the ruler down several times more. Each blow hurt more than the last and Cassy swayed on her feet, overcome by pain and fear. Then, as if by divine intervention, the door opened and the maid entered the room.

'You rang, Miss North?'

'Take this impudent girl to the dormitory and leave her to consider her misdemeanours. Cassandra will not be joining the girls for luncheon and unless she learns the house rules by five o'clock this evening she will go without supper too. Get her out of my sight, Moss.'

Cassy's hands burned and stung painfully as she stumbled from the room and when the maid thrust the heavy portmanteau at her she shook her head. 'I c-can't carry it,' she murmured, trying not to cry. 'Me hands hurt something chronic.'

'Me hands hurt,' Moss mocked. 'Take the bag, you ignorant little brat. I don't care if your hands drop off. I ain't waiting on the likes of a little guttersnipe like you.' She marched off towards a wide staircase and Cassy tried to ignore the agonising pain shooting from her bruised hands up her thin arms as she carried her case up two steep flights of stairs. On the second landing, Moss opened a door giving Cassy a spiteful shove so that she stumbled into a large room lined on either side with iron bedsteads. The sheets and blankets were neatly rolled on each bed and stacked at the head on top of a single pillow. The only other furniture was a chest of drawers at the far end of the room with a solitary candle set in a cheap enamel candleholder. The bare floorboards were scrubbed white as bleached bone, and black fustian curtains made it look as though the windows were in mourning for the loss of light. In stark contrast the walls were whitewashed and this added to the chilly atmosphere in the dormitory. There was a small cast-iron fireplace but the grate was empty and Cassy shivered as the cold seeped into her bones. For the first time since she parted with Bailey she felt completely overwhelmed and frightened.

Moss pointed to a bed in the corner. 'That's yours. A dark corner for a little half-caste. Very fitting, I'd say. Sit down and stay there until she says you can move. I don't fancy your chances if you disobey Miss North.' With a derisive snort, Moss left the room.

Cassy huddled on the bed, shivering uncontrollably. The maid's cruel words echoed in her head, although she did not fully understand their meaning. She wanted her ma and she was certain that the beautiful lady would be horrified if she knew the truth about Miss North's Academy for Young Ladies. The house was eerily silent, which she thought was strange considering that it was a school, and each of the beds in the room must belong to a girl like herself. Her stomach rumbled and she remembered Miss North's harsh words. There would be no dinner and no supper. It was worse than living in Three Herring Court. At least Biddy gave them bread and scrape and the occasional heel of cheese. Cassy curled up in a ball and closed her eyes. Bailey had promised to set up a home for them both when he was able, but where was he now? He could be anywhere in the world where the British army were sent to fight. And if he did come home, he would have no idea how to find her. She stuffed her fist in her mouth to muffle a sob. She would not let them see her cry. Her fingers closed around Lady Davenport's card, which she had secreted in her pocket, and she drifted into an uneasy sleep.

It was almost dark when she was awakened by small fingers tugging at her clothes. With a cry of alarm, Cassy snapped into a sitting position.

'It's all right. I'm sorry I scared you.'

'Who are you?'

'I'm Charlotte Solomon; my bed is next to yours. My friends call me Lottie.'

'I thought you was a ghost.' Cassy slid her legs over the side of the bed. Now that her eyes had become accustomed to the half-light she could see that Lottie was indeed a flesh and blood child.

'I'm real enough, but I'm not supposed to be here. I'll get what for if she catches me talking to you.' Lottie put her hand in her pocket and took out a bread roll. 'I expect you're hungry. I'm sorry it's not more, but it was all I could smuggle from the tea table. They watch every mouthful we eat.' She pressed the bread into Cassy's hand. 'What's your name?'

Cassy bit into the roll. 'Cassy,' she mumbled through a mouthful of bread. 'She called me Cassandra, but that ain't me name, and I ain't a half-caste. I don't even know what it means.'

Lottie perched on the end of the bed. 'That sounds like Moss. She's a spiteful bitch and ignorant too. You'd be surprised how many people judge a person by the colour of their skin or their religion.'

Cassy sensed the bitterness behind this remark. She

swallowed a lump of half-chewed bread, staring at Lottie's serene face in astonishment. 'My ma is from India and I don't know who my father was, but that can't be the same for you. You're beautiful and your skin is white.'

Lottie pulled a face. 'I'm Jewish. My pa is a tailor and we live in Whitechapel. There are some girls who never let me forget it, and they say things behind my back, calling me names and sniggering.'

'They won't do that when I'm around,' Cassy said, balling her small hands into fists. 'I come from Cripplegate which ain't so far from Whitechapel. You got to be tough to survive in Three Herring Court.'

Lottie's musical laughter echoed round the dormitory. 'We're sisters in adversity, Cassy.'

'I dunno what that means, but I ain't never had a sister. If I did, I'd like her to be just like you.'

Flinging her arms around Cassy, Lottie gave her a hug but she pulled away with a gasp of horror as the door opened and they were caught up in a beam of light from a lamp held in Miss North's hand. Her face contorted with rage and her lips disappeared as she bared her teeth in a feral snarl. 'Charlotte Solomon, I might have guessed it was you breaking the rules yet again.'

Lottie leapt to her feet and stood with her hands behind her back and her dark head bowed. Cassy froze, unable to move. Behind Miss North she could see Moss and a couple of girls in school uniform. Even in the shadows, Cassy could tell they were enjoying the spectacle as Miss North moved forward to seize Lottie by the ear. 'Wilful, obstinate and disobedient child. It's the coal hole for you.' She thrust Lottie at Moss. 'Take her downstairs and lock her in the cellar. She will stay there until she has learned her lesson. And as for you . . .' Miss North advanced purposefully on Cassy. 'Stand up and recite the school rules.'

Cassy opened her mouth to protest as Moss and one of the older girls dragged Lottie from the room, but before she could utter a sound she was yanked off the bed and sent sprawling onto the splintery floorboards. 'Get up and recite the rules.'

'I c-can't,' Cassy stammered.

'Can't or won't?' Miss North thrust her face close to Cassy's. 'Speak up, girl.'

'I c-can't read, miss.'

'We don't tolerate stupid girls here.' Miss North grabbed Cassy by the scruff of her neck and propelled her out of the room. 'You will be taught your first lesson. Norah, fetch the dunce's cap.'

Stifling a giggle, the remaining girl raced off into the darkness.

Minutes later, Cassy found herself standing on a stool in the common room with a pointed paper hat stuck firmly on her head. She tried hard to avoid the amused glances from the girls who were employing the period of free time before bed by writing letters home, darning their stockings, or reading books that were approved by Miss North. Cassy stared straight ahead, clenching her jaw so that no one would see her lips tremble. She was determined not to cry, and she tried not to think of Lottie locked in the coal cellar.

Her first day at school had been a nightmare and she prayed silently that she would wake up and find herself anywhere but here.

How long she stood on the small three-legged stool, Cassy had no idea, but the sudden ringing of a bell almost made her lose her balance, much to the amusement of the set of girls nearest to her. But their giggles were stilled by the entrance of a young teacher wearing a grey gown, the severe cut of which only served to enhance her youth and prettiness. She clapped her hands together. 'Bedtime, young ladies.' Her glance fell upon Cassy and her expression softened. 'Not you, I'm afraid, Cassandra. Miss North will tell you when you may get down.' She snuffed out the candles, leaving just one on the mantelshelf, and ushered the chattering girls from the room. As the sound of their footsteps faded away Cassy realised with a shiver of apprehension that she was all alone with just a guttering candle and the dying embers of the fire to keep the night terrors at bay.

Chapter Eight

The candle had gone out and there was only the faintest glow from the dying embers of the fire. The common room was cold and filled with strange shapes and shadows. There was a lingering smell of boiled mutton and cabbage from the girls' supper earlier that evening which did not quite overcome the overpowering smell of dust, chalk and carbolic that permeated the whole building.

Painful cramps were attacking Cassy's lower limbs and her empty belly was growling like a rabid dog. She peered into a dark corner thinking she had seen something move, but then she realised that it was she herself who was swaying dizzily from side to side. She tried to keep upright but suddenly her knees buckled and she felt herself falling, falling, falling . . .

'You poor child. This simply won't do.'

Cassy opened her eyes, blinking in the light of an oil lamp placed at her side. She tried to sit up but was pushed gently down on the cushion that the young teacher had placed beneath her head. 'I'm sorry, miss,' Cassy murmured. 'I must have fell off the bloody stool.'

A gasp was followed by a swiftly controlled giggle, and the teacher laid her hand on Cassy's brow. 'You aren't feverish, that's something, but I'd advise you not to swear in Miss North's hearing, however much provoked. Do you think you can sit up now, if I help you?'

Cassy nodded her head and with a little assistance she managed to raise herself to a sitting position. She eyed the stool warily. 'Do I have to get back on that thing, miss? I don't think I can stay up there much longer.'

'Certainly not. You should have been sent to bed hours ago. I simply can't imagine why Miss North allowed this punishment to go on for such a long time. However, I take full responsibility for releasing you from it. Let me help you to a chair, Cassandra, and then we'll get you upstairs to the dormitory.'

'Me name's Cassy, not Cassandra.'

'And I'm Miss Stanhope. I teach art, needlework and French.'

Cassy eyed her curiously. 'Are you a foreigner too, miss?'

Miss Stanhope's generous lips curved into a smile and her pansy-brown eyes twinkled. 'My mother was French, Cassy.'

'Then we're both half-castes,' Cassy said with a sigh of relief. 'That makes me feel much better, miss.' She scrambled to her feet but was almost overcome by a wave of dizziness and nausea.

'You'd better sit down, dear.' Miss Stanhope helped her to a chair. 'When did you last eat, Cassy?'

'Breakfast, I think. I dunno.' Cassy was not about to peach on Lottie who was already in enough trouble on her account. She shuddered as she thought of her new friend locked in the dank, dark coal hole.

137

'Sit there and I'll bring you some food. You can't go to bed on an empty stomach.' Miss Stanhope picked up the lamp but seemed to think better of it and put it back on the table. She eyed Cassy thoughtfully. 'I don't know where you heard that hateful term, but it's only used by ignorant people who know no better. If I catch any of the girls using it about you or anyone else, I'll make sure they are duly punished. Do you understand what I've just said, Cassy?'

'Yes, Miss Stanhope.'

'Good. Now I'm going to the kitchen to warm up some soup for you. I won't be long.'

An hour later, having consumed a bowl of broth thick with vegetables and pearl barley, mopped up with a generous hunk of bread, followed by a cup of warm milk, Cassy was feeling much better as she followed Miss Stanhope upstairs to the dormitory. The rest of the girls were sound asleep, their combined soft breathing punctuated by an occasional sigh and the creak of the iron bed frame as someone moved to a different position. Quietly and with the air of long practice, Miss Stanhope showed Cassy how to make up the bed. She waited patiently while Cassy undressed and put on the flannel nightgown purchased from the shop in Oxford Street. With a whispered 'Goodnight', Miss Stanhope tucked her in and blew her a kiss as she left the room. The door closed behind her and the darkness enveloped Cassy but she was asleep almost as soon as her head touched the pillow.

* * *

Next morning Lottie emerged from the coal cellar dirty, tired and with cobwebs in her hair but she managed a cheery grin when she saw Cassy. 'The rats were better company than some of the girls,' she whispered as she was marched past the refectory table where Cassy was having breakfast with the other boarders.

Miss North prodded Lottie in the back. 'Be silent. I haven't given you permission to speak, Charlotte Solomon.' She stopped, dragging Lottie to a halt in front of the table where the teachers sat. 'This is what happens to girls who disobey the rules. Unfortunately this child is a habitual wrongdoer, and I tremble to think what will happen to her in later life. The prisons are filled with women young and old who disobey the rules of society. Be warned, Charlotte. There but for the grace of God go thou.' She concluded by slapping Lottie round the head and giving her a push towards Moss, who stood by with a smirk on her pale features. 'Take Charlotte outside to the washroom and scrub her clean. I don't allow filth in my classrooms.'

Some of the girls sniggered softly behind their hands, but others kept their heads down, staring at their empty plates. Cassy was certain that Lottie winked at her as she was led from the room by Moss, who was obviously enjoying every minute of the unfortunate girl's disgrace.

'How do you stand it here?' Cassy whispered when Lottie came to sit by her in Miss Stanhope's art class. 'Why don't you run away?'

Lottie shrugged her thin shoulders. Her wet hair

gleamed black like coal and although it was tied back from her face drips of water trickled down her neck. She was shivering violently, but she managed a smile even though her teeth were chattering like castanets. 'My pa works night and day to pay for my education. He wants me to do well in life and I can't let him down.'

Cassy frowned as she made an attempt to draw the apple that Miss Stanhope had put on a table at the front of the class. 'Does he know how they treat you here?'

Lottie shook her head. 'No, and I'm not going to tell him. They can only get the better of me if I let them, and I intend to work hard and train to be a doctor when I'm grown up. Maybe old North will come to me as a patient and then I'll stick needles in her and laugh.'

Cassy clapped her hand over her mouth to stifle a giggle but Miss Stanhope saw her and frowned. 'I'm glad that you find sketching still life so amusing, Cassy.'

To explain would mean getting Lottie into further trouble. Cassy thought quickly. 'No, miss. It was a flea tickling me belly that made me laugh.'

The class erupted in giggles which were quelled by a glance from Miss Stanhope. She made her way between the desks to stand beside Cassy. 'That's not funny, Cassy. I hope you aren't going to be a disruptive influence in class.'

Lottie opened her mouth as if to own up but a paroxysm of coughing made speech impossible and had the effect of drawing Miss Stanhope's attention away from Cassy. 'Are you all right, Charlotte?'

'She's half froze to death, miss,' Cassy said urgently. 'I seen people die of lung fever after getting chilled to the marrow, and she spent the night in the coal hole.'

Miss Stanhope raised her hand for silence as the girls began to chatter between themselves. 'Get back to work, girls. I'll deal with this.' She turned to Lottie with a gentle smile. 'Come with me, and I'll see that you get some medicine.'

'I-I'm all right, thank you,' Lottie gasped in between spasms of coughing that wracked her small frame.

'You most certainly are not,' Miss Stanhope said firmly. She pointed to an older girl whom Cassy recognised as Norah, one of the girls who had found her initial ordeal so amusing. 'Norah Vickery, I'm putting you in charge of the class for ten minutes while I take Lottie to the sick room. I expect you all to behave like young ladies while I'm gone.' She hustled Lottie out of the room and as soon as the door closed behind her Cassy found herself being bombarded by paper pellets.

'She's got fleas,' someone chortled.

'The dirty half-caste has fleas.' Another voice took up the chant.

'She should be sent to the coal hole with the sheeny.'

Cassy had bent her head over her work, trying to ignore their taunts, but a pellet struck her on the side of her face and the obvious insult to Lottie made her furious. She leapt to her feet. 'Shut up, all of you. You should be ashamed of yourselves. Lottie is worth more than all of you put together.'

Norah marched purposefully along the aisle between

141

the desks, and picking up a wooden ruler she brought it down hard across Cassy's knuckles. 'You need to learn your place. One more word out of you and you'll be up before the North wind. She won't be so lenient this time, you ignorant little chi-chi.'

Even though the pain in her hands was so intense that it brought tears to Cassy's eyes, it was as nothing compared to the constant humiliation of being pointed out as being different from the others. In the melting pot of Three Herring Court she had been accepted and passed unnoticed amongst the throng of people with different coloured skins and ethnicity, but here amongst the girls who were supposed to be higher up the social scale she was an object of ridicule.

'She's crying. What a baby.' The remark from the far side of the room raised a titter.

'What colour are her tears, Norah?' a freckle-faced girl demanded. 'Are they the colour of river water thick with mud?'

The laughter that followed this cruel jibe seemed to have the opposite effect on Norah, and perhaps remembering her position of trust she called for silence. 'That's enough. Get on with your work.' She poked Cassy with the ruler. 'Stop snivelling, you silly little girl. Do you want to get the rest of us into trouble?'

Cassy wiped her eyes on her sleeve and was about to tell Norah and the rest of them to go to hell when Miss Stanhope returned. She cast a practised eye around the class, who were apparently engrossed in their efforts to draw the apples. She eyed the scattering of paper pellets surrounding Cassy's chair with a wry smile. 'It seems to have been snowing indoors.' She bent down to retrieve one of them, holding it between her thumb and first finger as if studying an object of scientific importance. 'It appears that I am mistaken.' Her voice became sharper and her expression hardened. 'Norah, you know who perpetrated this childish attack on Cassy. I expect you to see that the mess is cleaned up before those concerned leave the room.'

'Yes, Miss Stanhope,' Norah said sulkily, shooting an angry glance at Cassy as she made her way back to her seat.

'And,' Miss Stanhope continued in crisp clear tones. 'If I catch any of you calling anyone derogatory names they will spend the evening in detention, writing lines. Do I make myself clear?'

'Yes, Miss Stanhope,' the class replied in a singsong unison.

'Good, then you may continue to work. I'll come round to each one of you in turn and see how you are progressing.' Miss Stanhope patted her sleek dark hair, although there was not one strand out of place that Cassy could see, and her heart swelled with gratitude towards the pretty young teacher whose kind words had warmed her chilled heart. She grasped the stick of charcoal between her fingers and made a concerted effort to draw an apple, but never having used a writing implement of any kind she found it difficult and the result looked more like a cabbage than a piece of fruit.

'A good try,' Miss Stanhope said when she glanced over Cassy's shoulder at the mass of black squiggles.

143

'Write your name in the top right hand corner of the paper, Cassy. I'll mark your efforts later.'

Cassy stared up at her, uncomfortably aware of the blood rushing to her cheeks. 'I can't, miss.'

'What do you mean, Cassy?'

She hung her head. 'I dunno how to write me name, miss.'

Giggles were quickly stifled by a curt command from Miss Stanhope. 'I didn't know that, Cassy. You will need extra tuition to bring you up to the required standard, and I will personally see that you get it.' She spun round to face the rest of the class. 'You are dismissed. Go to your next lesson quietly. Remember that you are young ladies and not a herd of elephants on the rampage.'

Following the example of the other girls, Cassy rose to her feet as Miss Stanhope left the room. She was about to follow the others as they filed out to their next lesson when Norah caught her by the hair. 'Oh no you don't, chi-chi. You'll stay here and clear up the mess you made.'

'But it wasn't me,' Cassy protested, jerking her hair free from Norah's grasp. 'Miss Stanhope said . . .' A blow round the head cut her off mid-sentence.

'I'm head girl and you do as I say, worm. Pick up it up and put it in the wastepaper basket. Best hurry, chi-chi. If you're late for the North wind's Latin class, you'll be in for a wigging.'

Reluctantly, Cassy went down on her hands and knees to comply with Norah's command. As a result she was late for Miss North's Latin class and forced to stand in the corner for the whole lesson, all of which went completely over her head. The chanted chorus of declensions meant nothing to Cassy and it seemed a waste of time learning a language long dead. She spent the hour wondering how Lottie was but it was not until the break for their midday meal that she discovered her new friend was confined to the sickroom, and extremely unwell.

Cassy's troubles were of little moment compared to her concern for Lottie, who was feverish and seemed to have come down with a severe chill. Somehow Cassy managed to get through the lessons that day, and after supper in the common room she took the opportunity to slip away whilst the girls were enjoying their one period of free time and totally ignoring her. She found the sickroom without much difficulty and entered quietly, making certain that no one saw her. Embers of coal glowed feebly in the grate, and a single candle on the washstand emitted a straggly stream of light. There were two single beds in the room, and in the one nearest the wall Cassy could just make out the tumbled mass of Lottie's dark hair spread over the pillow like waterweed floating in the Thames. She moved swiftly to her bedside. 'Lottie, are you all right?'

Her worst fears were realised when Lottie did not answer. Her lips were moving and she was muttering feverishly but her eyes were closed and even in the poor light Cassy could see that her friend's face had a sickly pallor. She caught her breath in an agonised sob. She had seen symptoms like this amongst the infants in Biddy's care and the outcome had invariably been

145

fatal. Cassy's heart contracted with fear. She could not allow her one friend to die. She closed her eyes, struggling to remember the words of a prayer that Bailey had taught her, but all she could think of was to plead with God to spare Lottie. What would Bailey have done in these circumstances? She made an effort to gather her scattered wits. Panicking would not help. She must keep calm. She laid her hand on Lottie's forehead and frowned. Bailey had always insisted that fever must be brought down. She wished that he was here with her. He would know what to do.

Cassy made her way to the washstand and was relieved to find the pitcher filled with water. Miss North's obsession with cleanliness had its uses she decided as she dampened the washrag and wrung it out. She bathed Lottie's fevered brow, talking softly to her although she had no idea whether or not her friend could hear. The pealing of the bell made her jump but as she had no idea what it meant she ignored its urgent summons, and would have stayed there all night had not Miss Stanhope burst into the room. 'Cassy! I've been looking for you everywhere. You should not be here.'

Cassy eyed her warily. 'I'm sorry, miss. I was looking after Lottie.'

'That's not your responsibility, my dear. Matron will look in from time to time, and you must go to bed. When you hear the bell it's time for all the girls to return to the dormitory. Now hurry along, and if anyone says anything you may say that you were with me. But don't let this occur again.'

Cassy nodded vigorously. 'I won't, miss. But you will look after Lottie, won't you? I seen nippers taken off with the fever overnight.'

'She'll be well cared for. Now do as I say.' Miss Stanhope patted Cassy on the shoulder. 'Go to bed and get a good night's sleep.'

But Cassy could not sleep. She lay awake long after the other girls had drifted off, and apart from their rhythmic breathing and the faint creaking of timbers contracting in the cold night air, the house seemed to slumber in silence. Eventually, when she could bear it no longer, she slipped out of bed and tiptoed from the dormitory, making her way downstairs to the sickroom on the first floor. She opened the door carefully, peering inside in case Matron was on duty at Lottie's bedside, but the room was empty of anyone other than the sick girl. Cassy padded softly across the bare boards to stand by the bed. Lottie was mumbling feverishly, a jumble of disjointed sentences that made no sense to Cassy. Her nightgown was soaked with sweat and her thin fingers plucked irritably at the sheet.

All night, Cassy stayed at her friend's side, bathing her with cool water and whispering softly to comfort her when she cried out in a fevered dream. In the early hours of the morning, long after the embers of the fire had turned to grey ash, Cassy was chilled and aching with fatigue. She climbed into the bed beside Lottie and held her hand. 'I'm here,' she whispered. 'Don't be afraid. I won't leave you.' She closed her eyes and wriggled down beneath the coverlet, feeling the warmth creep back into her chilled flesh as exhaustion overcame her.

'It's the coal hole for you, miss.'

Cassy was yanked from the warmth of the bed to land on the cold, hard floor. She blinked sleepily up into Miss North's angry face. 'Why, miss? What have I done?'

'Matron told me you were here. Wicked child, you might have caught the disease and spread it around the whole school. You will have to learn obedience, Cassandra Lawson.' Miss North turned to Matron who was standing by the door, wringing her hands.

'I'm sorry, Miss North. I swear the child was not here when I last checked on the patient.'

'Cassy is a serpent,' Miss North said, narrowing her eyes. 'She wriggles into forbidden places and plants her poison there.'

'Cassy, is that you?'

Lottie's voice from the pillows made Cassy leap to her feet quite forgetting Miss North's anger. She clasped Lottie's hand and raised it to her cheek. 'You're better. You ain't going to die.'

'Of course she won't die.' Miss North yanked Cassy away by the scruff of her neck. 'The girl caught a chill, but she might have had typhoid or scarlet fever for all you knew, you stupid child. Coal hole, Matron. Cassy will stay there until supper time. I'll tame her rebellious spirit if it's the last thing I do.' She turned her fierce gaze on Lottie. 'You will remain in bed all day with no food. Starve a fever is what I was always taught. And if I catch you two naughty little girls behaving badly again you will be separated for the rest of your school days. Do you understand?'

'Yes, miss,' Cassy said, eyeing Lottie anxiously and being rewarded with a faint grin.

'Yes, Miss North,' Lottie murmured weakly. 'I'll try to be better.'

Matron grabbed Cassy by the arm. 'Come along, miss. It's the coal hole for you.'

During the next few weeks Cassy became well acquainted with the coal cellar. No matter how hard she tried to learn the school rules she seemed to fall foul of at least one a day. Sometimes the punishment was less severe and entailed spending the evening in solitary confinement in a classroom, attempting to write out lines. This itself was a struggle as she was only just coming to terms with the alphabet, and she found copying a sentence from the blackboard was both difficult and painfully slow. For more serious infringements of manners or as a penalty for her lack of learning, she would have to spend hours on a stool with the dunce's cap on her head. But all this harsh discipline only served to make her more determined to beat the punitive regime by studying hard. In this she was helped by Lottie, who took her under her wing and coached her in reading and arithmetic, at which Lottie was both proficient and advanced for her age. The other girls still called them names, but their attitude began to change subtly as they saw how Cassy survived the chastisements meted out by Miss North. She bore them all with the stoicism she had developed in order to cope with Biddy's beatings and neglect.

While Miss North did her best to break Cassy's spirit, Miss Stanhope was the voice of sweet reason. She encouraged Cassy to learn, giving her extra tuition while she was in detention and, whenever possible, ignoring Miss North's edict that Cassy and Lottie were to be kept apart. The strict routine of work, interspersed with long walks into the open countryside surrounding Highbury Hill, and a diet of plain but adequate food, had its effect on Cassy. They lived in Spartan conditions, getting up at five each morning and washing in ice-cold water in an unheated outside washhouse. The only warmth the girls experienced during the winter and cool spring months was in the common room after supper, when they huddled round the fire. Despite all this, Cassy had grown an inch or so in height by the end of the summer term, and she was now almost as tall as Lottie. As the prospect of a fortnight's holiday drew nearer, there was a buzz of excitement amongst the pupils and staff alike. Not everyone could go home for the last two weeks in August, as some of the girls had absent parents with fathers employed either in the army or in the colonial office abroad. If they had no relations in England who were willing and able to collect them, they were obliged to stay on in school under the care of Matron and Miss Stanhope. Cassy wondered if Ma would come for her, but she had not had word from her since her arrival at the school. Lottie was going home to Whitechapel to spend time with her widowed father, and she assured Cassy that she would be more than welcome to accompany her. Cassy was grateful but she still cherished the hope that Lady Davenport would allow Ma to come and collect her.

During one of her many detentions, Cassy had laboriously written a letter to Mahdu, begging her to come on the last day of term and take her back to Duke Street if only for a few days. Miss Stanhope had taken it to the post office and paid the postage herself; one of her many small acts of kindness kept secret from the North wind. Certainly there was a definite chill in the air whenever Miss North blew into the room, and Cassy had seen the more timid pupils freeze on the spot when confronted by the headmistress's icy stare. By the end of the summer term Cassy was almost beginning to feel like one of the girls, and they on the whole were treating her very nearly as one of them, but the difference between them still lingered in the atmosphere like the whiff of a strange and exotic scent.

On the very last day, the girls who were obliged to remain in school watched enviously as their more fortunate sisters stood in the hallway with their portmanteaux clutched in their eager hands as they waited for their families to collect them. Lottie had persuaded Cassy to accompany her, insisting that her pa would welcome her with open arms. 'He's always working,' Lottie explained earnestly. 'He keeps his shop open until all hours and sometimes he sits and sews all night if he has an important order to fulfil. My pa works harder than any man in London, and I'm going to do him proud. We'll help him, Cassy, so you won't feel you're imposing. We can pick up the pins and tidy the spools of thread, and sort out the bolts of material. There's lots we can do.'

Cassy had been persuaded, but she waited anxiously, watching the main entrance as the families arrived to squeals of delight from their offspring. Sometimes it was a coachman who strode in through the front door, or a maidservant or family friend, but gradually the girls disappeared one by one until it was only Lottie and Cassy left standing in the echoing silence of the tiled hallway.

'Papa will come,' Lottie said, squeezing Cassy's hand. 'He's probably had to work until the last moment, or sometimes he sends one of his tailors if he can't get away himself. We just have to be patient.'

Cassy nodded, unable to speak for the lump in her throat. Her hopes were fading fast. She would go with Lottie and be grateful for a good friend and a kind family, but that did not ease the pain in her heart or assuage the feeling of loneliness. Ma, it seemed, had forgotten her. Perhaps she had been relieved that her love-child was to be kept out of sight; tucked away and forgotten. Cassy's thoughts turned as they often did to Bailey. She still missed him and she knew that he would not have willingly abandoned her. She felt like a parcel left in the lost property department at a railway station, unclaimed and unwanted.

Just as Lottie was beginning to fidget, the doorbell clanged and Moss stamped along the tiled floor with a petulant shrug of her shoulders, making it plain that she would be glad to see the last of the young ladies for a fortnight. Cassy held her breath but Lottie ran forward with a cry of delight. 'Papa, you came.' She flung her arms around a small man, knocking his stovepipe hat sideways so that it sat at a comical angle on his dark head. He wore steel-rimmed spectacles and a well-cut if slightly shabby jacket over a waistcoat which he had forgotten to button, perhaps in his hurry to meet his only child. He clutched Lottie to his chest, and Cassy was surprised to see tears trickle down his sallow cheeks, but she could see by his smile that they were tears of joy and her heart swelled with happiness for her friend, even though a pang of something like envy caused a shiver to run down her spine.

Lottie drew away from her father, setting his hat to rights with a happy chuckle. She turned and beckoned to Cassy. 'Come and meet my dear papa. Don't just stand there. We're going home.'

Cassy was about to join them when a tall young man strode through the open door, coming to a halt as he glanced around and his gaze fell on her. She stared back at him, wondering who he could be, and why he was looking at her as though she ought to know him. She angled her head, suddenly curious. He was dressed in a smart grey suit that quite put the small tailor in the shade. He wore a red carnation in his buttonhole and he carried a silver-topped ebony cane which he pointed at her, grinning from ear to ear.

'Since you're the only one left, I suppose I must take you, brat.'

Cassy glanced over her shoulder just in case one of the other girls had entered the hall, but she was standing on her own. She pointed to herself. 'Who? Me?'

He swept off his top hat and a lock of blond hair flopped over his brow, which he dashed back with an impatient hand. Despite his arrogant stance, Cassy realised that he was little more than a boy, even younger than Bailey. He wielded his cane like an épée, pointing it at her throat. 'Name and number, brat.'

Cassy drew herself up to her full height although she only came up to his elbow. 'I dunno what you're talking about, mister. I got a name but as to a number I dunno what you're talking about.'

'Are you all right, Cassy?' Lottie hurried to her side, glancing anxiously at the stranger. 'Who's this?'

'I dunno,' Cassy whispered.

'Come home with me,' Lottie said urgently. 'He could be anybody.'

'I'm instructed to take Miss Cassandra Lawson to Lady Davenport's house in South Audley Street, but if she don't want to come then that's fine by me. I've got better things to do than run errands for a maidservant.' He set his hat back on his head with a pat of his hand and, turning on his heel, he strode out through the front entrance.

'No, stop,' Cassy cried. 'Stop, please. Wait for me.'

Chapter Nine

Belinda stood by the window in her boudoir, peering down at the traffic in South Audley Street. Her fingers drummed an agitated tattoo on the sill. 'Where is that boy? He should be here by now.'

Mahdu continued her task of folding freshly laundered undergarments and placing them neatly in the rosewood clothes press. 'Give him time, larla. It's a long way to Highbury and the roads will be busy at this hour of the day.'

'It seems such a long time since I last saw her,' Belinda said, sighing heavily. 'I've wanted so much to visit her in that wretched school.'

'I too, larla, but it would not do.'

'No, of course not. You're right, as ever, Mahdu. But I can't sleep at night for worrying about her. Are they being kind to her? Will the colour of her skin make her an object of derision amongst the so-called young ladies? I know how cruel children can be.'

'If the other girls treat her badly it will only be because they are jealous,' Mahdu said stoutly. 'When a child is as lovely as Cassandra it is only natural that she'll become the object of envy and spite, but from what I've seen of her she is a brave little girl and spirited just like her mama.'

Belinda's lips trembled into a smile. 'My spirit was broken ten years ago, Mahdu. I don't want that to happen to my daughter.'

'It will not.' Mahdu shut the drawer with more force than was strictly necessary as if to emphasise her point. 'While I have a breath left in my body I will do everything I can to protect her.'

'I know you will, darling Mahdu.' Belinda's eyes filled with tears but a sound from the street below made her resume her vigil and brought a cry of delight from her lips. 'They are here, Mahdu. Ollie has brought her home to us.' Picking up her skirts she hurried to the door. 'I can't wait to see her.'

Moving swiftly for a woman of her age, Mahdu crossed the floor to catch her mistress by the wrist. 'No, larla. Remember who you are. You must wait here and I will bring her to you.'

'You're right, as usual,' Belinda said, bowing her head with a sigh. 'I was forgetting myself and my position in my husband's house. Go downstairs and greet her, Mahdu. Give me time to compose myself. I'll see them both in the drawing room, where I'll try to act out my part in this sorry tale of deceit and lies.' Clinging to her last thread of self-control, she did not look up until she heard the click of the latch as Mahdu left the room. One sympathetic glance from her faithful servant would have undone her completely, and she could not afford to allow her emotions to get the better of her. She remained motionless for a few moments, telling herself that she must keep calm at all costs. If the truth were to come out now they would all be ruined and she would have no chance of helping her illegitimate child. Belinda was under no illusions as to Sir Geoffrey's reaction if he discovered that she had given birth to another man's baby. Divorce would inevitably follow, disgrace and ostracism by polite society. She would be cast off penniless and ill-suited to earning her own living. Poverty and destitution were the lingering threat that kept many women in unhappy marriages.

Belinda checked her appearance in the dressing table mirror, and pinched her pale cheeks until the colour returned to them. She bit her lips until they became rosy and she stretched them into a smile, but the eyes that stared back at her were hauntingly sad. She took a few deep breaths, held her head high and left the comparative security of her boudoir to make her way slowly to the drawing room on the floor below. She had just arranged herself on one of the elegant but uncomfortable sofas when Mahdu entered after a perfunctory tap on the door. She stood aside as Oliver breezed into the room as if he had not a care in the world. 'Ho there, Stepmother dearest. I'm delivering my charge to you, although goodness knows what you'll do with the skinny little thing. She's not spoken a word since I collected her from that ghastly mausoleum.' He turned to Cassy with a peremptory flick of his fingers, as if he were summoning a well-trained gundog to heel.

Belinda clutched her hand to her heart in an attempt to still its violent thudding against her stays. The blood was drumming in her ears, momentarily deafening her, and it was all she could do to remain seated when her instinct was to leap to her feet and enfold the small girl in her arms. 'Come here, child,' she whispered. 'Let me look at you.' Her breath caught in her throat as she saw once again her daughter's likeness to her beloved George; the love of her life who had died without knowing that he was to be a father.

Cassy approached her slowly, almost warily Belinda thought with a pang of dismay. Surely the child was not afraid of her? She held out her hand and smiled. 'Come closer, Cassy. Sit by me and tell me about yourself. Do you like school? Are they kind to you? I'm afraid I didn't enjoy my time there and was delighted when my parents sent for me to join them in India.'

Cassy's dark eyes widened. 'You was at Miss North's academy, missis?'

'My lady,' Mahdu said, stepping forward to lay her hands on Cassy's thin shoulders. 'You must learn proper manners, Cassy.'

'Sorry, Ma.' Cassy's hand flew to her mouth and she glanced anxiously at Mahdu. 'I never meant to call you that. It slipped out.'

'So that's it!' Oliver gave a hoot of laughter as he sprawled in a damask-covered chair by the empty grate. 'That's why I was sent halfway across London to bring her here. She's your brat, Mahdu. I should have guessed.'

Belinda shot him a withering glance. 'Be silent, Ollie. It's not a matter for discussion. You know nothing of the circumstances and I'd be grateful if you would keep this to yourself.'

Oliver tapped the side of his nose, grinning widely.

'Absolutely. I'm as silent as the tomb, as trustworthy as . . .'

'Thank you,' Belinda said firmly. 'We aren't playing similes. This is a serious matter.'

'Enough said. I'll just sit here and keep quiet.' Oliver folded his hands across his chest, making an obvious effort to suppress a chuckle.

There was something infectious in his ability to find humour in the most stressing situations and Belinda found herself relaxing a little. She shook her finger at him but she too was smiling as she turned her attention to Cassy. The child was eyeing her with those dark, almond-shaped eyes that would one day send men's hearts soaring heavenwards, of that Belinda had no doubt. There was a sweetness in Cassy's expression that had not been vanquished by her harsh upbringing or the rigours of school life. Belinda felt her own heart melt with love for her child who would soon be growing to womanhood, and she knew that she would give her own life to protect her. She took Cassy's small hand in hers. 'Don't be afraid, Cassy. Mahdu will fetch you some refreshments and you can tell me all about school. Is Miss North still called the North wind? She must be getting on a bit now as she was there twenty years ago when I was a pupil.' Belinda signalled to Mahdu with the barest inclination of her head, knowing that her faithful servant and companion would carry out her instructions without the need for further explanation.

'I'd like a glass of porter, Mahdu, my love,' Oliver said, flashing a smile in her direction. 'And a slice of pork pie would go down nicely, with a few pickles on the side.'

Mahdu inclined her head in acknowledgement as she left the room.

'Come on then, nipper,' Oliver said cheerfully. 'Let's hear all about that school of yours. What have you learnt? How about a few Latin declensions for a start?'

'Don't tease her, Ollie,' Belinda said, shaking her head at him. 'And don't take any notice of my stepson, Cassy. He was sent down from Eton for being drunk and disorderly, so he has no right to sit in judgement of anyone, let alone a child almost six years his junior.'

'That's something I know a bit about,' Cassy said eagerly, as if relieved to find a mutual topic of conversation. 'Old Biddy was drunk and very disorderly. She could put away a pint of gin with no trouble at all and not turn a hair, but another half-pint and she'd take on any of the men in Three Herring Court and win, but only if they was swipey too.'

Belinda caught her breath on an involuntary burst of laughter but she controlled her mirth with difficulty. 'I don't think you should repeat that story too often, Cassy.'

'Have I said something I shouldn't?' Cassy looked from one to the other, her mouth drooping at the corners and her eyes suddenly wary, like a young doe startled by a footfall and the crack of a twig.

'No, nipper,' Oliver said, making an obvious effort to be serious. 'You told the truth but it ain't exactly the sort of story you tell in a drawing room, if you get my meaning, but you can come to the pub with me and entertain my friends any time you like.'

'That's enough, Ollie,' Belinda said severely. 'Don't make fun of the child. It isn't her fault.' She turned to Cassy, who was looking extremely discomforted. 'You aren't to know any of these things, which is why I would like you to stay here with me for your summer holiday.'

Oliver leaned forward in his chair, suddenly alert and unusually serious. 'To what end, Stepmother? What's the point of educating a child from the slums when in all likelihood she'll go back there as soon as you finish with her?'

'That's not how it will be,' Belinda said, shocked into retaliating by his shrewd assessment of the case. 'With a good education and a little training, I'm sure that we can find a suitable position for Cassy. She's an intelligent girl and I intend to take her under my wing.'

Oliver shrugged his shoulders. 'Can't think why, but good for you, I say. Where's that pie and porter? A chap could die of starvation waiting to be fed in this house.' He winked at Cassy. 'What about you, brat? I bet they feed you on pigswill in school. I'm sure you could manage something tasty to eat.'

'I am a bit hungry,' Cassy admitted. She glanced up at Belinda. 'My ma can take care of me, mis— my lady. You shouldn't have to bother your head about a chi-chi from Cripplegate.'

Belinda gasped in horror, hardly able to believe her ears. She shot a warning glance at Oliver, who was grinning widely. 'Where did you hear that awful word, Cassy?'

161

'They call me that at school,' Cassy said wearily. 'I'm used to it now. I get teased all the time about my dark skin and hair, but so does Lottie and she's a Jew. She says that people are like that and you've just got to ignore it and get on with your life. Lottie's my friend and her papa said I could go and stay with them in Whitechapel where he has a tailor's shop. So if you find me too much of a handful, you can always send me there.'

'There you are; a solution to the knotty problem at last,' Oliver chortled. 'You can send us both to the tailor's shop in Whitechapel. Perhaps that could be my calling in life. I'm sure I'd make a damn fine tailor. Better that than a soldier, I daresay.'

He spoke with such a twinkle in his green eyes that Belinda was forced to smile despite her concern for Cassy. She held up her hand. 'No one is going to Whitechapel. It was very kind of the gentleman to offer you a home for the holidays, Cassy, but I want you here, and I know that Mahdu would be very unhappy if you were to go away so soon. As for you, Ollie, I think your plan of joining the army is a far better one. I can see you as a dashing young officer, but somehow the vision of you sitting cross-legged on the floor, sewing a seam, doesn't fit.'

Oliver opened his mouth to reply but closed it again with a satisfied sigh as the door opened and Mahdu ushered in a maid bearing a tray laden with food.

Belinda watched her daughter attack the food, stuffing bread and butter into her mouth as though she had not eaten for a week. The child's table manners were appalling but she could not bring herself to make a comment until Cassy cut a slice of pie and attempted to eat it off the point of her knife.

'No,' Belinda and Mahdu cried in horrified unison.

Cassy dropped the knife in fright, staring at them nonplussed. 'What did I do?'

Mahdu bustled towards her, snatching up the knife and a fork. She placed them in Cassy's hands. 'Don't they teach you anything at that school? You don't eat off a knife, my girl. Do you want to cut your tongue off and remain a mute for the rest of your life?'

'They don't let us have knives at school,' Cassy murmured, blushing and hanging her head. 'We have spoons and forks. I didn't know I done wrong.'

'Of course not,' Belinda said hastily. 'It's not your fault. Just enjoy your meal. There will be plenty of time for lessons in table manners. We have two whole weeks before you have to return to school.'

Mahdu frowned. 'Have you thought this through?' she whispered. 'Where is the child to sleep? And what do I tell the other servants?'

'A tricky question,' Oliver said, spearing a pickled onion on his fork. 'Dashed difficult thing to hide a ten-year-old kid, especially when she's got an appetite like a donkey.' He winked at Cassy who immediately put her knife and fork down, leaving her meal half eaten.

'It's none of your business, Ollie,' Belinda said severely. 'Cassy is my protégée and your father likes me to keep myself occupied with good works.'

Cassy pushed her plate away and leapt to her feet. 'Ta, lady. But I ain't a charity case. I'll work and pay for me keep like a good 'un. Bailey always said you don't get nothing for nothing, and I can see he was right.'

Shocked by the vehemence of her child's outburst, Belinda stared at Cassy in amazement. 'Don't upset yourself, my dear. You are my guest and there's no question of you having to work during your holiday.' She sent a questioning glance in Mahdu's direction. 'Who is Bailey?'

'I can answer for meself, missis,' Cassy cried angrily. 'Bailey is the best friend a girl could have. He looked after me since I was a baby and he was always there for me until Biddy croaked. He wouldn't have joined the army if he'd had any choice in the matter. He didn't want to leave me. It near broke his heart, and mine too.'

'Now there I can sympathise with this fellow,' Ollie said, his smile fading. 'I'm not so sure about a military career for myself either.'

'Be quiet, Ollie,' Belinda said more sharply than she had meant to. She moderated her tone. 'I mean, you have a choice as to your future, which it seems was denied to Cassy's friend.'

'Not much of a choice, Belle,' Ollie muttered. 'Pater wants me to enlist as an ensign in the 13th Hussars, but I'm dashed if I want to prance about on a horse all day.'

'The army might be the making of you,' Belinda said gently. 'You could do a lot worse, Ollie.' Despite his outward show of bravado she felt a degree of sympathy for Oliver, who although little more than a boy was to be flung head first into a man's world whether he wished it or not. Geoffrey had insisted that a spell in the army would be the making of his son, but Belinda was aware that military life did not suit everyone. She had known young men whose families had forced them into the service when they were emotionally unsuited for such a career. She had seen men not much older than her stepson whose spirits had been crushed and their nerves shattered after experiencing the reality of warfare. And of course there were the broken-hearted women left behind to mourn the loss of their loved ones. She knew only too well the pain and heartache, made even worse by being unable to grieve openly. She turned her attention to Cassy and once again her heart swelled with love for her daughter who was clearly on the verge of tears at the mention of her old friend. Belinda gave her a reassuring smile. 'Perhaps we can find out where Bailey is stationed and you might be able to see him, providing his unit has not been sent abroad.'

Cassy wiped her eyes on her sleeve. 'Do you think so, ma'am?'

'Tomorrow morning, my husband is going to take Oliver to the barracks to meet his commanding officer. A few discreet enquiries might well discover the where-abouts of your friend, or at least give us an inkling as to where we might go to find out more. Who knows, he might even be stationed at Wellington barracks.'

'I've met this boy,' Mahdu said hastily. 'I would know him again if I saw him in the street.'

'Then perhaps we will all go,' Belinda said happily.

'We'll support Ollie, and if we're lucky we may find Bailey.'

'In the meantime we must decide how best to present Cassy to the household,' Mahdu said firmly. 'And where is the child to sleep, my lady?'

Refusing to allow Mahdu's stern expression to dampen her enthusiasm, Belinda shrugged her shoulders and laughed. 'Don't make such a pother about small details, Mahdu, darling. Get someone to set up a truckle bed in your room and Cassy can sleep there with you to look after her.' Ignoring Mahdu's pursed lips, Belinda turned to Oliver. 'And you must cheer up, Ollie. You'll love being a cavalryman. I can just see you in uniform, riding a splendid horse and having the young ladies fall at your feet.'

Oliver drained the last drop from his glass of porter. 'I am a good horseman, and I'll look quite handsome in uniform. I suppose I might give it a go.'

Belinda awakened early next morning with a feeling that all was right with the world. She could hardly believe that her daughter was under the same roof and that they were to spend the best part of a fortnight together. She sat up in bed and pulled the bell rope to summon the maid with her morning hot chocolate and hot water to fill the washbowl. Sunshine streamed into her room through a chink in the curtains and she lay back against the pillows struggling with the important decision as to which gown and bonnet she should wear to the barracks. A frisson of excitement ran through her veins at the prospect of being back in the world in

166

which she had grown up, but if the idea of being amongst the military was like going home, it was also tinged with sadness and regret for the loss of her father and the man to whom she had given her heart. The pain of the old wound continued to ache like a scar that would never properly heal.

But this was not the time for sad memories. The future stretched before her and was all the brighter now that she was reunited in some small measure with her daughter. Belinda swung her legs over the side of the bed and went to the window to draw back the curtains. The sky above the rooftops was a cerulean blue with tiny puffballs of white cloud floating high up in the atmosphere. It was already warm and the day promised to be fine. She would wear her blue muslin gown sprigged with white daisies and tiny green leaves. It was a coincidence perhaps, but it was in a similar style and material to the one she had worn when she first met George all those years ago. If she closed her eyes she could still see his handsome face in minute detail, from the tiny scar on his top lip that made him appear to smile even when his dark eyes were serious, to the honeyed warmth of his gaze when their eyes first met.

'Good morning, my lady.'

Belinda turned with a start at the sound of the maid's voice. Her hand flew to her throat and she felt the colour flood her cheeks as if in thinking of her lover she had been caught out in a naughty deed. She struggled to regain her composure while the maid poured hot chocolate from a silver pot into a bone china cup patterned with violets and rosebuds. A smaller girl wearing a mobcap that was too big for her staggered into the room bearing a ewer filled with steaming water which she placed on the washstand, and stood waiting uncertainly for further instructions.

'Thank you,' Belinda said with a vague wave of her hand. 'That will be all.'

The maids left as quietly as they had entered, leaving Belinda to enjoy her chocolate. She settled down on the window seat, curling her feet beneath her and sipping the hot, sweet drink, but minutes later her husband strode into the room. Startled, Belinda slopped the hot liquid into the saucer. 'Geoffrey, I didn't expect to see you this morning.'

He was fully dressed and immaculately turned out as usual. A waft of Macassar oil and sandalwood preceded him as he came to stand at her side. His expression was serious. 'My dear, I've been called to an urgent meeting at the Foreign Office. I'm afraid I won't be able to take Oliver to the barracks, but I don't want him to miss his appointment with Colonel Masters.'

Belinda could barely conceal her relief that this incursion into her privacy was for other reasons than the infrequent calls on her marital obligations. She put the cup and saucer down on a side table and smiled at her husband. 'I can do that for you, Geoffrey. Colonel Masters was a friend of Papa's and I'm sure he'll remember me.'

'No one could forget you, my dear,' Sir Geoffrey said with an obvious effort to sound gallant, although it was plain that his thoughts were elsewhere. 'I particularly wanted to see Masters, as I think that Oliver ought to be taken under his wing as soon as possible, but I'll have to rely upon you, Belinda. I have a particularly delicate political situation to settle which will take hours if not days.'

'Don't worry, Geoffrey. Leave it all to me.'

Sir Geoffrey made to leave the room but he paused in the doorway, a frown creasing his brow. 'There's just one thing, my dear. I've seen a strange child wandering about the house. She seems to be wearing some sort of school uniform therefore I must assume that she isn't one of our servants.'

Belinda thought quickly. She had hoped that this conversation would not arise and that her husband would be too occupied with political matters to notice one small girl extra in the household. She flashed him a brilliant smile. 'Oh, dear. You've caught me out, Geoffrey. Cassy is one of my charity cases. I invited her here during the school holidays as the poor little thing had nowhere else to go.'

Sir Geoffrey shook his head and it was obvious that this time her smile had failed to charm him. 'You should have asked me first, Belinda.'

'But you might have said no.'

'I most certainly would. You know how I feel about children, and I certainly don't want my home invaded by street Arabs, however deserving their case may be. It won't do. If word got out that we were taking in waifs and strays we would have the whole of London's deserving poor importuning us at every turn. You must

169

find her alternative accommodation as soon as possible.'

'But, Geoffrey . . .'

'No, my dear. I'm perfectly happy to indulge your little whims in most cases but not this. Get rid of her. Send her to my sister if you must continue with this act of charity, but do it today.' He stalked out of the room, closing the door firmly behind him.

Sir Geoffrey's carriage drove through the gates of the barracks and to Belinda it felt like a homecoming. The mere sight of the soldiers in their smart uniforms and the sense of orderliness and discipline took her back to her girlhood, and for a moment she forgot her brief contretemps with her husband and her anxiety about Cassy. She gave Oliver a reassuring pat on the knee as she caught his eye and saw that he was apprehensive despite his outward show of bravado. Mahdu sat quietly by her side and Cassy was huddled in the opposite corner of the carriage, peering eagerly out of the window as if she hoped to find her friend amongst the soldiers on parade. Belinda felt her pain as though it were her own. The silken umbilical cord of mother love still bound her to her child, and she wished that she could conjure up the boy, Bailey, but he could be almost anywhere in the world by now.

At that moment the carriage drew to a halt and the groom leapt down to open the door. He pulled down the steps but even before her feet touched the ground Belinda had seen Colonel Masters striding towards them. His booming voice carried across the parade ground as he greeted her. He bowed over her hand, clicking his heels together. 'Lady Davenport, Belinda, my dear. How splendid it is to see you again after all these years.'

'It's good to see you too, Colonel,' Belinda said, smiling. 'May I introduce my stepson, Oliver: the young man in question.'

'How do you do, young man? I've heard a great deal about you from your father.' Colonel Masters eyed Oliver with a speculative stare, as if assessing him from head to toe like a prized stallion in Tattersalls. 'You look like a promising young fellow. How do you feel about a career in the army?'

Belinda held her breath. If Oliver chose to be difficult it would ruin all his father's plans, and put an end to his career in the army before it had even begun.

'I'm sure it would suit me very well, sir,' Oliver said meekly.

'Capital. That's what I wanted to hear.' Colonel Masters summoned a young lieutenant with an imperious flick of his hand. 'Carlton, show Mr Davenport around the barracks and the stables. You do ride, I take it, Davenport?'

'Yes, sir.'

'Splendid. I see you've come prepared.' Colonel Masters eyed Oliver's riding boots and breeches with a nod of approval. 'Good man. Get him mounted, Carlton. We'll see how he handles himself on horseback.'

Carlton saluted smartly and led Oliver off in the direction of the stables.

'Now then, my dear,' Colonel Masters said, proffering

his arm to Belinda. 'Mrs Masters is eager to see you and I'm certain you have plenty to talk about.' He angled his head, raising bushy white eyebrows as he stared pointedly at Mahdu and Cassy. 'I take it this is your maid, but who is the child? Not yours, I should think.'

For a moment Belinda thought she might faint. The Colonel's jocular comment was too close to the truth for comfort. She fanned herself vigorously. 'It is rather hot in the sun, sir. Might we all go indoors?'

'Of course. How stupid of me to keep you ladies standing outside in the heat of the day. Come with me and I'll take you to my quarters.'

Belinda exchanged relieved glances with Mahdu, who took Cassy by the hand as they crossed the parade ground. They entered the Colonel's private quarters where the air was pleasantly cool, and the mixed scents of lavender and beeswax were complemented by the perfume emanating from a vase of white lilies set on the hall table.

'Mrs Masters, our guest is here.' The Colonel's bellow echoed off the wainscoted walls and caused the lustres on the candle sconces to tinkle like fairy bells.

A door opened and a small, plump lady wearing a grey silk gown hurried out to envelop Belinda in a fond hug. 'My dear girl, you don't look a day older than you did ten years ago. I cried at your wedding, you were such a lovely bride.'

'Never mind that now, Mrs Masters. Our guest is in dire need of rest and refreshment after her carriage ride. I've sent Carlton off with the boy, and I'm going out to see how the chap handles a horse.'

'Yes, of course. Do come into the parlour,' Mrs Masters said, smiling fondly. 'It's good to see you again, Belinda. We have so much to talk about.' She glanced at Mahdu and if she was surprised to see Cassy standing a little way behind her, she did not bat an eyelid. 'Your maid and the little one can wait in the kitchen. Martha will make them most welcome. She is an old campaigner like me.'

Belinda had little choice other than to follow her old friend into the small but comfortably furnished parlour. She took a seat at the table where a silver kettle bubbled gently over a tiny spirit stove. Mrs Masters took a seat opposite her and busied herself making tea. 'Do have a slice of Cook's Madeira cake, my dear. It's very good. Martha has been with me since I was a young bride. We've been on more campaigns than the Iron Duke himself.' She chuckled at her own wit as she handed a cup and saucer to Belinda. 'Now tell me all about yourself. How do you find the life of a diplomat's wife? I'm sure it must be very interesting. And how is Sir Geoffrey? You made such a good match there. I'm not one to listen to gossip, but I had heard that you were seeing rather a lot of a young Anglo-Indian officer. I'm glad that was just a rumour, my dear. You know how people are about mixed marriages.'

Belinda choked on a mouthful of hot tea. She put the cup back on its saucer, wiping her eyes on a scrap of cotton and lace that served as a handkerchief. 'I'm sorry, the tea was hotter than I expected.'

'Did I say something to upset you, my dear?' Mrs

Masters eyed her anxiously. 'My husband is always telling me off for being thoughtless.'

'No, not at all,' Belinda lied. 'I'm happily married and I have nothing to complain about. Geoffrey is a kind man and a good husband.'

'Of course,' Mrs Master said hastily. 'Forgive a silly old woman's tactlessness, Belinda. Now tell me about the child who came with you today. What a beautiful little thing she is, but obviously of mixed blood. They are often the loveliest of creatures as I'm sure you are aware, and she is no exception.'

Having explained that Cassy was merely her protégée and that she was putting her through school in order to give her a better chance in life, Belinda was relieved when the Colonel reappeared, inviting them to go out onto the parade ground and see Oliver putting one of the horses through its paces.

Mahdu and Cassy joined them as they stood in the sunshine, sheltering in the shade of a parasol kindly loaned by Mrs Masters. Oliver appeared to be enjoying himself hugely as he rode the great black animal with complete confidence and expertise. The Colonel was obviously impressed by Oliver's display of horsemanship, and he took Belinda aside to tell her that there would be nothing to prevent Sir Geoffrey purchasing a commission for his son. Ensign Davenport would be accepted into the 13th Hussars without delay. If the rumours were true, it would not be long before the battalion was deployed to India. In his opinion, the boy would see active service before the year was out.

Belinda did not know whether to be pleased or

anxious when she heard this from the man in authority. She was determined to quiz her husband as soon as he returned home, and put the case to him that perhaps he ought to think again before sending his only child to war. She said nothing of this to Oliver when he rejoined them, and she gave him an encouraging smile as the Colonel drew him aside for a private conversation. It seemed that the interview had gone extremely well but Belinda was still a little anxious as she crossed the parade ground to her carriage. Oliver was still engaged with the Colonel, but Mahdu and Cassy were walking just a few paces behind her. The groom was holding the carriage door open and Belinda was about to climb into the carriage when she heard her daughter let out a shriek. Pausing with one foot on the step, she turned her head in time to see Cassy tearing across the parade ground, shouting and waving her hands above her head.

Chapter Ten

'Bailey,' Cassy shrieked, flinging herself at the young trooper standing stiffly to attention at the end of the line of soldiers on the parade ground. 'Bailey, I can't believe it's you.' His face flushed beneath his healthy tan, but he neither moved nor looked down at her. She tugged at his arm. 'Bailey. It's me, Cassy.'

Still he did not move. The soldier standing next to him stifled a chuckle, but his face froze as the sergeant major bore down on them with an angry roar. 'What's going on here?' He stormed up to Cassy, dragging her away. 'What d'you think you're doing, miss? You can't interfere with her majesty's soldiers when they're on duty. Clear off.'

'But he's my friend,' Cassy protested, casting an anxious glance at Bailey. She struggled with tears as he ignored her, staring straight ahead as if she did not exist. 'What's the matter, Bailey? Why won't you speak to me?'

'Go away, miss. Or do I have to carry you off?' The sergeant major breathed heavily down her neck, exuding the odour of stale beer and onions.

'Bailey, help me,' Cassy cried as she was lifted bodily and tucked beneath the sergeant's arm as he marched purposefully across the parade ground. She could not see where she was going, just the ground moving dizzily beneath her, until the sergeant came to a halt, stamping his feet and jolting her so that her head bobbed up and down like a cork floating on water.

'It's all right, Sergeant. Put her down. This child is known to me.'

She recognised the Colonel's voice and found herself staring at his shiny black leather boots, but with a sudden swift movement she was set on her feet and the world righted itself. 'Please, sir,' she said desperately. 'The soldier over there is my best friend, Bailey. I thought I'd lost him forever.'

'Young lady, you can't disrupt army routine on a whim.' Colonel Masters frowned at her so that his eyebrows met over the bridge of his nose.

'Don't scold her, dear,' Mrs Masters said, tucking her hand in the crook of his arm. 'She's just a child. Surely you could bend the rules a little, just this once?'

Cassy held her breath, crossing her fingers behind her back as she waited for the Colonel's response, but Belinda and Mahdu arrived at that moment, flushed and panting.

'I am so sorry, Colonel,' Belinda said breathlessly. 'Please forgive her. She knows nothing of military life.'

'Five minutes,' Colonel Masters said, addressing the sergeant major. 'The trooper may have five minutes with the child, as a special dispensation.' He turned to Oliver, who had been openly enjoying the scene, but a steely look from the Colonel wiped the smile off his face. 'Make yourself useful, Davenport.'

Oliver snapped to attention. 'Colonel, sir?'

177

'Take the young lady to her friend. Allow them five minutes together.'

Oliver held his hand out to Cassy. 'Come on then, brat. It seems the British army is prepared to mark time especially for you.'

Cassy needed no second bidding, and she trotted along at Oliver's side. 'Do you really want to be a soldier?'

'I think it might do,' he said casually. 'Splendid horses and good company might be the very thing for me.' He stopped as Bailey, at a command from the sergeant, broke ranks and walked stiffly towards them. 'There you are, brat. You've got five minutes so make it quick and let the poor chap get back into line without making him a laughing stock.' Oliver paused, eyeing Bailey up and down. 'So you're Bailey.'

'I am.' Bailey returned the stare with a suspicious glint in his grey eyes. 'Who are you?'

'You'd best get used to calling me sir,' Oliver said stiffly. 'I'll soon be Ensign Davenport, your superior officer, so show some respect when you address me, trooper.'

Cassy waited her turn with a sigh of resignation. Why, she wondered, did men have to be so silly? They were sizing each other up like bare-knuckle fighters about to launch into a fight. If she had been at home in Cripplegate she would have known how to handle this situation, but here in the toffs' world she knew she must try to behave with decorum. She longed to throw her arms around Bailey and hug him, but she managed to curb her instincts and suppress her desire

178

to whoop for joy at the mere sight of him. She stared at the two young men, who were facing each other with overt animosity. They were of a similar height and both fair-haired, although Oliver had green eyes and his face was rounded and youthful, whereas Bailey's eyes were as blue as the skies above them, and his suntanned skin was drawn taut over high cheek-bones. Years of privation as a child had made him look older than his eighteen years. Even so, she thought, given different circumstances they might have been taken for brothers. She drew away from Oliver and slipped her hand into Bailey's. 'Go away, Ollie,' she said boldly. 'I want to talk to my friend. It don't matter to me whether you're above him or he's below you.'

Oliver shrugged his shoulders and grinned. 'If you say so, brat.' He strolled off with a swagger in his step.

'He's going to be trouble,' Bailey observed, shaking his head, but his frown dissipated into a grin as he looked down at Cassy. 'I can't believe you're here, nipper. I thought I'd lost you forever.'

'Not me, Bailey. I was determined to find you one way or another, but I never expected to see you here, even though I hoped you might be.'

'I ain't sure that makes sense,' he said, chuckling. 'But how did you come to be with the toffs, Cassy? I've been worried sick about you. I tried to tell them that I needed to make sure you were all right but it was no use. They wouldn't listen to me.'

'I don't remember much about it,' Cassy admitted wistfully. 'It was raining and I was wet and cold, and then all of a sudden a carriage pulled up and it was my ma. She'd come to take me to a big house up West with servants and a mad old lady who took me on as a maid, but I broke things and was going to be sent away when Ma's mistress turned up. She's like an angel, the loveliest lady you ever saw, and she had tears in her eyes when she saw me. That's her over there.' Cassy pointed to Belinda who was still talking to Mrs Masters although the Colonel was no longer there. 'She's called Lady Davenport and she lives in another big house. She sent me to school, but that's another story. Anyway, I'm on holiday and staying with her and Ma, although I mustn't call her Ma, since it's a secret that must be kept from Sir Geoffrey and the other servants.'

Bailey pushed his shako to the back of his head. 'Blimey, Cass. What a tale. So you're going to be a young lady, then?'

'I dunno about that, but I think I might work in a shop up West when I leave school, or maybe I'll be a lady's maid like Ma. I ain't decided yet. They're teaching me manners and how to talk proper, I mean properly. And, Bailey, you must never eat off your knife. I learnt that much. It makes people stare at you, but I suppose you know that now.'

Bailey wrapped his arms around her and held her so tightly that the buttons on his tunic stuck into her flesh, but she did not complain. He smelt the same, only cleaner if she were to be honest. He was still her dear Bailey, and she felt safe in his arms.

'Time's up,' Oliver called out from a few paces away. 'Put her down, trooper.'

'I'll put him down in a moment,' Bailey muttered

into Cassy's hair. 'Officer or no, I ain't taking orders from a kid younger than me.'

Cassy clutched his arm, peering anxiously up into his face. 'Don't do nothing stupid, will you? And he ain't that bad, Bailey. He's just a boy and he's scared stiff really. Promise me you'll look out for him when he joins the regiment.'

Bailey pulled a face, but then he seemed to relent and he tweaked Cassy's nose. 'All right, nipper. If you say so, I'll keep me eye on the toff.'

'I got to go,' Cassy said, eyeing the sergeant major warily as he strode towards them. 'But at least I know where to find you now.'

'And where will you be?' Bailey asked anxiously. 'Where do I find you, Cass?'

'I'm staying in South Audley Street at the moment, but then I go back to Miss North's Academy for Young Ladies, Highbury Hill.'

'At least I know where you'll be for the foreseeable future,' Bailey said, backing away. 'They're sending me to the Riding Establishment in Maidstone tomorrow for more training, but we'll be together one day, Cass. That's a promise.' He froze to attention at a barked command from the sergeant major, and then marched briskly back into line.

'Come on, brat,' Oliver said, taking her by the hand. 'Let's go home. I'm starving. All this soldiering has given me an appetite for luncheon.'

The mahogany dining table was set with three places and the array of silver cutlery and crystal glasses left

181

Cassy both dazzled and confused. Oliver had taken his seat opposite her and when faced with a bowlful of soup she sent him a mute plea for help. Smiling, he demonstrated which spoon she should use, but intimidated by the poker-faced butler and the uniformed parlour maid who hovered at his side, Cassy struggled to remember the hints on table manners that Mahdu had given her before entering the room. She glanced anxiously at her hostess, but Lady Davenport seemed distracted and barely touched the cream of asparagus soup or the remove of poached turbot in tarragon sauce. Oliver on the other hand was filled with enthusiasm for his new profession and kept up a steady stream of conversation that required little input from his stepmother apart from the occasional nod of her head.

Cassy was too excited to eat much of the food no matter how tempting. Finding Bailey was like a miracle and even though he was leaving London for Kent the following day, she revelled in the fact that she had seen him again and that he knew where to find her when he was granted leave. The thought of returning to Miss North's establishment held no terrors for her now that she could cling to the hope of one day being reunited with Bailey. Despite the gap in their ages, they were closer than most brothers and sisters and she knew he would not let her down. They would set up home together and never again be parted. She jumped as she realised that Lady Davenport was speaking to her.

'Cassy, stop daydreaming and listen to me.'

'I'm sorry,' Cassy murmured guiltily. 'What did you say, ma'am?'

Belinda cleared her throat nervously. 'I was hoping that you would be able to stay here with me, but it seems that it won't be possible.' She shot a warning look at Oliver as he opened his mouth to speak. 'Let me finish, Ollie. As I said, it isn't possible for you to stay in South Audley Street, my dear. But I'm sure that Mrs Fulford-Browne will be only too delighted to have you as a guest for the remainder of your holiday.'

'Stepmother dearest, you're forgetting that she's married that Italian chap,' Oliver said, winking at Cassy. 'Old Fulford-Browne must be spinning in his grave.'

Belinda's lips twitched but she shook her finger at him. 'Don't be naughty, Oliver.'

'But I want to stay with you and Mahdu,' Cassy protested, ignoring Oliver's untimely interruption. 'Have I done something wrong, missis? I've tried to be good and do as I was told.'

Belinda's smile faded and she reached out to lay her hand on Cassy's arm. 'No, Cassy, darling. It's not your fault. If anything it is mine. I should have thought . . .' She hesitated, biting her lip. 'I ought to have arranged matters differently.'

'What's up anyway?' Oliver demanded, wiping his lips on a table napkin. 'Why can't the brat stay here? Is Pater being difficult again?'

'Your father is a good man, and I won't have a word said against him. He has a very important position to uphold and I'm afraid I might have compromised him in some way, although I don't quite understand how.'

'Poppycock, Stepmother,' Oliver said angrily. 'You're a saint if ever there was one and the old man is a stiff-necked old tyrant.' He rose to his feet, pushing his chair back abruptly. 'What possible harm can it do to give one small girl a place to stay for a fortnight, I'd like to know?'

'I didn't think you cared what happened to Cassy,' Belinda said sharply. 'As I recall you thought she was nothing but a nuisance just yesterday.'

'That was before I knew I was going to be an officer in the 13th Hussars,' Oliver said grandly. 'I'm a man now, Belle. I can stand up to Papa and I won't allow him to bully you or Cassy.'

'Oh, Ollie. You are so sweet, but your papa doesn't bully me or anyone else for that matter. However, we must respect his wishes.' Belinda turned to Cassy. 'You will be well looked after by my sister-in-law, and you'll be treated as a guest this time, not a servant. Mahdu and I will call every day to take you out for luncheon or tea, or perhaps to the Zoological Gardens or some other place of interest. What do you say to that?'

Cassy hesitated for a moment. She could see that the lovely lady was in earnest, although she did not understand why such a beautiful and rich person cared tuppence for a servant's offspring. It was obvious that she thought a lot of Ma, and perhaps that was why she was so concerned about the fate of one small girl. Whatever the reason for her benefactor's kindness, Cassy could not help wondering why there was a hint of sadness in Lady Davenport's beautiful blue eyes that never quite went away, even when she laughed.

'Well, Cassy?' Belinda said gently. 'What do you think of our plan?'

'I like it well enough, ma'am.' Cassy bowed her head. She did not want to return to Duke Street where the servants had plagued her, but it seemed she had little choice in the matter.

'There's no need to look so down in the mouth, brat,' Oliver said cheerfully. 'Aunt Flo is always good for a laugh.'

Flora Montessori looked anything but amused as Belinda stood before her with Cassy at her side and Mahdu, as usual, standing a couple of paces behind them.

'But I've just returned from my honeymoon, Belle,' Flora said, frowning. 'Leonardo will have something to say about this.'

'Since when did you care what anyone said, Flora?'

'I care about my darling Leo. He is the love of my life.' She took a cigarillo from the silver box on the table beside her chair and struck a vesta with the ease of long practice.

Belinda's eyes glistened with amusement. 'As I recall, you said the same about Gunter.'

Flora puffed on the small black cigar, exhaling a plume of blue smoke which made Cassy cough. 'I loved Gunter, it's true, but I told him not to go hunting and the silly man broke his neck on the eve of our second anniversary ball. I call that downright selfish.'

'And what about Captain Rivers?' Belinda asked innocently. 'You were only married for two weeks before he went off on that ill-fated expedition.'

'Alexander was an adventurer,' Flora said, sighing. 'He was such a good lover too. What a waste. Although I have to say that getting lost in the African jungle and being eaten by a crocodile was the result of bad judgement on his part.'

'I suppose it was Harcourt Fulford-Browne's fault that he died of apoplexy.'

Cassy was quick to hear the teasing note in Belinda's voice and she shot her a sideways glance. Their eyes met for a moment and Cassy had an almost uncontrollable urge to laugh outright, but a swift dig in the ribs from Mahdu made her remember her manners.

Flora however did not seem to be offended by Belinda's remark. She shrugged her thin shoulders. 'Harcourt was always delicate, and he was a greedy pig. I warned him time and again about his uncontrollable appetites, and I don't just mean for food and drink.'

'Flora!' Belinda gasped. 'Remember there's a child present.'

'And who brought her here uninvited, may I ask?' Flora tossed the butt of her cigarillo into the empty grate. 'Leonardo and I are just getting to know one another properly. I don't know what he'll say to a child running about the house, and no doubt spying on us.' She fixed Cassy with a cold stare. 'You caused chaos on your last visit, as I recall.'

'But you always have a house filled with guests,'

Belinda said mildly. 'Surely one small girl won't make any difference?'

'I've sent them all packing. There are elements of my past that Leonardo does not yet know about. He's a musician and has the true artistic temperament. I don't want him upset.' She tossed her head so that her diamond earrings swung like tiny chandeliers. 'We're in the first throes of romantic love, and we want to be alone.'

'You've only known him for a month. What possessed you to marry again?'

Flora raised an eyebrow, inclining her head towards Cassy. 'I don't need to spell it out to you as a married woman, Belle. I should have thought it obvious that a person, even someone in her prime like me, has certain needs. Although, of course, I'm forgetting that you married that old stick of a brother of mine. Perhaps I should find you an Italian lover like my Leo. That would bring the roses to your cheeks, my girl.'

Mahdu shuffled her feet and Belinda took Cassy by the shoulders, spinning her round and giving her a gentle push towards the door. 'We are obviously unwelcome here, Cassy. And anyway I don't think this is the right place for you. Go with Mahdu. I'm taking you home.'

There was an ominous silence in the carriage as they drove back to South Audley Street. Cassy only had a vague understanding as to what had passed between Lady Davenport and her sister-in-law, but whatever the problem between them it came down to the same thing. She was as unwanted in Duke Street as she was in Sir Geoffrey's house. She was a misfit, and an embarrassment. She belonged nowhere, and this point was made even more obvious when they arrived at the mansion simultaneously with her reluctant host. Sir Geoffrey's face darkened when he saw her alight from the carriage. He paused on the steps, glaring at her with brows drawn together and his lips clenched in a tight line.

'Geoffrey, I can explain,' Belinda began nervously.

'I told you to send the child back to wherever it was that you found her. I'm serious, Belinda. This won't do.'

Belinda shot an anxious glance at the footmen and the groom who were standing to attention staring straight ahead. 'Please, Geoffrey. May we continue this conversation indoors?'

'I have nothing further to say on the matter. I want the child gone as soon as possible. Do I make myself understood?' He strode into the house, tossing his top hat and gloves to the stony-faced butler. 'I'm going to my study. I don't want to be disturbed.'

'Please, ma'am,' Cassy said, tugging at Belinda's sleeve. 'I don't want to be no bother. I can go to my friend Lottie's house in Whitechapel for the rest of the holiday. She said so.'

Belinda's eyes brimmed with unshed tears. 'I won't be bullied into letting you go. Why is everyone being so unreasonable?' Seizing Cassy's hand she ran up the steps into the entrance hall.

'My lady, think carefully before you say anything you will regret later,' Mahdu said breathlessly as she caught

188

up with them. 'Let me take the child to Whitechapel, where I'm sure she will be most welcome.'

Belinda clasped Cassy's hand even tighter. 'I can't send her away like this. You don't want to leave us, do you, my dear?'

Cassy barely knew what to think or say at this sudden turn of events. She shrugged her shoulders. 'I don't want to make trouble for you, ma'am.'

'I can't bear this any longer,' Belinda cried, picking up her skirts and running towards the staircase. Her small feet made soft pattering noises on the marble tiles, and she brushed past Oliver who was coming down the stairs dressed for outdoors.

'Good Lord, what's wrong with her?' he demanded. 'Was she crying? Has the old man done something to upset her?'

Mahdu bowed her head, saying nothing, but in the face of her idol's distress Cassy was not going to remain silent. She caught hold of Oliver's arm. 'He made her cry,' she said angrily. 'Your pa is a mean old man and that sister of his ain't much better. I'll be glad to go to Lottie's house in Whitechapel if it means I don't have to see Lady Davenport upset time and again. It ain't fair and it ain't nice. She's a good sort and no one here appreciates her.'

Oliver stared at her open-mouthed. 'Well, by golly. That was heartfelt. What on earth has been going on? What have I missed, Mahdu?'

'It's not up to me to say, sir. I suggest you ask your stepmother, sir.' Mahdu laid her hand on Cassy's shoulder. 'Go to your room. I'll look after her ladyship.' She hurried off in the direction of the servants' staircase.

Cassy was about to follow her but Oliver caught her by the hand. 'Wait a moment, Cassy. What's been going on? And don't tell me it's nothing. I can see very well that something has upset my stepmother, and I want to know what's been said.' He hooked his arm around her shoulders. 'Come with me, brat. I know a very cosy little teashop nearby where we can sit and talk without being frowned upon.' He guided her past the footman who was still holding the door open. 'If anyone asks, Harris, I'm taking Miss Cassy out for afternoon tea.'

The teashop was filled with well-dressed ladies sipping tea from dainty bone china cups, nibbling cake and chatting. They were too engrossed in their gossiping to pay any attention to Cassy and Oliver, who were seated at the back of the room close to the kitchen door.

Oliver ordered tea and pastries and then settled down to listen to Cassy's account of what had happened to upset his stepmother to such a degree. 'Well, by George, the old man's done it this time,' he said at length, taking a bite out of a chocolate éclair. He chewed and swallowed, wiping his lips on a napkin. 'I think he's talking nonsense. Why would anyone take exception to a kid like you? I doubt if anyone would think twice about you staying with us for a couple of weeks. It's not as if the old man was going to adopt you.'

'He made it clear that I've got to leave,' Cassy said, licking her fingers and receiving a reproving frown.

'Not done,' Oliver said, waving his napkin at her. 'That's what this thing is for and don't you forget it.

I have to say that licking the jam off one's fingers is much more satisfying, but it just ain't the done thing. Look at the ladies taking tea and see how they behave. It's as well to do what they do and then no one can fault you for your manners.'

Cassy wiped her fingers on her table napkin. 'There's such a lot to learn, Ollie. I don't think I'll ever be anything but a street Arab.'

He frowned at her, shaking his head. 'Now that's not the sort of talk I want to hear from you, brat. You're as good as anyone here and don't you forget it. You'll be a stunner when you're a bit older and you'll have the chaps dangling after you. You could do very well for yourself and all you need is a bit of polish. I think my old man's quite wrong in sending you away, but as it is there's nothing much I can do to help.'

'I'll go to Whitechapel, Ollie. But you can do something for me. Let Bailey know where I've gone so that we don't lose touch again.'

'You're really fond of that fellow, aren't you, Cassy?'

She nodded her head. 'He's been my only family for as long as I can remember. I don't know what I'd do if I never saw him again.' She eyed the last cream cake. 'Can I have that cake?'

'May I have that cake?' Oliver corrected her with a grin. 'Go on, brat. Make yourself sick if you must. Enjoy yourself while you can.' He sat back in his chair watching her eat with obvious amusement. 'I wonder if your friend's pa would run me up a suit at special rates? You could ask him for me.'

* * *

Next day Cassy left the house in South Audley Street with Mahdu. Lady Davenport had not come down to say goodbye, but Mahdu explained that her ladyship was prone to headaches which sometimes laid her low for days. She had sent her best wishes to Cassy and hoped that she would enjoy her stay in Whitechapel. It had all been arranged with great haste. One of the footmen had been sent out the previous evening to ask the tailor if it was convenient for Cassy to spend the remainder of her holiday with them, and the answer had come back in the affirmative. It had not taken long to put Cassy's few belongings in a small portmanteau that morning, and the carriage had been summoned. Oliver had risen early and had given her a florin to spend as she liked. He had ruffled her hair and given her a brotherly hug, promising to pass her message on to Bailey as he too was going to Maidstone to polish up his equestrian skills, although he told her that he could probably teach the riding master a thing or two.

Cassy had left the house with mixed feelings. She experienced a sad little tug at her heartstrings on parting from the lady with the angel's face who had shed tears for her, and she had been sad to leave Oliver who had turned out to be a friend after all, even if he did treat her like a baby sometimes. She settled down in the comfort of Sir Geoffrey's carriage, casting a glance at Mahdu who was sitting opposite her, staring out of the carriage window.

'Will you come and see me when I'm back at school, Ma?' The question tumbled from Cassy's lips.

Mahdu turned her head to give her a straight look. 'I've told you not to call me that.'

'But no one can hear us,' Cassy protested. 'May I call you Mother when we are alone?'

'No, child. It's not right. You must not think of me in that way.' Mahdu stared down at her hands knotted together in her lap. 'You must forget about the past, larla. You will have to learn to live for yourself alone.'

'I don't understand, Ma. Are you ashamed of me?'

This brought Mahdu's head up and her face was contorted with pain. 'Never, larla. You are dear to me, and any woman would be proud to have you for a daughter.'

'Then why, Ma? Why can't you leave Lady Davenport and then we could live together? I don't want to go back to that school. I don't want to be a lady. I just want to be with you.'

'Don't talk like that,' Mahdu cried, clutching her breast with both hands. The colour drained from her face and her features contorted with pain. 'Be still, Cassy,' she gasped.

'What's wrong, Ma?' Cassy fell to her knees, taking Mahdu's clenched hands in hers. 'Speak to me. Tell me what to do.'

'It's nothing,' Mahdu managed to say through pale lips. 'Let me be quiet for a moment.' She collapsed against the leather squabs, breathing rapidly.

Cassy moved to sit by her side, clutching her hands. 'You need a doctor, Ma. I'll tell the coachman to take you to hospital.'

'No, larla,' Mahdu said with an effort. 'It's nothing.

The pain comes and then it goes. Let me rest for a moment and I'll be well again.'

Cassy sat on the edge of her seat, her gaze fixed on Mahdu's features as they began to relax and the colour returned to her cheeks. 'Are you feeling better, Ma?'

Mahdu opened her eyes. 'Cassy, I may not be with you always. There is something you ought to know.'

'Yes, Ma. Tell me, please.'

Mahdu placed her lips close to Cassy's ear. 'You are not my child, larla, although I love you as much as if you had been born to me.'

'But I've always thought you were my ma.'

'Larla, my time is close. I can't go to my maker with a lie on my lips. Your mother is . . .' Mahdu closed her eyes and a long drawn out sigh escaped from her lips.

Chapter Eleven

'I can't believe it's our last day at the academy,' Lottie said, putting the last hairpin in Cassy's coiffure and standing back to admire her handiwork. 'If I don't do well in medical school I might make a good lady's maid.' She clapped her hand over her mouth, meeting Cassy's eyes in the flyblown mirror above the dormitory mantelshelf. 'I'm sorry, Cass. I didn't mean . . .'

Cassy turned to her with a smile. 'It's all right, Lottie. Nothing you could say would offend me or hurt my feelings. We've been friends for too long to let silly little slips of the tongue come between us.'

Lottie enveloped her in a hug. 'You'll always be my best friend, Cassy. In fact you're more like a sister to me. I'll really miss the times we spent together in the school holidays. Papa wants you to know that you'll always have a home with us in Whitechapel, no matter what happens in the future.'

'I know that, and I love your pa. He's been the father I never knew and he couldn't have been kinder to me.' Cassy fumbled for her handkerchief. 'There, I told myself I wouldn't cry today.' Half laughing, half crying, she blew her nose.

Lottie dashed a tear from her eyes. 'Now you've started me off. Who would think that we'd be sad at leaving the North wind's academy for young ladies? I've hated this wretched school for almost every minute of the years I've spent here.'

'Well, today is definitely our last day. I just wish that Ma was here to see me get my diploma from Miss North.' Cassy sighed and turned away to fasten the lock on the portmanteau from South Audley Street that was now battered and worn with constant use. Memories of that fatal day when Mahdu had died in her arms were still fresh and painful even after five years. She remembered screaming for help until the carriage came to a halt and the groom wrenched the door open. The coachman had climbed down from his perch on the box and had given his opinion in sonorous tones that there was no hope for the poor woman, but he added in a half-whisper that Sir Geoffrey would not welcome the return of a corpse. After an agitated discussion, the coachman and groom had decided to take Mahdu to the London Hospital as it was in Whitechapel close to their destination, and leave the doctors to deal with the situation. The coroner would need to be informed, the coachman had said, seeming determined to impress his underling with his worldly wisdom. There would have to be a death certificate signed by a doctor and an inquest. Cassy had barely understood anything that was being said. All she knew was that the woman she had always thought of as her mother was dead, but even more painful, Mahdu's dying breath had been to renounce her as a daughter.

The coach had lumbered on through the heavy city traffic and Cassy had cradled Mahdu's lifeless body in her arms even after they reached the entrance to Spectacle Alley where Mr Solomon had his small shop. She remembered how she had clung to Mahdu's plump form, winding her small hands in her clothing so that her fingers had to be prised apart in order to make her let go. She had fought, scratching, screaming and begging to be allowed to stay with Ma, but strong arms had enfolded her and a merciful blackness had blotted out the terrible scene.

'You're daydreaming again, Cass.'

Lottie's amused voice brought Cassy back to the present with a start. She forced her lips into a smile. 'I'm almost ready to face the prize-giving.'

'Papa will be here by now,' Lottie said happily. 'He will clap loudly for both of us, Cass.'

'I know he will.' Cassy made an effort to sound cheerful, but she struggled with the awful feeling of isolation that sometimes overwhelmed her. It was a forlorn and lonely place in which she found herself. All the other girls had families of some sort, even if it was an aged aunt or a distant cousin, but she was alone. No one teased her now or called her a chi-chi, but she was still painfully aware of being different. The desperate aching void left by Ma's death was a private thing that only someone who had suffered a similar bereavement would understand. Even if Mahdu had spoken the truth and she was not her birth mother, Cassy drew some comfort from the fact that she had been loved dearly, but Mahdu's untimely death had left the question unanswered. Who was her mother and, equally important, who was it who had fathered her? Why had her birth been hushed up and kept secret for all of her fifteen years? What secrets about her lineage might never come to light?

'Lady Davenport might come,' Beck said, as if sensing Cassy's inner distress. 'She visits you quite often.'

'Yes, she has been good to me, and I wouldn't be here without her charity. But she travels often with her husband, and maybe they are away now. I haven't heard from her for some months.'

Lottie linked her hand through Cassy's arm with an affectionate squeeze. 'Never mind, you still have me and my pa. We'll be friends forever, and when I'm a Harley Street doctor, the first woman to practise in London, you can be my companion and housekeeper.'

'That would be one in the eye for Norah Vickery,' Cassy said, chuckling. 'Do you remember how she treated us when we were in our first year here?'

'I'll never forget the miserable bitch,' Lottie said with feeling. 'But darling Norah has hooked an earl, so I don't think she'll be very interested in us now. Come on, Cass. Let's go down and face the North wind for the last time. I'd like to whack her over the head with her blooming diploma, but I promise I'll behave.'

Laughing at the shared vision of Miss North's iron-clad self-control tested to the limits in such a ridiculous situation, Cassy and Lottie went downstairs arm in arm to the dining room where tables had been set aside and chairs lined in rows to accommodate the proud parents. Lottie spotted her father sitting on the far end of the back row and she blew him a kiss. Cassy stared straight ahead, not daring to hope that Lady

Davenport might have found time in her busy social life to attend such a minor event.

'Look, Cass,' Lottie whispered, tugging at her sleeve. 'There in the front row; I do believe that's your grand lady.'

Holding her breath and hardly daring to hope, Cassy craned her neck to get a better view through a forest of large hats and bald pates. Her heart gave a little leap inside her chest as Lady Davenport seemed to sense her presence, turning her head to look directly at her and smiling.

'Take your seats, and wait for your name to be called,' Miss Stanhope said, pointing to where the other girls were sitting demurely with their hands folded in their laps.

'Yes, Miss Stanhope.' The response was automatic and both Cassy and Lottie obeyed her instructions, moving swiftly to sit at the end of the row. Cassy fixed her gaze upon Lady Davenport's perfect profile beneath a confection of flowers, ribbons and lace that perched on top of her golden hair, coiled and piled high on her head. The soft curve of her cheek and the tenderness of her lips, parted slightly in a half-smile as she listened to the headmistress speaking at length, made her stand out amongst the other matrons as a vision of loveliness. Cassy was eager to speak to her patron but Miss North droned on and on about the achievement of her pupils, and the moral values that she had endeavoured to instil into girls who were now a credit to their school.

The parents and guardians listened politely but after

ten minutes they began shifting slightly on their hard wooden seats, and shuffling their feet. When someone coughed there was a veritable chorus of throat clearing, with a couple of stifled sneezes thrown in for good measure.

At long last Miss North seemed to realise that she had lost the attention of her captive audience and she began calling the girls one by one to collect their diplomas.

By the time she reached Cassy, who was last on the list, Cassy barely had time to take the scroll from Miss North's claw-like hand before the room erupted in a burst of noisy chatter as the girls were reunited with their families. Cassy threaded her way between groups of parents and daughters hugging and embracing each other and talking nineteen to the dozen. At first she could not see Lady Davenport and a feeling close to panic engulfed her. She felt suddenly like a small child who had lost her mother in a crowd. Perhaps Lady Davenport had decided not to linger, having stayed just long enough to see her protégée receive her diploma. Maybe Sir Geoffrey was waiting outside and they had already driven off in their carriage.

'Cassy, my dear. Congratulations.'

Cassy spun round and came face to face with her mentor. Six years ago she would have been looking up at Lady Davenport, but now they were roughly the same height and she was looking into a pair of smiling blue eyes. 'You came,' she murmured.

'Of course I did. I wouldn't allow an important day like today to go unmarked, Cassy. You've done so well and I'm proud of you.'

The urge to hug Lady Davenport and kiss her scented cheek was almost too much for Cassy but somehow she managed to stop herself. She was suddenly tongue-tied and did not know what to say. She felt the blood rushing to her cheeks and she clasped her hands behind her back, digging her fingernails into her palms to prevent herself from crying. So this was it. She had come to the end of her schooldays and this would almost certainly be the last time she would see Lady Davenport.

'Why are you looking so sad,' Belinda demanded, her smile fading. 'Is something wrong, my dear?'

'No. I mean, yes. I don't know, my lady.'

'Come with me, Cassy. It's so noisy in here that I can't hear myself think, let alone speak.' Lady Davenport started making her way to the door which led out into the hall but she paused as Lottie pushed through the crowd calling Cassy's name.

'Cass, you can't leave without saying goodbye.'

'This must be your special friend, with whom you spend your holidays,' Lady Davenport said, apparently unperturbed by the interruption. 'Won't you introduce us, Cassy dear?'

'Yes, my lady.' Cassy racked her brains in an attempt to recall something from one of Miss North's interminable lessons on etiquette. 'May I present Charlotte Solomon, ma'am.'

Lady Davenport embraced Lottie with a smile. 'How do you do, Charlotte? I'm delighted to meet you at long last.'

Bobbing a rather wobbly curtsey, Lottie glanced anxiously over her shoulder as her father barged his way between rows of empty chairs, knocking one over in his haste to join them, but once again Lady Davenport took matters in her stride. She turned to him holding out her hand. 'You must be Charlotte's father. I've never been able to thank you for your kindness to Cassy, but I do so now with all my heart.'

Eli Solomon peered myopically through the thick lenses of his spectacles and his lined face broke into a wide smile as he took her hand and raised it to his lips. 'I'm honoured to meet you, my lady. Cassy has always spoken of you with great affection.'

Lottie nudged Cassy in the ribs. 'She's so beautiful, Cass. You didn't do her justice.'

'I know,' Cassy said, relaxing for the first time since she had received her diploma. 'She's an angel. I've always told you that.'

'I hope one day to be able to repay your kindness to Cassy,' Lady Davenport said with obvious sincerity. 'If I were to send an invitation for you to take tea with us one day, I hope you would be in a position to accept.'

Cassy could only think that Lady Davenport was being gracious, and that Mr Solomon would accept out of politeness knowing that such an event was unlikely to happen. But a quick glance in his direction revealed a man struck almost dumb by Lady Davenport's charm and beauty. He was smiling broadly, exposing great gaps between his teeth, and nodding his head.

'Come along, Papa,' Lottie said, taking him by the arm. 'I think we should go now.' She raised her hand to pat Cassy on the shoulder. 'We'll wait for you outside, Cass.'

'Do by all means,' Lady Davenport said, acknowledging Eli's constant nodding with a slight inclination of her head and a smile. 'But Cassy will be coming home with me today. However, that doesn't mean to say that she cannot visit you in Whitechapel whenever she wants.'

'Thank you, my lady,' Eli murmured, gazing at her as if he could not bear to look away.

'Come, Papa,' Lottie said firmly, giving Cassy a meaningful glance as she led him away. 'I'll see you in a minute, Cass.'

Cassy turned to her mentor with a puzzled frown. 'Am I to go with you, my lady?'

'I would have come to see you sooner, but for matters beyond my control. However, if you are agreeable I would like you to be my personal maidservant. It's what I planned all along, and something that I know would please Mahdu, God rest her soul. I miss her very much, Cassy. She was an important part of my life, and yours too.'

Cassy could hold back no longer. 'She said she wasn't my mother.'

Lady Davenport's eyes clouded and her sunny smile faded. 'My carriage is waiting outside. We can speak more freely there. I've instructed Potter to fetch your luggage.' She hurried from the dining hall and Cassy was left with no other option than to follow her. She found Lottie waiting on the pavement outside while her father attempted to hail a passing hansom cab.

'Is everything all right?' Lottie asked anxiously.

'I think so. I'm to be her maid. It's more than I could

have hoped for.' Cassy gave her a quick hug. 'I have to go now but I'll try to keep in touch.'

'You know where we live,' Lottie called after her as Cassy quickened her pace in order to keep up with Lady Davenport, who by this time had almost reached the carriage which was waiting a little way down the hill. Potter leapt off the box to open the door.

When they were settled inside and the carriage was in motion, Lady Davenport broke the silence with an apologetic smile. 'I'm sorry if I appeared a little abrupt, Cassy. But Mahdu was more than just a servant; she was my friend and lifelong companion. She knew me better than anyone.'

'But she wasn't my mother.'

'No, my dear. She was not.'

'Did you know my real mother?'

'I knew her a long time ago, but that's all I can tell you. I'm sorry, but that's the way it must be.'

'I don't understand.'

'The secret is not entirely mine to reveal, but maybe one day I'll be able to tell you the truth. Until then I must keep silent, but I will look after you, Cassy. You'll be at my side as Mahdu was, and I will make sure that you are always treated well.'

Cassy was silent, considering this puzzling response to her question, but there did not seem very much she could say. Her future appeared to have been decided for her and she could scarcely have hoped for such an outcome as to be taken under Lady Davenport's wing. Even so, she was troubled, and the mystery of her parentage seemed even less likely to be resolved. Lost in her thoughts, she stared out of the window, barely noticing the buildings and traffic as the carriage made its way through the crowded street.

The smell of horse dung, rotting vegetables and sewage was enough to make Lady Davenport take a handkerchief impregnated with lavender oil from her reticule and hold it to her nose, but Cassy barely noticed the stench. If anything it reminded her of her childhood in Three Herring Court, and although her memories of that time were less than happy, they were made bearable by the fact that Bailey had always been there to look after her. It was four years since she last saw him, just before the 13th Hussars were drafted to India to fight the war against the Afghans. She had received the occasional missive from him, but his letters were few and far between. They were always brief and to the point, and did very little to heal the ache of separation. She had been able to take some comfort from the knowledge that he had been alive and well when he had written to her from Lucknow some weeks previously. He had reiterated his promise that they would make a home together when he returned to England, adding with some pride that he was up for promotion to the rank of corporal.

'We're here,' Lady Davenport announced as the carriage slowed down and came to a halt. 'Keep with me, Cassy. The servants have been told that there is to be a new member of staff, and that is all they need to know.'

Peering out of the window Cassy was surprised to

find herself staring at Mrs Montessori's butler, Poulton. 'We're not in South Audley Street,' she said, puzzled.

'No. The house has been shut up for some time now.' Lady Davenport gathered her skirts around her, avoiding meeting Cassy's enquiring gaze. 'Sir Geoffrey has been abroad for many months and it was more convenient for me to remove to Duke Street. It's purely temporary, but we're the guests of my sister-in-law. It works very well.' She stepped down from the carriage, assisted by Potter.

Cassy followed her, receiving a stony stare from Mrs Montessori's groom. It was only now that she recognised him as being a member of the staff who had treated her with such disdain all those years ago, but she had been too wrapped up in her own affairs to notice such details. 'Good afternoon, Potter,' she said politely.

He sniffed, staring straight ahead. Cassy smothered a sigh of resignation. So that was how it would be from now on. She had suffered the prejudice and bigotry of the servants during her last stay in this house, and it seemed certain now that nothing had changed. She raised her chin and marched up the steps, following her new mistress into the entrance hall where Poulton received them with an ingratiating smile for her ladyship, completely ignoring Cassy.

'Is Signora Montessori at home, Poulton?'

'No, my lady. Madam went out to luncheon and has not yet returned.'

Lady Davenport acknowledged his words with a

gracious nod of her head. She swept past him and ascended the stairs with Cassy hurrying after her.

The house was much the same as it had been when Cassy was employed there as a maid, although she had seen little of the upper floors. Lady Davenport's bedchamber was on the second floor, overlooking the courtyard garden and the mews beyond. It was a large room, as befitted her status in the household, and elegantly furnished in the Regency style. Cassy could not help but be impressed. After the starkness of the school dormitory this room seemed the height of opulence and luxury. The cream and blue curtains and bed hangings were of finest silk damask, and the carpet was delicately patterned with flowers and foliage in matching shades.

'It's a lovely room,' Cassy said in answer to Lady Davenport's amused glance. 'Better than the one you had in the other house.'

'I'm glad you think so, but as I said, it's only temporary. It's my hope that we'll return home very soon.' Lady Davenport crossed the floor in quick agitated steps, a fact that was not lost on Cassy. She flung open a door on the far side of the room. 'This is my dressing room, and it's where you will sleep. There's a couch which I think might do for the time being at least. I want you to have as little to do with the other servants as possible, Cassy. Do you understand?'

Recalling the treatment she had received as a terrified ten-year-old from Nancy and some of the other servants, Cassy was only too pleased to concur. 'Yes, my lady.'

'And we must get you fitted out with a suitable uniform. You can't go around dressed like a school-girl. In fact, I think we'll go shopping now. I won't bother to change my gown, but when we return you will help me dress for dinner. It's always a long and tedious affair in this house. Flora still crams the place with guests. It's no wonder that Leonardo spends most of his time in his club.' She studied her reflection in the cheval mirror, adjusting the angle of her hat and smoothing the creases from her skirts. 'I think we'll walk to Oxford Street. It's not very far and I'm sure the exercise will be beneficial. We will walk and talk without being overheard by anyone who matters. You can tell me all about yourself. You'll find me a very good listener.'

To her surprise, Cassy found that Lady Davenport had spoken the truth. By the time they had reached Peter Robinson's store in Oxford Street, Cassy had told her everything there was to tell about life in Miss North's Academy for Young Ladies and of the happy times she had spent in Whitechapel with Lottie and her father. Her story came to a faltering halt as they were seized upon by an imposing woman who welcomed them to the store and enquired as to their needs. It seemed that Lady Davenport was a valued customer and they were escorted from one department to another. Chairs were produced for their comfort while Lady Davenport made her selection and minions were sent scampering off to pack her purchases.

After the serious business of buying garments suit-able for a lady's maid, Cassy was surprised and delighted when Lady Davenport insisted that she should have a print gown for Sunday best and encouraged her to choose undergarments made of fine cotton lawn, trimmed with broderie anglaise. It was obvious from the raised eyebrows of the shop assistant that such items were considered far too good for a servant, and she had the temerity to suggest that perhaps calico might be more serviceable, only to be put down sharply by Lady Davenport. Overwhelmed by such generosity, Cassy was almost speechless. By the end of the afternoon she found herself the proud possessor not only of practical everyday wear, but of a brand new pair of black leather boots which fitted perfectly, a fine woollen mantle for winter wear and a cashmere shawl that was as soft as gossamer. If the shop assistant had thoughts about these extravagant purchases she kept them to herself this time, merely enquiring whether the packages were to be taken to Madam's carriage or delivered to her home. Cassy would gladly have carried them all, even if some had to be strapped to her back, but it was decided that the goods should be delivered to Duke Street. Then, declaring herself to be completely exhausted, Lady Davenport insisted on taking Cassy to Brown's Hotel for afternoon tea.

'I am not generally known here,' she said with a mischievous smile. 'We can pretend that you are my daughter and I am taking you out for a special treat. It could be a birthday or some other anniversary, or maybe to celebrate your leaving school with a diploma, which is true.'

Cassy took a seat at the table, glancing round nervously. 'I don't think Sir Geoffrey or his sister would approve. I should really wait outside.'

'What nonsense. Geoffrey is in Brussels and Flora would think it a great lark. At least she isn't stuffy, although poor thing she's made a dreadful mistake in marrying the Italian.' Lady Davenport leaned across the table, lowering her voice. 'Her husband is a charming rogue with a penchant for the gaming tables. Apparently he was penniless when she married him, although she did not know it at the time. I fear he will run through her fortune, gambling it away as he did his own considerable inheritance.'

Cassy glanced over her shoulder to see if anyone was listening, but the waiters were fully occupied and the other patrons appeared to be deep in conversation. Even so, such confidences made her feel uneasy. 'I'm not sure you should be telling me this, ma'am.'

Lady Davenport tossed her head and laughed. 'You're forgetting our game, Cassy. You are my daughter and I can say anything I like.' She looked up as a waiter appeared at her elbow, hovering like a crow in his black swallow-tail coat. 'Tea for two,' she said, beaming up at him. 'I would like Earl Grey but my daughter prefers Darjeeling. Isn't that so, Cassandra?'

Cassy nodded her head, hardly daring to look at the waiter in case he saw her for what she was, but he was obviously too well trained to show any emotion and he simply bowed and glided away, returning moments later with a silver cake stand laden with tiny bite-sized sandwiches and pastries oozing with cream. She realised suddenly that she was extremely hungry and her hand shot out to take a sandwich but she hesitated, not wanting to appear greedy. She met Lady Davenport's twinkling eyes and suddenly she was at her ease.

'Help yourself, my dear. I doubt if we'll be able to do this again, so let's enjoy ourselves.' Lady Davenport selected a cucumber sandwich and took a bite, smiling with approval as Cassy tucked into her meal. 'When we are in company I will have to treat you quite differently, but I want you to know that I am very fond of you, Cassy. If it were in my power I would adopt you as my daughter and bring you out into society, but I'm afraid that's simply not possible.'

'Good heavens, no.' Cassy almost choked on a strawberry tartlet. 'I mean, I never expected anything like this, my lady. I know I'm a charity girl and I'm truly grateful for everything you've done for me . . .' She broke off in astonishment at the sight of tears rolling unchecked down Lady Davenport's pale cheeks. 'Have I said something to upset you, ma'am?'

Lady Davenport plucked a handkerchief from her reticule and dabbed her eyes. 'No, of course not, my dear. I'm just a little tired. Will you go outside and ask the doorman to find us a cab? I should like to go home now.'

In the days and weeks that followed, Cassy gradually settled into life as a lady's maid in the chaotic household in Duke Street. Although she had nothing to do with the house guests, it would have been impossible to ignore their existence. There were dinner parties every evening and drunken carousing which went on well into the night. The smell of tobacco smoke and a substance that Cassy recognised as opium from her days in the East End hung about the reception rooms in a thick cloud each morning, together with the odour of stale wine and strong spirits. Strange people wandered about the house, some still wearing evening dress at midday, and others were to be found slumped in the hallway waiting to be helped into hansom cabs by Harris. On certain occasions Potter had to be summoned from the stables to exercise his muscle on those who were reluctant to leave. Poulton was the overseer of these physical ejections and his stoic expression barely hid his obvious contempt for Flora Montessori's guests.

Lady Davenport took no part in the late night parties. Cassy was aware that she graced the dinner table in deference to her sister-in-law, but more often than not against her own wishes, and when she returned to her room Cassy was waiting there to help her undress. Although she never uttered a word of complaint, Cassy knew that Lady Davenport was not happy with her current situation. Questions buzzed round in her head like a hive filled with bees. Why had she not accompanied Sir Geoffrey on his trip to Brussels? Why had he seen fit to close up the house in South Audley Street? And was he aware of the invidious position in which he had placed his wife? Cassy did not think that the Montessori household was a suitable home for her mistress. In the short time she had been with Lady

Davenport, Cassy had become her devoted admirer. She would have walked through fire if it had been of benefit to her idol.

But if Cassy had learned anything in Miss North's academy, it was fortitude. She could do nothing to alter a difficult situation other than look after her mistress and attend her every need. In return, Lady Davenport had seen to it that Cassy had little to do with the rest of the servants and was kept safe from possible prejudice and spiteful tittle-tattle. She took her meals alone in the morning parlour, and these were brought to her by Nancy, who was now the parlour maid. Cassy remembered her only too well and her friend Clara, the scullery maid who, Nancy said, had left some time ago to marry the butcher's boy. He had been compelled to make an honest woman of her when it was discovered that she was in the family way. There had been quite a to-do at the time and it was said that Poulton put pressure on the butcher, threatening to stop patronising his shop unless the boy married his pregnant sweetheart.

Nancy had been pleased to pass on this titbit of gossip on Cassy's first day in the house, and each time she brought Cassy her meals she complained bitterly about something or someone. The house guests came in for the most savage criticism, and in her opinion their appetite for food and drink was going to bankrupt Mrs Fulford-Browne. The servants, she added, refused to call Madam by the outlandish Italian name. Her husband was a rake and a gambler, intent on ruining his wife and spending her fortune. It was rumoured that he had done this before, marrying rich older women in order to get his hands on their money. It was all the talk below stairs. 'Foreigners and play actors,' Nancy said with a curl of her lip. 'Musicians and artists, they're all the same. He fills the house with his cronies, who eat like horses and they drink like fishes. We'll all be in the poorhouse if this goes on. You don't know what you let yourself in for, Cassy my girl. This house is facing ruin. We're all looking for positions elsewhere. If you've got any sense you'll get out while the going is good.'

'You shouldn't pass on this sort of gossip,' Cassy said severely. 'Lady Davenport has been good to me and I'll never leave her.'

'Good luck to you then,' Nancy said, shrugging her thin shoulders. 'She'll be the next one to lose everything. It's well known that Sir Geoffrey lives above his income. He don't come from landed gentry although he chooses to live like a toff. It's said that he plays the stock market and he'll end up in Carey Street with his sister and the gigolo. It won't be long before your fine lady will be forced to earn her own living like the rest of us. Mark my words.'

Chapter Twelve

'What do you mean – dead?' Belinda sank down onto the nearest chair. The drawing room had begun to spin around her in wearisome circles as she tried to assimilate the young man's words.

'Where's my sal volatile?' Flora murmured. 'I don't know who needs it the most.' She stared at her brother's aide, who had brought the horrific news that Sir Geoffrey had been found dead of gunshot wounds in his Brussels apartment. 'Are you certain of your facts, sir?'

'It must be a mistake,' Belinda murmured, holding her hand to her head. 'Geoffrey wouldn't commit suicide. He just wouldn't do a thing like that, Alastair.'

'I was closer to Sir Geoffrey than most, Lady Davenport,' he said gently. 'He has been under a great strain recently.'

'Alastair Kennedy, stop shilly-shallying and tell us the truth,' Flora snapped. 'Did my brother deliberately take his own life or was he murdered?'

'There was no one else involved, ma'am. The Belgian police are certain of that.' Alastair ran his finger round the inside of his high shirt collar, the starched points appearing to be in danger of cutting into his throat as he gulped and swallowed. 'I'm terribly sorry to be the bearer of such sad tidings.'

'But why?' Belinda struggled to make sense of his words. 'Why would my husband do such a thing? If only he'd allowed me to accompany him to Brussels this would never have happened.'

'My lady,' Alastair began tentatively, 'I think there may be circumstances of which you are unaware.'

Flora reached for a silver vinaigrette half hidden beneath a pile of papers on a table at her side. She flicked it open and inhaled the pungent fumes. 'You mean that he was deep in debt and facing bankruptcy. We aren't children, Alastair. I think Belinda and I deserve to be told the truth, even if it is painful.'

'I believe it was so, ma'am.' Alastair bowed his head, staring down at the top hat clasped tightly in his hands, his knuckles showing white above the black brim. 'I am not fully conversant with the exact details.'

'But that can't be true.' Belinda rose shakily to her feet and began pacing the floor. 'The house in South Audley Street must be worth hundreds of pounds, and then there are stocks and shares, apart from my husband's salary.'

'Ma'am, it's not for me to say.' Alastair cast a pleading look at Flora.

She shook her head. 'I only know that Geoffrey was just as much a gambler in his way as my present husband, except that Leonardo plays the tables and Geoffrey dabbled in the stock market. There's little difference between the two of them as far as I can see.' She sent the pile of papers flying up into the air with a careless sweep of her hand. 'Bills – all of them unpaid. I wish that Leonardo would take the coward's way out and shoot himself before he runs through my entire fortune.'

Belinda came to a halt, staring at Flora in horror. 'That's a dreadful thing to say, even for you; especially when you've just lost your only brother.'

'We were never close. He was a little sneak who used to delight in telling tales on me and getting me into trouble. I've still got the scars on my backside from being caned thanks to his tittle-tattling to Father.'

Alastair shifted from one foot to the other, a dull flush suffusing his pale cheeks. 'Perhaps I should leave now, ladies. I have to report to the Foreign Office. As you can imagine there are many questions that have to be answered.'

Belinda turned to him with an attempt at a smile. 'You were devoted to my husband, Alastair, and I'm grateful for everything that you tried to do for him.'

He took her hand and raised it to his lips. 'If I can ever be of service to you, my lady, you have only to send for me and I'll come at once.'

'I know that, and I thank you from the bottom of my heart.' She averted her eyes so that he would not see the tears welling up in them. She knew that her emotions were in a fragile state and at any moment she might break down in an outpouring of grief and guilt. Grief for the death of the man who had been her husband for more than a decade, and the feelings of guilt which had plagued her since marrying Geoffrey when she knew that she did not and could never love him.

'Will you be all right, ma'am?' Alastair asked anxiously. 'Perhaps you ought to go to your room and lie down? Should I summon your maid?'

'Stuff and nonsense,' Flora said irritably. 'She's not as delicate as you think. A tot of cognac will do the trick. Ring the bell for the maid, Alastair, and then go about your business. We'll wait for the foreign minister to arrive in person and offer his condolences. Or will the whole sorry affair be brushed under the red carpet?' Her hollow laughter echoed round the room as he made a hasty retreat, casting an apologetic smile in Belinda's direction as he tugged at the bell pull on his way out.

As the door closed on him, Belinda spun round to face her sister-in-law. 'That was cruel and uncalled for. You know how devoted he was to Geoffrey.'

'The fellow is a toady and a social climber. He'll probably end up with Geoffrey's position in the Foreign Office. Maybe he loaded the gun, who knows?'

Belinda gasped in horror. 'What a thing to say. You know it's not true.'

'Of course it's not,' Flora said wryly, 'but being waspish makes me feel a bit better about my own position. Leonardo has just about ruined me, Belle. He married me for my money, that's perfectly clear to me now, and it serves me right for being a conceited old woman who wouldn't admit that her attractiveness to men was now purely financial. I don't know about Geoffrey, who was always a weakling, but perhaps I should put a gun to my head too.'

'Don't talk like that, Flora. All is not lost. I have the house in South Audley Street and my jewels must be worth something.' She plucked the diamond earrings from her ears, holding them in the palm of her hand. 'Take them, please. You've given me a roof over my head since Geoffrey went abroad.'

Flora shook her head. 'Paste, my dear. I've always suspected that they were fakes.'

'No,' Belinda cried in horror. 'These were a wedding present from my husband. He wouldn't have been so false.'

'I expect the originals were real enough, Belle. But you're such an innocent. Didn't you suspect anything when he kept taking your diamonds back to the jeweller?'

'They were to be cleaned and polished,' Belinda said helplessly. 'Geoffrey said so.'

'They were being copied in paste and base metal, my dear. Any fool can see that those aren't real diamonds, and as to your house – did he never tell you that it was rented? It isn't being renovated, even I knew that. There are new tenants living in South Audley Street.'

'But why didn't you tell me? How could you let me go on believing that everything was all right?' Belinda clasped her hands to her chest as sobs racked her slender body. 'How could you be so cruel?'

'To tell you the truth would have been like pulling the wings off a butterfly,' Flora said tersely. 'You're such a baby. A spoilt child idolised by your papa and cosseted by my brother. You've never had to face the real world, Belle. But I fear all that is about to change.'

'No. I can't believe that Geoffrey wouldn't have made provision for me, for both of us if it comes to that. You'll see I'm right when the Will is read.'

A sharp rap on the door prevented Flora from replying. 'Enter.'

Nancy burst into the room, her face alight with curiosity. She bobbed a curtsey. 'Yes, ma'am?'

'Brandy,' Flora said. 'Bring the decanter over here and two glasses.'

Nancy shot a sidelong glance at Belinda as she carried out Flora's instructions. It was obvious to Belinda that the servants had already heard the news and were prepared for the worst. She took a deep breath, dabbing her eyes with her handkerchief. 'I expect the news of my husband's death is common knowledge in the servants' hall, Nancy?'

'Yes, my lady. We was all very sorry to hear of your loss, ma'am.'

'And if you breathe a word of the circumstances of my brother's demise outside this house there will be, in common parlance, hell to pay,' Flora said, tossing back a tot of brandy. 'Pour me another and then get back to your work.'

With a mutinous look on her face, Nancy did as she was told. She shot a pitying glance at Belinda as she left the room after being dismissed by a casual wave of Flora's hand.

'Really, Flora,' Belinda protested. 'Is is necessary to speak to the servants in that way? The poor girl was only trying to be kind.'

'Nonsense. They'll be gossiping their heads off below

stairs. You have to keep them in line, Belle. Didn't Geoffrey teach you anything?'

'He was a kind man and he always treated everyone with great consideration,' Belinda said angrily. 'I won't allow you to speak ill of the dead, even if he was your brother.'

'Just you wait and see,' Flora said, sipping her brandy. 'He may be dead but this act of cowardice will not be forgotten by those in high places, who will be suffering enormous embarrassment. Suicide, in case you've forgotten, is a criminal act and my dear brother has created a scandal that will live long after his bones have turned to dust.'

The funeral was a quiet affair, hushed up by those in authority and conducted under the cover of darkness in a small church south of the river. The arrangements had been made by Geoffrey's superiors, and Belinda suspected that a sizeable sum of money had been donated to the church funds in return for his interment in consecrated ground. Against all advice, Belinda had insisted on attending. Flora had refused to accompany her at first, but she relented at the last minute.

Heavily veiled and leaning on Alastair's arm, Belinda stood at the graveside, scarcely able to believe that it was her husband who lay cold and dead in the simple oak coffin. As the last words of the funeral service drifted off into the night air, she tossed a handful of soil onto the coffin, and the vicar closed his prayer book with a snap that reverberated off the flint church walls like a pistol shot. An owl flew overhead shrieking its hunting cry, and a chill breeze whipped through the trees that surrounded the graveyard, sighing and sending down a shower of dead leaves. The first sign of autumn, Belinda thought inconsequentially. Summer was over and winter was on its way bringing hardship to those least equipped to deal with harsh conditions. It was a fitting metaphor for her present situation. She had enjoyed a life of ease and luxury but that was about to end. Flora's dire predictions had proved to be only too accurate. Earlier in the day Sir Geoffrey's solicitor had informed them that his client had left nothing but debts. The furniture from the house in South Audley Street, which had been put in store while the supposed refurbishment was carried out, had been seized by the bailiffs. They had also paid a visit to the establishment in Duke Street and would have taken Belinda's jewels if Flora had not had the forethought to conceal the more valuable pieces in her own jewellery casket. The bailiff had left with a handful of paste replicas, worth very little when compared to the original precious metals and gems, but to Belinda it had felt like being stripped naked in public. Her humiliation had been complete.

'Come, my lady,' Alastair said gently. 'It's cold and you must be chilled to the bone. Let me help you to the carriage.'

'Yes, do stop daydreaming, Belle,' Flora said briskly. 'I could do with a glass of hot rum punch to take away the taste of soil and sewage which fills the air in this dreadful spot. No one in their right mind comes south of the river. If Geoffrey weren't already dead I could kill him for putting us through this farce.' With a defiant swish of her black cloak, she marched off towards the waiting carriage.

'She doesn't mean it,' Belinda said, slipping her hand through the crook of Alastair's arm. 'My sister-in-law is distraught and she doesn't know what she's saying.'

'I understand, my lady. It's a bad business and no mistake.'

Belinda clung to his arm as they made their way across the rough ground with only the glimmer of the coach lamps to light their path. Alastair had been a pillar of strength since he first broke the news of Geoffrey's suicide to them, and she realised only now that she had given little thought to his situation. 'What will you do, Alastair? Will my husband's actions have any effect on your career?'

'I'm being sent to the British Government House in Cairo. It's a junior position, but it's all valuable experience.' He handed her into the carriage and climbed in to sit beside Flora, who twitched her skirts away as if to emphasise the fact that he was a subordinate and should think himself privileged to ride in their company.

Belinda reached across to pat his hand. 'You've been such a comfort to me through all this, Alastair. I haven't thanked you for sending word to Ollie. I really couldn't face telling him that his father had died in such a way, even by letter.'

'The boy is tougher than you imagine, Belle,' Flora said, taking a flask from her reticule and taking a sip of its contents. She offered it to Belinda. 'It's good cognac, the best thing for keeping chills at bay.'

Belinda shook her head. 'No, thank you, but I would like a nice hot cup of tea.'

'You have such plebeian tastes,' Flora said with a shudder. She put the stopper back in the flask and closed her eyes. 'Don't speak to me until we are north of the river and closer to home. All this gallivanting about in the middle of the night is not for me.'

Belinda settled down in the corner of the carriage and they travelled on in silence for what seemed to her like an eternity. She was cold, cramped and exhausted both physically and mentally. They had laid Geoffrey to rest and that part of her life was well and truly over. Who knew what the future would bring.

On returning to Duke Street the door was opened by Harris, the footman whose set expression revealed neither surprise nor curiosity. Alastair saw them into the house, bidding them a reluctant farewell as he announced that he was due to leave for Egypt the following day, or as Flora pointed out irritably later that morning as it was well past midnight. Belinda stood on tiptoe to kiss him on the cheek, thanking him once again for his kindness. He raised his hand to touch the place where her lips had come in contact with his skin and she was vaguely surprised to see that a blush had reddened his face. She had not given a thought to the fact that Alastair's concern for her welfare might have been fuelled by a boyish crush, but she was tired and emotionally drained. No doubt he would recover soon enough when a younger and prettier face took his fancy.

He backed out of the door, lingering on the top step

only to have Harris close it firmly in his face. Belinda turned away with a sigh and was about to make her way to the staircase when she realised that Flora had come to a sudden halt outside the dining room. The sound of men's deep voices and drunken laughter were punctuated by female screeches and giggles, which grew louder as the door opened and a man tottered out of the room. Ignoring Flora, he staggered crabwise across the floor calling loudly for his hat and cane.

Harris moved swiftly to guide him out of the house, slapping the top hat on the drunken man's head and thrusting the cane into his hand. 'I'm sorry, ma'am,' he muttered, eyeing Flora nervously. 'The master is still entertaining his friends.'

'We'll see about that,' Flora snapped, thrusting the door open again. She recoiled as a waft of cigar smoke enveloped her in a foggy cloud. 'Gentlemen, I think it's high time you went home.'

There was a stunned silence and Belinda glanced anxiously at Harris. He raised his eyebrows, saying nothing, but she could tell from the way he clenched his fists that he was expecting trouble. She moved to stand beside Flora, and peering into the smoky dining room she was horrified to witness a scene of utter chaos and depravity. Leonardo was sprawled in his chair at the head of the table, which was scattered with bruised fruit and nuts lying in pools of wine that dripped like blood onto the floor. A woman was dancing on the table, exposing a great deal of bosom and bare legs. Several other females all equally scantily clad were either sitting on the guests' laps or standing in provocative poses around the room.

'This is a disgrace,' Flora said angrily. 'I won't have my home treated like a common bordello.'

Leonardo rose from his seat. 'It's my home, cara mia. You are my wife and everything belongs to me, including you. So go to bed like a good little English lady and leave the gentlemen to their pleasures.' He stubbed his cigar out on a plate, making a point of grinding it until it crumpled into shreds. His lips were smiling but the look in his eyes made Belinda shiver.

'Come away, Flora,' she said, catching her by the sleeve. 'Leave them to their silly games.'

Flora seemed to freeze. She looked around the assembled group of men, some of whom had red wine spilt on their ruffled shirt fronts, which made them look as though they were bleeding from stab wounds. Others who were lolling in their chairs, fondling the semi-naked women, were obviously too drunk to stand up. Flora seemed to be rooted to the spot, and Belinda's attempts to drag her from the scene met with failure.

'This is intolerable,' Flora said, controlling her erratic breathing with obvious difficulty. 'You are behaving like animals.'

Someone baaed like a sheep and another man made an attempt at neighing like a horse but only succeeded in having a choking fit.

'Go to bed, Flora,' Leonardo hissed, his mask slipping to reveal the anger beneath his smile. 'I will deal with you later.'

'Yes, Flora,' Belinda insisted. 'Please come away.'

Reluctantly, Flora allowed herself to be led from the room and someone slammed the door.

'Is there anything I can do, ma'am?' Harris asked nervously.

'You can throw those drunken sots out of my house,' she said firmly. 'I'm a broad-minded woman and I enjoy parties, but my husband has gone beyond the limits of decency and I won't have it. I simply won't stand for it.'

'I'm under orders to remain at my post, ma'am,' Harris muttered, shame-faced but obdurate.

'Please go to your room, Flora,' Belinda urged gently. 'This can all be sorted out in the morning.'

'It is the morning, you little idiot,' Flora snapped. 'I will have this out with that Italian gigolo once and for all.' She made as if to return to the dining room, but Belinda caught her by the arm.

'No, don't. They're drunk and beyond reasoning. Get some sleep, and perhaps Leonardo will be more amenable in the morning.'

Flora subsided and seemed to shrink in stature. 'You're right, of course. But I won't stand for this. Leonardo must learn that he cannot treat me this way.'

'Of course,' Belinda said, leading her towards the stairs. 'And I'm sure when he sobers up he will be thoroughly ashamed of himself.'

With a peremptory nod of her head, Flora ascended the staircase. Watching her, Belinda thought sadly that her sister-in-law seemed to have aged ten years after that unpleasant encounter. She might be well past sixty, but Flora Montessori was still a handsome woman and one of great spirit, even if some of her actions were misguided at times. Belinda followed her more slowly up the wide staircase as a wave of exhaustion swept over her. She was too tired to think and it was an effort to put one foot in front of the other, but somehow she managed to get to her room and as she opened the door she breathed in the lingering aroma of her favourite French perfume. The mixed scents of tuberose, frangipani and jasmine were sweet and pure compared to the stench of corruption that had assailed her nostrils when faced with the apparent orgy in the dining room. She smiled as she saw her nightgown laid out on her bed and the covers pulled down. A fire had been lit in the grate and carefully banked up so that it still glowed with a warm welcome. She knew that she had Cassy to thank for all this and she looked into the dressing room to make sure that her daughter had gone to bed and not attempted to wait up for her. Cassy's dark head lay on her pillow and her thick eyelashes formed black crescents on her cheeks. She looked younger in sleep and as innocent as a damask rose. Belinda's heart swelled with love for her child who was growing rapidly to womanhood. She tiptoed over to the truckle bed and leaned over to drop the lightest of kisses on Cassy's forehead.

If only she could reveal her true identity to her. The temptation was ever present but the consequences of such a selfish act would have involved admitting her youthful indiscretion to Geoffrey. To acknowledge an illegitimate child publicly, especially one of mixed blood, would have created a scandal, and the possible loss of his position in the Foreign Office. Even worse, Cassandra would bear the label of illegitimacy for the rest of her life and her chances of a good marriage would have been ruined. As it was, her prospects in that direction were little better. It was almost impossible for a maidservant, even one with a good education, to marry above her station in life. Even so, Belinda had always hoped that a respectable match could be arranged and that one day she would see her precious daughter cared for and protected by a good man who loved her for herself and not for her lineage or fortune. What would happen now was something that she could not begin to consider. Bankruptcy and ruin were staring her in the face, but she would not think about that now. Her tired brain could not cope with matters of such import.

Belinda slipped off her mourning gown, allowing it to fall to the floor unheeded, and was struggling with the laces on her stays when suddenly the door flew open. Uttering a cry of fright, she snatched at the silk robe which Cassy had laid out for her, but Leonardo was at her side in an instant and plucked it from her hands.

'Don't cover yourself, cara mia. Such lovely flesh should be seen and enjoyed by a man who can give you what you want.'

She attempted to push him away but he was strong and he was drunk. 'Let me go.'

'I've wanted to do this for a long time,' he said, nuzzling her neck while he fumbled with the laces on her stays. 'Such a young and beautiful body should belong to a man who appreciates it, not an old fool like Geoffrey.'

Struggling and kicking out with her feet, Belinda was close to panicking. 'Don't say such things. Let me go at once or I'll tell Flora.'

'I'll tell her myself.'

He raised his head to look into her eyes, and she was appalled and terrified by the naked lust in their dark depths. Her stays fell to the floor and he ripped her shift, exposing her naked body with a grunt of satisfaction. He lifted her off her feet and carried her to the bed, tossing her onto the coverlet and throwing himself on top of her. Belinda opened her mouth and screamed but her cries were stifled by his kiss, his tongue probing her mouth and his hands raking her flesh.

'No. Stop. Get off her.'

The sound of Cassy's shrill voice caused Leonardo to raise his head, although Belinda could not move for the weight of his body pinning her to the bed. 'Get out,' he roared.

Cassy threw herself on him, her fingers clawed. 'Get off her, I said. Leave her alone.'

Leonardo took a swipe at her, but he was in no position to fight and too drunk to aim well. The punch landed on the pillow beside Belinda's head. Seizing her opportunity she bit the soft flesh of his forearm, causing him to cry out in pain and rage. He struggled to his knees but a clout on the jaw from Cassy caught him off guard and he fell backwards onto the floor, shouting what were obviously obscenities in Italian. Belinda could not understand the words, but their meaning was abundantly clear. Raising himself swiftly Leonardo lashed out at Cassy, striking a blow that sent her tumbling to the floor.

Incensed and forgetting her state of undress, Belinda leapt off the bed. 'Cassy, are you all right?'

Cassy lay for a moment, staring dazedly up at the ceiling. 'I think so,' she murmured, attempting to sit up.

Belinda snatched her robe from the floor and slipped it on. She knelt at Cassy's side. 'Are you sure?'

Leonardo slithered off the bed, standing up and adjusting his clothing. 'Send her away. I haven't finished with you, Belle.'

'Get out,' Belinda snapped. 'Leave my room immediately.'

'I'm the master here,' he said, advancing slowly towards them. 'I do as I please in my house.'

'It's Flora's house,' Belinda cried furiously, wrapping her arms around her daughter who was trembling from head to foot. 'You are a gigolo, you bastard.'

'She is the bastard,' Leonardo said, pointing to Cassy. 'Your little half-caste pet is someone's bastard. I've often wondered why you favour her as you do. She can't be Geoffrey's by-blow, so where does that leave you, Belle?'

'Leonardo. What is going on? I could hear the noise from my room.' Flora stood in the doorway, her face deathly pale in the lamplight.

'He tried to rape me,' Belinda said through clenched teeth. 'This man, your husband, attacked me and he hurt Cassy when she came to my aid.'

'Take no notice of her, cara mia,' Leonard said smoothly. 'She tried to seduce me. She has lost her protector and now she looks for another.'

'You bastard,' Flora hissed. 'You're a liar.'

Leonardo shrugged his shoulders. His eyes narrowed and were filled with malice. 'I am not the bastard here. You think that your sister-in-law is as pure as the driven snow. I think she is the mother of that child she holds so dear. If you have any doubts, ask Belle who fathered the little chi-chi.'

Chapter Thirteen

Cassy felt her knees buckle beneath her as she sank to the floor. She bent her head, unable to believe the vicious accusation she had just heard levied at her adored mistress. She would have gladly given her life to save Lady Davenport, but she had never for a moment thought that she might be the woman who had abandoned her so many years ago. She had mourned for Mahdu's loss, thinking of her always as her birth mother, but the cruel words of a drunken man had turned her fragile world upside down. She bowed her head, covering her face with her hands. 'Stop. Don't say any more.' She rocked to and fro, shutting her ears to the angry voices raging above her head. Then there was silence and she felt herself wrapped in a tender embrace. The soft sound of Lady Davenport's voice soothed her like a barely remembered lullaby, although for a moment her words made no sense at all.

Belinda gave her a gentle hug. 'Cassy, my darling child. It is all true. I cannot live a lie a moment longer. I am your mother, and giving you up was the cruellest blow. It almost killed me and it's been a cross I have had to bear all these long years.'

'Belle, what are you saying?' Flora said angrily. 'Have

you gone mad? Has this devil made you lose your mind?'

'I won't listen to any more of this nonsense.' Leonardo spat the words at them as he strode out of the room, slamming the door behind him.

Belinda helped Cassy to her feet. 'I am not mad. I'm doing now what I should have done fifteen years ago. I was a coward then but I've paid for it with my heart's blood.'

'I don't understand, my lady,' Cassy murmured dazedly. 'Tell me the truth, I beg you.'

Belinda sank down onto the bed, tears coursing down her cheeks. 'It is a secret I have borne all this time. The pain has eaten into my heart until it is little more than a husk.'

'For heaven's sake stop this pathetic drivel and come to the point,' Flora said impatiently. 'I can scarcely believe that the saintly Belinda would have given birth to a child out of wedlock.'

'I was young and very much in love with Cassy's father.'

'I can't believe it,' Cassy whispered. 'There must be some mistake. I thought Mahdu was my mother.'

'She loved you dearly,' Belinda said, dashing the tears from her eyes with the back of her hand. 'But you are my child, and your father was a gallant soldier, killed in action on the North-West Frontier.'

Flora shot her a speculative glance. 'So why did you marry Geoffrey? If you'd kept the matter quiet and given the baby to a childless couple, you could have taken your pick of young officers.'

A wry smile curved Belinda's lips. 'As soon as he discovered the truth, my father arranged the match, and I had little choice but to follow his wishes. To be perfectly honest, Flora, I didn't care if I lived or died, but I had my baby to think about. I knew that I couldn't keep Cassy with me, but I simply had to be in a position to pay for her upbringing. I needed to keep her as close to me as possible.'

'And Mahdu helped you,' Cassy whispered. 'That's why I thought she was my mother.'

'And the child's father was an Indian,' Flora said, nodding her head. 'I can see your problem, Belle.'

Belinda winced as though the words hit her like a slap in the face. 'He was handsome, brave and charming and I loved him with all my being, just as I love you, Cassy.'

'You could have told me before,' Cassy murmured. 'I wouldn't have asked you for anything, ma'am. I would have served you all my life and wanted nothing more.'

'I couldn't tell you before, my darling. If the truth had come out while Geoffrey was alive, the scandal would have ruined us all. The only way in which I could support you and make sure that you were cared for was to conceal your true identity. Can you ever forgive me?'

'I've had enough of this sentimental twaddle,' Flora said, throwing up her hands. 'Your youthful indiscretions are past history, Belle. I'm going to bed. Tomorrow, or rather later on today, I'm going to have stern words to say to that Italian weasel who calls himself a husband.'

She stormed out of the room, leaving the door to swing on its hinges.

Belinda wiped her eyes on the back of her hand. 'We will never be parted again, my darling girl. I don't know what the future holds for us but we'll face it together this time.'

Cassy threw her arms around her mother's neck. 'I'm the happiest girl in the world. Nothing matters to me now, my lady.'

'Mother,' Belinda corrected, smiling through her tears. 'I want you to call me Mama from now on. I want everyone to know that you are my own dear daughter.'

Cassy stifled a giggle. 'Bailey will laugh when he hears the news, and so will Ollie.'

'I'd almost forgotten Oliver,' Belinda said, frowning. 'I wonder how he will take this piece of news. Poor boy, he has lost his father and his home. He will inherit nothing but debts and disgrace.' She ruffled Cassy's hair with an affectionate hand. 'Get some sleep, dearest. Tomorrow we will need to make plans for our future. It's plain that we cannot remain here.'

Next morning, despite only having had a few hours' sleep, Cassy awakened feeling refreshed and filled with energy. At first she thought she had dreamt the whole thing, but when she raised herself from her cot in the dressing room and went into the main bedchamber, the events of the previous night came flooding back to her in minute detail. The bedclothes were still tumbled from the struggle that ensued when Leonardo had forced himself on Belinda. There were garments spread about the floor like fallen leaves in autumn, and an upturned chair which she righted as she made her way to stand at the foot of the bed. She gazed at the sleeping woman she now knew to be her mother with a feeling of awe and disbelief. With her golden hair spread about her head like angel's wings, Belinda looked young and innocent: a snowdrop of a girl, unsullied and untouched by grief or passion.

'Mama,' Cassy whispered. The word tasted like honey on her lips. It was wonderful and yet terrifying. Supposing there had been a mistake and she was not the infant that Mahdu had left in Biddy's care. Many babies had died in Three Herring Court. Perhaps the real Cassandra Lawson had been one of them and she was someone else's fatal mistake.

Belinda stirred and opened her eyes. 'Cassy, darling,' she murmured, holding out her arms. 'Come and give me a kiss.'

Forgetting everything, Cassy moved swiftly to hug her mother and covered her face with kisses. Their tears of joy mingled as Belinda sat up in bed, hugging her daughter to her breast. 'You don't know how I've longed for this moment,' she whispered. 'I thought it might never come, but we must be practical, darling. We have to find somewhere else to live, especially now that Leonardo has shown himself in his true colours.'

Cassy drew away from her mother, brushing her hair back from her face with an impatient movement of her hand. 'I'll find work, Mama. I'll look after you.'

'You are a dear child, and you'll never know how

237

much I love you.' Belinda pushed her gently away. 'But I must get up and dress. We have a new life to begin and it starts today, Cassy. From now on it will be you and me, as it should have been all those years ago if I had not been such a young fool.'

'You and me,' Cassy repeated, smiling. 'It makes me want to shout for joy, Mama.'

'We will be ourselves,' Belinda said happily. 'We will find a small house in a cheaper part of town, and perhaps I can earn money by sewing or painting pictures. I used to be quite good with watercolour when I was a girl.'

Cassy leapt off the bed and began sorting through the clothes press for a suitable morning outfit, quite forgetting that she was no longer a servant, but the daughter of a titled lady. 'What will you wear today, ma'am, I mean, Mama?'

'It doesn't matter,' Belinda said, swinging her legs over the edge of the bed and rising gracefully to her feet. 'You choose, and pick a gown for yourself. We are about the same size now, and you must dress according to your station in life. We will go down to breakfast together and you will sit at the table next to me.'

'But what about the master? Have you forgotten what he did to you last night?'

'Leonardo must be faced sometime and I intend to stand up to him. My life has been dominated by men for too long; first there was my father and then my husband, but now things are going to change. Pass me the grey silk gown, Cassy. I won't wear widow's weeds, and I refuse to bow to convention. You would look lovely in that emerald-green tussore: it would bring out the colour of your eyes. We are going to face the world; mother and daughter together.'

'And you'll tell me all about yourself and my real family, Mama?'

'Nothing could give me more pleasure, my darling.'

Cassy found it hard to swallow any of the food she put in her mouth at breakfast. Belinda toyed with a forkful of buttered eggs but it was obvious that she had little appetite. Summoned by the bell, Nancy brought the coffee and almost dropped the silver pot on the floor when she saw Cassy dressed like a lady and taking breakfast with the mistress. A small nerve throbbing in Poulton's temple, and an even more rigidly controlled expression than usual was the only indication that he had noticed anything untoward. He moved swiftly to pull out a chair as Flora entered the room. She took a seat without looking at him. 'That will be all, Poulton.'

His mouth worked soundlessly, as if in silent protest at being sent from the room before he had discovered the reason for Cassy's sudden elevation in status. Flora dismissed Nancy with a wave of her hand. 'Put the pot down, girl. I'm not incapable. I'll help myself to coffee. Now go away.' She waited until both servants had left the room, making a show of pouring coffee into her cup. 'I am not helpless,' she repeated. 'But I need to see my solicitor without delay.'

'Why, Flora?' Belinda demanded anxiously. 'What has Leonardo done now?'

'He's sold the house,' Flora said, slamming the coffee pot down on the polished surface of the dining table. 'I went to his room to demand an explanation for his outrageous behaviour and an apology for turning my home into a den of iniquity.' She took a mouthful of coffee, swallowing convulsively. 'He sat in bed grinning at me and announced that he has sold my home and its entire contents in order to pay off his gambling debts. It was all I could do to prevent myself from slapping his smug face. I can't believe that I ever imagined myself to be in love with that creature.'

Belinda's eyes widened in horror. 'But he can't do that. Can he? Surely the law will not allow him to sell the property without your consent.'

'A woman loses all control of her fortune when she marries. It becomes her husband's property as she does herself, but my former husbands all died and left their money to me. This was a turn of events that I had not anticipated.' Flora took another sip of coffee and pulled a face. She reached for the sugar bowl and cream jug. 'I can't drink this without cream and sugar. How will I live without the luxuries to which I am accustomed?'

Cassy shot a nervous glance at her mother. What had started as the happiest day of her life seemed to be turning into a disaster. She knew by the expressions on their faces and the tone of their voices that matters were serious, and, worst of all, she could do nothing to help.

'Your solicitor will sort things out,' Belinda said hopefully. 'You must go and see him straight away.'

'I trusted him,' Flora said slowly. 'They say that there's no fool like an old fool, and I have been the biggest idiot of them all. I thought he had married me for myself alone, and my conceit has led me to this pretty pass. I will see my solicitor in the hope that he might be able to salvage something from my ruined finances, but I hold out little hope.'

'I'm so sorry,' Belinda said softly. 'I've been selfish, thinking only of myself and my joy in having my daughter restored to me.'

Flora shrugged her shoulders. 'You weren't to know that I'd married a rake and a libertine, and it was my duty to protect you after Geoffrey's unfortunate demise.' She turned her head as the door opened and her expression darkened as Leonardo sauntered into the room.

He stopped with a dramatic wave of his hands. 'Ah, such beauty all assembled at my table, and my wife is here also. Still, nothing is perfect.'

'What do you want, Leonardo?' Flora snapped. 'Have you come to gloat?'

'Cara mia, would I be so insensitive?'

'Say what you have to say and be done with it,' Flora said icily. 'I'm going out and I've sent for the carriage.'

'I am afraid you will have to walk. The carriage is gone and also the horses. It was a damnable hand of cards.'

'You used my carriage and pair to cover a bet?' Flora's voice rose to a screech.

'You are forgetting that they belong to me. At least,

they did, but no more.' He threw up his hands with a wolfish smile that did not reach his eyes. 'You have until tomorrow to vacate the house as the new owners will be moving in at the end of the week. I am leaving today for Italy. I feel the call of my native land.'

Flora rose majestically to her feet. 'How dare you treat me like this, Leonardo? I have done nothing to deserve such cavalier treatment. I'm still your wife and you have a responsibility towards me.'

'You are free to petition for divorce, cara mia. I will not be here to contest the proceedings.' He was about to leave the room, but he paused, addressing himself to Belinda. 'Should you wish to accompany me, I would be happy to take you with me.'

'Never,' Belinda said emphatically. 'I'm insulted by your remarks, Signor Montessori. You would not be so bold if my husband were alive.'

'He left you with nothing. I can offer you my protection, after all, Lady Davenport, you have nothing to sell other than your body or that of the child who is masquerading as a lady. I could get a high price for a beautiful young virgin.'

Cassy had heard enough. She leapt to her feet and looking round for a missile, her eyes lighted on the silver epergne which normally graced the centre of the dining table but had been set on a chiffonier whilst breakfast was being served. Seizing a handful of fruit, she pelted Leonardo with plums and grapes, catching him squarely in the face with a ripe peach. His shocked expression might ordinarily have made her laugh, but it quickly changed to one of rage and he advanced on

242

her, fists clenched and teeth bared in a snarl. She was saved from a certain beating by Poulton, who entered the room to announce that a hansom cab was waiting to take the master to Victoria station.

'I should wash your face before you leave, Leonardo,' Flora said, stifling a giggle behind her hand. 'An unfortunate accident with flying fruit, Poulton. Perhaps you would be good enough to assist the master?'

Poulton stood his ground. 'I am no longer in his employ, ma'am. I wouldn't wipe his face any more than I'd wipe his blooming arse.' Having rendered them all temporarily speechless, he stalked out of the dining room. Leonardo followed him, shouting something in Italian, the tenor of which made Cassy suspect it was a stream of expletives which would undoubtedly have impressed Biddy and the rest of the inhabitants of Three Herring Court.

Belinda had risen from her seat, but she sank down again. 'He's gone, and good riddance I say.'

'And we must be gone soon too,' Flora said decisively. 'Pack a few necessities and what valuables you still possess, and I'll do the same. I've seen this sort of thing happen to people of my acquaintance and the bailiffs will descend on us like wolves on the fold. Bring only what you need. We must not be too obvious.' She moved swiftly to the door, almost bumping into Poulton.

'They're here, ma'am,' he said in a low voice. 'I sent them to the master's study on the pretext that he was there, but he left the house by the back door some minutes ago.'

'Cassy, run up to my room and bring my jewel case,'

Flora said sharply. 'Belle, you do the same. Even your paste baubles will fetch something. Pack a few necessities but be quick; those men don't waste time on niceties.'

'I'll find you a cab, ma'am,' Poulton said, holding the door open for Cassy. 'Best hurry, miss. The bailiffs are up to all the dodges.'

Flora laid a hand on his arm. 'We'll be gone soon. I hope the new owners will take you and the others on, Poulton. You've served me well all these years.'

Cassy hesitated in the doorway, hardly able to believe her eyes as she witnessed tears running down Poulton's cheeks. It seemed as though the stiff-necked butler had suddenly melted into a shivering mass.

'Hurry, girl,' Flora commanded in a voice that had to be obeyed. 'Belle, go with her and make certain you bring my best bonnet with the ostrich feathers and my velvet mantle. I'm not leaving them to be sold at auction to tradesmen's wives and daughters.'

Lugging two large portmanteaux packed with what both women termed were absolute necessities, they escaped down the back stairs and out through the servants' quarters. Sounds of hysterical female voices coming from the kitchen were drowned out by the shouts of the bailiffs, who had apparently become suspicious and realised that the master and mistress of the house had absconded. Poulton had found a cab and they bundled into it with the aid of one of the grooms, but two of the bailiffs erupted from the house just as they were about to leave.

'Hold on a minute, mate.' The more senior of the

men raised an imperious hand to the cabby. 'I need to speak to the owner of the establishment.'

Flora leaned across Cassy, smiling sweetly. 'Then you must find my husband, officer. Everything I had belongs to him. I'm just a poor deserted woman, left to fend for herself by a faithless rogue. Drive on, cabby.'

'Where to, missis?'

For once, Flora appeared nonplussed. She turned to Belinda with a puzzled frown. 'I hadn't thought that far.'

Belinda bit her lip. 'I don't know anywhere else. What will we do?'

Cassy leaned out of the cab window. 'Spectacle Alley, Whitechapel, please cabby.'

'Good grief, girl,' Flora exclaimed. 'Whitechapel? What are you thinking of?'

'It's somewhere we can be sure of a welcome,' Cassy said firmly. 'My best friend, Lottie, lives there with her father. They took me in during the holidays when I had nowhere to go. I'm certain they'll help us now.'

Flora cast a despairing glance at Belinda, who nodded her head. 'Mr Solomon is a tailor: a very respectable man, and a kind one too. I met him at Cassy's school and he was most polite and courteous, a real gentleman. Perhaps he can help us find a house to rent while we sort ourselves out. I mean, your solicitor might be able to salvage something of your fortune, Flora, and then we can move back to the West End where we belong. I have to think of Oliver too. He will need somewhere he can call home when he returns on leave.'

And Bailey, Cassy thought, although she dared not

voice his name. If Oliver had home leave then perhaps Bailey would also be allowed time away from the Afghan conflict. Her pulses quickened at the thought of seeing him again. If Bailey were here now he would know what to do. He had promised to find them a home and she knew in her heart that he would keep his word.

'Very well then,' Flora said slowly, 'but tomorrow I will see my lawyer. I don't intend to spend more than a night or two in that part of town. It's rife with crime and filth, which may be acceptable to the lower classes, but it isn't for us, Belle. We won't stay for a day longer than necessary.'

'Have you enough money to pay the cab fare?' Belinda whispered.

Cassy saw Flora flinch, as though this was a question of huge impertinence, and one which had never entered her head. For a moment it looked as though she was about to dismiss the matter as a mere triviality, but she seemed to reconsider and she opened her reticule, taking out a small purse. She opened it and counted the contents. 'I was going to buy a new pair of gloves with this,' she muttered, 'but I suppose someone has to pay the cabby, although I haven't the faintest idea how much it will cost. One leaves that sort of thing to those in one's employ.' She turned her head to stare out of the window as if daring the world to encroach any further upon her.

Cassy squeezed her mother's hand. 'We'll be fine, Mama. I'll look after you.'

'My dear girl, I know you will, but it should be the

other way round. I should be taking care of you, Cassy.'

'It don't matter, Mama. I was used to caring for the nippers, though most of the poor little things died and I could do nothing to save them.'

'Oh do be quiet,' Flora said wearily. 'Isn't it bad enough we have to come crawling to a little tailor without you reminiscing about your atrocious experiences in the slums of Cripplegate? Don't say another word or I'll scream.'

The carriage came to a halt and as Cassy looked down the narrow street she could see her friend's dark head bent over a seam she was sewing. She leapt out, waving frantically, and when Lottie looked up her face creased into a delighted grin. Abandoning her work, she ran from the shop with her arms outstretched, but she stopped short when she saw Belinda alight from the cab. She bobbed a curtsey. 'This is an unexpected pleasure, ma'am.'

'I see they taught you something of manners at that school.' Flora stepped down onto the pavement, accepting the proffered arm of the cabby who tipped his hat respectfully as she thrust a silver coin in his outstretched hand. Cassy could tell that she had overpaid him quite ridiculously, and she was tempted to demand some change, but thought better of it as Flora dismissed the man with an imperious wave of her hand. It was obvious to Cassy that the toffs never bothered to ask the cost of anything, but that would have to change. Every penny would count in their impoverished circumstances.

'Won't you come inside?' The bell jangled as Lottie thrust the shop door open. 'Pa, look who's come to see us.'

Eli Solomon appeared from the dark depths of the shop, his eyes red-rimmed and his posture bent from long hours hunched over his work. His lined cheeks cracked into a wide smile as he recognised Cassy. 'You are always welcome in my home, Cassy.'

'It's lovely to be here again, Mr Solomon.' She rushed forward to give him a hug, but she drew away, realising that his gaze had wandered to her mother. He stared at Belinda as though transfixed. Cassy had seen this happen a dozen times in the past. Her mother's radiant beauty was enough to render any man speechless. 'May I introduce you to my mother, Lady Davenport,' Cassy said, struggling to remember the lessons in etiquette that the North wind had drilled into her pupils.

Belinda's smile seemed to light up the dingy little shop as she held her hand out to Eli. 'We met once before at Miss North's academy, Mr Solomon.'

His jaw dropped and he stared at her open-mouthed before recovering himself enough to murmur, 'I remember it well, my lady, but . . .' He turned his head to send an appealing glance to Cassy.

'Yes, Mr Solomon,' she said happily. 'You heard right. This is my mama. I am her daughter.'

Flora pushed past Cassy with an impatient sigh. 'Come to the point, Cassy. I'm not standing all day in this dreary little shop while you discuss your parentage.' She fixed Eli with a stony stare. 'I am Lady Davenport's sister-in-law, and as you might surmise when given a chance to catch your breath, we find ourselves in dire straits, which is why we have been forced to come to you for help.'

Eli took a step backwards as Flora towered over him. 'I – I don't understand, ma'am.'

Lottie had been holding Cassy's hand, but she let it slip from her grasp, eyeing her friend in awe. 'Are you really her daughter?'

'Yes, isn't it wonderful? I have a mother at last,' Cassy whispered. She would have liked to shout the news from the housetops, but this was neither the time nor the place. 'It's a miracle,' she added softly.

Lottie folded her hands in front of her, casting her eyes down and refusing to look at Cassy. 'Congratulations. I'm happy for you.'

If Lottie had slapped her across the face, Cassy could not have been more shocked by her friend's reaction to her news. 'What's the matter? What's wrong, Lottie?'

'You shouldn't have brought her here,' Lottie said in a low voice. 'She's a lady and she doesn't belong in Whitechapel. Just look at the other one; you can tell what she thinks of us. How could you do this to my pa, Cassy? You've embarrassed him and me. I'll never forgive you for this.' Choking on a sob, Lottie pushed past her father and disappeared into the back of the shop.

Chapter Fourteen

Cassy made to follow her, but Belinda caught her by the arm. 'Let her go, Cassy. Give her time to get over the shock.'

'Yes,' Eli said, nodding. 'This has come as a surprise, but not an unpleasant one. I must congratulate you on your daughter, my lady. Cassy is a good girl and she deserves to be happy.'

Belinda encompassed him with her radiant smile. 'I am the most fortunate one, Mr Solomon. It's a long story, but I was forced to give up my child when she was just a baby, which is something I will regret for the rest of my life.'

'I understand, my lady. Only a parent could appreciate the pain that must have caused you.'

'Poppycock,' Flora said angrily. 'This sentimental drivel is getting us nowhere. If you can't bring yourself to tell him the truth, Belle, then I will.'

'I should go after Lottie,' Cassy said urgently. 'I need to speak to her.'

Belinda swayed on her feet and Eli rushed to pull up a chair. 'Please sit down, ma'am. I can see that this is very distressing for you.' He turned to Cassy. 'Fetch a glass of beer for your mother, my dear.'

'Beer!' Flora almost spat the word. 'My sister-in-law doesn't drink beer, sir.'

Fanning Belinda vigorously with his hands, Eli's mouth twisted into a grim smile. 'She will have to drink ale while she's in this part of London, ma'am. The water is putrid and would kill her as easily as a dose of arsenic.'

'Then give her brandy. For heaven's sake, use your head, man. Can't you see that Belinda is a lady and used to better things?'

'I'll get the beer,' Cassy said hastily.

'No need,' Belinda said, rallying a little. 'It was just a dizzy spell. I'm quite all right now, and I think we ought to leave. Coming here was a mistake and an imposition on Mr Solomon.' She looked up at Eli with an apologetic smile trembling on her lips. 'I am sorry if we've upset you and your daughter. It wasn't our intention to cause trouble.'

Cassy hesitated, longing to go after Lottie, but unwilling to leave her mother in this delicate state. She could see that Eli had fallen under her mother's spell, but that only seemed to make matters worse. She twisted her hands behind her back, wishing that there was something she could say or do that would help matters, but Flora was obviously not in a mood for using tact and diplomacy. She took a lace handkerchief from her reticule and made a point of dusting off the seat of a chair kept for valued customers before sitting down. 'A woman's touch would make this apology for a business premises much more profitable,' she said, arranging her skirts around her. 'What no one seems prepared to admit is that we are destitute, or very nearly. For reasons which don't concern you, Mr Solomon, we are homeless and virtually penniless. We need to find a property that is cheap to rent until our fortunes are restored.'

Eli straightened up, adjusting his spectacles and angling his head thoughtfully. 'I'm not sure how I can help you, ma'am. I would offer you accommodation here, but as you can see it is not what you have been used to and there is barely room for myself and my daughter. When Cassy stayed here she had to share Lottie's bed, although that did not seem to bother the pair of them. I could hear them chattering away and giggling until late into the night . . .'

'I'm not interested in your personal sleeping arrangements, sir. Do you or do you not know of clean, respectable lodgings suitable for ladies of quality?'

'Please don't speak to Mr Solomon in that tone of voice, Flora,' Belinda said, frowning. 'We are all equals now and we are throwing ourselves on his mercy, so to speak.' She looked up at Eli with an expression that Cassy thought would have melted the hardest heart, and it was becoming apparent that Eli could gainsay her nothing. He took her hand and raised it to his lips.

'I am at your service, my lady. If you will rest here for a while, Lottie will look after you while I go out and do my best to find you suitable accommodation.'

'At reasonable rates,' Flora said sternly. 'And don't mention that there is a titled lady in question.

Tradesmen always charge more when they think the gentry are involved. You may refer to me as plain Mrs Brown and my sister-in-law as Mrs Smith. I think that sounds common enough for us to pass unnoticed.'

Eli shot her a shrewd glance. 'It almost sounds as though you are evading the law, if you'll forgive the impertinence, ma'am.'

'I won't. Go about your business, my man. When I have settled matters with my lawyer, I'll see to it that you are suitably reimbursed for your pains.'

Cassy smothered a gasp of dismay. She could cheerfully have slapped Flora's arrogant face, but she managed to control her anger. There were more pressing matters on her mind and making her peace with Lottie was one of them.

Eli snatched his slightly battered top hat off its peg on the wall and crammed it onto his head. Ignoring Flora, he addressed himself to Belinda, speaking in a gentle tone he might have used to a child. 'I won't be long, my lady.' Crossing the floor, he opened the door that led into the private parlour. 'Lottie, come here this minute. I want you to look after these ladies while I am out.' Without waiting for a reply he hurried out into the street, leaving the shop door to jangle on its spring.

'Flora. How could you speak to him like that?' Belinda said in an undertone. 'The poor man must have been mortified and yet he has gone out of his way to help us.'

'Fiddlesticks! You have to keep these people in their place, Belle. I would have thought you'd have learned

253

how to control underlings from your father, the colonel.'

'My father treated his men with respect. He was a fair man and a good soldier.'

'Stop it,' Cassy cried passionately. 'Leave Ma alone. You're one of us now, Mrs Montessori or Brown, whatever you choose to call yourself. You should be grateful to Lottie's pa for agreeing to help. He's a real gentleman if ever there was one.'

'That's true. My pa will do anything for anybody.'

The sound of Lottie's voice made Cassy turn with a sigh of relief. She rushed to her side and seized her by the hand. 'I'm sorry if I hurt your feelings, and I never intended to embarrass your pa. You're my best friend and I brought them here because I knew that he would help us.'

Lottie hesitated for a moment, and then she flung her arms around Cassy. 'I'm sorry too. It was a shock but I'm all right now, and I'm glad you found your real mother. Mine died when I was born and I suppose I was a bit jealous.'

Belinda rose from her seat. 'Cassy is lucky to know you, Lottie. She told me how you befriended her at school and for that I will always be truly grateful to you.'

Lottie's pale cheeks were suffused with a blush and she bobbed a curtsey. 'That's very kind of you, my lady.'

'You must call me Belle. Flora is right. We're all equals and the past is dead and buried. From now on I am plain Belinda Smith.'

Cassy shook her head. 'No, Ma. If I'm Cassy Lawson, then you should be Mrs Lawson. It's a good name, and one you gave to me all those years ago.'

Belinda turned away with a sigh. 'Belinda Lawson,' she murmured.

'Smith, Lawson, pumpernickel – it doesn't matter.' Flora fixed her gaze on Lottie. 'I thought you were getting us some refreshment, girl? I'm parched and something to eat wouldn't go amiss.' She fished in her reticule and brought out two silver shillings. 'Go out and buy some food and a bottle of brandy.' She thrust the money into Lottie's hand with a sigh. 'That's almost the last of my money. Is there a pawnshop in the vicinity? I must see my lawyer as soon as possible and I'll need the cab fare to Lincoln's Inn.'

'I'll come with you, Lottie.' Cassy could not help smiling as she followed Lottie out of the shop. Their predicament might be dire, but having found her real mother at last made her the happiest girl in London and nothing could take that away from her. She linked her hand through Lottie's arm as they walked towards Whitechapel High Street. 'Why were you working in the shop, Lottie? I thought you were going to be a doctor?'

'I was. I mean I am; at least I've started after a fashion.'

'What does that mean?'

'It's all very well for the government to pass an act allowing women to study medicine, but it's only well-off families who can afford to send their daughters to medical school. I've started at the London Hospital, working as a ward maid, and I'm saving up every penny I can in the hope of studying at Mrs Garrett Anderson's hospital in Bloomsbury.'

'You'll do it, I know you will.' Cassy gave her arm a comforting squeeze. 'But shouldn't you be at work?'

'I'm on night shifts, so you can have my bed tonight, although I expect that snooty aunt of yours will take it,' Lottie said with an irrepressible chuckle. 'Come on, Cass. Let's get some pie and pease pudding.'

'Don't forget the brandy.'

'Anything to keep the old lady happy.' Lottie's smile froze as Cassy dragged her to a halt outside a shop door where a woman lay sprawled on the pavement. Sitting beside her was a small boy of about five or six, holding out a ragged cap.

'Spare a copper, miss?'

'Come away, Cass,' Lottie said, tugging at her arm. 'The old woman is drunk. If you give her money she'll only spend it on jigger gin.'

Memories of Biddy and Three Herring Court flashed through Cassy's mind. She looked closer at the filthy urchin who was staring up at her. His eyes were dull and she could see his collar bones sticking out through the shreds of his tattered shirt, but there was something about him that was achingly familiar, and her suspicions were confirmed when she saw the silvery line of a scar on the bridge of his nose. 'Freddie?' she murmured. 'Is it you, Freddie?'

The boy's expression barely altered as he shook his cap at her. 'A farthing will do if you can't spare a copper, miss.'

'What's the matter with you, Cass?' Lottie demanded. 'I don't know who Freddie is, but this is just a beggar boy.'

Vague memories of being told that Freddie had been taken in by a soldier's widow from Whitechapel came back to her now as Cassy leaned down to take a closer look at the old woman. Her mouth was slack and a trickle of saliva dribbled from her lips. Strands of greasy grey hair escaped from her mobcap to cling round her neck like the snakes on Medusa's head, but even though her clothes were filthy and threadbare, Cassy could see that they had originally been of good quality. Pinned to her shawl, just discernible beneath a coating of grime, was a military badge. Cassy gave her a shake. 'Wake up, Mrs Wilkins.'

'How do you know her?' Lottie asked anxiously. 'You must be mistaken, Cass. This woman is a drunkard and the child is probably a pickpocket as well as a beggar.'

'I don't think so,' Cassy said, bending lower so that her face was close to the boy's. 'Don't be afraid, I won't hurt you. Is your name Freddie?'

He nodded his head and Cassy scooped him up in her arms. 'I knew it. I brought this boy up from a baby, Lottie. He was only nine months old when I last saw him, but I'd know Freddie anywhere. He's got the biggest brown eyes I ever saw, and that tiny scar on his nose is where he fell over when he was trying to stand for the first time. It bled and it bled, so that I thought it would never stop.' She rocked him in her arms, but he was having none of it and he struggled to get free.

'Leave us alone, missis. I ain't going to the orphanage. You can't make me.'

She went down on her knees, laying her hands on his shoulders and looking him in the eyes. 'Freddie, I don't expect you to remember me, but I'm Cassy. I took care of you when you were a baby. We were separated through no fault of mine, but I've always wanted to know what happened to you.'

Before Freddie had a chance to absorb this piece of information, the woman stirred in her sleep and opened her eyes. She stared blearily at Cassy, blinking owlishly. 'What's going on?' she demanded in a slurred voice. She raised herself on her elbow. 'You leave the boy alone, miss. He's mine and you ain't taking him away from me.'

'I doubt very much if a woman your age could be the mother of this child,' Lottie said sharply. 'I think you use him to get money so that you can drink yourself into oblivion. I've seen it all before.'

'I'm a respectable widow, miss. Annie Wilkins is the name, and there ain't no call to speak to me in that tone.'

'Maybe not,' Lottie said sternly. 'But can you prove that this boy belongs to you?'

Mrs Wilkins attempted to rise but only managed to struggle to her knees. 'I raised him,' she said thickly. 'Freddie, come away from the lady. She's one of them who take children away from a good home in the name of charity. She'll put you in an orphanage as soon as look at you.'

Cassy scrambled to her feet. 'No, you've got it all

wrong, ma'am. My grandfather was Colonel Phillips, and I believe that your husband served under him in India. I'm right, aren't I?'

Mrs Wilkins focused her eyes on Cassy's face with obvious difficulty. 'You're Miss Belinda's daughter?'

'Yes, I am.'

'Come away from them, Ma,' Freddie said, tugging at her. 'Don't let 'em take me away.'

'I can't think straight.' Mrs Wilkins ran her hand across her eyes as if hoping such an action would clear her fuddled brain. 'I need a drop of porter to set me up again.'

'Leave them,' Lottie urged. 'We've got things to do, Cass.'

'I can't abandon Freddie for the second time.' Cassy held her hand out to the boy who was hiding behind Mrs Wilkins, and sucking his thumb. 'I won't put you in an orphanage, Freddie. I won't take you away from your mother if you want to stay with her, but I will find a way to help you both.'

'Don't need charity, young miss,' Mrs Wilkins said, leaning heavily on Freddie as she clambered to her feet. She clutched her hand to her bosom, gasping for breath. 'I need a drink, miss. It keeps the rheumatics at bay.'

'Don't look at me like that, Cass,' Lottie said as if reading her thoughts. 'It's not your money to give away.'

'Look at the boy, Lottie. He's a mass of skin and bone, and he was such a lovely baby.'

'I take good care of him, miss.' Mrs Wilkins held her

hand out. 'If you give us a few pence I promise to spend it on food for Freddie.'

'I heard that excuse time and again from old Biddy,' Cassy said, shaking her head. 'You must come home with us. We'll see to it that you both have something to eat, and I'm sure my mother will think of some way to help you and Freddie.'

Mrs Wilkins screwed her lips into the shape of a prune, angling her head and eyeing Cassy speculatively. She gave a brief nod. 'You're on, but I don't want Miss Belinda to see me like this. I was a respectable woman before my luck changed.'

'It can happen to anyone,' Cassy said with feeling. 'Follow us, Mrs Wilkins. I don't know how I'll do it, but you and Freddie will never want for food and shelter again.'

Lottie walked on muttering beneath her breath and Cassy had to run to keep up with her. 'What's the matter? I couldn't leave them in such a terrible state.'

'You're making promises you can't hope to keep, Cass. Have you forgotten how hard life is in the East End, and you without a penny to your name?'

'No, I haven't, and that's why I won't leave Freddie to die of want or turn to a life of crime. He was my baby, just like little Anna, and Samuel, and the twins Charity and Mercy. There were many others who passed away before they'd had a chance to live, but I've been lucky. I found my real mother and I've had a good education. I owe it to the dead babies to try and make a difference in the world, Lottie. I've seen how the poor struggle to survive and I've lived with the toffs who take what they want without any thought for others.'

'All very fine,' Lottie said, glancing over her shoulder at Mrs Wilkins who was staggering along behind them, aided by Freddie who was supporting her to the best of his ability. 'But if you give her money she'll fritter it away on drink, and tomorrow she and Freddie will be in the same state they were today.'

'Not if I've got anything to do with it,' Cassy said with a defiant toss of her head. 'You want to heal the sick and I want to help poor children, just like the ones that Biddy took in and then neglected shamefully. You might not agree with me, but I know who would.' If she concentrated hard, blotting out the sound of horses' hooves, the rumble of wagon wheels, and the shouts of the costermongers and cabbies, she could hear Bailey's voice, cheering her on and encouraging her to follow her heart.

'Be it on your own head, then,' Lottie said as she stopped outside the pie shop. 'I'm not going to get my head bitten off by snooty Mrs Brown. You can take full responsibility for this, Cass.'

Sniffing the air laden with the delicious aroma of hot meat and freshly baked pastry, Cassy felt her stomach growl with hunger. She could remember exactly what it was like to be so hungry that your stomach felt as though it was eating itself. She turned to Mrs Wilkins and Freddie with a confident smile. 'Pie and pease pudding all round, then?'

'And a drop of porter to keep out the cold?' Mrs Wilkins said hopefully.

'No!' Cassy and Lottie spoke in unison.

'Have you gone quite mad, Cassy?' Flora stood in the tiny living room behind the tailor's shop, arms akimbo, glaring at Mrs Wilkins and Freddie as if they had suddenly sprouted two heads apiece. 'What were you thinking of? We've problems enough without you collecting beggars along the way.'

'Hold on, missis,' Mrs Wilkins protested. 'I'll have you know that I'm a respectable widow. My husband was in Colonel Phillips' regiment.'

Belinda stopped slicing the pie. 'It's Mrs Wilkins, isn't it? I remember you well. You used to give me toffees when my ayah wasn't looking.' She turned to Flora with an anxious smile. 'I know this woman, and it was through Mahdu that I arranged for her to take the boy and bring him up as her own.' She hesitated, her smile fading. 'Poor Mahdu. I miss her terribly.'

'The Indian lady used to bring money once a month but it stopped suddenly,' Mrs Wilkins said, ruffling Freddie's blond hair. 'I love me boy as if he was me own, but I can't take in sewing like I used to, what with the rheumatics knotting me poor fingers so that I can't hold a needle. We struggled on, but in the end I couldn't pay the rent and the landlord threw us out on the streets.'

Flora sniffed the air like a gun dog scenting a kill. 'And you drink to drown your sorrows. You smell like a distillery, madam.'

'I don't think you are in a position to criticise,' Belinda said with unusual asperity. 'We might all be driven to drink if we can't find a way out of this mess.'

Cassy moved to her mother's side. 'You won't throw them out, will you, Ma? There must be something we can do.'

'It will be up to Mr Solomon, Cassy,' Belinda said gently. 'This is his house and we are already greatly in debt to him for giving us a roof over our heads.'

'My pa is the best-hearted man in all of London,' Lottie said, spooning pease pudding onto the plates. 'He's never turned anyone from the door or walked past a beggar on the streets.'

'You exaggerate, my dear.'

Conversation ceased as everyone turned to stare at Eli who was standing in the doorway, holding his hat in his hands. Lottie dropped the spoon and ran to him, giving him a hug. 'Naughty Pa. You shouldn't have been eavesdropping.'

'I wasn't. On my life, I swear it.' Eli's walnut face cracked into lines as he smiled down at his daughter. 'I see we've got more guests,' he added, bowing to Mrs Wilkins. 'Are you part of the family, ma'am?'

'No indeed.' Mrs Wilkins bristled like an angry hedgehog. 'I should have more manners than her.' She jerked her head in Flora's direction.

'Insolent creature.' Flora drew herself up to her full height. 'I think I should like to lie down, Mr Solomon, if your daughter would be so good as to show me to my bedchamber.'

Lottie glanced at Cassy, her delicate winged

eyebrows raised. 'It's my room, Mrs Brown. I'm afraid you'll have to share it with Cassy and Lady Davenport. We've only two bedrooms; the attics are filled with bolts of material.'

'You can have the bed, Flora,' Belinda said hastily. 'Cassy and I will sleep anywhere. On the floor if necessary.'

'And I won't stay where I ain't wanted.' Mrs Wilkins dragged Freddie away from the table where he was tucking ravenously into a plate of pie and pease pudding. 'We've been sleeping in shop doorways for a fortnight or more; another night won't kill us.'

'Madam, I don't know who you are, but no one in this room will sleep rough tonight. Mrs Brown may take my bed, and the attic is clean and dry. You are welcome to make yourself and the boy as comfortable as you can up there.'

Mrs Wilkins eyed the pie. 'Maybe I will take a little sustenance before I retire for the night.'

'For goodness' sake sit down and stop complaining,' Flora said, taking a seat at the table and reaching for a plate of food. 'Think yourself lucky that Mr Solomon is a generous man.'

Ignoring Flora's sudden change of heart, Belinda turned to Eli with a smile. 'You will join us in our meal, I hope, Mr Solomon?'

'Nothing would give me greater pleasure, my lady.'

'Belle, please. I'm to be plain Belinda Lawson from now on.'

Mrs Wilkins paused with a forkful of food halfway to her lips. 'I recall a handsome young officer by the name of Lawson. I'm sure he was my Albert's superior officer. He was the handsomest man I ever saw: a touch of the tarbrush maybe, but a gent all the same. You must remember him, ma'am.'

'It was a long time ago, Mrs Wilkins,' Belinda said, blushing. She handed a plateful of food to Eli who took it with a beatific smile on his face.

'You could never be described as being plain, ma'am. No one would ever call you anything but beautiful.'

'Never mind the flattery,' Flora said impatiently. 'Did you find us alternative accommodation, Mr Solomon?'

He shook his head. 'I'm afraid not, ma'am.'

'I'll go out tomorrow and look,' Cassy said, helping Freddie to another slice of pie even though it meant that there would be only a small piece left for her.

'You will not.' Flora put her plate down with a decisive thud. 'That was ghastly, but at least it was food. Cassy, I have plans for tomorrow and they include you. I intend to visit my solicitor and I want you to accompany me as my maid.' She held up her hand as Belinda seemed about to protest. 'No, Belle. I won't allow my standards to drop, and I don't want to give a mere lawyer the impression that I am desperate for money.'

'But we are, and I don't want my daughter to be treated like a servant.'

'You were happy enough to do so when it suited you,' Flora said acidly. 'I'm not asking the girl to scrub floors, although if we don't get money from somewhere it may come to that.'

'I don't mind, Ma.' Cassy gave the last piece of pie

to Freddie. 'I'll do anything to help get us out of this tangle.'

'Good for you,' Lottie said, clapping her on the shoulder. 'I'd love to stay and chat, Cassy, but I've got to go to the hospital to begin my shift. I'll see you tomorrow.'

The living room with its dark painted walls and bare window overlooking the back yard seemed even smaller and gloomier without Lottie's cheerful presence. The black marble clock on the mantelshelf had a loud tick when it could be heard above Flora's complaining tones, and the shop bell called Eli away several times before he had finished his meal. It was a comfortless room, Cassy thought, as she cleared the supper things off the table. Lottie's attempts at making it more homely, which she had proudly shown Cassy before the meal, included a crimson satin cushion on the saggy old chair by the hearth, and several cheap china ornaments vying for position on the shelves with bolts of cloth and reels of thread. These feminine touches did little to relieve the stark masculinity of the room, which Cassy found depressing, and there were too few chairs to seat everyone.

It was a relief when night fell and they made their way upstairs. Eli elected to sleep in his chair by the fire, and although Flora complained bitterly that the bed he had given up for her was hard and the sheets coarse and not very clean, she was asleep almost as soon as her head hit the pillow. Cassy could hear her aunt's snores reverberating throughout the house, while she herself tried to make the best of sleeping on the bare floorboards covered by a thin blanket, with Lottie's crimson cushion for a pillow. She knew by the way the iron bedstead creaked and groaned that sleep was not coming easily to her mother, and the darkness gave Cassy the courage to voice the question that had been burning on her lips. She had sensed her mother's discomfort when Mrs Wilkins recalled the handsome young officer whose surname she bore, and she could hold back no longer. 'Ma, may I ask you a question?'

'Of course, Cassy. What is it?'

'Who was the man that Mrs Wilkins spoke of and why did you choose his name for me?'

Chapter Fifteen

Next day during the cab ride to Lincoln's Inn Fields, Cassy was still pondering over her mother's reluctance to talk about the young officer, whose name she had discovered was George Lawson. That was the only fact that she could elicit. Ma had been vague to the point of mysterious when questioned further. He was one of the officers in her father's regiment, she said. A brave man, killed in action. There was little else to say about him. Why had she given Cassy his name? Why not? It was as good as any other, and the first that had come to mind. It was late, time to go to sleep, but as Cassy lay on her makeshift bed on the floor she could tell by her mother's breathing that she too was still wide awake.

It had taken Cassy a long time to doze off, and she had dreamt that she had found her father. She could not see his face clearly but she knew that he was tall and handsome, dashing and brave. He was calling her name and holding out his arms as she ran towards him. She tripped and stumbled and she was falling, falling . . . She had awakened to find daylight streaming through the window and her mother's bed empty.

'Did you hear me, girl? I don't want you to say a

word when we're in the solicitor's office,' Flora said, snapping Cassy out of her reverie.

'No, ma'am.'

'You've been trained as a servant, so just remember your place.'

'Yes, ma'am.'

Flora peered out of the window. 'We're nearly there. Thank goodness for that. I hope I've enough money to pay the fare.'

'If you haven't I'll keep him talking while you go inside, and then I'll make a run for it.'

'I hope you're joking.' Flora eyed her suspiciously. 'But should the necessity arise, I think it best if I give you my purse. Ladies of quality do not handle money. I'll walk on ahead, and if there isn't enough to pay the fare you know what to do, but don't look to me to get you out of prison if the law catches up with you. I'll deny all knowledge of you.'

'Yes, ma'am. I rather thought you would.'

The cab drew to a halt outside the solicitor's chambers in Lincoln's Inn Fields. Flora alighted and stalked off, mounting the steps as though, Cassy thought, she owned the place. It was left to her to pay the cabby, who was quite plainly not in the best of moods and kept blowing his nose into a rather dirty red handkerchief. He glowered at her when she did not give him a tip, but she closed her fingers tightly around the remaining coins and followed Flora into the building.

The waiting room appeared to be crowded with people, and to Cassy's astonishment one of them, a rustic-looking man wearing a billycock hat and gaiters, had a large calf tethered to his wrist by a rope. The animal wore a desultory expression as if it had detached itself from the proceedings, but the agitated persons surrounding the farmer were anything but calm. 'He's ours and you stole him.' A thin woman with the hint of a dark moustache and a mop of thick black hair shook a bony finger at the man holding the animal.

'I never did. He'd got loose from the pen in Smithfield, 'tis true, but he's mine all the same.'

'He was one of ours,' the woman argued. 'I'd know him anywhere.'

The calf began to roll its eyes and prance about, but the farmer jerked on the rope and with a swift movement pulled the animal onto its haunches, holding it between his knees. It relaxed instantly, staring straight ahead with glazed eyes. 'See how it is?' the farmer said. 'He knows who's master here.'

'We shall see what the man of the law says about that, mister.' A tall rangy man standing just behind the woman made a move to grab the calf but his action seemed to startle the animal and it struggled to free itself, scrabbling to its feet, bucking and shaking its head as it tried to slip free of the noose tied around its neck. The farmer threw himself on the calf and the tall man fell upon the farmer.

'Good gracious, what is the world coming to?' Flora demanded, holding up her skirts and backing towards the door. 'This is a madhouse. Where is Mr Nixon? I want to see my solicitor.' She spun round as a worried-looking clerk entered the room clutching a sheaf of papers.

'Gentlemen, please,' he murmured, waving his hand ineffectually. 'This is a law office, not a farmyard. I beg of you to take the animal outside.'

Cassy leapt sideways as the calf made a break for the open door dragging the farmer along behind it. The irate woman and her companions hurried after them, shouting and demanding that the animal be brought back to face justice.

The clerk mopped his brow with a spotless white handkerchief. 'My apologies, madam. A most unfortunate incident.'

Flora dusted her skirts as if expecting them to be covered in mud, although Cassy could see that it was an unnecessary piece of theatre.

'What makes the yeoman stock think they can mingle with their betters?' Flora glared at the unfortunate man as though the whole episode was his doing. 'Have you no control over who comes into your rooms?'

'Farmer Mullins is a very wealthy man, ma'am. He may smell of the farmyard but he's been a client here ever since I can remember, and he pays his bills on the nose.'

'How vulgar. But that is no concern of mine. I wish to see Mr Nixon right away.'

'Certainly, ma'am. He's waiting for you. Please follow me.'

'I'll think seriously about changing my lawyer,' Flora said in a loud whisper as she left the waiting room. 'Come, Lawson. Don't dawdle.'

Cassy would much rather have gone outside onto the green to witness the struggle to gain control of the calf, but she knew better than to disobey Flora. She followed them down a long dark passageway to the back of the building, where the clerk ushered them into a large room which was more like a gentleman's study than an office. A mahogany breakfront bookcase was crammed with tomes bound in leather and a large aspidistra occupied pride of place on the windowsill. A strong smell of Macassar oil and bay rum wafted gently in the warm air and a coal fire blazed in the grate. In one corner, standing like a naughty child doing penance, a long-case clock struck eleven.

The solicitor rose slowly from his seat behind a mahogany pedestal desk to acknowledge Flora with a courteous bow and an ingratiating smile. 'My dear Signora Montessori, it is always a pleasure to see you. Won't you take a seat?'

Flora remained standing. 'I've reverted to my former name of Fulford-Browne,' she said stiffly. 'I want nothing to do with the libertine who ruined me.'

Mr Nixon rubbed his hands together vigorously, as if washing them with soap and water. 'I understand your feelings, ma'am. A most regrettable outcome to what should have been a happy union.'

He pulled up an ornately carved chair, and, somewhat reluctantly, Flora lowered herself onto the seat. Cassy stood to attention by the door. She would have liked to move closer to the fire as the damp chill of early autumn still clung to her clothes, but she had been well trained by Mahdu and knew how to melt into the background so that she became almost invisible.

'It was a damnable outcome, Nixon,' Flora said with feeling. 'The Italian rat has sold my house and apparently run off back to his native land so that he can avoid supporting me. He has left me with nothing.'

Mr Nixon resumed his seat, resting his elbows on the desk and steepling his fingers. 'It's true that your fortune became the property of your husband on your marriage, but thanks to the Married Women's Property Act, which was passed a few years ago, you are entitled to keep the house in Duke Street which was left to you by your previous husband.'

Flora shot a triumphant look at Cassy. 'I can keep my home.'

Mr Nixon shook his head. 'Not exactly. Unfortunately, Signor Montessori sold the property apparently with your blessing, as you signed the deeds over to him.'

'I did no such thing,' Flora protested. 'The question never arose.'

'Nevertheless, Mrs Fulford-Browne, you did sign the document. I have seen it myself and verified that it is indeed your signature.'

'You're all in it together,' Flora cried angrily. 'You lawyers are all the same.'

'I resent that, ma'am. But I can understand why you are upset. Perhaps you signed the document unknowingly?'

Flora frowned thoughtfully. 'I did put my name to some business transaction that Leonardo said would make us a fortune, but . . .' Her voice trailed off and her mouth drooped at the corners. 'The bastard duped me.'

'Precisely so, ma'am. An easy mistake to make when one trusts the perpetrator of such a dastardly deception. Anyway, I believe that the proceeds from the sale went to your husband's creditors, and that bankruptcy proceedings have been initiated against him for the remainder of the monies owed.'

'So I am completely without funds?'

A slow smile spread across Nixon's urbane countenance. 'Not entirely, ma'am. Your former husband left a sum of money in trust for you, which cannot be touched by your present husband's creditors.'

'God bless Fulford-Browne. How much did he leave me? Tell me, man. How much have I to live on?'

'Fifty pounds a year.'

'Fifty pounds!' Flora sat back in her chair, staring at him aghast. 'I can't live on fifty pounds a year. I spend as much as that on gloves and shoes.'

'Nevertheless it is quite a respectable sum, ma'am. My clerk has raised a family of ten children on less than half that amount.'

Flora rose to her feet. 'When do I get this princely sum, Nixon?'

'It will, according to the terms of your late husband's will, be paid to you quarterly. I can advance the first payment right away, but there is a little matter of my fees.'

'Send the account to me,' Flora said airily. 'I'm residing temporarily in Whitechapel, but I'm looking for more suitable accommodation. I don't suppose you know of anywhere that might be acceptable?'

Nixon reached for a wicker filing basket and rifled

through a sheaf of documents. 'I think I might have just the place, ma'am. A client of mine has taken up a position as estate manager on a sugar plantation in Jamaica. He wanted me to find a respectable person to rent his former home for an indefinite period.'

Flora sat down again. 'Tell me more. I might be interested.'

Outside on the neat lawns of Lincoln's Inn, the calf was demonstrating its desire for independence by refusing to budge, despite the efforts of Farmer Mullins and the irate couple who claimed ownership of the animal. A youth, who appeared to be related in some way to the man and woman, was plucking handfuls of grass from beneath a tree in an attempt to lure the animal back into the building. The clerk stood at the top of the steps, arms folded across his chest, patently prepared to repel any further invasion by livestock. A small group of onlookers, mainly consisting of junior clerks and passers-by, had gathered round to watch the spectacle. Some were cheering and it was impossible to tell which side they were supporting, or whether it was the calf that was getting all their sympathy.

Flora stopped and tapped the farmer on the shoulder. 'My good man, can't you see that the animal is scared out of its wits? If it had any in the first place, that is. Why not tie it to a tree and leave the boy to watch over it while you and these people go inside and sort matters out once and for all?'

A small cheer rippled through the crowd and someone started clapping. Cassy took the rope from the farmer's hand and gave it to the youth. 'Hold this and don't let it go.'

Farmer Mullins scratched his head. 'Seems like a good idea. What d'you say, mate?'

'It's probably a trick. If us goes inside he'll get his men to snatch the animal from young Percy. They're probably hiding round the corner as we speak.' The man glanced around as if expecting to discover a small army of cowmen concealed in the bushes.

'Don't be ridiculous,' Flora said coldly. 'I'm sure the boy is able to stand up for himself.'

'Of course he is, Ted.' The woman gave her husband a shove towards the lawyer's rooms. 'Get inside, you great booby. The market will be over and done with if we hang about here any longer and we'll get nothing for the animal.'

'Thank you, ma'am,' Farmer Mullins said, tipping his cap. 'I'm much obliged.'

'Don't mention it, my man.' Flora walked on with a satisfied smile on her lips. 'There you are, Cassy. All it takes is a little commonsense. Now let's go back to that ghastly little shop and tell them that we've found ourselves a nice little house in – where was it?'

'Pedlar's Orchard, Stepney, ma'am.'

'I hope Stepney is a salubrious area. I've never been there myself.'

'No,' Cassy said. 'Neither have I.' She did not want to spoil Flora's moment of triumph by telling her that it was still in the East End, and most probably not what she was expecting.

*   *   *

276

'You can smell the gas works,' Belinda said, wrinkling her nose.

Flora sniffed, saying nothing, but Cassy could tell by her expression that she was unimpressed by the exterior of the house in Pedlar's Orchard. The name had conjured up visions of green grass and trees laden with blossom in the spring and rosy red apples in autumn, but the reality was far different. On either side of the mean street, terraced houses were stuck together in higgledy-piggledy fashion. Some of the houses boasted three storeys, others only two. A squat, half-timbered pub occupied the corner site, its top storey leaning precariously over the pavement, giving it a drunken look. Most of the properties had seen better days and the one to which Flora held the key looked as though it had once stood on its own, surrounded by gardens and the possibility of an orchard. Now it had the appearance of an old statesman, bowed by age, and shabby from neglect.

'It looks quite promising,' Belinda said hopefully.

Eli pushed his black bowler hat to the back of his head as he looked up and down the street. 'At least there is an open aspect at the back, even if it does encompass the gas works and the cemetery. In Spectacle Alley I could reach across from my front door to rattle the knocker on the house opposite.'

'I'm not sure about the cemetery,' Belinda said, following his gaze. 'It might be a bit frightening at night.'

Eli patted her hand. 'But at least your neighbours will be quiet, my dear Lady Belle.'

'You're right, of course, but please, it's just plain Belle. My title means nothing now.'

'Never plain,' Eli said with obvious sincerity. 'As I said before, and will say again, no one would ever use that term in connection with you.'

'It's beginning to rain,' Cassy said hastily as Flora opened her mouth undoubtedly to utter a caustic comment on Eli's clumsy attempt at gallantry. 'We'd better go inside and take a look round.'

Flora handed her the key. 'You go first, Cassy. Heaven knows what horrors lurk in there.'

She unlocked the door and pushed it open. The still air was musty with the hint of stale cooking smells, and a pile of circulars and pamphlets lay on the doormat, but as she crossed the threshold she was pleasantly surprised to find that the interior was in much better shape than the exterior. At the far end of a narrow hallway the fading daylight filtered through an arched window halfway up the staircase. The first door on the right led into a small parlour with a single tall window overlooking the street. Cassy looked round with an approving nod of her head. This would do, providing Flora did not object. The furniture was old-fashioned and rather shabby, but the armchairs by the fireplace looked comfortable, if a little saggy, and the chimney recesses were lined with bookshelves, although the owner had not left any books for them to read. A fire burning in the black cast-iron fireplace would make all the difference, she thought, glancing anxiously at Flora who was unusually quiet. Surely she could see that all the room needed to make it more

278

homely and inviting were small personal touches: some ornaments on the mantelshelf and pretty pictures to cover the damp patches on the faded wallpaper.

Eli must have thought so too as he broke the silence. 'This is a very nice parlour, ladies. I can just see you both sitting either side of the fire of an evening.'

Flora turned on him with a curl of her lip. 'You have a vivid imagination, Solomon. My dressing room in Duke Street was bigger than this poky little hole.'

'But it's reasonably clean and the furniture is passably good,' Belinda said with a cheerful smile. 'What do you think, Cassy?'

'It's perfectly fine, Mama. I think we might be quite comfortable here.'

With a toss of her head, Flora led the way to the dining room, which was of similar size with a window overlooking a small garden, but the view across allotments beyond the garden wall was spoiled by four huge gasometers silhouetted against the darkening sky. 'I don't like this at all,' Flora snorted. 'It isn't what I've been used to.'

'I'm sure it's only temporary, dear lady,' Eli said cautiously. 'Your fortunes will take a turn for the better, I hope.'

Flora turned on him with a stony stare, but Belinda moved swiftly between them. 'There is another room to see before we go upstairs,' she said lightly. 'There seems to be a basement, which is probably the kitchen. Shall we go downstairs and have a look?'

'I don't need to see the servants' quarters. I want to take a look at the bedrooms before I decide whether or not to take this doll's house, and even then it will be on a purely temporary basis. Lead on, Lawson,' Flora said, giving Cassy a none-too-gentle shove in the back. 'You go first. I can't abide spiders and cobwebs.'

'She isn't your servant, Flora,' Belinda said sharply. 'Please remember that Cassy is my daughter and should be treated as such.'

Cassy could see that Flora was going to argue. She shook her head. 'It doesn't matter, Ma. I'm prepared to earn my keep, so if Mrs Fulford-Browne chooses to treat me like a servant, that's up to her.'

'At least someone has their priorities right,' Flora said with a satisfied smirk. 'Let's go upstairs while we still have some daylight.'

Cassy led the way to the first floor where there were two bedrooms, the larger at the front of the house, which Flora reluctantly agreed might suit her well enough, and a smaller room overlooking the garden, and, of course, the gasworks, which appeared even more foreboding as the light faded and gaslights flared in the compound. 'This will have to do for you, Belinda,' Flora said in a tone that brooked no argument. 'The bed looks lumpy, and there is a frightful draught whistling through that ill-fitting window.'

'I think it will suit me very well,' Belinda said, squeezing Cassy's hand. 'Let's go upstairs to the top floor and see which room you would like, my dear.'

'I'm not trailing up there in the dark.' Flora picked up her skirts. 'Solomon, come downstairs with me. I want you to go out and find a cab to take us back to

Whitechapel. I've had quite enough excitement for one day.'

Leaving Eli to follow Flora's instructions, Cassy and Belinda ascended the steep staircase to the top floor where they found two smaller rooms. It was cold beneath the mansard roof, and the windowpanes were cracked and grimy. Cobwebs hung from the ceiling in the room at the back of the house. Empty boxes and tea chests were scattered about the floor, and it appeared that the former incumbent had used this space to store unwanted items. However, the room at the front was clean and boasted a single brass bedstead and a deal chest of drawers with a matching washstand.

'It's very nice,' Cassy said, clutching her mother's hand. 'I'd be quite happy up here, Mama.'

'You're a good girl,' Belinda said, raising Cassy's hand to her cheek. 'You haven't once complained about the way you've been treated, nor have you ever criticised me for the neglect you suffered on my account. I don't deserve a daughter like you.'

Cassy snatched her hand away only to throw her arms around her mother. 'I love you, Mama. What happened in the past doesn't matter a bit. We've found each other and I don't care where we live as long as we can be together.'

Belinda fished in her pocket and brought out a handkerchief. She dabbed her eyes, sniffing and smiling through her tears. 'Your papa would be so proud of you, Cassy.'

'But you won't tell me who he is.'

'He died a hero, Cassy. I can't bear to talk about it, even to you. One day, when the time is right, I'll tell you everything, but until then I beg you to be patient, and be proud to be the daughter of a fine man.'

Cassy was about to press the matter further but the sound of Eli's voice made them draw apart.

'Lady Belle, Cassy. Mrs Brown wishes to leave now.'

'We're coming.' Belinda brushed Cassy's cheek with the lightest of kisses. 'We mustn't keep Flora waiting.'

They arrived back in Spectacle Alley to find Lottie waiting anxiously in the shop.

'Why aren't you at the hospital?' Eli demanded. 'Are you ill?'

'No, Papa. There's nothing wrong with me, but I am finished at the London.'

'You've been dismissed?' Eli said faintly. 'Surely not. I can't believe that a daughter of mine has suffered such a slight.'

Lottie's serious expression melted into a wide grin. 'No, Papa. I left of my own free will. Matron called me in to tell me that I've earned a place at the New Hospital for Women in Bloomsbury. I'm to study medicine just like Mrs Garrett Anderson. One day I'll be a doctor, Papa.'

Cassy seized both her hands and danced Lottie round the shop floor, almost knocking over a dummy clad in a suit that Eli had been altering. 'Congratulations,' she cried. 'Well done. I knew you'd do it one day, Lottie.'

Belinda clapped her hands. 'This calls for a

celebration, Eli. We should have wine so that we can toast your clever daughter.'

'I'm not made of money,' Flora said primly. 'Don't look at me.'

Belinda slipped off her gold wedding ring. 'Take this to the pawnbroker, Cassy. Get what you can for it and we'll spend the proceeds on a special supper with wine.'

'I can't allow you to do that, Lady Belle,' Eli murmured, his eyes moist and his voice thick with emotion. 'I will pay for the celebration.'

'No need to waste money on food.' Mrs Wilkins hobbled into the shop, wiping her hands on her apron. 'Miss Lottie told me her good news and I've roasted a fowl with all the trimmings.'

'Where did you come by the money to purchase poultry?' Flora demanded. 'And why are you still here? I was against you remaining here from the start.'

'I said she could stay. It is my house, Mrs Brown,' Eli said, eyeing Flora warily as if expecting her to strike him down. 'I couldn't turn them out on the streets, and she is a good cook. I haven't eaten so well since . . .' He broke off, biting his lip.

'You are kindness itself,' Belinda said hastily. 'But are you sure you will have enough food to go round, Mrs Wilkins? I mean, a small boiling fowl has very little flesh on its bones.'

'It seems that Mrs Brown has an admirer,' Lottie said, winking at Cassy. 'A gentleman calling himself Farmer Mullins left a large capon as a thank you for services rendered. I can't think what they could be.'

Flora's dumbfounded expression was enough to send Cassy into a fit of giggles, but somehow she managed to avoid Lottie's eye and to curb her desire to laugh, although she could not quite control the tremor in her voice. 'It must have been Farmer Mullins.'

'Who is he?' Belinda asked innocently. 'Do you know him, Flora? A farmer?'

'She prevented two farmers resorting to fisticuffs,' Cassy explained as Flora appeared to have temporarily lost the power of speech. 'I'm surprised that it wasn't in the newspapers. There was quite a crowd outside the solicitor's office in Lincoln's Inn. They were squabbling over a real live calf. It was quite a sight.'

'Well, there's a fine supper come out of it. We'll eat like royalty this evening and that's the truth.' Mrs Wilkins turned on her heel. 'I've left Freddie in the kitchen, so you'd all best come before he gobbles the lot.'

'I'll go to the pub on the corner of Angel Alley and buy some wine,' Eli said, making for the door. 'We'll toast your success, my love, and eat like royalty thanks to Mrs Brown.'

'Mrs Fulford-Browne,' Flora corrected, finding her voice at last. 'As to Mullins, well, the man may be a peasant but he has manners, I'll allow him that.'

'And he obviously admires you, Flora,' Belinda said with an innocent air that belied the mischievous twinkle in her eyes.

The move took several days and many trips to Pedlar's Orchard with items that Flora insisted they could not live without. She took Belinda and Cassy on a spending spree that both alarmed and thrilled them. Belinda urged caution and Cassy could see that Flora's quarterly allowance would not go far if she continued to squander it at this rate, but Flora was unrepentant. The curtains must be replaced with something more suitable. The bedding was probably riddled with bed bugs and lice, and needed to be replaced. The furniture would have to do for the time being, but silk cushions would make the chairs more comfortable and add colour to a drab room. She purchased pictures in gilded frames and silver candlesticks, although as a compromise she chose plate instead of solid silver. She insisted that fine bone china was an absolute necessity unless they wanted to live like artisans, but Belinda managed to persuade her to attend an auction sale. After some lively bidding, which Cassy was afraid was going to prove even more expensive as Flora was determined to outbid her rivals, she secured a dinner service and tea set with only a few cracked plates and five cups instead of six. Cassy found a set of bone-handled cutlery that was a fair copy of ivory, although not as desirable as silver, but by this time Flora was beginning to realise that she must cut her costs or they would have to live on bread and scrape for the remainder of the quarter.

It was decided that they would move into the house the day after Lottie left to take up her place as a medical student. It seemed to Cassy that it was an ending and a new beginning all rolled into one. She was sad to lose her dearest friend, but Lottie assured her that nothing would change between them. Cassy accompanied Lottie and her father to Huntley Street and it was a tearful farewell, with hugs and kisses, tempered with promises to keep in touch. A uniformed doorman took Lottie's luggage inside the hospital and she paused on the step, waving to them as the cab drove off. Cassy craned her neck to catch the last sight of her friend, who looked a tiny figure as she stood beneath the portal of the New Hospital. Eli blew his nose loudly. 'My little girl,' he murmured. 'I'll miss her, but it's for the best. She'll be a proper doctor. I'm so proud.'

'She'll do well,' Cassy said softly. 'And she's not that far away. I'm sure she'll visit you often.'

He nodded his head, but was obviously overcome with emotion and Cassy lapsed into silence, pretending not to notice when he blew his nose constantly in a vain attempt to staunch his tears.

The excitement of moving was overshadowed by Lottie's leaving, and that evening Belinda insisted on taking them all to the Pavilion Theatre, where they saw Mr Isaac Cohen's production of *Little Red Riding Hood and the Goblin Wolf*, with some subordinate acts of singers and a comedian whose crude jokes made Flora laugh quite uproariously. Cassy enjoyed herself hugely as this was her first experience of the theatre, but she noticed with some regret that her mother's wedding ring was missing, and she realised that it had been pawned in order to pay for their night out. However, the desired effect had been achieved as Eli left the theatre with a smile on his face, and he walked back to Spectacle Alley with a lighter step.

The next day, travelling in two hackney carriages at

Eli's expense, they made their way to Pedlar's Orchard. Flora, Belinda and Eli travelled in the first carriage with Cassy, Mrs Wilkins and Freddie following on in the second vehicle. Flora had decided that they needed a cook-general and that Mrs Wilkins had proved herself in the culinary department and would be an ideal person for the job, even if that meant taking Freddie in as well. Cassy was delighted with the arrangement, and the room next to the kitchen had been made ready with a single bed and a truckle bed for the boy.

That evening, when supper was over and Freddie had been put to bed, Mrs Wilkins was happy to spend the evening by the kitchen range with her knitting, and Flora was snoozing in her chair by the fire in the front parlour. Cassy had cleared the table in the dining room and had finished tidying everything away ready for breakfast next morning when she heard Eli and her mother talking in the hall. She put her head round the door, meaning to say goodnight to him, but she was startled to see Eli take her mother's hand and instead of raising it briefly to his lips, he clutched it to his heart as though he could not bear to let her go.

'Goodnight, Eli,' Belinda said gently. 'Thank you for everything that you've done for us. I will always be in your debt.'

'Goodnight, sweet lady. I can't bear to say goodbye.'

Cassy stole another peep around the door, wondering whether to go and rescue her mother from her over-sentimental admirer. She held her breath as Eli rather clumsily drew Belinda into an amorous embrace. She

287

struggled free, pushing him away. 'Mr Solomon, don't spoil things.'

'I want to spoil you, Lady Belle. I'm not good with words, but you must know that I adore you. I mean no disrespect.' He threw himself down on his knees. 'I worship you, Belle. I love you with all my heart and I would be most honoured if you would consent to be my wife.'

Chapter Sixteen

Belinda glanced anxiously down the hallway. She thought she had heard the dining room door creak on its hinges, but there was no one in sight. However, it was only a matter of time and Flora might appear from the parlour, or, even worse, Cassy would emerge from the dining room to find her mother in a compromising situation. She did not want to hurt Eli's feelings but she could not allow the poor man to harbour hopes that were never going to be fulfilled. 'Please get up, Eli.'

He clutched his hands to his heart. 'I love you, Belle. Say you'll marry me and make me the happiest man in the world.'

'I'm so sorry, but I can't. If I've ever given you the slightest encouragement or the wrong impression as to my feelings, then I'm truly sorry.'

He scrambled to his feet, dusting off his trousers at the knee. 'I've spoken too soon. I should not have allowed my feelings to run away with me. Forgive me, dear lady.'

Belinda laid her hand on his arm. 'There is nothing to forgive. You've done me a great honour, and I'm touched, but I cannot marry you, or anyone for that matter.'

He bowed his head, avoiding her gaze. 'I'm too old for you, I realise that.'

'No, you're a man in his prime,' Belinda said in desperation, fearing that any moment he might break down and weep. 'Any woman of sense would be proud to be your wife.'

He glanced at her beneath his brows. 'Is it because I am a Jew?'

'No, never think that, Eli. Race and religion have nothing to do with my feeling for you. I'm very fond of you, and I have the greatest respect for you. You are the kindest, sweetest man I've ever met.'

A wry smile twisted his lips. 'But you do not love me.'

'I'd be lying if I said anything else. My heart is buried in the grave, and I'll never marry again.'

'Your husband was a most fortunate man, Lady Belle. How I envy him.'

Belinda realised that he was referring to Geoffrey, but she did not correct his mistake. Her heart had been frozen in time and was buried in an unknown grave somewhere in India with George, the only man she had ever loved or could ever love. 'I'm sorry to cause you pain, Eli. I hope this won't spoil our friendship.'

'I should not have spoken. I knew it was a vain hope.' He opened the front door and a gust of cold wind whipped around their legs, sending in a shower of dried leaves and bits of straw. 'I'll go now. Goodbye, dear lady.' He stepped out into the gathering gloom.

'For heaven's sake shut the door. The draught blew my candle out.'

Flora's irascible voice made Belinda turn with a start. She closed the door with an effort. 'I'm sorry, Flora. I was just saying goodnight to Eli.'

'That man has designs on you,' Flora said, retreating into the warmth of the parlour. 'I suppose you could do worse,' she added as Belinda took a seat opposite her. 'He's not very prepossessing, and he may be in trade, but at least he's got a good business.'

In spite of everything, Flora's pragmatic approach was such a turnabout for the grand dame who had mixed with London society that Belinda could not suppress a giggle.

'What's funny?' Flora demanded. 'Have I said something amusing?'

'No, not really. It's just that a few weeks ago you wouldn't have entertained such an idea.'

'Nor would I,' Flora agreed, nodding her head. 'But times change and we've had to change with them. Look at us, Belle. Two unattached women, forced to live in a hovel on fifty pounds a year. Fulford-Browne, God bless him, would be turning in his grave if he knew what a sorry pass I've come to.'

'At least he had the foresight to set something aside for you, Flora. If only Geoffrey had been as thoughtful I wouldn't be in this plight now.' Belinda stared into the fire, watching the orange tongues of flames lick around the coal. She sighed. 'I'm still young and I could earn my living, if only I could think of something at which I excelled. But my education was limited to subjects that were considered suitable for a young woman whose only purpose in life was to be a good wife and mother. Unfortunately I failed at both.'

'Nonsense. You were as good a wife as Geoffrey deserved, and as to the mother business, well, you did what you thought was for the best. You were a child yourself, and you had little say in the matter.'

'But I'm grown up now, and I must take control of my destiny. One of the first things I must do is to write to Ollie and give him our new address. Poor boy, he's the one who will suffer most from his father's disgrace.'

'It will build his character,' Flora said, slipping off her shoes and wriggling her toes in front of the fire. 'The coal scuttle is empty, Belle. Ring for Wilkins.'

Belinda rose to her feet. 'She's not a young woman. You can't expect her to run up and down the stairs with buckets of coal.'

'Then send young Cassy to fetch it. She's hale and hearty and you look as though a puff of wind would blow you away. I hope you're not pining for my brother, Belle. He wasn't worth it and you'll find someone else. I've no doubts on that score.'

Snatching up the coal scuttle, Belinda made for the door. 'I'm stronger than I look, and for your information, I turned Eli down when he proposed to me this evening.'

'I know,' Flora said with a smug smile. 'I was listening at the door. You handled that quite well.'

'You're incorrigible,' Belinda said, chuckling. 'But I hope I haven't hurt his feelings too much. He's a dear and he's been a perfect gentleman.'

'And he's a useful contact. Think about it, Belle. Eli makes bespoke garments for wealthy merchants and men of business. I could use my knowledge of society to send him clients of a higher standing, and in doing so I might find husband number five. I'm not completely past my prime.'

'Then perhaps you should marry Eli,' Belinda said, keeping her face straight with difficulty. 'You could do well together and even set him up in Savile Row.' She left the room without waiting for a response and she was still smiling when she almost bumped into Cassy in the dark hallway. 'Oh Lord, Cassy. You gave me a fright. I thought you were a ghost.'

Cassy took the coal scuttle from her mother's hands. 'Let me fetch the coal, Ma. I said I'm going to earn my keep and I meant it.'

'Thank you, dear. I am a little tired. It's been a long day.'

Cassy turned towards the basement steps, and then hesitated. 'I overheard some of your conversation with Mr Solomon, Ma. I'm glad you turned him down.'

Belinda felt the blood rush to her cheeks. 'I did nothing to encourage him, Cassy. You must believe that. I know how fond you are of Eli and Lottie, and I wouldn't hurt him for the world.'

'I know, Ma. He couldn't help himself, poor old fellow.'

'Oh, Cassy, he's not so old. I doubt if he's more than forty-five, but I was just the same as you when I was young. Anyone over twenty was middle-aged, and people in their thirties were ancient. Now I'm thirty-three and I don't feel any different from when I was seventeen.'

'Well, he's too old for you anyway,' Cassy said defensively. 'You should marry a rich lord or an earl, or someone who can take care of you in a proper manner.'

'I'll never marry again. I'm going to find a way to earn my own living and keep both of us in style. Now, are you going for the coal before Flora starts shouting, or shall I?'

Later that evening, Belinda was sitting up in bed with her feet on a hot brick wrapped in a piece of flannel, hugging a shawl around her shoulders as she attempted to compose a letter to Oliver. She had penned a brief missive informing him of his father's death, but now she needed to let him know that there was a home waiting for him when he returned to England. She would make sure that the spare room on the top floor was kept in readiness to receive her stepson whenever he chose to visit them. She dipped the pen into the inkwell she had borrowed from Flora, but the nib scratched on the paper and made a large blot. Then the words started to run into each other like a colony of ants racing across the page, and her eyelids were becoming increasingly heavy. She decided to leave the task until the morning, and setting aside the writing implements, she blew out the candle and snuggled down in the bed, which was comfortable thanks to Flora's insistence that they purchase new feather mattresses for everyone, including young Freddie. Belinda closed her eyes and abandoned herself to sleep.

*   *   *

The first weeks in Pedlar's Orchard were spent settling in and making the house as comfortable as possible. As the days progressed, Belinda set about finding suitable work, writing advertisements to place in shop windows offering her services to teach young ladies painting and deportment, which was all that she could think of that might be useful. She received one or two enquiries, but the women who contacted her merely needed someone to look after their young children while they went out to work in the manufactories, and were offering very little by way of payment. Belinda was only too well aware that Flora must have spent her entire first quarter's allowance, but somehow there was always food on the table, coal for the fires and candles to light when the dark winter evenings drew in.

Cassy took Freddie to the ragged school each morning and collected him at midday when lessons ended. She helped Mrs Wilkins in the kitchen as well as cleaning out the grates, dusting, sweeping and polishing and in general acting as a maid of all work. Belinda was not happy to see her daughter being used as a domestic and she attempted to help, but her inexperience was all too evident and she found herself struggling with the most simple of household tasks. Flora went out each day, wrapped in a slightly moth-eaten but serviceable cloak which she had purchased in a dolly shop. It smelt strongly of naphthalene and camphor, used to keep moths at bay, but it was lined with rabbit fur and as the winter approached even fashion-conscious Flora had to admit it was a necessary adjunct to her depleted wardrobe. The reason for her long walks went unexplained until one foggy afternoon Belinda simply had to ask the question that had been burning on her lips.

'Where have you been?' she demanded as Flora slipped off the heavy cloak and let it fall onto the sofa, where no doubt Cassy would be expected to retrieve it and hang it on its peg in the hall. 'Where do you go each day? And don't tell me it's for a constitutional because I won't believe you. You hate exercise, you know you do.'

'I'd love a cup of tea and a slice of Mrs Wilkins' seed cake,' Flora said calmly, taking her seat by the fire. 'It's getting colder each day now. I wouldn't be surprised if we had some snow.'

'Flora, stop teasing me. If you don't tell me, I'm afraid I might scream.'

'I've been out walking with a gentleman friend.' Flora leaned over to unlace her boots. 'Fetch me my slippers, there's a good girl.'

At a loss for words, Belinda picked up the satin slippers that she had left warming in the hearth. She held them behind her back. 'I'm not giving them to you until you tell me everything. Who is this man? Has he a name and how did you meet him?'

'It's Mullins. I didn't tell you because I knew you would make fun of me. Now please give me my slippers.'

Handing them to her, Belinda sat down on the sofa, deflated and shocked. 'Farmer Mullins? The man with the calf?'

'Yes, Farmer Mullins. The man who gave us the capon and has been providing us with eggs, butter and cheese for the last few weeks, to say nothing of the odd boiling fowl and the leg of lamb we ate on Sunday.'

Belinda ran her hand across her brow. 'But I still don't understand how this all came about.'

'It seems that the fellow isn't so simple after all. He managed to persuade Nixon to give him our address, although I'm certain that is not the done thing.'

'That doesn't explain why you've been meeting him in secret, Flora. What could you two have in common?'

'It isn't like that, silly girl. Mullins is a decent sort of chap, despite speaking with that awful Essex accent and wearing clothes that smell of the farmyard. We've been meeting in the Gunmaker's Arms, in a private parlour, of course, and I've been teaching him to read and write.'

'And he pays for his tuition with farm produce.' Belinda eyed Flora with growing respect. 'Who would have thought it?'

'I don't know why you're so surprised, Belle. I can be practical when the occasion demands. Now I would really appreciate that cup of tea and a slice of cake. I think I've earned it.'

Despite the continued gifts of farm produce from Farmer Mullins, money was in short supply. Belinda had pawned her last piece of jewellery in order to buy coal, candles and lamp oil as well as other staples such as flour, sugar and salt, but a spell of unusually cold weather at the beginning of December was making their life even more difficult. Flora's quarterly allowance was not due until the beginning of January, and, despite her continued efforts, Belinda had failed to find suitable employment. Against her mother's wishes, Cassy had found a job in a pub kitchen where she worked six nights a week washing dishes. It brought in a few pennies but it was nowhere near enough to pay the rent, and Belinda was becoming desperate, although Flora remained unworried. 'The landlord is in Jamaica,' she said with a shrug. 'I'm sure his agent will give us time to find the money.'

The rent collector was unsympathetic, but Belinda managed to persuade him to give them another week. Although Flora brushed her worries aside, Belinda continued to be anxious. She was desperate to find work, and when Eli arrived at the house one evening on the pretext of giving them news of Lottie's progress at the hospital, Belinda decided to ask his advice. After all, he was a successful businessman and if anyone could help, it was he. She sat on the sofa with Cassy, listening while he talked about his beloved daughter. She was, he said, studying hard and had earned praise from all her tutors. One day he was certain that she would become a fully qualified doctor, if the stuffy old men at the top of the profession ever gave women the chance they deserved. It was an insult to womanhood that Mrs Garrett Anderson had been forced to go to France in order to get her degree in medicine. His eyes misted over whenever he spoke about the struggles ahead for Lottie.

Belinda was quick to sympathise. 'We do the best we can as parents,' she said with feeling.

'Of course we do, dear lady.' Eli beamed at her over the top of his spectacles. 'I'm sure no one could be a better mother than you.'

She could not allow this fulsome praise to pass unremarked, and she shook her head. 'You don't know the full story, but I'm doing my best to atone for my past mistakes.' She held her hand up as Cassy opened her mouth as if to disagree. 'You only know part of our story, Eli. The past may be gone but we still bear the scars, and the most lasting is our lack of funds. In short, I must find work. I'm quite competent with a needle. Perhaps I could do some sewing for you. We're quite desperate, or I wouldn't ask.'

'My dear Lady Belle, your honesty breaks my poor heart. Why didn't you tell me this sooner? I'm not a rich man but I would gladly help out financially.'

She reached out to lay her hand on his sleeve. 'You are a true friend, Eli. But I wouldn't accept a loan from anyone unless I could see my way to repay it. I want to work, and I've tried my best to find employment, but it seems I'm unsuited for anything other than making polite conversation, and other equally useless accomplishments.'

Eli did not answer immediately. He sat staring into his teacup, a frown making deep furrows in his brow.

'I could do a few mornings as well as evenings at the King's Arms,' Cassy said eagerly. 'It doesn't pay very well but it's better than nothing.'

Belinda shook her head. 'You do enough already, my

darling. You help Mrs Wilkins and you take young Freddie to school each day and fetch him when lessons end. I'm the only one in the house who doesn't earn their keep, and it can't continue.'

'Lady Belle,' Eli said slowly. 'You told me that Mrs Brown teaches the farmer to read and write.'

'Eli, please call me Belle. I'm not an aristocrat and I have no right to that form of address.'

'You are in every sense a lady, and I think I might have a suggestion which would bring in a modest income.' Eli placed his cup and saucer carefully on the tea table. 'I have many clients, some of whom are wealthy, others are not. But many of the rich merchants and ambitious bank clerks have wives who want to advance themselves in the social scale, if you know what I'm saying?'

His dark eyes twinkled as he met Belinda's anxious gaze and she was quick to get his meaning. 'Yes, I think I do. Go on.'

'Lessons in etiquette and advice on fashion might prove to be both popular and profitable when given by a titled lady, even though you scorn its use.' His mouth twisted into a whimsical smile. 'I could put these ladies in touch, if you so wished. With the festive seasons and soirées soon upon us, I think this would be an ideal time for you to start.'

'Mama, that's a wonderful idea. You must do it,' Cassy cried enthusiastically. 'You are so clever, Mr Solomon.'

Belinda was too stunned to comment. She had never thought of herself as a leader of fashion or an expert in style and manners, but both Cassy and Eli were looking at her with such expectation on their faces that she had not the heart to dampen their enthusiasm. 'It might work,' she murmured. 'If you think anyone would be interested, Eli.'

Two days later, a carriage with bright yellow wheels drawn by a pair of matched bays drew up outside the house in Pedlar's Orchard and a small, fussily dressed woman in her early thirties stepped down onto the pavement. Belinda had been peering out of the parlour window as she waited somewhat nervously for her first student to arrive. 'It's Mrs Ponsonby, the wine merchant's wife. She's arrived.'

Cassy leapt to her feet. 'I'll let her in, Ma. She'll think I'm the maid.'

She had gone before Belinda had a chance to argue. She stood by the fireplace, smoothing the creases from her skirts with hands that shook despite her attempts to keep calm. Flora was out for the afternoon giving Farmer Mullins his twice weekly reading tuition, and Mrs Wilkins was below stairs in the kitchen with Freddie. Belinda glanced anxiously in the mirror above the mantelshelf; so much depended on the success of her new venture. They were down to the last of their supply of coal and there were only enough candles to light them to bed tonight. After that, if Mrs Ponsonby did not prove to be a satisfied client, they would quite literally be in the dark, and the rent collector would call on Friday.

The door opened. 'Mrs Ponsonby for you, Lady

301

Lawson.' Cassy curtsied deeply, keeping her face straight with an obvious effort as the woman sidled into the room, looking even more nervous than Belinda was feeling.

'How do, love.' She paused, looking critically around the room.

'How do you do, Mrs Ponsonby,' Belinda said, motioning her to take a seat. 'Please make yourself comfortable.'

'May I take your mantle, ma'am?' Cassy held out her hands to take the expensive but garish red-velvet garment trimmed with gold frogging.

'Ta, ever so.' Mrs Ponsonby juggled unsuccessfully with her reticule and an umbrella, but eventually and with Cassy's assistance, she managed to take off her gloves and her jacket before subsiding onto the sofa. 'This house couldn't hold a candle to ours and you a lady. I call that very queer.'

Belinda perched on the edge of her chair by the fire. She realised that she would have to work hard to earn her fee with Mrs Ponsonby. She shot a warning glance at Cassy who was openly grinning. 'Thank you, Cassy. You may bring the tea tray now.' Belinda waited until the door closed on her daughter before turning to Mrs Ponsonby with an attempt at a smile. 'How may I be of service to you, ma'am?'

'My hubby has made a success of his business and he says I need to speak proper and polish up me manners. What goes in Stepney ain't good enough it seems for entertaining the toffs who buy his wine. Although it don't seem as how a title's done you much good, or you wouldn't be teaching the likes of me and living close by the gasworks.' She clutched her hands to her chest, closing her eyes and groaning softly.

Alarmed and thinking the woman must be ill, Belinda jumped to her feet. 'What's the matter, ma'am? Are you feeling faint?'

Mrs Ponsonby opened her eyes and belched. 'That's better out than in. Blooming lobster always does that to me. Sits heavy in me belly for hours after dinner. I don't suppose you've got a drop of port and brandy, have you?'

Belinda shook her head. 'No, I'm sorry. Perhaps a cup of hot water might help?'

'Lawks, d'you want to poison me?' Mrs Ponsonby emitted a series of small burps. 'A cup of tea will have to do. Now let's get on with the business. How long d'you think it will take you to turn me into a proper lady?'

Forever wouldn't be long enough, Belinda thought, forcing her lips into a smile.

At the end of the session Belinda had a florin and a headache. But she was able to send Cassy out to purchase a pound of candles, kindling and matches and to pay for a sack of coal to be delivered before nightfall. There was something left to put towards the rent of three shillings a week, although even with Cassy's wages from the pub they would still be short when the rent collector came to call. Belinda could only hope that Eli would find more clients for her soon, or they would face a less than merry Christmas.

Amazingly the clients kept coming. The next morning a timid woman arrived on foot purporting to be the wife of a bank clerk who was seeking promotion to assistant manager. She was a gentle soul, eager to please, and blessed with natural good manners. All she needed was confidence, Belinda decided, and a little town polish. Then at the end of the week, just in time to make up the rent money, a couple of middle-aged ladies arrived in the pouring rain, climbing down from a hansom cab and scuttling into the house chattering like magpies. They were dressed in identical costumes, short capes over dark blue bombazine dresses with white piqué collars and cuffs. Their black bonnets trimmed with matching crepe were commensurate with mourning wear, and their hands were encased in black mittens leaving work-worn fingers exposed to the elements. The Misses Dobson, it transpired, had a brother who was in holy orders and had decided to volunteer to become a missionary in East Africa. Whilst having a tropical suit made by Eli he had mentioned that his sisters wanted to join him, but their humble background made it difficult for them to be accepted by the Missionary Society. 'We need to speak proper,' Miss Mattie announced boldly. 'Our brother learns real quick, but we was at home looking after Ma and Pa until they passed away. We never had a chance to go to school, although Ma taught us to read and write.'

'Pa was a waterman,' Miss Mary added, as if continuing her sister's train of thought. 'He didn't hold with women working outside the home. We need to learn what's what, if you know what I mean.'

Belinda smiled. 'I think I do, and I hope I can be of assistance, ladies.'

'Ladies,' Miss Mattie breathed, clasping her hands together. 'Did you hear that, Mary? She called us ladies.'

'That's a miracle, sister,' Miss Mary said, wide-eyed and smiling. 'And we've only just walked in the door. Henry will be pleased with us.'

'Please sit down, Miss Mattie, Miss Mary,' Belinda said patiently. 'We've a little way to go yet, but you're halfway there already.'

At the end of the session Belinda could not in all conscience charge them four shillings for what had been a touching and illuminating experience. She could hardly believe that two women, several years her senior, had led such sheltered lives although dwelling in the roughest part of Limehouse. It appeared that they had been kept at home and never allowed to venture out unless accompanied by their father or brother. They had lived as unpaid servants, cooking, cleaning and taking in washing to help with the family finances, but more carefully chaperoned than most young ladies from higher up the social scale. They had never experienced romance or been given the chance to form a relationship with the opposite sex. They were like two children in ageing bodies, but so eager to accompany their brother to a foreign land in order to spread the word of God that they made Belinda feel humbled and guilty for taking all her previous good fortune for granted.

'We'll come again next week,' Miss Mattie said, following Belinda into the hallway with her sister hurrying after her.

'We've learnt so much from you today,' Miss Mary added breathlessly. 'Henry will be pleased.'

Opening the door, Belinda glanced outside and realised that it was still raining, a fine misty drizzle that would soon soak them to the skin. It was getting dark and the gas lamps created golden pools on the wet pavements. 'Ladies, you should get a cab,' she said anxiously.

'We'll find one in the Commercial Road, I expect,' Miss Mattie said bravely.

'Henry gave us the money,' her sister added proudly. 'He is such a good brother.'

The sound of a horse's hooves made Belinda peer out into the gloom. 'There's a cab, ladies. And it's coming this way.' She stepped down onto the pavement, waving her hand to attract the cabby. 'It's stopping.' She was about to step back into the house but something caught her attention as the cab drew to a halt a little way down the street and the occupant swung the half-door open and prepared to alight from the cab. She could not make out his features clearly but she would have known him anywhere. Disregarding the fact that her gown was already soaked through, Belinda picked up her skirts and ran.

Chapter Seventeen

Cassy was about to go into the front parlour to retrieve the tea tray, but the noise from outside the house added to the fact that the front door was wide open made her pause in the hallway. She had seen her mother step outside to say goodbye to the two strange women, but she had thought little of it until now. Holding the oil lamp in her hand, she was about to investigate further when Belinda entered the house, smiling excitedly and seemingly oblivious to the fact that her hair and clothes were soaked with rainwater. 'Cassy, darling, you'll never guess who's just arrived.'

Cassy held the lamp a little higher but she almost dropped it as she recognised the young man who had followed her mother into the house. Standing there, resplendent in his officer's uniform, his shako tucked beneath his arm, he looked her up and down with a slow smile radiating from his lips to his eyes. 'Cassy, by all that's wonderful. I hardly recognised you.'

'Ollie.' Shock, surprise and delight rendered her almost speechless.

'Don't keep him standing in the cold hallway, Cassy,' Belinda said, taking the lamp from her as she disappeared into the parlour. 'Come in and get warm, Ollie.'

With a deft flick of his wrist Oliver tossed his shako onto a peg, and before she had time to collect her thoughts he enveloped Cassy in a hug that took her breath away. 'By God, Cassy. You've turned into quite a young lady. What happened to that little girl I left behind?'

'I'm nearly sixteen,' she protested, laughing. 'You've been away a long time. I hardly recognise you if it comes to that. You look so dashing.' It was true, she thought, as he held her at arm's length, staring at her as if he could not quite believe that she had grown up. His face was thinner and the skin drawn tightly over high cheekbones. Even though he was smiling, there was a veiled look in his eyes as though he had seen many dreadful things and had locked them away at the back of his mind. She realised then that the boy she had known was gone forever and in his place was a man who was almost a stranger. Perhaps he was thinking the same about her. The moment was shattered by the sound of booted feet on the steps and another uniformed figure entered the house staggering beneath the weight of a small cabin trunk and several valises. He dumped them on the floor and leaned against the door to shut out the wind and rain.

Forgetting Oliver, Cassy pushed past him and ran towards the soldier with her arms outstretched. She would have known him anywhere. He was as much a part of her as the heart that quickened its beat inside her breast. 'Bailey. Oh, Bailey. You've come home.'

He caught her to him, swinging her off her feet in a hug. 'Cass, is it really you?' He set her down, but he kept his arms around her, staring into her face as if committing every detail to memory. 'You've grown up, my little Cass.'

Halfway between laughter and tears, she traced his jawline with the tip of her finger. His face was also tanned and much leaner than when she had last seen him. His body felt taut and muscular and there were white lines at the corners of his eyes where he had squinted against the hot Indian sun, which made him appear to be smiling even when his face was in repose. She touched his eyelids, and running her finger down his cheek she felt a scar. 'Oh, Bailey. What happened? You've been injured.'

'He fought a duel over a beautiful Indian maiden,' Ollie said, laughing. 'See to the luggage, Corporal Moon.' He strolled into the parlour, leaving them alone in the dark hallway.

'Did you really fight a duel?' Cassy asked, although safe in the circle of his arms she knew the answer even before he shook his head.

'It's his idea of a joke, Cass. It was nothing, just a scratch from a piece of shrapnel.'

She sighed, inhaling the scent of him. Beneath the mixed odours of saddle soap, leather and the damp wool of his uniform, he still smelled like Bailey, her friend and protector for as long as she could remember. 'You might have been killed,' she murmured. 'If you died, I'd die too, Bailey.'

He dropped a kiss on her forehead. 'Still the same passionate girl you always were. I'm glad you haven't changed, Cass. You're the reason I've worked hard to better myself. I'm Captain Davenport's batman now. Wherever he goes, I go too.'

'You're here and that's all that matters,' Cassy said, taking him by the hand and dragging him into the parlour where she found Oliver standing with his back to the fire and Belinda was seated.

'This is wonderful, Ollie,' Belinda said, smiling up at him. 'I can't believe that you're really here.'

'I received your letter, Belle,' Oliver said gently. 'I was due a spell of leave anyway, but the Colonel allowed me to come home earlier on compassionate grounds. It was a bad business about the old man.'

'It's almost harder for you, my dear,' she said, averting her gaze.

'But to leave you with nothing. That's simply not on. No wonder he took the coward's way out.'

Belinda raised her head to look him in the eye. 'I won't have you speak of your father in that way, Oliver. He found himself in a position that he couldn't control. It's not for us to judge him.'

Cassy could see that Oliver was angry and that Ma was upset. She drew Bailey into the circle of lamplight. 'Look who's here, Ma. It's Bailey, my dear brother.'

Bailey released her hand abruptly, and stood stiffly to attention, staring straight ahead.

'At ease,' Oliver said casually. 'We're not on the parade ground now, Corporal.'

'Yes, sir.' Bailey relaxed a little, but still looked as though he wished he was somewhere else.

'What's the matter with you both?' Cassy demanded. 'Why are you treating him like a servant, Ollie?'

310

'They're soldiers, my dear,' Belinda said gently. 'Discipline is strict and all-important in the army.'

'I don't care about the army,' Cassy cried, swallowing convulsively as a lump in her throat threatened to choke her. 'They're at home now. We're all together. Can't they forget rules and regulations for a while?'

'It's up to you as his superior officer, Ollie,' Belinda said firmly. 'But I think Cassy's right.'

'Sit down, man,' Oliver said, grinning. 'There's no need to stand on ceremony within these walls.' He glanced around the small room. 'This is a bit of a comedown, if you don't mind me saying so, Belle. Stepney of all places too. What would the pater say if he could see us now?'

'It's all we can afford,' Belinda countered, a frown creasing her smooth brow. 'We lost everything, Ollie.'

Cassy glanced at the clock. 'Oh my goodness, I'll be late. I must go or the landlord will dock my pay.'

'What's this?' Bailey demanded, seeming to forget that he was in the company of a superior officer and speaking out. 'Where are you going?'

'She has to work,' Belinda said before Cassy had a chance to reply. 'We all have to work in order to pay the rent. Flora has a small income but the old days are gone and we have to manage the best we can.'

Oliver moved away from the fire and sprawled in the chair which was Flora's favoured seat. 'Where is Aunt Flora? You said she'd left the Italian gigolo.'

'It's a long story,' Belinda replied wearily. 'She'll tell you the details herself, but she's out at present giving reading lessons to a farmer.'

'Aunt Flora and a farmer. That conjures up a pretty picture,' Oliver said, chuckling. 'Come now, Belle. You can't leave it there.'

She shook her head. 'There's so much you don't know, but I can't go into it all now.'

Cassy reached for her shawl which she had laid in readiness on a chair by the door. 'I have to go.'

'Where are you going?' Bailey rose to his feet. 'What's this all about, Cass?'

'I work in a pub kitchen. I wash dishes.'

Bailey turned his head to cast an accusing look at Belinda. 'Do you mean to tell me that you allow your ward to go out alone at night to work in a common public house?' His voice shook with suppressed anger.

Cassy caught him by the sleeve. 'It's all right. I'm quite capable of looking after myself, and we need the money. Besides which, there's something you don't know.' She glanced nervously at her mother. 'Will you tell them, or shall I?'

Belinda rose slowly to her feet. She moved to Cassy's side, slipping her arm protectively around her daughter's shoulders. 'I'm her mother,' she said simply. 'Cassy is my daughter.'

Bailey let out a long whistle between his teeth and Oliver shook his head in disbelief. 'Come now, Belle. You're joking, of course.'

'I was never more serious in my life.' Belinda managed a smile, but to Cassy's concern she saw the colour drain from her mother's face.

'Don't upset yourself, Ma. They don't need to know

the whole story. It's your business and has nothing to do with anyone else.'

'But I thought the Indian maidservant was your mother,' Bailey said, staring at Cassy as if seeing her for the first time. 'How long have you known this, Cass? And why didn't you tell me sooner?'

'I only found out a short time ago. I wanted to tell you in person.'

'It's complicated,' Belinda said, laying her hand on his arm. 'But it makes no difference, Bailey. Cassy is still the same girl you cared for and protected for all those dreadful years when I was unable to help her. I'll always be grateful to you for that.'

'It's a bit of a shock, but I always knew she was special,' Bailey said, winking at Cassy. 'I'm glad you found your ma at last, Cass.'

'I need a drink, Corporal Moon,' Oliver said, rising to his feet. 'This is too much information to take in at once. What say we escort my new stepsister to her place of employment?'

'Flora will be home soon,' Belinda murmured. 'She'll want to see you, Ollie.'

His stern expression melted into his old, charming smile. 'We won't be long, presuming of course that you have room to put us up for a week or two. Otherwise, Moon and I will have to find another billet.'

'Of course you must stay here,' Belinda said, rallying. 'I'll tell Mrs Wilkins to make up the bed in the spare room, although I don't suppose you two want to share.'

'No, that would be going a step too far,' Ollie said, chuckling. 'Moon can take the sofa. He's slept in far less comfortable circumstances, haven't you, old chap?'

Bailey acknowledged this truth with a nod. 'The sofa would be luxury compared to sleeping rough, ma'am. As to the Captain's room, I'll see to that if your housekeeper would be kind enough to give me the bedding.'

This made Cassy giggle. 'It's like old times, Bailey. Only instead of looking after babies, you're taking care of a grown man.' She shot a mischievous glance at Oliver. 'Although I'm not so sure if Ollie is as grown up as he makes out.' She uttered a screech as Oliver swept her off her feet and slung her over his shoulder, almost knocking the oil lamp over in the process.

'You're not so much of a lady that I can't give you a good spanking, young Cassy. And being your big brother gives me the right to chastise you at my pleasure.'

Bailey took a step towards his senior officer. 'Put her down, sir. She's not a toy. Treat her right or you'll have me to deal with.'

'Boys, please remember that this is my parlour and not the barrack room,' Belinda said sternly. 'We may have come down in the world but I won't stand for brawling and bad manners. Cassy is a young lady and you will both treat her as such.'

Bailey had the grace to look shame-faced but Oliver set Cassy back on her feet with a casual shrug of his shoulders. 'It's all in fun, Belle.'

'I know your larks of old, Oliver,' Belinda said, frowning. 'Now, if you'll excuse me, I'll go downstairs and ask Mrs Wilkins to prepare supper for two extra.'

'Don't go to any trouble on our account, Belle. We'll dine at the pub. I'm sorry if I've offended you.'

'I'm sorry too,' Bailey added apologetically. 'We've been away from home for far too long.' He hooked his arm around Cassy's shoulders. 'I'm sorry, nipper. I'll have to get used to you being all grown up and a lady too.'

'I'm still the same girl I ever was,' Cassy assured him.

He eyed her speculatively. 'No, that's not true, and I was a fool not to see it coming. You were always different; a cut above the rest. Now I know why.'

Oliver clapped him on the shoulder. 'Come along, Moon. Let's go and reconnoitre this place where Cassy works. I don't want my sister working in a cheap grog-shop. We need to have a decko at this place.'

It was still raining. A fine mist hung in damp cloud above the Regent's Canal and the lights from the King's Arms twinkled in fractured reflections on the dark water. The stench from the gasworks and the manu-factories that had grown up along the banks of Limehouse Cut lay heavily in the air, pressed down by a thick blanket of cloud.

'This ain't a nice place,' Bailey said, as they made their way along the footpath. 'You shouldn't be walking this way alone at night, Cass.'

'I've been doing it for weeks,' she protested. 'It's not that bad.'

'I'd swear that Belle doesn't know the half of it,' Oliver said grimly. 'I've seen better place in the slums of Bombay.'

Even as he uttered the words, the doors of the pub were flung open and two drunks were ejected forcibly onto the pavement. Bailey clutched Cassy's arm a little tighter. 'Let's go. I've seen enough.'

'But I'll lose my job,' Cassy protested as Oliver tucked her free hand into the crook of his arm.

'You'll lose more than that if you continue to work here,' Bailey said through gritted teeth. 'It's as well we turned up when we did. I think Lady Davenport should be put straight, Captain. I'll leave that to you, sir.'

'Point taken, but you can drop the formal address, Moon. We're on leave and we don't want to make the ladies feel uncomfortable.'

Cassy found herself wheeled around and propelled homewards with her feet barely touching the ground. 'Don't I get a say in all this?'

'No,' they replied in unison.

'Well, at least stop and get something in for supper,' she urged. 'Mrs Wilkins has made boiled mutton and caper sauce, but there won't be enough to go round.'

'Take us to the nearest eel pie shop or a fish and chip shop,' Bailey said, licking his lips. 'I haven't had a decent meal since I left England.'

'I've never had eel pie,' Oliver said thoughtfully. 'But a nice steak and kidney pudding with oysters would be just the thing.'

Cassy sighed. She was hungry too, but she would undoubtedly have lost her job and when their leave was ended, Bailey and Oliver would return to India, leaving the family to face a long hard winter. 'All right,' she said reluctantly. 'I know a good place, but you'll have to pay.'

Oliver tweaked her cheek. 'Of course, sweetheart. And don't worry about anything. We'll take care of you from now on. Your troubles are over.'

They arrived back at the house laden with parcels of food wrapped in yesterday's newspapers, but just as Cassy was about to knock on the door a dog cart drew to a halt at the kerbside. Oliver and Bailey stood back as Farmer Mullins clambered down from the driver's seat and assisted Flora to alight. Wrapped in the fur-lined cloak she stood on the pavement staring at Oliver in disbelief.

'Goodness gracious, boy. Where did you spring from?'

'I'll be taking me leave now, ma'am,' Farmer Mullins said, tipping his cap. 'Ta for the lesson. I'll see you again the day after tomorrow, if that's still convenient.'

Flora waved him away with a waft of her hand. 'Yes, of course, Mullins.'

'And I'm doing passable well, ain't I, ma'am?'

Farmer Mullins seemed reluctant to leave and Cassy felt a twinge of guilt for the cavalier way in which Flora was treating him. 'Perhaps Mr Mullins would like to come in and share our supper,' she suggested.

He opened his mouth to reply but a look from Flora made him snap his jaws together like a steel trap.

'Mullins has to drive back to Essex,' Flora said in a voice that brooked no argument. 'He has a farm to run and livestock to feed.'

'Begging your pardon, ma'am, but I employ men to do most of the hard labour.'

'Yes, Mullins, I'm sure you do. Now go home, there's a good fellow. I expect your wife is waiting for you with a hot meal on the table.'

'I'm a widower, as I've told you several times, Mrs Brown.'

'Fulford-Browne,' Flora corrected. 'Goodnight, Mullins.' She held out her hand. 'That will be half a crown, please.'

He fumbled in the pockets of his corduroy breeches, producing a coin which he placed in her palm. 'It's a long drive back to East Ham, Mrs Fulford-Browne, ma'am.' He looked longingly at the open doorway and the interior of the hall illuminated by the light from a lamp held in Belinda's hand. 'It's cold and wet and a cup of something hot wouldn't go amiss, ma'am.'

'For goodness' sake come indoors, man,' Oliver said genially. 'We've food enough for all and one more at table won't make the slightest difference. Beside which, I'd be interested in your views on farming. I've toyed with the idea of working the land myself when my army career comes to an end.'

'Oliver, don't talk nonsense.' Flora glared at him, but he ignored her warning glance and strode into the house, brushing Belinda's cheek with a kiss as he walked past her.

'Come inside, sir,' Cassy said, beckoning to Mullins. 'Will your horse be all right left to himself?'

'He'll not move unless I say so.' Mullins took off his cap as he mounted the steps. 'After you, miss.'

Bailey came in last, closing the door behind him. He caught up with Cassy, taking her by the arm. 'What's all this about, Cass? What's been going on since I went away?'

'Not now,' she whispered. 'I'll tell you later.'

If Belinda was surprised to see Farmer Mullins shamble into the dining room she was too well-mannered to say so. She set another place while Bailey served the food from a side table. Oliver produced two bottles of wine that he had purchased on the way home, and he pulled the corks with a practised hand. Flora took her seat at the head of the table and proceeded to quiz him about his military exploits. To Cassy's surprise, the normally ebullient Oliver was reticent when speaking about the war against the Afghans. It seemed to her that it was something he wished to leave behind him, and she could tell by Bailey's shuttered expression that he felt the same. With her usual tact and diplomacy, Belinda managed to steer the conversation round to farming, which drew an immediate response from Oliver, who bombarded the unfortunate Mullins with questions until the poor man began to look slightly dazed.

Cassy tried in vain to think of another topic of conversation but matters were made worse when she met Bailey's amused glance and she saw his lips twitch. She had an almost overwhelming desire to giggle but was saved by Freddie bursting into the room demanding to know if anyone wanted treacle pudding and custard.

'Well now, who's this?' Bailey said, staring at Freddie. 'Is this your housekeeper's boy, Cassy?'

The laughter that she had been trying hard to suppress bubbled to the surface in a throaty chuckle. 'Heavens no. Don't you recognise him, Bailey? Can't you see the scar on his nose where he took that tumble when he first started to toddle?'

Bailey beckoned to Freddie, who was standing staring at him with his thumb plugged in his mouth. Sucking his thumb was a habit that Mrs Wilkins was trying to break with the use of bitter aloes, but Cassy was only too well aware that Freddie had always had a will of his own. She held her breath, watching Bailey's expression change from frankly baffled to one of wonderment. 'Freddie, is it you?' he said, holding out his hand. 'I'm Bailey. Do you remember me?'

Freddie's face split into a grin and he took his thumb out of his mouth. 'Bailey.' He scrambled onto Bailey's lap and began examining the brass buttons on his tunic as if it were the most natural thing in the world.

'Well,' Cassy exclaimed. 'He remembers you, but he'd forgotten all about me.'

'It's my personal charm,' Bailey said, smiling. 'We were good friends, weren't we, Freddie?'

'You're a soldier.'

Freddie was obviously impressed and in no hurry to take a message back to the kitchen. Cassy rose to her feet. 'Anyone for pudding?'

By the end of the meal, Farmer Mullins had become quite expansive, aided no doubt by several glasses of claret, and Freddie clung steadfastly to Bailey, refusing to go to bed unless his new idol took him downstairs and tucked him in. At this point, Belinda rose from her seat, suggesting that if the gentlemen wanted to smoke they were most welcome to do so, but the ladies would retire to the parlour.

Cassy could not help thinking that it was a bit silly to carry on as though they were still living in a grand house, but she began clearing the table, motioning Bailey to remain seated when he started to rise.

'Quite right, Moon. At ease,' Oliver said, tossing him a cigar. 'We're all one family until we return to duty.'

Belinda left the room, but Flora remained seated, watching eagerly as Oliver offered his silver cigar case to Mullins. He selected one with an appreciative smile. 'I dunno when I last had a fine Havana, Captain.'

'Only the best for me, Mullins old boy. Now tell me more about your acreage.' Oliver struck a vesta and warmed his cigar before lighting it.

'Where are you manners, boy?' Flora demanded. 'I haven't smoked a cigar since we left Duke Street. I'm sure you can spare one for your aged aunt.'

'Of course, Auntie. Apologies,' Oliver said, passing the case to her. 'Help yourself. I admire a woman who can appreciate good tobacco. Don't you, Mullins?'

'Your aunt's a remarkable woman, if you don't mind me saying so, Captain.'

'There's no need to toady, Mullins,' Flora said tartly. 'The fact that you were invited to join us for dinner doesn't mean that you can take liberties.' She allowed him to light her cigar, and she puffed out a cloud of smoke with a satisfied smile.

Cassy paused as she was about to pick up a pile of

plates. She could see that Farmer Mullins was discomforted by Flora's sharp words. 'I hope you enjoyed your supper, Mr Mullins.'

'I did indeed, Miss Cassy.' He shot her a grateful glance beneath bushy black eyebrows. 'I was going to suggest that I repaid the kindness by inviting you all to my farm, but that might be considered presumptuous by someone sitting at this table.' A smile transformed his craggy, weather-beaten features and his brown eyes glowed with warmth. They were rather fine eyes, Cassy thought, observing him properly for the first time. She realised with a degree of surprise that he might once, when he was much younger, have been quite a fine-looking man.

'What rot, Mullins,' Oliver said scornfully. 'I say it's a capital idea. I for one will be pleased to accept your offer. When shall we come?'

'Don't include me in your plans,' Flora said icily. 'I can't abide mud and large animals.'

'I told you that I detest the countryside,' Flora grumbled as Oliver helped her down from the old-fashioned and slightly decrepit barouche that Farmer Mullins had provided in order to transport them to his farm just outside the straggling village of East Ham.

'You'll have a splendid time keeping Mullins in his place,' Oliver said, winking at Cassy who had clambered down and was holding her skirts above her ankles to prevent them from trailing in the mud.

'Just because you're an officer in the Queen's army doesn't give you the right to cheek your elders and betters,' Flora said, slapping his hand away. 'I'm not decrepit. I can manage on my own, boy.'

'Of course, Auntie.' Oliver proffered his hand to Belinda. 'Stepmother, may I assist you or would you rather leap from a great height into the mud and muck.'

Belinda smiled, laying her hand on his arm. 'Don't torment your aunt. She'll sulk for the rest of the day and take it out on poor Farmer Mullins.'

Bailey climbed down from the box where he had travelled beside the driver, a silent individual who drove with a pipe clenched between his teeth and a battered bowler hat set squarely on his head.

'What a pity young Freddie couldn't come with us,' Bailey said, looking around at the wide expanse of the farmyard where chickens wandered freely, pecking the ground, and a colourful rooster strode amongst them protecting his feathered harem. On the other side of the fence was a large pond with a reed bed which provided nesting places for ducks and geese, and as far as the eye could see there was green pasture where cows grazed peacefully. To Cassy, who had never ventured into the countryside, this was an idyllic scene of rural tranquillity. They might have been a hundred miles from the stews of East London instead of a mere eight.

'Fresh air,' Oliver cried triumphantly. 'Just take a breath of that, Aunt Flora. It's like inhaling champagne.'

Flora screwed up her face. 'I can smell nothing but mud and animal droppings. It's freezing out here. Let's hope the farmhouse is warmer, although looking at that ramshackle building I have my doubts. Where's

Mullins? I call it very bad manners for the host to be absent when his guests arrive.'

As if acting on cue, Farmer Mullins emerged from the door and came striding across the yard to greet them. Cassy thought he looked like a different man, filled with confidence and comfortable in his own setting. 'Welcome to my home, ladies and gentlemen. Won't you come inside and partake of a glass of buttered rum punch? It's a raw day and no mistake.' He proffered his arm to Flora.

'I don't know why I came,' Flora muttered as she laid her hand on his sleeve.

'Come inside, ma'am. I have a fire burning in the parlour and my housekeeper, Dora Cope, has aired the room specially. She took the Holland covers off yesterday and beat the carpets on the washing line. You'd think the Queen herself was coming to dine.'

Oliver pulled a face but any remark he might have made was quelled by a look from Belinda. 'I'll hold on to your arm, if I may, Ollie,' she said sweetly.

He clasped her hand as it lay small and white against the dark green of his uniform. 'This should prove very entertaining, Belle.'

'Behave yourself, Ollie.' A dimple in her cheek and the twinkle in her eyes belied the frown she gave him.

Bailey took Cassy by the hand. 'You're shivering, Cass. Let's get you inside out of the cold.'

They followed the others across the farmyard and into the house, which was a long, low half-timbered building, but the inside was surprisingly spacious. The large entrance hall had a flagstone floor and an oak staircase leading up to a galleried landing. The wainscoted walls were bare of any form of embellishment and the only furniture was a hallstand and a carved wooden chest. Farmer Mullins led the way into the parlour where a log fire burned in an inglenook fireplace. Rag rugs made splashes of colour on the flagstones and the smell of beeswax and lavender mingled with the scent of burning apple wood. The low-beamed ceiling and the small windows with leaded lights made the room seem dark even though it was barely midday, but oil lamps had been lit and placed on a polished oak table, surrounded by ladderback chairs with rush seats.

'How rural,' Flora murmured, gazing round the room as if it found little favour in her eyes.

'It's very cosy,' Belinda said hastily. 'A charming room, Mr Mullins.'

He puffed out his chest. 'Aye, it is to be sure. My late wife made the rugs with her own hands, ma'am. My Emily was a fine woman, but she died young.'

'How sad.' Belinda's lips drooped in a sympathetic sigh. 'And you have no children?'

'My wife died in childbirth, ma'am. The infant perished with her. They're buried in St Mary Magdalene's churchyard, along with several generations of the Mullins family.'

'I have every sympathy with them,' Flora said, shivering. 'Did you mention hot rum punch, Mullins?'

He beamed at her. 'I did indeed, ma'am. If you'll excuse me, I'll go and fetch it from the kitchen.' He backed out of the door as if bowing to royalty.

'Flora,' Belinda said sternly. 'Stop tormenting the poor man. Can't you see he's doing his best?'

'I knew that I shouldn't have come.' Flora subsided onto a wooden settle by the fire, wrapping her cloak around her even though the others had discarded their outer garments.

There was an awkward silence as they waited for Mullins to return with the rum punch, and at the sound of his booted feet on the flagstones, Cassy ran to open the door. He gave her a cheery grin as he strode past her carrying a large pan filled with steaming liquid. 'This will warm the cockles of your heart,' he said, setting it down on the hearth. He ladled the punch into earthenware cups which had been laid out in readiness on a side table. He offered the first cup to Flora. 'Ma'am. Will you partake?'

Flora almost snatched it from him and raised the cup to her lips. Her eyes opened wide as she swallowed a mouthful and she took a deep breath. 'Excellent punch, Mullins, if I do say so.' She held the cup out for a second helping and a hint of pink tinged her pale cheeks.

By the time everyone had had their share, Flora had downed three cupfuls of hot buttered rum punch and she was exuding goodwill. 'I'd like to have a tour of the house, Mullins,' she said, rising to her feet. 'Are you girls coming with me?'

Cassy glanced nervously at Farmer Mullins. She was not at all sure that he would welcome three women traipsing around his home, but he was nodding his head and smiling. 'Splendid idea, ma'am. I'll have Dora show you the house while I take the gentlemen round the farm. Then we'll have a bite to eat afore I drive you home.'

Dora Cope turned out to be an elderly lady with white hair and a stick-thin body. She did not look as though she had the strength to raise a duster, let alone clean and polish such a large house, but her movements were sprightly and there was a martial sparkle in her eye when she addressed herself to Flora. They followed her from room to room, and Cassy could tell by her silence that Flora was impressed. She made no comment at all on the size and shape of the dining room, which boasted a refectory table large enough to seat twenty people, as well as a slightly rusting suit of armour perched precariously on a plinth by the stone fireplace. Neither had she anything to say about the enormous farmhouse kitchen. It was left to Belinda and Cassy to admire the sheen on the copper pots and pans and the cleanliness of the scrubbed pine table where luncheon was being prepared. A plump girl from the village was in the scullery peeling vegetables and the aroma of roasting beef made Cassy's mouth water. Two apple pies with crusts glistening with sugar had been set aside to cool, and a bowl filled with eggs and a pitcher of warm cream hinted at custard waiting to be made.

The dairy was tacked on to the side of the house, and a quick scrutiny revealed equal attention to cleanliness and order. The milk churns shone like silver and the skimming ladles, ewers and butter churn were spotless. Cassy could imagine that any flies which dared

327

to trespass into Dora's domain would meet a swift and brutal end.

There was a smaller parlour on the far side of the kitchen and a room sparsely furnished with a desk and a chair and shelves lined with ledgers, which Dora explained up until now had been kept by a bookkeeper, but Mr Mullins was hoping to take over this task himself once the good lady had brought him up to scratch with his reading and writing. Numbers he could do, she added proudly. There wasn't a man in Essex who could tot up figures like Farmer Mullins.

An inspection of the rooms upstairs revealed four good-sized bedrooms. Their exploration was interrupted by the scullery maid who raced upstairs puffing and panting to say that something was burning in the oven. Dora flew off after her flapping her arms like a demented crow, and she could be heard scolding the unfortunate creature all the way down the stairs until the sounds faded as they reached the kitchen. This left Belinda and Cassy free to examine the master bedchamber in greater detail, although Flora feigned lack of interest and perched on the edge of the four-poster bed complaining that it was too soft. Belinda opened the clothes press and marvelled at the neat array of flannel shirts, neckties, and starched white collars, presumably for Sunday best. She opened a drawer and closed it hastily, blushing rosily when she admitted that it contained undergarments and perhaps they should stop prying into Farmer Mullins' private things. Cassy had lost interest in clothes and had picked up a small daguerreotype of a young woman with a merry face and laughing eyes. 'How sad,' she whispered. 'This must be poor Emily, who died in childbirth. She looks such a lively soul too.'

'Let me see.' Flora had risen to her feet and come up behind them unnoticed. She snatched the frame from Cassy's fingers. 'Hmm, she looks common.'

'Flora, how can you speak so of the dead?' Belinda took it from her and placed it back on the chest of drawers amongst an untidy litter of cufflinks and collar studs.

'I speak as I find,' Flora said airily. 'Anyway, I've seen enough of the house and I'm hungry. Let's go downstairs and see if the woman can turn out a passable meal that won't leave us all with bellyache.'

Cassy and Belinda exchanged despairing glances. 'She's determined to be difficult,' Belinda whispered in Cassy's ear as they followed Flora down the wide, shallow stairs.

'I may be difficult,' Flora snapped, 'but I'm not deaf. I only came here on sufferance. I shan't come again. Ever.'

Chapter Eighteen

The gaslight outside the parlour window glowed orange and blue before turning a golden yellow as the lamplighter did his bit to keep the night at bay. It was late afternoon and darkness was swallowing the city in great greedy gulps, but the parlour in Pedlar's Orchard formed a warm cocoon around Cassy and Lottie as they sat by the fire.

'Do you mean to tell me that the farmer has invited all of you for Christmas dinner?' Lottie's eyes shone with amusement.

'He did. He asked Flora in front of me and Ma,' Cassy said, giggling. 'She was so taken aback that she gave in without a murmur and said yes.'

'I'd love to have seen Mrs Brown lost for words. Tell me more about this budding romance between the grand lady and the farmer.'

This image made Cassy laugh outright. 'Don't be absurd, Lottie. Flora treats the poor man as if he were less than nothing as it is, and can you imagine her living in the country, let alone being a farmer's wife?'

'Stranger things have happened,' Lottie said, tapping the side of her nose and grinning. 'They say that opposites attract. Maybe she's ready to take on husband number four.'

'Number five, I think.'

'Never.'

'First there was Gunter, who was killed in a hunting accident,' Cassy began counting them off on her fingers. 'Second there was Captain Rivers who was lost during an expedition up the Amazon. I think some wild animal ate him or he died of a fever, I can't remember which. Number three was Harcourt Fulford-Browne who died of apoplexy and number four was the Italian gigolo. You know all about Leonardo.'

'Four husbands,' Lottie said, shaking her head. 'I doubt if I'll even marry once.'

Cassy was about to shovel coal onto the fire in the parlour but she stopped, staring at her friend in surprise. 'Why would you say that, or even think such a thing?'

Lottie shrugged her slender shoulders. 'I'm what they call a bluestocking. Gentlemen don't like clever women.'

'Who told you that, Miss Solomon?'

Cassy turned with a start to see Oliver standing in the doorway. 'Ollie, you shouldn't be eavesdropping,' she said, noting the flush that coloured Lottie's cheeks. She could sense her friend's embarrassment as if it were her own. The bond that they had developed during their school years was too strong to be broken now that they were approaching womanhood. She loved Lottie as if she were her own sister. 'You should have said something,' she added.

'I did,' Oliver retorted unabashed. 'I said . . .'

'I know what you said.' Cassy cut him short. 'What

do you want anyway? I thought you were going to meet your friend Captain Peters.'

'Not today, my sweet. Peters is attending some boring charity function in the City, run by an ex-army officer who set up a hospital for wounded soldiers or some such thing. He invited me to go, but it sounded deadly dull, although the ball this evening might prove entertaining. Anyway, I'm at a loose end at the moment and there's nothing I'd enjoy more than to sit by the fire on a bleak December day and take afternoon tea with two beautiful young ladies.'

Lottie rose to her feet. 'I really should go home. Pa will worry if I don't get back before dark.'

Oliver held up his hand. 'No, I insist that you take tea with us, Miss Solomon. I went out earlier and bought some muffins, which hopefully Mrs Wilkins will have toasted to perfection. You must stay and I will see you safely home later, if you agree.'

Lottie glanced at Cassy, her slanting black eyebrows raised in a silent question.

'Yes, do stay,' Cassy said, tossing coal onto the fire and clambering to her feet. 'I'll fetch the tea things while you chat to Oliver. Perhaps you can teach him some manners.'

'I hear you're training to be a doctor, Miss Solomon,' Oliver said, motioning her to resume her seat. 'I'm impressed by your courage and determination. I'd say if you were a fellow and a soldier, you'd make general before you were thirty.'

'It might be easier than trying to break into the male

world of the medical profession,' Lottie said, smiling up at him.

Satisfied that peace was restored, Cassy left the room and made her way down the back stairs to the basement kitchen where she found Bailey and Freddie divesting themselves of their outdoor garments. 'Is your friend still here?' Bailey asked as he unwound Freddie's muffler and draped it over a chair. 'She's a nice girl, Cass. Clever too.'

'Lottie's staying for tea. Ollie insisted on it, having embarrassed her so much that she was ready to leave there and then.' Cassy took a plate of buttered muffins from the range where Mrs Wilkins had left them to keep warm. 'We'll miss these treats when you and Ollie go back to your regiment.'

'It's a crying shame they have to leave so soon,' Mrs Wilkins said, placing the teapot and hot water jug on a large wooden tray. 'It's livened the place up having two young gentlemen to stay.'

'You're a brick, Mrs W,' Bailey said, giving her a hug. 'I'm going to adopt you to be my mother, and send you violets on Mothering Sunday, when I'm in England, of course.'

'You and your soft soap,' Mrs Wilkins said, chuckling. 'Get on with you, Bailey. You'll have forgotten about us the moment you set foot on that boat back to India.'

'Never,' he said, clutching his hand to his chest. 'My heart will stay here in London with all of you.' He was smiling but Cassy knew that he meant every word he said.

'I wish you didn't have to go,' she murmured. 'And I wish this horrible war with the Afghans would end soon so that you can all come home.' She picked up the tray, but Bailey took it from her hands.

'Amen to that,' he said softly. 'I haven't forgotten my promise to look after you, Cass.'

'Me too,' Freddie cried, grasping Bailey's coat tails. 'Don't forget me.'

'As if I would, young 'un. Go on ahead and open the door, and maybe there's a poke of toffee in my pocket for you.'

'You spoil that boy,' Mrs Wilkins said in a sombre voice. 'I dunno what he'll do when you go. He'll take it bad, mark my words.' She slumped down on her chair by the range. 'Wars,' she muttered as they left the room. 'It men's madness.'

As they reached the top of the stairs, Bailey allowed Freddie to search for the toffees and he sent him back to the kitchen with a promise to read him a story after supper.

'You do spoil him,' Cassy said, smiling. 'He really looks up to you, Bailey.'

'He's a good boy. I won't let him down, nor you neither, Cass.'

'We'll be together some day soon, like a real family,' she said softly. 'When the war is over we'll find a house and take in youngsters like Freddie, and give them a proper home. Not like old Biddy's dreadful baby farm in Three Herring Court.'

'Is that what you want? For us to be a family?'

'Of course,' she said, surprised. 'It's what we've

always planned, isn't it? You're my dear brother and I love you, like always.' She opened the door and preceded him into the parlour. 'I hope Ollie hadn't been boring you with army stories, Lottie.'

Lottie shook her head. 'No, he's been most entertaining.' She glanced up at Bailey. 'Is something wrong? You look as if you've lost a shilling and found sixpence.'

'No, it's nothing,' Bailey said, curving his lips into an attempt at a smile. 'I just realised that our leave is nearly over and we'll be returning to the battlefield as soon as Christmas is out of the way.'

'And we're going to make the most of every minute,' Oliver said, taking the plate of muffins and offering them to Lottie. 'I say, I've just had a thought.'

'There's always a first time for everything,' Cassy said, chuckling.

'I'll ignore that, miss.' Oliver took a muffin before returning the plate to the tray. He bit into it chewing thoughtfully. 'What say we take the girls to the charity ball, Moon?'

Bailey almost choked as he sipped his tea. 'You're joking.'

Oliver shook his head, his eyes bright with mischief. 'Not at all. Peters gave me an open invitation, and we have two lovely young ladies with time on their hands. What about it, Miss Solomon, or may I call you Lottie?'

She shot a questioning glance at Cassy. 'You may call me Lottie, but I really should be going home now.'

'But you'd like to go to a ball, wouldn't you?' Oliver gave her his most disarming smile. 'One might say it was your patriotic duty to accompany two gallant soldiers to a charity function.'

Cassy frowned. 'That's not fair, Ollie.'

'War isn't fair, my dear,' Oliver said, adopting a sepulchral tone.

'Hold on, sir,' Bailey protested. 'Perhaps Lottie doesn't want to accompany you to the ball, and even more likely, her father might disapprove of such a jaunt.'

'And I haven't anything to wear,' Cassy protested. 'I'm not Cinderella. I haven't got a fairy godmother to turn a pumpkin into a coach and conjure up a ball gown from nothing.' She glanced over her shoulder as the door opened and her mother glided into the room.

'What's the matter?' Belinda asked, eyeing them curiously. 'It sounds as though you were having an argument. Is there anything I can do to help?'

'You could produce two ball gowns, Belle,' Oliver said lightly. 'I wanted to take the girls to a charity ball this evening, but they say they haven't anything to wear.'

Belinda smiled. 'I think it's a splendid idea. After all, Cassy, tomorrow is your birthday. I've been racking my brains trying to think of something we could do to celebrate, and this might be just the thing.'

'But Ma, I can't go in rags,' Cassy said, lifting her skirt to demonstrate the patch just above the hem.

'And I have nothing suitable,' Lottie added. 'I'd have to ask my pa, and I'm not certain he'd allow me to go.'

'He might if I asked him,' Belinda said thoughtfully.

'As to the gowns, I have two that I couldn't bear to leave behind in Duke Street. I was going to take them to the pawnshop so that I could buy Cassy a present for her seventeenth birthday, but I think this might be a better use for them.'

Cassy and Lottie exchanged eager glances. 'It might be fun,' Cassy whispered.

'If your mother could speak to my pa, he might let me go.'

'My dear Lady Belle, how can I refuse when you put it that way?' Eli spoke with obvious sincerity. 'You've been kind to my Charlotte, and I can't deny her this chance to enjoy herself. She works so hard at her studies.'

'I'm sure she does,' Belinda agreed. 'My stepson will look after her and bring her home when the ball is over.' She sent a warning look to Cassy and Lottie as they whooped with delight.

'Alas, they grow up too soon,' Eli said, sighing. 'I know my daughter must move on, but her leaving has left a gap in my life that only another parent could understand.'

Cassy shifted nervously from one foot to the other. She thought for a terrible moment that Mr Solomon was going to change his mind and withdraw his permission.

'I do sympathise, Eli,' Belinda said gently. 'And we owe you a debt of gratitude for the way you took us into your home. I realise you might not celebrate Christmas as we do, but perhaps you could stretch a point and accompany us to Whitegate Farm in East Ham. Mr Mullins has invited all of us to join him for Christmas dinner, and I know he would be only to happy if you and your daughter would join us.'

'Oh, please say yes, Pa,' Lottie said clapping her hands. 'I've never visited the countryside, and I don't have to return to my studies until after Christmas.'

Eli took Belinda's hand and raised it to his lips. 'You're very kind, Lady Belle. We would be happy to accept, providing the gentleman has no objections.'

'I'm sure he won't mind. And can I take it that Lottie is allowed to go to the ball? It is a sort of birthday present for Cassy, after all.'

'Please say yes, Pa,' Lottie urged. 'I'll work twice as hard when I get back to my studies.'

Eli took off his glasses and polished the lenses on a scrap of cloth. Without them he looked suddenly small and defenceless. Cassy had to resist the urge to give him a hug. He nodded his head. 'Go and enjoy yourself with my blessing, dear one.'

Outside in the street, Bailey was waiting for them in a hackney carriage. 'How did it go?'

'Pa said yes,' Lottie cried excitedly. 'I'm allowed to go to the ball, and we've been invited to join you for Christmas at the farm.'

'I do hope Farmer Mullins doesn't mind,' Belinda said, climbing into the cab with Bailey's assistance. She arranged her skirts around her, making room on the seat for Cassy. 'I felt so sorry for poor Eli, left on his own. He needs a good woman to look after him when you are at your studies, Lottie, but you can't give your

338

life up for your father, it wouldn't do at all. You're destined for great things, my dear.'

'I don't know,' Lottie said doubtfully. 'Being a bluestocking isn't much fun. The male medical students either tease me or ignore me. They've made it quite plain that they resent my being there.'

'All the more reason to stick to your guns,' Bailey said firmly. 'You'll show them, Lottie. I know you will.'

An hour after they arrived back in Pedlar's Orchard, Cassy and Lottie descended the narrow staircase to find Oliver and Bailey resplendent in their uniforms and eager to be off.

'Cassy, you look absolutely spiffing,' Oliver said enthusiastically.

'And you don't look in the least like a bluestocking, Miss Charlotte.' Bailey bowed from the waist. 'It's a pity those medical students won't be at the ball to see you in your finery.'

'Who knows,' Cassy said, tucking her hand into his arm. 'They might be there and you'll knock them skywise and crooked, Lottie.'

'Such vulgar parlance, Miss . . .' Oliver stopped short, turning to give Belinda a questioning glance. 'If it's a formal do we'll have to be announced and I don't know Cassy's surname.'

'She used to say she was Cassy Moon when we were nippers,' Bailey muttered, glaring at Oliver. 'And I knew her long before you did.'

Cassy's smile faded. It was a question that had bothered her for a long time and one which she could never quite put out of her mind. She looked to Belinda for an answer, but her mother's expressive face was shuttered, as if a door had closed on her soul. 'Perhaps it would be easier to use Davenport, for now,' she suggested vaguely. 'We are a family, are we not?'

'Of course we are,' Cassy said before Oliver had a chance to comment. She sensed that there was something deeper behind her mother's casual words, but this was neither the time nor the place to pursue the matter. 'Davenport it is then. Even you should remember that, Ollie, unless you forget your own name.'

Oliver set his shako on his head, proffering his arm to Lottie. 'There have been times when I've been celebrating a little too heartily that I couldn't remember who I was, but tonight won't be one of them. Shall we go, ladies? Our carriage is outside and no doubt the cabby will be adding the waiting time onto the fare.'

Cassy was about to follow them but Bailey caught her by the wrist. 'Wait a moment, Cass. I've got something for you.' He put his hand in his pocket and drew out a small package wrapped in brown paper. 'I was going to give it to you tomorrow, but I'd rather you opened it now.' He laid it in her upturned palm. 'Happy birthday, Cassy.'

She caught her breath as she peeled back the paper to reveal a silver locket on a wisp of a chain. 'Oh, Bailey, it's beautiful. It's the best present I ever had. Thank you so much.' She stood on tiptoe to kiss him on the cheek. 'Will you fasten it for me, please? I'm so excited, I'm all fingers and thumbs.'

*   *   *

340

The journey to the Guildhall passed quickly enough in the confines of the hackney carriage with Oliver and Bailey vying with each other to determine which one could be the most amusing. Cassy could feel excitement bubbling up inside her like a mountain spring as she sat beside Bailey, nervously clutching his hand as she had done when they were children and they were faced with a difficult situation. What if she were to trip over the long skirts of her borrowed gown? What if she said the wrong thing to one of the eminent personages present? What if they saw through the thin veneer of manners and fine clothes and saw the girl who had been raised in Three Herring Court? She might be Lady Davenport's daughter, but when all was said and done she had been born on the wrong side of the blanket, and of mixed blood. Would the great and the good turn their backs on her? She squeezed Bailey's fingers and he turned his head to give her an encouraging smile. Dear Bailey, she thought, my loving brother. What would I do without you?

'We're here,' Oliver said, opening the window and leaning out. 'Just look at that, girls. They've laid the red carpet out for us.' He leapt out, barely giving the cabby time to draw his horses to a halt, and he handed Lottie out and then Cassy. He turned to Bailey as he stepped down onto the pavement. 'Pay the cabby, Moon.'

With Cassy on one arm and Lottie on the other, Oliver led them into the Guildhall while Bailey settled with the cabby. Cassy smothered a gasp of surprise and awe. Never in her life had she seen anything as grand or as imposing as the Great Hall with its Gothic arched roof and stained-glass windows. The huge room seemed like a cathedral to Cassy's inexperienced eyes, and it was packed with elegantly dressed couples standing in groups, conversing sociably. The hum of voices rose to echo off the high ceiling and in the background there was the sound of the orchestra tuning up. The air was heavy with the mixed scents of hothouse flowers and expensive perfume, with the occasional waft of champagne cup laced with out-of-season strawberries.

She glanced up at Oliver but he was scanning the faces in the crowd. He raised his hand and waved. 'Peters, you old dog,' he said cheerfully as a young officer wove his way between the couples to join them. 'We made it after all.'

'So you did, Davenport, and you brought two charming companions, I see.'

'Ladies, may I present Captain Horatio Peters of the 13th Hussars,' Oliver said with a degree of formality. 'Peter, this is my sister Cassy and her friend, Miss Charlotte Solomon.'

'How do you, Miss Davenport, Miss Solomon?' Captain Peters bowed from the waist. 'It's Horry, if you please. Horatio might have been a suitable name for our great hero, but I am not he.'

Cassy liked the way his eyes twinkled and the humorous quirk of his lips when he smiled. She giggled, but receiving a frown from Ollie she lowered her gaze and bobbed a curtsey. 'How do you do, Captain Horry?'

'Just Horry, Miss Davenport.'

His undeniable good looks and easy charm made Cassy feel quite light-headed, but she was determined to be on her best behaviour. 'And this is Lottie,' she said, giving Lottie a gentle nudge so that she had no choice but to step forward.

'How do you do?' Lottie blushed as Captain Peters raised her hand to his lips.

'I'm honoured to make your acquaintance, Lottie.'

'Enough of this nonsense,' Oliver said impatiently. 'I could do with a drink and a cigar. Moon, look after the ladies while Peters and I go in search of refreshment.'

'Where are you manners, Davenport?' Captain Peters demanded as the orchestra struck up the grand march. 'May I have the pleasure of the first dance, Cassy?'

Bailey moved to her side and she met his questioning look with a reassuring smile. 'Don't worry,' she whispered. 'I'm quite capable of looking after myself.' She allowed Peters to lead her onto the dance floor, and after a few false steps she began to relax. The grand march gave way to a gavotte and Peters showed no sign of wanting to relinquish his partner, and Cassy was beginning to enjoy herself. She was glad that she had paid attention to the rather boring dancing lessons in Miss North's academy, when the girls had to partner each other and Miss North's aged mother accompanied them, playing the pianoforte as if she had two left hands.

Oliver had been whirling Lottie round the floor with more energy than expertise, and as the dance ended the two couples made their way back to their table where Bailey had glasses of champagne cup waiting for them. As Peters held out Cassy's chair and thanked her for being a perfect partner, Bailey eyed him askance, but if he had any criticisms of his superior officer he kept them to himself. Cassy sipped her drink slowly, savouring every moment of this new and wonderful experience. She gazed in awe at the beautiful gowns worn by ladies who in ordinary circumstances might be described as plump, overly thin or even plain, but they all looked beautiful in their silks and satins with their jewels sparkling in the candlelight. The men were equally resplendent either in full dress uniform or severe black evening suits and crisply starched shirtfronts.

'Who is that?' Cassy whispered, nudging Ollie and pointing her fan in the direction of a man who had just entered the Great Hall. He was surrounded by people but there was something about him that made his presence notable.

'I don't know,' Oliver said casually. 'Never seen the fellow before. Who is it, Peters? You're the one who's into all this charity business.'

'That, Davenport, is the chap who started this particular charity. He bought a near derelict mansion in Stepney Green, and converted it into a home for badly injured soldiers who have no one to care for them.'

'A laudable deed,' Ollie said, serious for once. 'I've seen fellows survive with hideous wounds, but little prospect at home other than to sit on the streets and beg. I'd like to shake his hand. What's his name?'

'Captain Cade. I've only met him once before, but the pater is keen on supporting charities. He'd be here tonight but he's otherwise engaged.' Peters rose to his feet. 'May I get you another glass of champagne, ladies?'

Cassy shook her head. The bubbles had already gone to her head and she was feeling pleasantly muzzy. 'No, thank you, Horry.'

Lottie smiled and nodded. 'I'd like another glass, if you please.'

'A girl after my own heart.' Peters gave her a mock salute. 'I'm going to get something a bit stronger for myself. What about you, Davenport?'

Oliver pushed back his chair and stood up. 'I'll give you a hand, old boy. Moon will look after the girls.' He followed Peters, disappearing into the crowd.

'I'd like to meet Captain Cade,' Cassy said thoughtfully. 'I think he's done a splendid thing.'

, 'It looks as though he's been in the wars himself,' Lottie murmured. 'Look, Cassy, see how badly he limps and that terrible scar all down the left side of his face. Poor man, no wonder he feels for the wounded soldiers.' She turned to Bailey, who had been unusually silent. 'What do you think, Bailey? What would cause such an awful injury?'

'He might have been caught in the blast from a grenade, or it could have been hand-to-hand fighting. Cade must have seen active service. You don't get injuries like that from duelling.'

'Which is illegal anyway,' Cassy said, staring at the tall figure of Captain Cade. Despite his scars he was a handsome man who commanded attention. His hair was dark, almost black, with silver wings at his temples, and as he turned his head to speak to one of his companions Cassy could see the extent of his disfigurement. His eyes rested upon her for a brief moment, and she felt herself blushing. She looked away but she could not resist taking another peek at him, and she could have sworn that there was a smile lingering in his dark, almond-shaped eyes.

'I think he likes you,' Lottie whispered, nudging Cassy in the ribs. 'Be careful. My pa has warned me about older men liking young girls.'

Bailey slipped his arm around Cassy's shoulders. 'I'll see him off, Cass. You don't have to worry about old roués while I'm around.'

'He's coming this way,' Lottie said, her voice shaking with excitement. 'How thrilling. We're going to meet the great man. I've heard all about his work at the hospital.'

Bailey leapt to his feet, standing to attention as Cade approached them. His limp was pronounced and he walked with the aid of an ebony cane. He stopped at their table. 'At ease,' he said with a lopsided smile which made him look suddenly younger and more approachable. 'Good evening, ladies. I hope you are enjoying yourselves, although you seem to have been temporarily deserted.'

Cassy angled her head, staring at him in fascination. He must, she thought, have been an extremely handsome man before the injury that had left a livid white scar standing out against his olive skin. She experienced a sharp pang of sympathy and an overwhelming sense of fellowship. She knew better than most how hard it was to be just that bit different from everyone else. Her days of torment in school were gone but not quite forgotten. She smiled up at him as he turned to her with a question in his eyes. 'I'm having a lovely time, and I think your charity is doing wonderful work. If I had any money I would willingly give it to you.'

He threw back his head and laughed, causing a ripple of interest amongst the people nearest to them. There was a hush as they waited for him to reply, and it was only then that Cassy realised she was talking to someone highly respected and of considerable importance.

'May I know your name?' Cade asked. 'I don't recall seeing you at any of our previous functions.'

Bailey laid his hand on Cassy's shoulder, but she met his anxious gaze with a slight shake of her head. She was not afraid of Captain Cade. 'My name is Cassandra Davenport, and this is my friend Charlotte Solomon, and my very dear friend and brother, Bailey Moon.'

'Corporal Moon, sir,' Bailey said, snapping to attention and saluting.

'As I said before, at ease, Corporal. You're not on duty now.' Cade extended his hand. 'So you're Miss Davenport's brother?'

Shyly, Bailey shook his hand. 'Not exactly, sir. But we grew up together and I've always tried to look after Cassy.'

'I'm sure you do very well on that score.' Cade

347

inclined his head. 'It's been a pleasure talking to you, Miss Davenport, and to you, Miss Solomon. I hope you enjoy the rest of your evening.' He was about to walk away, but he hesitated, turning back to give Cassy a long look. 'If you are genuinely interested in my work, I would be delighted to show you round the institution, and you also, Miss Solomon. The men are always cheered by the sight of a pretty face.' He walked away and was instantly claimed by a group of people patently eager for his attention.

'What a charming man,' Lottie breathed, clasping her hands to her bosom. 'I would love to work for someone like him if I ever qualify as a doctor.'

'He's a bit too charming for my liking,' Bailey muttered. 'I don't trust him and I didn't like the way he was looking at you, Cass.'

'Don't be silly, it wasn't like that.' Cassy had spoken more sharply than she intended, and she could see by the stubborn set of Bailey's jaw and the small nerve twitching at the edge of his lips that he was going to argue. 'If you say another word I won't speak to you for the rest of the evening, Bailey Moon.'

'I'm sorry, Cass,' he said, reaching out to hold her hand. 'Maybe I overreacted a bit.'

'I should just think you did.'

'Dance with me then? I can do the polka and I promise I won't tread on your toes.'

Her momentary flash of anger forgotten, Cassy smiled. 'If you ruin Ma's only pair of satin slippers she'll never forgive you.' She rose to her feet. 'Will you be all right left on your own, Lottie?'

'I can see Oliver heading this way,' Lottie said, smiling. 'Perhaps he'll ask me to dance.'

'It seems he's lost Peters,' Bailey said, leading Cassy into the dance. 'I don't trust that fellow.'

'You don't trust anyone.'

'You don't know anything about men, Cass. You're a beautiful young woman and you have to watch out for men who'll take advantage of your innocence.'

'No one could have a better brother than you, but you mustn't worry. I'm not stupid, Bailey.'

He spun her into a turn making conversation impossible as they executed the energetic steps of the polka, but halfway through the dance Peters appeared as if from nowhere to tap Bailey on the shoulder. 'My dance, I think, Corporal,' he said.

'I think not, sir.' Bailey tightened his hold on Cassy as if fearing that Peters would wrest her from him. 'Cassy promised this one to me.'

Peters pushed his face close to Bailey's. 'Are you daring to argue with a superior officer, Moon?'

For a moment, Cassy thought that Bailey was going to challenge Peters' authority. She knew little about army regulations but she had seen enough to realise that Bailey was in no position to argue. She broke free from his grasp, giving him a warning look. 'It's all right, Bailey.' She allowed Peters to take her in his arms, although he was holding her much too close and she could detect the smell of strong spirits on his breath. He was dancing at a wild pace, pushing through the other dancers and incurring angry words from the gentlemen, but Peters seemed oblivious to anything other than his desire to dance her off her feet. Breathless and dizzy, Cassy realised too late that he had guided her into an alcove at the far end of the hall, away from the main body of dancers. She tried to push him away but he had her banded in arms of steel. His breath reeked of brandy and the buttons of his uniform were cutting into her flesh. 'Let me go, Captain Peters. This isn't the behaviour of a gentleman.'

He gave a throaty laugh and pressing her against a marble pillar, claiming her mouth with a brutal kiss that almost suffocated her. She struggled with all her might, turning her face away and gasping for air, but he clamped his hand behind her head and forced her lips open with his tongue. She was dimly aware of his fingertips caressing her slender neck and shoulders, but she was close to panic when he slipped his hand beneath her bodice to cup her left breast. Beating at him with her clenched fists her attempts to kick him were hampered by her voluminous skirts. He drew back his head, looking drunkenly into her eyes. 'Don't tell me you've never been kissed before, you little doxy. We all know what girls like you really want.'

'Get off me, you brute,' Cassy hissed furiously. 'If you don't let me go this instant I'll scream.'

Chapter Nineteen

'If you don't let her go, Peters, you'll find yourself on a charge and I'll be more than happy to report you. I may no longer be a serving officer but I know your commander well.'

Peters released Cassy with a startled grunt. 'Captain Cade, sir. It wasn't what you think. She's nothing but a cheap whore.' His eyes widened with surprise as Cade grabbed him round the throat and thrust him back against the pillar.

'She's little more than a child,' Cade said through clenched teeth.

'She led me on, sir. I swear it.'

'Get out of my sight before I do something I'll regret.' Cade let him go, wiping his hands together in disgust. His expression softened as he turned his attention to Cassy. 'Are you all right, Miss Davenport?'

Controlling her erratic breathing with difficulty, she managed to nod her head. 'I didn't lead him on, Captain. I did nothing to deserve such treatment.'

'She's lying,' Peters muttered, straightening his jacket. 'I know her sort.'

Cade rounded on him angrily. 'You don't deserve to wear that uniform, and if you continue in this vein I'll do my best to see that you are stripped of your rank and end up a foot soldier. You'll apologise to Miss Davenport and then you will leave or I'll have you thrown out.'

Peters stared down at his highly polished shoes. 'I apologise.'

'Sound as though you mean it.' Cade took a step closer to him and Peters shot a resentful glance at Cassy.

'I'm sorry. I was in the wrong and I apologise.'

Cade eyed him coldly. 'Now go. Explain yourself to her brother if you can.'

'He's not her brother,' Peters said venomously. 'She's his stepsister, and Davenport's father committed suicide having run into debt and ruined himself and his family. At least my family are all honourable.'

'There's always one black sheep,' Cade said, glaring at Peters as he strutted off like a disgruntled rooster. Taking a spotless white handkerchief from his pocket, he gave it to Cassy. 'Dry your eyes, and then I'll escort you back to your party, Miss Davenport. My carriage is at your disposal if you wish to go home.'

'I'm all right now, sir,' Cassy said, blowing her nose in the soft white Egyptian cotton. 'I don't want to make a fuss.' She dabbed her eyes and was about to return the hanky to its owner, but he smiled and shook his head.

'Keep it, my dear. You've had an unpleasant experience and you have every right to make a fuss, as you put it. Most young ladies would have had hysterics by now or fallen to the floor in a dead faint.'

His crooked smile brought a swift reaction from

Cassy and she felt suddenly at ease. 'I'm made of sterner stuff, Captain. But I want you to know that what Peters said was not the whole truth. I never really knew him but Ollie's father wasn't a bad man; he was just unlucky and unwise. My mother wouldn't have married Sir Geoffrey if he'd been the wrong sort.'

Cade paused, staring at her thoughtfully. 'Sir Geoffrey Davenport was your stepfather?'

'Yes, sir. Well, no, not exactly.' Cassy found herself floundering. 'It's a long story.'

'And it's getting late and you've had a trying time to say the least. I don't want to pry, Cassy. We'd best get you back to your friends before they start looking for you.'

The Great Hall was filled with music and reverberating with the sound of feet tapping out the rhythm of the dance on the polished floorboards. Cassy saw Lottie waltz past in Oliver's arms, and both of them were flushed with exertion and smiling as if they were enjoying themselves. They made a handsome couple, Cassy thought, as Cade escorted her to the table where Bailey was sitting alone, drumming his fingers on the white cloth. He leapt to his feet as they approached. 'Cassy, I was getting worried. Where've you been, and where is Peters?'

'Cassy will tell you in her own good time,' Cade said calmly. 'Let's just say that Captain Peters may be an officer but he's no gentleman. I'll send for my carriage and I suggest that you take her home when she feels able to make the journey to . . .' He paused, allowing the question to hang in the air.

'We live in Pedlar's Orchard,' Cassy said wearily as a wave of exhaustion threatened to swamp her. 'It's in Stepney, sir. Quite a way from here.'

Cade nodded. 'I know the area well. Take care of her, Corporal Moon.' He walked off, only to be accosted by an earnest-looking gentleman who appeared to have rather a lot to say for himself.

'What happened, Cass?' Bailey demanded anxiously. 'What did Peters do? I'll kill him if he's harmed you in any way.'

'No, Bailey. He didn't hurt me. He embarrassed and humiliated me but I'm fine, thanks to Captain Cade.' She uncurled her fingers and realised that she had been clasping his handkerchief as if it were a good luck talisman. 'It's his,' she murmured. 'I'll wash it and make certain that he gets it back.'

'You're feverish,' Bailey said, rising to his feet. 'I'll go and find Oliver and we'll take you home. Belle will know what to do for the best.'

'He was kind to me, Ma,' Cassy said sleepily as her mother tucked her up in bed. 'I don't know what would have happened if Captain Cade hadn't come along then.'

'Oliver and Bailey should have been keeping an eye on you,' Belinda said, pulling the coverlet up to Cassy's chin. 'And that Captain Peters should be shot for making advances to a girl of your age.'

'He said I led him on, but I didn't.' Cassy's eyelids felt heavy as the dose of laudanum did its work. 'I only danced with him, Ma.'

'He's a brute, and I owe Captain Cade a huge thank you,' Belinda said gently. 'Now go to sleep, darling. Forget all about Peters and tomorrow everything will look brighter.'

'Must wash his hanky and return it to him,' Cassy murmured, closing her eyes.

'That can wait until Monday, my dear. I'm sure that Captain Cade has more than one handkerchief to his name.'

On Monday morning the back yard was powdered with snow, and the iron latch on the outhouse door was slippery with frost. Inside the small brick building the warm air was filled with steam and the smell of lye soap. Cassy took the lid off the copper and dropped the handkerchief into the bubbling water to join the rolling mass of white linens. Mrs Wilkins would be out a little later to put the sheets and pillow-cases through the mangle before the final rinse, and it was Freddie's job to turn the handle, but Cassy could not wait that long and anyway the hanky was not badly soiled. She fished it out with wooden tongs and rinsed it in the stone sink, adding the blue bag to the water as she had seen Mrs Wilkins do a dozen times or more. Satisfied with her efforts, she returned to the kitchen where Freddie was finishing a bowl of porridge. He waved his spoon at her. 'What are you doing, Cassy?'

She ruffled his curly hair. 'None of your business, young man. Eat up or you'll be late for school.'

'He's got to help with the mangling first,' Mrs Wilkins

said, ladling porridge into a bowl. 'You seem a bit better today, miss. You looked quite peaky yesterday.'

Cassy spread the handkerchief over the brass rail on the range. 'I'm well, thank you. I was just a bit tired yesterday.'

'I heard all about it,' Mrs Wilkins said, pursing her lips. 'Nice carryings on I must say. It was lucky for you that nice gentleman come to your rescue.'

'This is his hanky. I've washed it and I need to iron it before I return it to him.'

Mrs Wilkins thrust a bowl of porridge into Cassy's hands. 'Eat your breakfast and I'll put the flat iron on the range. That fine material will dry quickly.' She fingered the hanky with a nod of approval. 'Best Egyptian cotton if I'm not mistaken. Your Captain Cade must be a gentleman of quality.'

'And he's old enough to be my father,' Cassy said, laughing. 'He's no knight in shining armour, but I'm sure he's very heroic and he was very kind to me.'

Mrs Wilkins searched in the cupboard and produced a flat iron which she placed on the range. 'My Albert was a hero, poor devil. He got hisself killed during a skirmish in the Khyber Pass in the first war against them Afghans. Poor Bert, he weren't much of a husband, but he was a good soldier. Eat up, Freddie. You've got work to do afore you goes to school.'

'I'm going to be a soldier like Bailey,' Freddie announced proudly. 'He's a hero, he told me so.'

'Aye, and he'll be gone as soon as Christmas is over,' Mrs Wilkins said grimly. 'They're all the same these military men, here one minute and gone the next. How we'll manage without their money, I don't know.'

'I don't want him to go away.' Freddie's bottom lip trembled.

Cassy could see that he was close to tears. 'He'll be home again before you know it, Freddie,' she said, hoping she sounded more confident than she was feeling. 'The war can't go on forever.'

An hour later, Cassy was standing outside the Home for Wounded Soldiers in Stepney Green. It was only a few minutes' walk away from Pedlar's Orchard but the deepening snow had slowed her progress and the pavements were treacherous underfoot. She gazed up at the Georgian façade of the four-storey building, and felt suddenly and unaccountably nervous. She braced her shoulders; after all, she was only going to return a cotton handkerchief and thank a gentleman for an act of kindness. She raised the iron ring of the doorknocker and let it fall on the metal plate. The resounding clang seemed to reverberate throughout the building and it was answered almost immediately by the clatter of footsteps. The door was opened by a middle-aged woman wearing a white cap and a grey gown with a starched white collar and cuffs. 'Can I help you, miss?'

Cassy cleared her throat nervously. 'I'd like to see Captain Cade.'

'If you've come about the position of scullery maid, it's been filled.'

357

'No, I haven't. I mean I didn't know there was a vacancy. It's a personal matter.'

The woman sniffed and shrugged her shoulders. 'You'd best come in then. Wait here.' She scuttled off, disappearing down a long passageway, leaving Cassy standing in the vestibule. She waited for a good five minutes, shifting nervously from foot to foot. The sound of male voices came from deep within the building with the occasional burst of laughter, which she found surprising. She had imagined the home to be a dark and dismal place filled with moans and groans and the smell of disinfectant. The reality seemed to be quite different and the atmosphere was one of a comfortable and reasonably well-to-do home. The wallpaper in the entrance hall was surprisingly exotic with a pattern of golden lilies and warm orange tones. The floorboards were polished until they shone like horse chestnuts, and the aroma of freshly baked bread wafted from the basement kitchen. The hands on the long-case clock moved almost imperceptibly but Cassy was beginning to think that she had been forgotten when she heard the tapping sound of Cade's ebony cane on the bare boards. She went to meet him, feeling suddenly shy as she held out the freshly laundered handkerchief. 'I came to return this, Captain.'

He took it from her, acknowledging its return with a slight inclination of his head. 'I wouldn't have expected you to venture out in the snow simply to return a handkerchief, Miss Davenport.'

'I wanted to thank you for saving me from an

embarrassing situation. I still don't know quite how it happened.'

Cade's serious expression melted into a lopsided smile. 'If I were being kind I'd put it down to Captain Peters' youthful folly and too much brandy, but if I was your father I wouldn't be so charitable and I would probably want to horsewhip the bounder.'

The humorous glint in his eyes belied his stern tone and Cassy responded with a chuckle. 'Then it's as well that we are not related, sir. Anyway, I am very grateful and I'm sorry to have taken up so much of your time.' She turned and was about to leave but he called her back.

'Miss Davenport, I seem to remember that you voiced an interest in my work here. I believe I promised to show you round.'

Cassy hesitated. 'I would like that, but only if you have the time.'

'I have plenty of time. Come with me and meet some of the brave men who have had to combat crippling disabilities as well as pain and suffering.'

If she had thought about it at all, Cassy had vaguely imagined that Cade's wounded soldiers would be lying in bed, heavily bandaged and reliant on nurses for all their needs. But the reality was far different as he showed her round the premises. There was a large communal dining room, where long tables were laid in readiness for the midday meal. A vase filled with jewel-coloured chrysanthemums added its spicy aroma to the fragrant scent of pine from the logs burning in the grate. A cursory glance at the table settings revealed attention to detail that even the most particular hostess would appreciate. The glassware and cutlery had been polished until they shone and starched white table napkins were folded neatly at each place.

'We try to make it as much like home as possible,' Cade said as he led her across the hallway into the drawing room. 'This is where the men come when they want to relax.'

Cassy gazed round the large room and could not help but be impressed. Every effort seemed to have been made to make the establishment welcoming and homely. Comfortable-looking armchairs were dotted around in groups and two large sofas faced each other on either side of the fireplace. The Turkey red carpet and emerald-green curtains gave the room a masculine look, and the walls were hung with pictures. She studied the paintings with interest, and was even more impressed when Cade explained that they had been painted by men who had discovered hidden artistic talents. 'Most of them are in a bad way when they first arrive. It takes many months for the worst cases to recover their former spirit. We find that music often helps to heal the mental wounds they bear with such stoicism,' he said, following Cassy's gaze as she spotted a pianoforte standing in the far corner of the room. 'Do you play the piano, Miss Davenport?'

She shook her head. 'No, at least not very well. We had lessons at school but I'm afraid I have no talent for music.'

He acknowledged this admission with a smile and a slight shrug of his shoulders. 'But you like to read?'

She glanced at the bookshelves which occupied a whole wall and the piles of magazines and periodicals on a table beneath one of the tall windows. 'Yes, but we had to leave the books and everything else in Duke Street. We can't afford luxuries like that now.' Cassy stopped, biting her lip. She could not think why she had allowed such an admission to slip. She felt the colour rise to her cheeks and she picked up a chess piece from a set laid out on a small table. 'I'm sure the men are extremely comfortable here,' she murmured, changing the subject.

'Some of the men will never leave here as they have nowhere else to go and no one to care for them. Others will leave as soon as they are fit enough to earn their own living. Come with me and you can see the workrooms.'

'I thought it would be like a hospital,' Cassy said as they went from room to room on the ground floor. She listened intently as Cade explained that the men were being helped to rebuild their lives by mastering new skills or simply relearning old ones which had been made almost impossible by their injuries.

From a window overlooking the garden at the back of the house, he pointed to the washhouse where smoke belched from the chimney and trickles of steam escaped through gaps in the door. 'We do everything we can to help the men return to as normal a way of living as possible. Those who are able work in the laundry, and we grow our own vegetables and fruit. Some of them choose to work in the kitchen, and we encourage those who show promise to find work in hotel kitchens, or take up positions in large houses. Part of the charity is set up to find households willing to take on men who would in general be overlooked by other employers.'

Cassy felt her throat constrict as she watched a young man attempting to paint a picture using his left hand, when he was obviously right-handed but had lost that arm below the elbow. He was frowning and holding the tip of his tongue between his teeth as he concentrated. He looked up at her and grinned. 'Don't think it'll ever get in the Royal Academy, miss.'

She moved closer, studying the work with a critical eye, realising instinctively that fulsome praise would not be welcome. 'I'd think I was clever if I could do half as well.'

He angled his head. 'Ta, miss. I take that as very encouraging. If I had both me legs I'd stand up and give you a kiss, but as you see I'm waiting for me peg to be made.'

Cassy looked down and realised with a sickening feeling in her stomach that his right leg had been amputated below the knee. She felt the colour drain from her face but she forced her lips into a smile. 'I'll keep you to that when we meet again.'

'I should have me peg leg in time for Christmas, miss. I'll make certain we've got a big bunch of mistletoe.'

'I think Miss Davenport might have other commitments on Christmas Day, Jack,' Cade said, patting him on the back.

Cassy met the young soldier's gaze and saw pain, cynicism and a hint of despair in their blue depths.

Suddenly she was seeing Bailey sitting there, terribly disabled and needing to feel that he was still a man. 'I'll be here,' she said softly. 'And make sure you get the biggest bunch of mistletoe you can find.'

'That was kind, but you shouldn't make promises that you don't intend to keep,' Cade said as they left the room and made their way towards the entrance hall.

'But I will keep it. I meant every word I said, Captain. That poor boy deserves all the encouragement he can get if he's to survive outside this place. I know how hard life can be for people who are even slightly different from the rest, so how will it be for a young man like Jack? I'll come on Christmas morning, if you'll allow it.'

He acknowledged her words with a slight nod of his head. 'You're welcome here at any time, Cassy. Just the sight of a pretty face and a friendly smile will have worked on the men better than any tonic that a physician could prescribe.'

'But you can't go to that place on Christmas Day,' Flora said, pausing as she was about to close the parlour curtains against the darkness outside. 'What were you thinking of, Cassy? Mullins is expecting us at Whitegate Farm. Had you forgotten?'

'No,' Cassy said, meeting her angry gaze with a straight look. 'I hadn't forgotten, but I think this is more important. If you'd seen those poor men, you would want to do anything you could to make their lives more bearable.'

'It sounds as though this Captain Cade fellow is doing well enough without your help,' Flora snapped. 'Really, Cassy, I won't have my arrangements put out because you want to play angel of mercy.'

'That's not fair.' Belinda looked up from darning one of Oliver's socks. 'Cassy is following her conscience and I think she should be allowed to do as she pleases.'

'You were always too soft, Belle.' Flora went to sit by the fire, holding her hands out to the blaze. 'I say we should take care of our own. After all, Oliver and Bailey will be sailing for India on the Friday after Christmas, and we should make certain they have happy memories of home. Never mind fussing around after strangers.'

'I understand what you're saying, Flora, but I think Cassy must do what she thinks is right.'

'I can come on later,' Cassy said, fingering the silver locket that hung round her neck, which she had made a vow not to take off until Bailey was safely home again. 'Perhaps I could travel with Lottie and Mr Solomon. I believe he said he was going to hire a dog cart for the day.'

Flora twitched her shoulders and her mouth drooped at the corners, a sure sign that she intended to have the last word. 'We would be in a sorry plight without the money that Mullins pays me for his lessons, not to mention the gifts of eggs, meat and poultry. He may be a yeoman but he's a good man and should be given the respect he deserves.' She rose to her feet and flounced out of the room.

'Well,' Cassy said. 'I think she has a soft spot for Mr Mullins.'

'I believe you're right,' Belinda said with a smile that brought the dimples to her cheeks. 'But we've grown to rely on his generosity, and once the boys have gone we'll need every penny we can get. It's going to be a long, hard winter, Cassy.'

'I'll find work, Ma. I should have been out looking instead of gallivanting about with Oliver and Bailey.'

'You're young, my love. You deserve to have a bit of fun and the boys are only here for a short time. I'll put an advertisement in the newspaper offering my services to ladies who wish to learn etiquette and deportment. With a few more clients I can make up for the loss of your earnings in the pub, and I don't want you to go back to that sort of place. It isn't for a girl like you, Cassy.'

Cassy frowned. 'Who am I really, Ma? I was a servant, and then I was educated like a young lady. I'm your daughter but I'm not a Davenport, and at the ball the other night it was even more obvious that I'm not like the other girls. Would Captain Peters have treated me like that if he'd thought I was a lady?'

Belinda dropped the sock and clasped both Cassy's hands, looking deeply into her eyes. 'You are yourself, my dear sweet daughter. And your suffering was caused by my youthful folly, for which I'll never forgive myself, but your father was a good man and I loved him with all my heart. If he were here now he'd dispel all the doubts your have about yourself.'

'Tell me about him, Ma. Who was he? What was his name?'

'I can't tell you, my darling. If I speak his name my heart will break all over again. I will love him until I die, but I beg of you don't ask me any more. It's my secret and it's too painful to share, even with you.'

Cassy wrapped her arms around her mother, and their tears mingled. 'I'm sorry,' Cassy whispered. 'I won't ever mention him again. You're my mother and I've found you; that's all that matters.'

The snow was several inches deep by Christmas morning and a pale primrose sun beamed down from a whitewashed sky. The roofs and pavements sparkled beneath its rays and a powdering of snow that had fallen during the night had temporarily covered the black slush churned up by horses' hooves and wagon wheels. After breakfast, when they had exchanged small gifts, Cassy set off for Stepney Green accompanied by Bailey who refused to let her go on her own. 'I want to see this place for myself,' he said with a stubborn lift of his chin. 'I know that Cade is well respected but we don't know anything about the men in his care.'

Walking along at his side, Cassy slipped her hand through the crook of his arm. 'From what I saw they're decent men who've suffered dreadful injuries. Captain Cade seemed to think it was a good idea, and I'm only going there to give Jack a kiss beneath the mistletoe.'

'What?' Bailey came to a sudden halt, staring at her in horror. 'You didn't mention that when you told your mother about the visit.'

A gurgle of laughter escaped from Cassy's lips and she squeezed his arm. 'It's only a peck on the cheek, Bailey. My virtue isn't in any danger.'

'Not with me at your side it isn't. I don't know what that fellow Cade was about when he agreed to such a thing.'

'Don't look so disapproving. When I saw poor Jack I thought that it could have been you or Ollie wounded and in need of someone to show that they cared about you.'

He patted her hand as it rested on his arm. 'I know you meant well and I'm being a bear, but I'm still coming with you. The slightest hint of disrespect and I'll soon put them in their place.'

'Come along then. It's only round the corner and if we don't hurry Mr Solomon and Lottie will call for us before we've had time to wish them a merry Christmas.' She tugged at his arm, laughing as their feet skidded on the frozen surface of the snow. 'It's like skating,' she giggled. 'You'll think of this when you're back in the heat of India.'

Bailey's hand tightened on her arm, and as she saw the muscles in his jaw tighten she felt a pang of remorse. The day after tomorrow she would have to say goodbye to him yet again. Bailey and Oliver would sail on the tide for a war in a far-off land that meant nothing to her. He would risk his life along with hundreds of other young men, some of whom would never return. Their time together was precious and she must not waste a second of it.

They arrived flushed and breathless and were

admitted by Cade himself. 'So you came,' he said. 'I wasn't sure if you'd remember.'

'Of course I did. I wouldn't let Jack down and I've brought my friend Bailey with me, as you can see.'

'We met at the ball, I believe, Corporal Bailey.'

'Yes, sir.' Bailey snapped to attention.

'There's no need for formality,' Cade said, smiling. 'It's many years since I was a serving officer. Come inside and meet some of the men. They've been looking forward to this for days, Cassy. I hope I may call you that as we're being informal.'

'Of course,' she said, gazing in admiration at the swags of holly and ivy that had been draped over picture frames and around the doorways. 'It looks very festive.'

'We try,' he said, leading the way to the drawing room. A gust of warm air and the tempting aroma of hot mince pies greeted them as they entered the room. The men who were able rose to their feet, and others whose injuries made it impossible for them to stand unaided began to clap their hands and cheer.

Overwhelmed and embarrassed by the sudden glare of attention, Cassy felt the blood rush to her cheeks. 'Merry Christmas,' she murmured.

Jack limped towards her leaning heavily on his crutches. He glanced upwards and following his gaze she saw a bunch of mistletoe hanging from the gasolier. She leaned forward and kissed him on the cheek, receiving a round of applause. 'How are you, Jack,' she asked shyly.

From his jacket pocket he produced a small picture

in a gilt frame, pressing it into her hand. 'Merry Christmas, miss. I done this one just for you.'

Her vision was blurred with tears as she gazed at the painting which was obviously meant to be a portrait of her. It was childish in execution but somehow he had managed to capture her likeness. Large doe-like eyes gazed back at her from an oval face and what it lacked in technical ability was more than compensated for by the way he had managed to capture a sense of tenderness and serenity. 'It's lovely,' she breathed. 'You are very clever, Jack. Thank you.' She showed it to Cade and then to Bailey, who nodded and agreed that it was a good effort.

'Sit down, miss,' Jack said, indicating an empty chair. 'You'll take a glass of Christmas cheer and a mince pie with us, I hope. Old Badger made them so I can't vouch for the pastry, but he does his best.'

This remark was received with a ripple of comments and laughter and an older man with a patch over one eye and two fingers missing off his left hand shuffled forward with a plate of mince pies. Cade served the punch and Cassy found herself besieged by well-wishers, all of them simply wanting to speak to her or to give her a whiskery kiss on the cheek. With Bailey standing close by her side and Cade watching their every move, not even the boldest amongst them would have said or done anything to embarrass her. She was beginning to enjoy herself when the housekeeper announced that Mr Solomon had come to collect the young lady. Reluctantly, Cassy said goodbye to her new friends, and she thanked Jack yet again for the painting.

'You will come again, won't you, miss?' he asked anxiously. 'You've really brightened out day.'

'I'm only sorry I haven't anything to give you in return for the lovely picture,' Cassy said with genuine regret.

'Just promise to come again and that'll be the best present ever. We hardly ever see a pretty face, let alone get the chance to touch a soft cheek.'

'Come on, Cass,' Bailey said, moving closer to her side. 'We'd best not keep Mr Solomon waiting out there in the cold.'

Cade followed them out into the vestibule where the front door had been left ajar and they could see Lottie seated alongside her father in the dog cart. 'Where is it you're going?' Cade asked, eyeing the rickety contraption and aged pony with a worried frown.

'To East Ham, Captain,' Bailey volunteered. 'Whitegate Farm, to be exact.'

'That's a long way to go in an open cart which has obviously seen better days, and the horse looks tired already.' He stepped outside and returned after a brief discussion with Eli. 'This isn't the weather to be travelling any distance in an open carriage,' he said by way of explanation. 'I've offered to take you in my barouche. I'll be happy to drive you there and bring you safely home.'

Lottie stepped inside the house rubbing her hands together. The tip of her nose glowed pink and she was shivering. 'Are you sure, Captain? We'd be most grateful but we don't want to impose on your good nature.'

'Yes,' Cassy added hastily. 'We can't take you away from your men on Christmas Day. It wouldn't be fair.'

Cade smiled and shook his head. 'By the time the punch bowl is empty they won't care who is there to serve them their turkey and Christmas pudding. My housekeeper will cope magnificently, as always, and I wouldn't think of allowing you to travel to the wilds of Essex in that contraption. I suggest you go into the small parlour where there is a fire burning and I'll send for the carriage.'

'I'm obliged to you, sir,' Eli said, having followed Lottie into the vestibule, 'but this is too much to ask of you, particularly on such a short acquaintance.'

'Nonsense,' Cade said genially. 'I feel like a jaunt into the country and I've given my coachman the day off to spend it with his family. I was wondering how I would spend the rest of the day, and this will give me a chance to get out of the city for a few hours.'

'I do hope that Flora and Mr Mullins won't mind,' Cassy whispered to Lottie as they settled themselves in the luxury of Captain Cade's barouche.

'One more won't make any difference,' Lottie said, leaning back against the leather squabs. 'I wonder what Bailey and the captain are talking about out there on the box.'

'Army men always have something in common,' Eli murmured, closing his eyes. 'It's been a busy week with so many orders to complete. Wake me up when we get there, Lottie my dear.'

There was little traffic on the roads, and, despite the

371

hard-packed snow, they arrived at Whitegate Farm in a little over an hour. Dora Cope let them into the farmhouse, taking their outer garments from them and hanging them on the oak hallstand. She glanced at Cade in some surprise and Cassy moved swiftly to his side. 'Mrs Cope, this is Captain Cade, who was kind enough to drive us here in his barouche.'

Cade inclined his head as he met Mrs Cope's curious gaze. 'If my presence here causes you any inconvenience, ma'am, I can take myself off to the local tavern and return at a given time.'

'I'll have to ask the master, sir.'

'What's this?' Mullins demanded, joining them with a welcoming smile almost splitting his face in two. 'Why do you keep our guests standing about in the hall, Dora? Come into the parlour, everyone, and have a glass of sherry wine before we have our dinner.'

'Luncheon, Mullins,' Flora said sternly as she emerged from the parlour to greet them. 'You took your time,' she added, and her eyebrows shot up as she spotted Cade. 'And who may you be, sir? I can see by your apparel that you aren't the coachman.' She rounded on Eli. 'I thought you were driving them in your cart?'

Faced with the fierce woman, Cade seemed unperturbed. 'I apologise for arriving uninvited, ma'am. I'm just about to leave.'

'No, please, don't go, Captain Cade.' Cassy turned to Farmer Mullins with a beseeching look. 'The captain was kind enough to drive us here in his barouche. He could have left us to travel in the dog cart and it's bitterly cold outside.'

'No, really, I'm quite happy to go to the tavern and wait,' Cade said pleasantly.

'What sort of fellow would I be to turn a man out in the snow?' Mullins demanded, shooting a warning look at Flora. 'You must stay, Captain. There's food enough to go round and plenty of room at my table.'

'Why are you all standing out here?' Belinda hurried from the parlour to hug Cassy. 'We were getting worried, darling. I thought you'd had an accident on the road, it's so treacherous . . .' She broke off, staring at Cade. Her eyes widened and her cheeks paled alarmingly, as if, Cassy thought, she had seen a ghost.

'Belle?' Cade's voice shook as he murmured her name and he stood perfectly still, as if rooted to the spot.

Moving like a sleepwalker she took a step towards him and collapsed in a dead faint.

Chapter Twenty

Belinda opened her eyes. At first she had no recollection of what had caused her to tumble into unconsciousness, but as the mists cleared from her brain she realised that she was lying on the sofa in Farmer Mullins' parlour. She struggled to raise herself on one elbow, but firm hands pressed her back against the cushions and Cassy held a glass to her lips.

'Sip this, Ma. It's only water.'

Obediently, Belinda allowed the sweet fresh spring water to slide down her throat. A sea of faces hovered above her but standing close behind Cassy she saw a tall man with one side of his face disfigured by a livid white scar. For a moment she wondered what a stranger was doing in their midst, and then the truth hit her once again like a bolt of lightning. She sat up straight, staring at him in wonderment. 'George,' she whispered. 'You've come back to me.'

Cassy turned to Cade with a worried frown. 'My mother isn't well, Captain. She must have mistaken you for someone else.'

'I thought I was dreaming,' Belinda murmured, unable to take her eyes off his face. Despite the disfigurement and the lines of suffering etched on his otherwise handsome face, she would have known him anywhere. 'Are you really here, George?'

'Who the hell is George?' Flora demanded crossly. 'What's going on, Belle? Have you lost your mind?'

Cade moved swiftly to kneel at Belinda's side. He took her hand gently and raised it to his lips. 'I'm here, Belle. It's a miracle. When Cassy told me a little of her history I thought it must be you, but I wasn't sure. I couldn't wait any longer to find out, which is why I came today. Can you forgive me for giving you such a shock?'

'What's this all about, Ma?' Cassy whispered, reaching out to clutch Bailey's hand.

Belinda heard her daughter's voice but the words were muffled by the beating of her own heart and the rhythmic sound of the blood drumming in her ears. She had no words for anyone other than the man whom she had believed to be dead for almost seventeen years. She raised her hand to touch his face, tracing the scar with the tip of her finger. She had thought at first that he was a phantom or a figment of her imagination, but the warmth of his breath on her face convinced her that he was a living being and he was there by her side, holding her hand. She gazed into his dark lustrous eyes and was lost in their depths. She could feel their souls uniting once again and the years fell away. 'I was told that you died,' she said softly. 'They said you'd been killed in action.'

'I was left for dead and when I eventually returned to my regiment I was told that you had married and gone to live in England. I never thought I would see you again, Belle.' He bowed his head and she felt his warm tears caress her flesh. She slid her arms around his neck. 'George, my dearest, darling George.' Holding him close, she looked up at Flora. 'Might we have some moments alone, please?'

For the first time since she had known her, Belinda saw her sister-in-law disconcerted and at a loss for words. Cassy was leaning against Bailey with her hand covering her mouth and her eyes wide with shock, and the others had moved to the doorway as if preparing to make a rapid exit.

'Please, Flora,' Belinda said again. 'I'll explain everything later.'

'Outside.' Flora recovered enough to shoo those lingering in the doorway from the room. 'I don't know what this is all about,' she added, grabbing Cassy by the arm, 'but I'm sure we'll find out in good time. That means you too, Ollie.' She hustled everyone into the hallway, closing the door behind them.

The room was strangely silent. All Belinda could hear was the ticking of the black marble clock on the mantelshelf and the crackling of the log fire. 'George,' she whispered. 'I can't believe it's you.'

He raised his head and his eyes were magnified by tears. 'My God, Belle. I thought I'd lost you forever.' He rose from his knees to sit beside her, enfolding her in his arms and holding her as if he would never let her go. 'I knew you had married Sir Geoffrey, and of course I heard that he had died. I even went to your house in South Audley Street but was told that Lady

Davenport no longer lived there. You seemed to have disappeared off the face of the earth and I had no way of discovering your whereabouts, until I met Cassy at the ball.'

Resting her hands on his chest, she could feel his heart beating in time with hers. It seemed as though the years had rolled away and they were young lovers stealing a few moments together in secret. She looked into his eyes, hardly daring to believe that the only man she had ever loved had been restored to her. It was, she thought, a Christmas miracle. 'It doesn't matter,' she whispered. 'Nothing matters now we're together again.'

He smoothed her tumbled blonde locks back from her forehead, brushing her eyelids with his lips, kissing her cheeks and finally claiming her mouth in a long and tender kiss. 'I love you, Belle. I've always loved you.'

'And I love you, George.' She raised her face, parting her lips and giving herself up to the rapture of his kiss. The scent of him was the same; the taste of him had not changed. He still had the power to make her go weak at the knees and forget everything except her desire for him. When he finally released her, she laid her head against his shoulder. 'What happened to you, my love? You were listed killed in action. It broke my poor heart and I thought I'd die too.'

'I was left for dead after a skirmish with local tribesmen. We were outnumbered and it was carnage, although I didn't know that at the time. We were close to the border and I remember very little of what followed, but somehow I managed to crawl away from the dead and dying to a place of relative safety amongst the rocks. I was found several days later, half dead, by a Pathan farmer who was searching for some of his goats that had strayed. He took me back to his tribe and they tended me as if I was one of their own, which of course I am, partly anyway, and speaking their language was an advantage. Gradually I began to recover, although for a time I was wracked with fever and it was many months before I could walk again. Eventually I made my way on foot back to the garrison only to discover that you were beyond my reach forever.'

'Oh, George, my darling, it wasn't what I wanted. In the end I had no choice.'

He clutched her hand to his heart. 'You thought I was dead. I wouldn't have expected you to give up your life for someone you would never see again.'

'You don't understand,' Belinda said softly. 'I was carrying your child, George.'

'Belle, if only I'd known.'

His voice cracked with emotion and she raised her hand to stroke his cheek. 'I didn't know myself until after the news came that you'd been killed. I wanted to die too but I had another life to consider. My father arranged the match and I had little choice but to agree to marry Sir Geoffrey. I gave birth to our daughter in Bombay and Mahdu cared for us both. She accompanied us to England and she found a woman in Cripplegate who promised to care for the baby as if she were her own.'

Cade looked deeply into her eyes, his lips parted in wonder. 'All these years I've had a daughter and I knew nothing of her existence.'

'She was the most beautiful thing I'd ever seen and it tore my heart in two when she was taken from me at only two months old. Sir Geoffrey was much older than me and he already had a son and heir. He didn't want any more children and he would never have married me had he known about my baby.'

Cade gripped her by the shoulders, his eyes searching her face. 'Do you mean to tell me that Cassy is my daughter?'

'Couldn't you tell just by looking at her, George? She is so obviously your child.'

He shook his head. 'I thought she must be Davenport's daughter, although somehow I think that deep down I knew the truth all along.'

'Cassy is ours, George. It almost killed me to give her to that woman, but I was able to send money to support her even though being married to Geoffrey meant that I could never see her. If I had gone to that terrible place in Three Herring Court I wouldn't have been able to leave without her, but Mahdu went there in my stead, once a year on Cassy's birthday under cover of darkness.'

A slow smile spread across his face. 'I can't believe that we're together at last, and that we have a wonderful daughter.'

'She's a remarkable girl. We only found each other a short while ago, but I wouldn't give her up for all the titles and wealth in the world. She is so like you, darling George. I wonder you didn't see it the first time you clapped eyes on her.'

'Something drew me to her that evening in the Guildhall. I thought she was the loveliest little thing I'd ever seen, and I wanted to protect her. Now I know why.' His smiled faded and his lips twisted as if he were in pain. 'How can I ever make it up to both of you? My suffering is as nothing to the pain I caused you and our daughter.'

'Ma?'

Cassy's voice from the doorway made Belinda turn her head, and Cade released her with a guilty start. She rose from the sofa, holding out her arms. 'Cassy, you must have guessed the truth by now.'

Cassy looked from one to the other, her puzzled frown fading into a look of wonderment. 'Are you telling me that he's my father?'

Belinda nodded her head, struggling to keep back tears of joy. 'It's a miracle, Cassy. He has come back to us. George is the man I've always loved and he is your father.'

'I had no knowledge of your existence, Cassy,' Cade said, eyeing her as if she were a fragile piece of glass that might shatter at any moment. Rising slowly to his feet, he hooked his arm around Belinda's shoulders. 'You can't imagine how happy this makes me. I loved your mother all those years ago and I love her now, more than ever, and I'll love you too, if you'll let me.'

Cassy's shuttered expression sent a shiver down Belinda's spine. She could not understand why her daughter was not as overjoyed as herself. The fairytale ending to their story seemed to be slipping from her grasp. 'George is your father, my darling. That's why I gave you his name.'

'I'm Cassy Lawson, not Cade.' Cassy tossed her head, staring at Cade with a challenge in her dark eyes.

They were so alike, father and daughter. There could be no doubting Cassy's parentage. Belinda could have cried with frustration. She opened her mouth to explain but, as if sensing her distress, George gave her shoulders a reassuring squeeze. 'My full name is George Cade Lawson,' he said quietly. 'But when I was at Sandhurst there were several Georges in my year and I was known by my middle name. The only people who ever called me George were my father and your mother. The memory of our love was sacred to me and it was too painful to hear others using my Christian name. When I first opened the home I became Captain Cade. It was never meant to deceive, it just came about.'

Belinda held her breath, but she could see that Cassy was shocked and wary as a stray cat faced with a new owner. 'Aren't you happy for me, darling?' she said anxiously. 'I know it will take time to get used to the idea, but we'll be a real family at last.'

'They're sitting at table,' Cassy said stonily. 'Aunt Flora sent me to tell you that Mr Mullins is carving the turkey.' Turning on her heel, she left the room.

Belinda made as if to follow her but Cade caught her by the wrist. 'Let her go, my love. Give her time to get used to the idea of having me as her father.' He pulled Belinda into his arms, gazing into her eyes. 'I can hardly believe it myself.'

His kiss was everything that Belinda had dreamed about and more. When they drew apart she met his tender gaze and saw the man she had fallen in love with all those years ago, unscarred and handsome. 'Never leave me again, George,' she murmured.

'I don't intend to, Belle. I'll get a special licence and we can be married next week, if you agree.'

'Next week? That's too soon. I have arrangements to make and then there's Flora. I can't leave her to fend for herself. We've all had to work to support ourselves, George.'

'Don't you want to marry me, Belle?'

'Of course I do, silly. I want nothing more in the whole world, but there are other people involved. There's Cassy for one. We need to be gentle with her. She's just a child.'

Cade smiled and dropped a kiss on the tip of her nose. 'By my reckoning she's about the same age as you were when you became a mother. Your little girl is a woman now, Belle. And unless I've mistaken, both Bailey and Oliver are aware of the fact. Perhaps it's just as well they're leaving for India the day after tomorrow, or who knows how the situation might have developed.'

Belinda stared at him, shocked out of her euphoric state. 'What are you saying?'

He chuckled. 'Unless I've misread the situation, those two young men are head over heels in love with our daughter.'

'Nonsense,' Belinda said firmly. 'Bailey is like a brother to Cassy and as for Ollie, he falls in and out of love on a regular basis. I think he's far more interested in Lottie than in Cassy.'

The door flew open before Cade had a chance to respond and Flora stood there, glaring at them, arms akimbo. 'I think you're both a bit old to be playing Romeo and Juliet. Are you joining us for luncheon or are you going to loiter in here like a pair of star-struck adolescents?'

'You must forgive us, ma'am,' Cade said, slipping his arm around Belinda's shoulders. 'We've only just found each other after what seems like an eternity.'

'Then another hour or so won't make much difference,' Flora said tartly. 'I'm as romantic as the next person, but you're making the rest of us feel distinctly uncomfortable. Perhaps you should give more consideration to Cassy. She looks as though she's been poleaxed, and I don't wonder at it.' Flora swept out of the room leaving the door swinging on its hinges.

'We're being very selfish, George,' Belinda said guiltily. She forced herself to move from the shelter of his arm and made her way towards the door. 'We must join the others and try to behave naturally.'

He followed her, catching hold of her hand before she reached the hallway. He gave her fingers a squeeze. 'It won't be easy, but you're right, my love. Perhaps we could spend tomorrow together?'

She paused in the hallway, smiling up at him. 'That would be lovely.'

'I'll call for you at ten o'clock.'

* * *

The clock on the mantelshelf struck the quarter as Belinda waited by the parlour window, barely able to control her excitement as she waited for Cade's barouche to arrive. She was alone in the house except for Mrs Wilkins. Flora had elected to stay on at the farm, ostensibly to help Farmer Mullins sort out his chaotic bookkeeping, although in her heightened emotional state Belinda was beginning to suspect that there might be a romance budding between the oddly assorted pair. Oliver, Bailey and Cassy had already left the house, taking Freddie with them. They planned, Oliver had said, to collect Lottie on the way to Victoria Park where the lake was reputedly frozen hard enough to allow them to skate. Tomorrow they would be embarking on a ship taking them to India but today they intended to enjoy themselves to the full.

Belinda wished that she had been able to get Cassy on her own for a heart to heart, but there had been no opportunity during the Christmas celebrations at the farm, and Cassy had retired to bed as soon as they returned home. She had been quiet during breakfast, and had left with the others as soon as the meal was finished. Mrs Wilkins had said she was glad of a chance to put her feet up all day and do nothing. She had enjoyed herself immensely during her day out, but her bunions were playing up something chronic after joining in the dancing, accompanied by Dora on the harpsichord. Belinda closed her eyes, reliving the moments when George had held her in his arms as they waltzed around Farmer Mullins' parlour. She had been in heaven then and now she felt like a young girl, waiting for her beau to take her out for the day. Only this time there would be no chaperone to accompany them and George was no longer just a beau; he was the husband of her heart if not in law.

She gazed at the snowy scene outside. The houses opposite snuggled beneath roofs blanketed by pure white snow, and the pavements glistened in the pale morning sunlight. The dreary, dirty street had been transformed into a vision of pristine purity, but it was an illusion that would not last. By the end of the day, the gleaming surface of the road would be churned to black slush, but at this moment she felt she was in fairyland, and nothing could spoil her joy. She pressed her nose against the ice-cold windowpane and her breath fogged the glass in an instant. Giggling and feeling seventeen again, she drew her initials and George's entwined together in a heart. Then, at the exact moment the clock struck ten, the barouche drew up alongside the kerb. Snatching up her bonnet and struggling into her merino mantle, Belle hurried from the parlour and ran to open the front door.

He stood there in a caped greatcoat, momentarily blocking out the daylight. 'Belle, my love.' Taking off his top hat, he swept her into his arms, kissing her in full view of the neighbours across the street who had come out to take a closer look at the expensive equipage driven by a coachman in a many-caped greatcoat.

Laughing, she pulled free, adjusting her bonnet. 'George, you'll have the whole street talking about us.'

He handed her out across the pavement and into the barouche, climbing in beside her. 'I want them to see us together,' he said, wrapping her in a fond embrace. 'I want the world to know that you and I will soon be husband and wife, never to be parted. That's what you want, isn't it, my love?'

She snuggled against him. 'Of course it is, but I want Cassy to get used to the idea before we rush into anything. She needs to get to know you, my darling, and to love you as I do.'

'She's our daughter and she must come first, but today is ours, my darling Belle.'

'Where are we going?'

'I want to show you my house, which will be our home but only if you approve. If not we'll sell it and buy something more suitable. I'd like you to see the soldiers' home too, and meet some of the men who live there. They loved Cassy and I know they'll adore you too.'

Cade's house was situated in Lemon's Terrace, Stepney Green, just a short way from the soldiers' home. Belinda was ready to be impressed as she alighted outside the once elegant but slightly dilapidated three-storey, double-fronted Georgian town house. Iron railings surrounded the area leading down to the basement, and stone steps led up to the front door, where a sadly tarnished brass lion's head doorknocker gazing soulfully into space. Cade took the steps two at a time in order to unlock the door and usher Belinda into the square entrance hall. She did not know what she was expecting as she stepped inside but she was surprised by the echoing emptiness of the large house. It smelt slightly damp and it was almost as cold inside as it was out on the pavement.

'I haven't done much to the house since I moved in four years ago,' Cade said apologetically. 'I don't spend much time here and I'm afraid I've concentrated all my efforts on the soldiers' home.' He took off his top hat and hung it on the newel post at the foot of a sweeping cantilevered staircase that was also in a sad state of repair. The mahogany banister rail was muddy with greasy fingerprints and the treads were dusty and in need of a good polish.

'Come into the drawing room,' Cade said, eyeing her warily. 'I had Mrs Porter light a fire early this morning so it should be a bit warmer in there.' As he opened a door on the far side of the hall the doorknob came away in his hand. 'As you can see there is a bit of work to do on the old house.'

He looked so downcast that Belinda struggled to find an encouraging remark. 'It must have been a fine home when it was built.' She had already lost the feeling in her toes and her fingertips were tingling from the cold, and she made her way to the marble fireplace where the coal burned feebly, sending out occasional belches of smoke and filling the air with smuts. It barely took the chill off the large room, which was light and would be pleasantly airy in summer. The floor to ceiling windows were draped with faded velvet curtains which might once have been a delightful shade of blue, but were now grey with age and brown-tinged with dust blown in from the street. The only furniture was a slightly saggy sofa and a wingback chair set close to the fireplace. Placed beneath one of the windows a console table groaned with papers, magazines and a jumble of books.

'It needs a woman's touch,' Cade said sheepishly. 'But the rooms are well proportioned and . . .' He hesitated, gazing at her with a frown puckering his brow. 'You hate it, don't you?'

Belinda threw back her head and laughed. 'Of course I don't hate it, George. It's just going to take a small army of women to clean it and a great deal of money to refurbish it, to say nothing of the cost of carpets and new furniture. Perhaps we should sell it and get something smaller and cheaper to renovate.'

Cade took her in his arms, answering her with a kiss that robbed her of speech and sent the blood thundering through her veins. 'My darling, you can have anything you want. Money isn't a problem; I'm a comparative wealthy man.'

Confused, Belinda gazed up at him. 'But how? I don't understand.'

Shrugging off his overcoat, he tugged at a rather tatty bell pull by the fireplace. 'I'll get Mrs Porter to bring us some tea, if she bothers to answer the bell, that is. I'm afraid I inherited her with the house but she has a weakness for jigger gin and laudanum, and is probably the worst cook in the world. I'd sack her but the poor soul would end up on the streets, and so I take most of my meals at the home.'

Taking off her bonnet, Belinda sank down on the sofa, avoiding a hole where the horsehair stuffing protruded in a tangled mass. 'You really do need someone to look after you, and you still haven't told me how you managed to make your fortune after you left the army.' She shivered as she watched her breath curl up in a cloud with every spoken word, and she hugged her mantle a little closer around her chilled body. 'I think my first task will be to find a chimney sweep and to order coal enough to fill the cellar.'

Cade rang the bell again with an exclamation of annoyance. 'I'll go below stairs and see what she's doing,' he said, making for the door.

'I'm coming with you.' Belinda stood up again, glad for an excuse to move away from the hideously uncomfortable sofa. At least walking about would keep her warm, and she was curious to see the rest of the house.

The basement kitchen was in semi-darkness. A desultory fire burned in the range, which had not been cleaned since the turn of the century, or so Belinda thought as she gazed around the room. Considering that it was the place where food was stored and prepared, the kitchen was surprisingly empty and unnaturally tidy. There was not a pot or a pan to be seen and even the mice seemed to have moved out to find a better home. Mrs Porter was sprawled in a chair by the range with her booted feet propped up on a three-legged stool. Her mouth was open and her chins sagged onto her bosom, which rose and fell with each loud snore. On the floor by her side lay an empty stone bottle, which had presumably contained the spirits that had lulled her into the arms of Morpheus. The smell of stale alcohol, sour milk and rancid fat made Belinda cover her mouth and nose with her hand.

Cade stared dispassionately at his housekeeper and shrugged his shoulders. 'Dead to the world,' he said, lifting the blackened kettle off the hob. 'Boiled dry,' he added, shaking his head. 'I think we'll forget the tea. The chaps in the home have a constant brew on the go. I made certain that there were two large water boilers when we had the new range installed.' He strode to the door and held it open. 'Best leave the old girl to sleep it off.'

Hand in hand they ascended the staircase to the ground floor. 'This isn't a good first impression,' Cade said regretfully. 'I wanted you to like the house, Belle. But I understand if you think it's past saving.'

She smiled up at him, knowing that she might regret her decision tomorrow, but she could deny him nothing, and she was ready to take up the challenge. 'It's a splendid house, George. It just needs a little love and a lot of hard work. We'll make it into a wonderful home, but I'd like Cassy to see it before we make any firm decision.'

'I love you, Belle. Have I told you that recently?'

'Not for the last five minutes, my darling.'

He swept her into his arms as if to prove a point. 'Now then, where were we? I know, I was showing you round our new home. I'm afraid the dining room is a bit of a mess, and the morning parlour leaves a lot to be desired. As to the bedrooms, well I've only used one and that isn't a fit sight for a lady's eyes.'

'I think I can bear it, George,' Belinda said stoutly.

He led her into the morning parlour where the wall-paper was hanging off in shreds and the paintwork peeling. The grate was filled with soot and rubble and the windows were fogged with dirt. 'You see what I mean, Belle? This isn't a job for the fainthearted.'

'I'm a soldier's daughter, George. And you're a rich man, so you say. Or is that a story you've made up to lure an innocent woman into matrimony?' Angling her head she smiled mischievously. 'I'd still love you, even if you'd robbed a bank.'

He leaned against the mantelshelf, kicking at the burnt remains of a log and sending a shower of ash onto the hearth. 'I was discharged from the army as being medically unfit, and I'd lost you. I really didn't care what happened to me. I had some discharge pay and I travelled about India for a while, searching for something although I didn't know what. My money ran out and I found myself in Bombay, penniless and destitute. I remembered visiting my grandfather's house when I was a child. My father took me there only once before he sent me to school in England. I was desperate and my fever had returned. I remember very little of the first few weeks after I had been taken in. My grandfather was very old and not a well man, but it turned out that I was his only heir. My uncles had produced daughters who were all married off to wealthy men and had already received generous dowries. During my long convalescence I became close to my grandfather and I was with him when he died. He was a wealthy man and he left me everything.'

'And yet you chose to return to England?'

'I had to find you. Even if I couldn't have you, I wanted to be close to you. I thought if I could see you now and again it would heal the rift in my heart, but on the occasions when I did see you with your husband I found it was too painful to bear. Eventually I gave up, until as I told you I heard of Sir Geoffrey's death, and then it seemed that I was too late. I had no idea where you'd gone and I thought I'd lost you forever.'

She walked into his arms. 'But we're together now, thanks to our daughter. Who would have thought we'd have a happy ending?'

He held her close. 'Now all we have to do is to convince Cassy.'

'She's your flesh and blood, George. Give her time and she'll come to love you.' Belinda shivered. 'But could we go somewhere warmer? I'm freezing.'

Late that afternoon as the carriage stopped outside the house in Pedlar's Orchard, Belinda left the shelter of Cade's embrace with the greatest reluctance. She blew him a kiss as she hesitated in the doorway, waving until the barouche turned the corner and was out of sight.

'So you've been with him all day.' Cassy's voice was as brittle as the icicles that hung from the area railings.

Her smile faded as she came hurtling back to earth with a bump. 'Yes, I have. Do you mind very much?'

'I don't want to see you get hurt, Ma.'

'But your father and I love each other, darling. We love you too.'

'He doesn't know me,' Cassy said coldly. 'And I know very little about him except that he got you with child when you were a girl just like me. What would you say if the positions were reversed, Ma? If I went with a man and had his baby out of wedlock, how would you feel then? Would you trust him to make me happy if he turned up suddenly, many years later?'

'I-I don't know,' Belinda murmured, lost for words and taken aback by the anger smouldering in Cassy's eyes.

'I'd say you're the one who needs to get to know him,' Cassy went on, her voice trembling with suppressed fury. 'I'm not going to put my life in his hands. You did it once before when you married Sir Geoffrey and now you're going to do it again. I say shame on you, Ma. Are you never going to learn?' Her voice breaking on a sob Cassy turned away and ran up the stairs. The sound of her door slamming made Belinda cover her ears with her hands.

Chapter Twenty-one

Cassy barely slept that night, despite an enjoyable and energetic day spent skating on the frozen lake in Victoria Park and the ensuing snowball fights on its banks. Things had started to go wrong after she had returned home; in fact the pleasurable outing had turned into something of an emotional nightmare. She had been waiting for Ma's return, desperate to confide in her and ask her advice. Never had she needed her mother more than at that moment, but the sight of Ma in Cade's arms had come as a shock. They had been kissing passionately and were totally oblivious to the world around them. Cassy had felt sick with embarrassment. She had liked Cade well enough in the beginning; indeed she had been drawn to him as if by an invisible thread, but to accept him as her father was a different matter entirely. He was not the image she had fondly cherished as a child. When she had thought that Mahdu was her mother, she had imagined her father to be of medium height and slender build with light brown hair that curled a little at the ends, and smiling eyes; a perfect English gentleman. In her mind he had been sensitive and intelligent, more like a poet than a soldier. He had been a cross between William Wordsworth and St Francis of Assisi. Animals, birds and children had flocked to him in their droves, and his love for her mother had been spiritual rather than carnal. Now, faced with the unquestionably virile, dashing and battle-scarred reality of Captain Cade, she was in a state of denial. Her mother had fallen under his spell once again, apparently forgetting that he had taken advantage of her when she was an innocent young girl. And worse still, they were so wrapped up in each other that they had forgotten that it was she, Cassy, who was the real victim of their youthful indiscretions. What would they say if she had given in to passion when Oliver kissed her that same afternoon? Would they even care?

The memory of that moment brought a blush to her cheeks. Bailey and Freddie had volunteered to see Lottie home after Cassy had started to shiver, complaining that her boots leaked and that she had lost the feeling in her toes. She and Ollie had come on ahead, hand in hand and giggling like schoolchildren as they entered the house and made for the warmth of the parlour. It was dark outside and the flickering firelight had created shifting shadows on the walls. She had been about to light the candles but Ollie had said it was cosier like this. He had made her sit on the sofa and had knelt before her, unlacing her boots. His hands had been warm and gentle as they chafed her cold feet. He had teased her about the hole in her stocking where her big toe peeped through, and she had slapped his wrist, tucking her feet out of sight beneath the sofa. She remembered how his smile had faded and his eyes had darkened as they held hers in an almost hypnotic gaze, and then to her surprise he had seized her hands in his and clasped them to his chest. He had said that his feelings for her were anything but brotherly, and he had risen from his knees to enfold her in his arms. His kiss had been tender and yet demanding, thrilling and a little frightening. Being held in a warm embrace and being kissed with undoubted expertise was a new experience. It had been shocking and at the same time exciting.

Cassy pulled the coverlet up to her chin as she lay staring at the ceiling. Today she would be waving goodbye to Ollie, sending him off to war with nothing but a kiss and a smile to remember her by. He would be facing dangers on the battlefield, and she might never see him again. He had been too much of a gentleman to press his suit, but the thing that shocked her most was the fact that she had wanted him to make love to her. She was hazy as to the mechanics of the whole thing. It had been the topic of many whispered conversations in the dormitory at school, and no one really knew what went on in the privacy of the marital bedchamber, but there had been a lot of supposition accompanied by even more giggling. Now, as night faded into morning, Cassy was lost in guilt as she remembered the lover-like words that Ollie had whispered in her ear. She could still feel the caress of his hands on her breasts as he helped her take off the damp woollen mantle, and how the touch of his fingers on her nipples had caused them to harden and sent shivers of delight down her spine. His mouth had sought hers again and her lips had parted with a sigh of pleasure.

It had gone no further as Ollie released her suddenly, shame-faced and with an apology, but it had left her wanting more. Had it been the same for Ma when she was just a girl and had given herself to Cade?

'I love you, Cassy.' Oliver's parting words still rang in her ears.

'And I love you too.' The reply had tripped off her tongue. Oliver's embrace had awakened strange and potent desires. The remnants of childhood had been torn away by feelings that were intense and thrilling. It must be love.

In the cold light of day she was not so sure. Cassy swung her legs over the side of the bed, grimacing as her bare feet touched the cold linoleum. Having had to break the ice before pouring water from the ewer into the washbowl, her ablutions were brief. She dried herself on a piece of coarse towelling and with her teeth chattering she dressed as quickly as her numbed fingers would allow. She was searching through the chest of drawers for a pair of stockings that were not too much darned when her gaze fell upon the portrait of herself that Jack had given her. She had intended to give it to Ollie as a keepsake, but then she remembered with a pang of remorse that Bailey was also leaving today. Her much loved friend was returning to the battlefield, and until this moment she had barely given him a second thought. Guilt, shame and the need to make reparation, even though he had no knowledge of her slide from grace, made it imperative that she give him something to remember her by. She slipped the portrait into her pocket, put on her stockings and boots and went downstairs, bracing herself to face Ollie at breakfast. If what she felt for him was love, it was a complete jumble of emotions and very disturbing.

She looked round anxiously as she entered the kitchen and was relieved to find that he was not there. Mrs Wilkins was stirring a pan on the range and Freddie and Bailey were sitting at the table eating their breakfast.

Bailey gave her a searching look. 'You look pale. Are you feeling all right this morning, Cass?'

Avoiding his intense gaze she busied herself pouring tea. 'I'm fine. Where's Ollie? Is he still in bed?'

'He was up hours ago,' Mrs Wilkins volunteered as she ladled porridge into a bowl and set it on the table in front of Cassy. 'Had his breakfast and went out to look for a cab about five minutes ago.'

'You'd gone to bed by the time Freddie and I got home,' Bailey said, frowning. 'I thought you must have caught a chill or something.'

'I stayed up later than you, Cassy,' Freddie said with a mischievous grin. 'I'm a big boy now.'

Cassy leaned across the table to ruffle his hair. 'Yes, you are. Now put your coat on and I'll take you to school.'

Bailey jumped to his feet. 'No, you won't. It's still freezing outside. We'll drop him off on the way to the docks.'

She nodded, sipping her tea. 'He'll miss you terribly.'

'Will you miss me, Cass?'

'Of course I will. I always do, silly.'

398

He raised her to her feet. 'Give me a hug, Cass. And then I think you ought to go and sit by the fire in the parlour. You look done in.'

'I'm coming to see you off at the docks.'

'No, I won't hear of it. There's no point you catching your death of cold, and I want to remember you at home, safe and warm. That's the picture of you I'll carry with me always.'

Suddenly the war in that far-off country seemed to invade the kitchen. Cassy shivered as a sudden chill made her heart contract with fear. She wrapped her arms around him. 'You will come back to me, Bailey. Promise me you will.'

He held her for a moment and then gently disengaged her hands from around his neck. 'I have to go now, but I'll do my best to stay alive, girl.' His words were cheerful but the expression in his eyes was bleak.

'Bailey,' she said, slipping her hand in her pocket and pulling out the framed portrait. 'I've got something I'd like you to have.'

'What's that, Cass?'

She pressed the picture into his hand. 'Something to remember me by when you're far away.'

He stared at it for a moment and she could see his mouth working as if he was at a loss for words. He brushed his hand across his eyes. 'I don't need anything to remind me of your face, girl.' Clutching the picture, he held it to his heart. 'You're here, Cassy. Everywhere I go, I take you with me.' He sniffed and his lips twisted into a smile. 'You're part of me, Cass. Nothing can ever come between us.' His voice broke and he turned to Freddie, holding out his hand. 'Come on, Freddie. You're travelling to school in style today, old chap.'

Mrs Wilkins bustled over to throw her arms around Bailey. 'Take care of yourself, boy. Let's hope this blooming war don't go on for much longer.' She gave him a hug and then released him. She bent down to retrieve a pair of coarse woollen socks from her chair, thrusting them into Bailey's hands. 'Here, I knitted these for you. Keep your tootsies warm in them cold Afghan nights.'

He tucked them into his pocket, bending down to kiss her cheek. 'Ta, Mrs Wilkins. I'll think of you and your boiled mutton and caper sauce every time I put my socks on.'

She slapped him on the arm. 'Get on with you. Best hurry or Master Oliver will put you on a charge.'

The mere mention of his name made Cassy tremble. How would she face him today? Would he have forgotten the moments they had shared in the parlour yesterday? She watched Mrs Wilkins fussing round Freddie as Bailey helped him into his coat, and although she would have liked to remain hiding away in the kitchen, Cassy knew she had to see Ollie alone. The last thing she wanted was to send him off to war thinking that she did not care, even though her own emotions were in a desperate muddle. Leaving the room with a murmured apology, she hurried up the back stairs. Oliver was in the hallway standing by the open front door while the cabby loaded their luggage into the waiting cab. His face lit up at the sight of her. 'There you are, Cassy. I thought you'd overslept and I'd have to come up to get you.'

She raised her eyes to his face and her heart skipped a beat at the warmth of his smile. 'I wanted to come to the docks to see you off, but Bailey doesn't think it's a good idea.'

'I should think not. We'd be selfish brutes if we expected you to freeze on the dockside just to wave us off.' He swept her up in his arms, kissing her thoroughly until her lips parted with a sigh, and she slid her arms around his neck. She was dizzy with desire as he set her back on her feet. He held her for a moment, gazing deeply into her eyes. 'When I come back home I'm going to ask you to marry me, Cassy. You've plenty of time to think it over while I'm gone.' He glanced over her shoulder as Freddie came clattering up the stairs, followed by Bailey. 'Come along, Corporal Moon. We'll be in trouble if we miss the boat.' He patted Freddie on the head. 'Hop in the cab, boy. We've no time to lose.'

'Look after yourself, Cass.' Bailey brushed her cheek with the tips of his fingers. 'Don't forget me, girl.' He hurried down the steps into the waiting cab.

Cassy stood in the doorway, shivering in the cold and fighting back tears. She did not want them to see her crying, but as soon as the cab was out of sight she gave way to great shuddering sobs. All the tensions of the last few days seemed to bubble to the surface as she leaned helplessly against the doorpost, regardless of the icy chill from the snowy pavements.

'Come inside, my love.' Belinda had come up behind

her unheard, and she slipped her arm around Cassy's waist, drawing her gently back into the house. She closed the door, shutting out the bleak weather. 'Come and sit in the parlour, and I'll fetch you a nice hot cup of tea.'

'They might be killed,' Cassy whispered. 'I love them both and I may never see them again.'

'You mustn't think like that,' Belinda said firmly. 'There's always hope, and they've survived so far. We can only wait and pray that this dreadful war in Afghanistan comes to an end very soon.'

She guided Cassy's steps into the parlour and was about to leave the room but Cassy reached out to hold her hand. 'I'm sorry, Ma. I was hateful to you yesterday. I didn't mean it.'

Belinda squeezed her fingers, smiling. 'I know you didn't, darling. You've had so many changes in your short life that I don't wonder you have difficulty in accepting George as your father. But he is, my love. He is your father and I love him. I hope one day you will see what a good man he is and find it in your heart to love him too.'

'I'll try, Ma. I promise you, I will do my best to get to know him.'

'I want us to be a family, Cassy. George has asked me to marry him, but I won't accept his proposal unless I have your blessing.'

Cassy bowed her head. 'Everything will change, Ma. We've been happy here.'

'Yes, we have, but nothing stays the same for ever, and it's been a struggle to make ends meet.'

'We've managed,' Cassy murmured. She wanted to

tell Ma to go ahead and marry her man, but somehow the words stuck in her throat, although she did not know why.

'Yes, darling. We've scraped by with Mr Mullins' help and with the money I get from teaching Mrs Ponsonby and the Misses Dobson, but since you lost your job at the pub things have been a bit more difficult. Anyway that's not the life I want for my daughter. Your father and I love each other and we want the best for you too, Cassy. Can't you see that?'

She nodded her head. 'Yes, Ma.'

'Good girl. Now, you can say no if you don't want to come with me, but George is sending the carriage round this morning and I'm going to the house in Lemon's Terrace. I'd love you to see it, Cassy. It will be a wonderful home when it's been refurbished, and I'd value your help in choosing paint and wallpaper. Then there'll be visits to warehouses to choose curtain material, carpets and furniture. We could do it together, if you agree.'

Cassy met her mother's eager gaze and her resistance melted away. She had never seen Ma look so happy and she had not the heart to refuse. 'Of course I will, Ma.'

She was rewarded by a hug and a smile. 'Get your outdoor things on then, darling. The carriage will be here at any moment. George will be so pleased to see you.'

Cassy could not help but be impressed by the size of the house in Lemon's Terrace and the faded elegance of the rooms. Belinda's enthusiasm was infectious and Cade insisted that no expense should be spared in turning the house into a home. He would, he said, leave it entirely in their capable hands, and he was as good as his word. In the weeks that followed he was fully occupied attending meetings of the various charitable institutions of which he was a patron. A part of each day was spent at the soldiers' home and he encouraged Cassy to accompany him. Gradually and almost imperceptibly she was drawn into his world. He was endlessly patient with her, never once reprimanding her when she challenged his authority. Belinda was kept busy organising the renovations to the house. She spent many hours checking the work of the painters, carpenters and plumbers and kept a keen eye on the work of the gas fitters who were installing gasoliers and gas mantles in all the rooms. 'It's going to be the most modern house in Stepney,' she told Cassy gleefully. 'Just think of it, darling. We'll have a bathroom with running water. There wasn't one in Duke Street or South Audley Street, and we'll have gas lighting in all the rooms too. No more candles or oil lamps.'

'It's amazing, Ma,' Cassy said dutifully.

'Just wait until you see the kitchen.' Belinda's eyes sparkled with excitement. 'The new range is the very latest thing, and there's a new copper in the scullery. I'll have to let Mrs Porter go, of course, when we all move in, but I'll advertise for a cook-general, and I've told your father that we'll need a much larger staff if we're to keep up our standards.'

'Yes, Ma.' Cassy was growing weary of talk about wallpaper, colour schemes and the endless trips to warehouses to look at swatches of material and an astounding array of carpets from all over the world. She tried to look interested for her mother's sake, but her thoughts kept wandering and she struggled daily with an uneasy feeling that Ollie and Bailey were in even more danger than before. Perhaps she was being fanciful, or maybe it was due to the fact that she had not enough to occupy her mind.

The house in Pedlar's Orchard seemed very quiet and dull without them. Freddie was at school all day and Flora spent most of her time at Whitegate Farm. Mullins came daily to collect her in his new and extremely stylish gig. Under Flora's influence, he had smartened himself up. He no longer wore nankeen breeches and leather gaiters, or the corduroy jacket with frayed cuffs, but sported a tweed suit and cap more suited to a country squire than a yeoman farmer. Gone was the spotted neckerchief. His newly clean-shaven chin rested on starched collar points, and his cravat was held in place with a gold stickpin. Flora was patently proud of her protégé, and boasted that since she had taken over his bookkeeping and accounts, the farm income had almost doubled.

It seemed to Cassy that everyone had found their niche in life except herself. She saw little of Lottie now that she was immersed in her studies, and Cade had given her an allowance which meant she did not need to go out to earn her living. When she was not needed to accompany Ma on her trips to warehouses or to the large stores in Oxford Street to purchase items of clothing, Cassy spent as much time as she could at the soldiers' home. Even here there was little that she could do as the household tasks were taken care of by the staff and the inmates, but she played chess with some of the older men, and read to the unfortunates who had lost their sight. She had learnt to play the pianoforte at school, although she was far from being a concert pianist, but she could play a polka or a popular tune, and some of the men had excellent singing voices. At other times she went into the art room to clean brushes and palettes, and to admire Jack's work which was improving daily as he gained better use of his left hand. His paintings were pinned to the walls, creating a wonderful display of colour and light. They were admired by everyone who visited the home, and he had even sold a couple to a wealthy gentleman with mutton-chop whiskers who had made his fortune in cheese, and was now looking for worthwhile causes to support. Cassy had been witness to this burst of generosity and it gave her an idea. She waited until the mutton-chop gentleman had left the building before broaching the matter with Cade.

'I'd like a word with you, Captain,' she said, waylaying him as he was about to enter his office.

He eyed her with a hint of a smile in his dark eyes. 'I'm listening. Come in and tell me what's on your mind, Cassy.'

She followed him into the small room, which was just large enough to house a desk, some bookshelves and two chairs. It was little bigger than a broom cupboard, but Cade was not a man to wallow in self-importance. She had learnt that early on in their slowly improving relationship, but she still could not bring herself to call him Father.

She sat down on the hard wooden seat. 'I think we could sell Jack's work,' she said, getting straight to the point. 'That man paid five pounds for one of his paintings. It's a small fortune, and if Jack could have an exhibition somewhere, who knows how much it might raise?'

Cade perched on the edge of his desk. 'That's a very good idea. I wonder I didn't think of it myself.'

She eyed him suspiciously. 'Are you laughing at me?'

'Not at all; it's a good plan, and if successful might lead to Jack being able to gain his independence. My aim has always been to help the men lead a normal life.'

'Then you agree that an exhibition would be possible?'

'Absolutely, and as you are the one who thought of it, I think that you should organise it.'

Cassy blinked and swallowed hard. This was something she had not foreseen. 'Me? I wouldn't know where to start.'

He smiled. 'I'll be there to help out if you get stuck, but I think you're perfectly capable of organising such an event. I can give you a list of the right people to invite, and some possible venues. You've been saying that you'd like something to occupy your time other than shopping, which your mother adores, so here's your chance, my dear. Show me what you can do.'

It was a challenge that she could not resist. She leapt to her feet. 'I'll do it. I'll start right away.'

Keeping busy took her mind off the niggling fears for the safety of Oliver and Bailey. She could not understand why now, after they had been involved in skirmishes and fighting for so long, she had become more anxious about their chances of survival. Perhaps it had something to do with the realities of warfare that came home to her every time she visited Jack and the other wounded soldiers. Or maybe her heightened sensibilities were due to a deeper emotion – love. Even that was confusing. Being kissed by Ollie had revealed a side of her nature that had lain dormant, like a flower in bud, waiting for the warmth of the sun to encourage its petals to unfurl. Her one and only experience of genuine love and tenderness had left her restless and unsettled. She could still feel the imprint of his lips on hers and she could recall the way her blood had fizzed in her veins at his touch. His kisses had been as intoxicating as the champagne cup she had drunk at the ball where she first met Cade.

The memory of that evening came back to her often during her troubled relationship with the man who was her father. She knew that Ma loved him deeply and that he adored her. She wanted to be a good daughter and to love him unreservedly, but deep down she was wary, and she could not quite dispel the feelings of resentment against him for being the unwitting cause of her mother's suffering. For herself she did not care. Life had been tough in Three Herring Court, but she had had Bailey to look after her. She would always love Bailey, but there had been a slow and subtle change in their relationship. She had not seen it coming and she had not been prepared for the look in his eyes when he told her that he loved her.

It seemed to Cassy that now she was a woman her life was both dominated and complicated by men. Sometimes she longed to be a child again, taking everything for granted and able to give unconditional love to those closest to her. Bailey was her oldest and dearest friend. She often wondered what she would do if he were killed in battle. In some ways she had grown independent of him, and yet she could not imagine a world where he did not exist. He would come home soon, she told herself. Both Bailey and Ollie would return as conquering heroes and life would return to normal.

In the meantime she had an exhibition to arrange and she threw herself into the preparations. Cade had been as good as his word and had introduced her to influential people who took an interest both in art and in raising funds for charity. They were all middle-aged City men who had been successful in business and now wanted to give something back to those less fortunate. A venue had been found and a date set for the first week in May. Cade had made time to take her to art galleries and private showings of works by such famous artists as Dante Gabriel Rossetti, Millais and the other members of the Pre-Raphaelite Brotherhood. Jack's paintings were nothing when compared to those of the masters, but there was an honesty and an almost child-like quality in his art that both intrigued and enchanted everyone who had so far had the chance to view them. Cassy was certain that the exhibition would be the making of him.

Then there was the wedding. Cade had spoken to her one day as they made their way back from the Royal Academy, humbly asking Cassy's permission to marry her mother. She knew him well enough by now to realise that he was sincere, and if she were to admit the truth she had never seen Ma look so beautiful or as happy. She had gladly given her consent, and the date had been set to coincide with the completion of the renovations to the house in Lemon's Terrace in June. Belinda had insisted that they wait until after Jack's exhibition, and anyway it was to be a quiet affair. She said it would be inappropriate to make a fuss when Oliver was risking his life for his country. She would have liked to wait until her stepson returned home, but the war was dragging on with no sign of ending in the near future.

The church was duly booked and Belinda's bridal gown was being made by a dressmaker in New Bond Street who was alleged to have made gowns for no lesser personage than the Princess of Wales. Belinda had argued that this was an unnecessary expense and that she had seen an advertisement in the *Young Ladies' Journal* illustrating the latest Paris fashions, which were obtainable from Nicholson's Warehouse in Cheapside, but Cade was adamant in his refusal to countenance such folly. His fiancée, he said, was not going to the altar in a ready-made creation. Nothing but the best would do for the future Mrs Lawson. Belinda, Cassy and Flora had no choice but to accede to his wishes, although Cassy suspected that both her mother and Flora were secretly pleased to return to the height of fashion.

Then there was the problem of who would give Belinda away. Cassy suggested Mr Solomon, but the look of consternation on her mother's face was answer enough. Belinda, Flora and Cassy were discussing the final preparations for the wedding over supper one evening in Pedlar's Court. Everything had been arranged apart from this last detail.

'I have no surviving relatives,' Belinda said sadly. 'At least none that I know of. Papa lost contact with his family when he went into the army, and I don't think he was close to any of them even before he left the country.'

Flora cleared her throat, eyeing them warily. 'I have a suggestion.'

Cassy was suddenly alert. Flora was not usually reticent about putting her opinions forward. She opened her mouth to speak, but was silenced by a warning frown from her mother.

'Tell me,' Belinda said eagerly. 'I've run out of ideas.'

'Mullins.'

'Farmer Mullins?' Belinda raised her eyebrows. 'No, surely not.'

'We're getting married.' Flora glared at each of them in turn, as if expecting an argument. 'I can't go on visiting the farm day in and day out without causing tongues to wag.'

Cassy thought for a moment that she was joking, but one look at the set expression on Flora's face was enough to convince her otherwise.

'Marriage is a huge step,' Belinda said, eyeing Flora warily. 'Are you sure you're doing the right thing?'

'Mullins needs a firm hand and someone with a head for business. The farm could be a goldmine if it was run properly, and I find I have quite a talent for organisation.'

'But you dislike the countryside, Flora. You've lived all your life in town. How will you cope when the novelty wears off?'

Flora shrugged her shoulders. 'I was bored with London anyway, and it's a challenge. Mullins is a challenge too. I'll soon whip him into shape; in fact I have already. He's a different man from the clodhopping yokel I first saw arguing over a prize calf.'

Setting aside the picture conjured up in her mind of the extremely odd couple living together as man and wife, there was another and even more pressing concern on Cassy's mind. 'This is all very fine, but what will happen to Mrs Wilkins and Freddie? Everyone's making arrangements for themselves, but when we leave this house where will they go? I'm not leaving here without Freddie; I'll tell you that for nothing, Ma.'

'It's all arranged, darling,' Belinda said, reaching across the table to give Cassy's hand a comforting squeeze. 'I was going to tell you tonight anyway. I've found a place for Mrs Porter in the soldiers' home. She's going to live in and work in the kitchens, although I hope they won't allow her to do any cooking. We need a housekeeper, and Mrs Wilkins has agreed to come with us to Lemon's Terrace. Naturally Freddie will come too. I wouldn't leave the little fellow behind, and he'll go to a better school. We'll make a gentleman of him yet.'

What Freddie thought of the plan to make him into a gentleman was never likely to be put to the test, but when Cassy asked him how he felt about the move, she found to her relief that he was looking forward to living in the big house and did not seem to be worried about the change of school. Mrs Wilkins was thrilled to think she would be elevated to the position of housekeeper with staff to do her bidding. Everyone seemed happy, but Cassy still had the nagging feeling that something was wrong. She could not put her finger on what it was that worried her, but she knew that something somewhere was amiss. She had vivid dreams that verged on nightmares when she was searching for someone or something in a suffocating dust storm that howled about her ears and filled her eyes and mouth with grit. She was about to find what she was looking for when she awakened, sweating and panic-stricken.

She told no one, not even Lottie when she came to visit one Sunday afternoon. It was just an irritation of nerves, Cassy told herself, due to an over-active imagination aggravated by all the emotional upheavals of the last few months. Putting her personal problems behind her, she listened avidly to Lottie's experiences at the hospital. The male doctors were frankly hostile, she said, but the female students were determined to overcome their prejudices. They were sisters in adversity, and in some ways it was like being back in Miss North's academy. This made them both dissolve into giggles, and then it was Cassy's turn to tell Lottie about her hopes for promoting Jack Bragg as an artist. Lottie was enthusiastic and promised to attend the exhibition. There was nothing she would love more than to help support the brave soldiers who had given so much to their country.

With this encouragement in mind, Cassy threw herself even more keenly into making arrangements for the first public showing of Jack's art. After a great deal of thought she had decided to include as many of the inmates of the home as possible. One-legged, one-eyed Sidney was a dab hand at making wicker baskets, having worked at that trade before he enlisted in the army. Ronald, blinded by an exploding grenade, could throw a clay pot as well as any sighted man and his sensitive fingers had created some amazing results. These were fired in a kiln at the bottom of the garden paid for by Cade, who was more than generous in providing the men with everything they needed to encourage and develop their skills.

Cassy sent out dozens of invitations and on the day of the exhibition she had the men dressed in their Sunday best, waiting to meet their prospective patrons. At first she was afraid that no one would turn up, but by midday the hall was packed with people all showing great interest in the soldiers' work. The well-heeled, expensively attired guests made all the right noises, congratulating the men on their efforts and praising them to the skies, but Cassy saw very little money change hands. At the end of the afternoon when the crowds had drifted away, Cade organised cabs to take the men back to the home, leaving Cassy and Jack to take stock of their success.

As he slipped the last coin into a leather pouch, Jack looked up at Cassy with a rueful grin. 'They wasn't exactly in the mood for spending, it seems, miss.'

Cassy had been taking down what was left of his artwork, but she stopped and hurried to the table where he had the account book open in front of him. 'How did we do?'

He shook his head. 'Put it this way, miss. The toffs weren't about to spend a fortune on works by the likes of us. We won't get no champagne suppers from what we took today.'

'Let me see.' Cassy leaned over to examine his neat rows of figures and her heart sank. 'They haven't been over-generous, that's for sure,' she said angrily. She did not tell him that their takings would barely cover the cost of hiring the hall. She forced herself to smile. 'It's a start, Jack.'

He gave her a straight look. 'No, miss. I ain't a fool. This is more like the finish for the likes of me and the boys. You've got to face facts.' He picked up the pouch and shook it so that the coins jingled. 'I'll bet this don't cover the expense of setting up all this. It's the end for me, and I know it.'

Chapter Twenty-two

'Nonsense,' Cassy said firmly. 'We were just dealing with the wrong sort of people, Jack. I was aiming too high, but it's given me an idea.' She paced the floor, stopping to pick up a basket and looping it over her arm. 'What we need is a shop where we can sell things to people who would be only too pleased to buy something handmade by the men who were prepared to give their lives for their country. I had it all wrong when I invited all those stuck-up snobs who make their money out of ordinary people's hard work, paying them a pittance for their labours. It was my mistake, Jack, not yours. You'll see.'

'I'm no artist, miss. Maybe I should give up now.'

'If you do I'll never speak to you again. Just wait until I've discussed it with my father. We won't let one small setback put us off.'

Jack's face split into a cheerful grin and his eyes twinkled. 'Well now, Miss Cassy. I ain't never heard you call him that afore.'

She shrugged her shoulders. 'It slipped out. Anyway, I'll talk to him as soon as we get home. Wait here while I go outside and look for a cab.'

Reaching for his crutches, Jack hauled himself off the chair. 'I ain't completely helpless. You stay here.

I'll find a cab even if I has to hook one in with me crutch.'

Next day, after staying up late the previous evening drafting out her ideas for a shop run by the men themselves, Cassy went to Cade's study to put her proposition to him.

He listened intently to what she had to say. 'I think you're right,' he said with a nod of approval. 'Perhaps I should have seen it coming, but I didn't. The merchants and industrialists on my lists are always very open-handed when it comes to giving publicly at charity functions and paying lip service to helping those less fortunate than themselves, but it appears that they don't practise what they preach.'

'I think we were aiming too high. Perhaps we should have started off in a smaller way. Anyway, I won't allow one setback to put an end to the men's hopes and dreams. I started this and I'm going to see it through.'

Cade patted her on the shoulder. 'Cassy, I'm proud of you. Go ahead with your plans and I'll give you any help you need.'

She smiled. 'Money is the main thing, Pa. Can I rely on you?'

'You know you can, my love. You can have the top brick off the chimney, as my English nanny used to say.'

The next few weeks were spent in a flurry of activity. There were fittings not only for a gown for the wedding, but to Cassy's astonishment Cade had insisted that both she and her mother were to have a whole new wardrobe. This also entailed visits to shoemakers, milliners and to department stores where they purchased gloves and stockings, not to mention lace-trimmed undergarments, stays and nightgowns. Cassy's protests that it was all too much were swiftly quelled by her mother. 'Darling, you must remember that your father has never had the chance to spoil his daughter. Allow him the pleasure of seeing you dressed like a lady.' Belinda selected a fan from the array set before them by an eager shop assistant. She unfurled it and closed it again with a flick of her wrist. 'I didn't realise how much I missed having pretty things,' she added with a mischievous smile. 'I am a worldly creature, Cassy. You are much more like your father, and I admire what you're doing for those poor unfortunate men who have given so much for Queen and country.'

'It's little enough, Ma. They're all so brave and cheerful. I love them all and I want to do my best for them.'

Belinda angled her head. 'What about Oliver? I know there was something going on between you two at Christmas.'

Cassy turned away as the ready flush flooded her cheeks. 'He kissed me once, Ma. That's all.'

'I'll take this one,' Belinda said, handing the fan to the shop assistant who was shamelessly eavesdropping on their conversation. 'Have it wrapped, if you please, and add it to my other purchases.' She led Cassy away from the counter, making a show of looking at cashmere shawls hanging like angels' wings from the ceiling. 'You don't have to explain to me, darling. Ollie is a charming boy and I don't wonder that you are attracted to him.'

'I'm not,' Cassy said hastily. 'I mean, I suppose I am, but there's so much I want to do in life. I don't want to be tied down by marriage and babies. Not yet anyway.'

Belinda chuckled, slipping her arm around her daughter's waist. 'You've plenty of time, my dear. All I want is to see you well established in life and above all happy. Now, what about the white shawl? It looks like a spider's web in lace, and it will be just right for a hot climate.' She clapped her hand over her mouth. 'Now I've spoilt the surprise.'

'What surprise? Why do I need something for a hot climate? What are you saying?'

'George will be so cross with me,' Belinda said, giggling. 'But I was dying to tell you. It was supposed to be a surprise. We were going to spring it on you after the wedding.'

'Ma, stop chattering like a magpie and tell me.'

'George is going to take me back to India for our honeymoon, and we want you to come with us. We feel that you should see the land of your birth, and the place where your grandmother's family came from. George thinks that if you come full circle you will be able to relate to both cultures, and there's a possibility that we might be able to see Oliver and your friend Bailey, if it could be arranged. What do you say, Cassy?'

'I – I can't play gooseberry on your honeymoon, Ma.'

'Darling, I'm not seventeen and this isn't my first marriage. Your father and I both want this, Cassy.

After all that has gone before we both think that it is important for us to be a family. Please don't refuse before you've had time to think it over.'

Fingering the soft gossamer-like material of the shawl, Cassy raised her eyes to her mother's face. She could see herself mirrored in their blue depths and she was overcome with emotion. She had tried hard to emulate Ma in everything she did, but she knew now that she was more like Cade. Perhaps that was why she had not warmed to him at first, but things were different now. She realised that the same blood ran in their veins, and that he was just as much a part of her as her beloved mother. She nodded her head slowly. 'I'd love to come with you, Ma. And if I could see the boys, that would be wonderful. I've been so worried about both of them.'

Belinda uttered a cry of delight, bringing a sales assistant hurrying to her side.

'Is there anything wrong, ma'am?'

'No,' Belinda said happily. 'Everything is wonderful, thank you. We'll take this shawl and the blue one too, and could you direct me to the department which sells cabin trunks?'

After days of searching, Cassy found a likely shop premises in Rowland's Row almost exactly opposite the soldiers' home. It could not have been in a better position. Goods could be transported across Stepney Green in a handcart, and it was only a short distance from Lemon's Terrace. Cade signed the lease on behalf of the men and paid the required deposit and six months' rent in advance. Although Cassy would have liked to spend more time preparing the premises for business, the wedding was only a few days away and arrangements had to be made for the voyage to India. This left her little choice but to put Jack in charge of overseeing the refurbishment of the shop, which had hitherto been the premises of a cobbler and before that an ironmonger. The smell of tanned leather and rusty nails still prevailed, but not for much longer if the men from the home had anything to do with it. When she was satisfied that they could manage on their own, Cassy left them to it and turned her attention to helping her mother prepare for her big day.

Then, much to everyone's astonishment, Flora returned from Essex a married woman. She brushed aside their protests. 'Mullins obtained a special licence,' she said airily. 'Dora and her daughter were witnesses and we were married in the village church.'

'But Flora, we would have liked to be there.' Belinda's eyes filled with tears. 'We're still family even though we aren't blood related.'

'Oh, Lord. I knew you'd make a fuss, Belle, which is why we chose to do it quietly and without a song and dance. At our age, what does it matter anyway?'

'Well, I think it's romantic,' Cassy said, giving her a hug. 'It doesn't matter how old or young you are, Aunt Flora. It's lovely to think that you and Mr Mullins will have each other.'

Flora pulled a face. 'Mullins will do as he's told and I don't have to keep coming back to this wretched hovel. At least I'll have a degree of comfort in my old age, especially when I've finished modernising that draughty old farmhouse. Mullins doesn't know it yet, but I have plans.'

Avoiding her mother's gaze in case she burst out laughing, Cassy kissed Flora on the cheek. 'I hope you'll be very happy, and I can't wait to visit you when we come back from India.'

'Yes, Flora,' Belinda said earnestly. 'I was going to ask if you would oversee the removal of our things to Lemon's Terrace, but I can see that you will be far too busy.'

'Nonsense. I'm more than capable and my time is my own. I'll see to it that Mrs Wilkins does the hard work. You're to go on your honeymoon and leave everything to us.'

Cassy opened her mouth to ask if Flora and Farmer Mullins were going away on a romantic wedding trip, but Flora forestalled the question. 'I know what you're going to say, young Cassy, and the answer is no. We're past all that sort of nonsense, and I'll thank you not to giggle, miss. You'll be old one day, like me.'

'You'll never be old, Aunt Flora. Not if you live to be a hundred.'

'Humbug,' Flora said sharply, but her lips twitched and she fluttered her eyelashes.

'Well then,' Belinda said, smiling. 'Now all we've got to do is to make the final arrangement for next Monday. I can hardly believe that we're getting married at last.'

Although Belinda and Cade had wanted a quiet wedding, St Dunstan's Church was packed with well-wishers. The men from the home were there, some in Bath chairs pushed by the more able-bodied, and others who had walked the short distance with the aid of crutches. All the staff were there, including Mrs Porter who appeared to be remarkably sober, clean and tidy. Eli and Lottie sat in the front pew with Flora and Cassy, and on the opposite side of the aisle Mrs Wilkins and Freddie sat beside Dora and her daughter, a robust countrywoman who looked as though she would not stand for any nonsense.

The scent of summer flowers filled the cool air and the fragrance of roses, sweet peas and lilies mingled with a hint of mustiness from old hymnals and damp hassocks. At a signal from the verger standing in the doorway, the organist began to play the processional march, and heads turned to see Belinda walking down the aisle on Farmer Mullins' arm. Cassy had always thought that her mother was beautiful but today she was a vision of loveliness in a deceptively simple gown of muslin and lace with a delicate wreath of rosebuds crowning her golden head. She looked radiant, like a young girl rather than a woman in her mid-thirties, and Cade obviously thought so too. Cassy's heart missed a beat when she saw the rapt expression on his face. If she had any remaining doubts they were stripped away in that brief moment. She knew for a certainty that Cade loved her mother truly and deeply, and their love would last for eternity. Tears flowed down her cheeks but they were tears of joy.

Flora nudged her in the ribs. 'For goodness' sake,' she

hissed. 'Stop blubbing. This is supposed to be a happy occasion.'

'I am happy,' Cassy whispered. 'This is the best day of my life.'

The ceremony went off without a hitch and afterwards everyone congregated outside to congratulate the newlyweds. Cade invited everyone back to the house in Lemon's Terrace where he had arranged for a small army of caterers to provide food and drink for the guests. Cassy had to admire his forethought, or perhaps he had known that it would be impossible for a man of his standing in the community to get away with a quiet wedding. It seemed that the gods were on their side as the weather was perfect. The birds trilled away in the churchyard trees and the wedding party walked in a slow procession to the house that would soon be Cassy's new home. Inside it was almost unrecognisable. The builders, decorators and plumbers had left and the furniture, carpets and curtains had been set in place. The result was elegance without opulence, and comfort with style and good taste. Waiters in black tie and tails held silver trays laden with glasses of champagne ready to serve to thirsty guests, and there was fruit cup and ale for those whose tastes differed.

Cade and Belinda stood in the entrance hall to receive their guests and the once silent old house seemed to have taken on a new life, filled with the sound of laughter and conversation. The bride and groom were circulating and Cassy was just crossing the hall on her way to the dining room where the wedding breakfast had been laid out when someone crashed on the door-knocker. The girl newly employed as a parlour maid hurried to answer its urgent summons, and Cassy stood rooted to the spot as she saw the unmistakeable uniform of a telegram messenger boy. For a moment she could not move or breathe. It seemed that time itself had stood still. The maid was talking to her but all Cassy could see was the movement of the girl's lips.

'It's for Lady Davenport,' the maid repeated. 'I dunno who she is, miss.'

Slowly, as if wading through a swamp, Cassy forced her feet to move and she managed somehow to take the envelope from the messenger. 'It's all right,' she said breathlessly. 'I'll take it to her ladyship.'

'Any reply, miss?'

With trembling fingers she managed somehow to extract the flimsy sheet of paper.

'Any reply wanted, miss?' the boy repeated.

She shook her head, allowing the envelope to flutter to the floor. 'No,' she murmured, 'thank you.' She walked slowly into the drawing room, looking for her father.

Cade turned to look at her as she approached holding the telegram out to him in a mute plea for help. 'What is it? What's wrong?'

'It's Ollie,' she said faintly. 'And Bailey. It says missing in action, believed killed.'

The next twenty-four hours passed in a haze of grief and uncertainty. Cassy refused to believe that they were dead. She had felt for weeks that something was wrong, but death was so final. She would surely have known if Bailey or Ollie had gone to a world other than her own. Bailey was part of her, he had always been there for her; he simply would not go away and leave her on her own. She was barely conscious of life going on around her. She recalled afterwards that Lottie had been constantly at her side until it was time for them to board the ship sailing for Bombay. It was not the happy beginning to her parents' honeymoon they might have expected. Their journey had become a pilgrimage to the land where their loved ones had given their lives for their country.

Five weeks later, almost to the day, their vessel docked in Bombay. The voyage had been uneventful and being far from land had a soothing effect on Cassy's troubled nerves. There was nothing she could do other than to survive each day as best she could. She was listless, but took comfort from gazing at the vast vista of ocean that changed colour minute by minute. Her mother and Cade made every effort to keep up her spirits, but even though they tried hard to entertain and amuse her, theirs was a relationship that was exclusive and all-consuming. Cassy understood and accepted this and she was glad that her mother had found happiness at last, but that did nothing to assuage the gnawing anxiety that kept her awake well into the night until eventually the movement of the ship slicing through the waves lulled her to sleep.

Once ashore, Cade took over. He was on home ground now and he had their luggage taken to a hotel that resembled a huge white palace. They stayed there for several days, and would have moved on sooner but for the fact that Belinda was feeling unwell. She put it down to the change of diet or perhaps it was simply travel fatigue, but Cade was anxious and insisted that she must rest before they undertook the long journey by rail to Lucknow where the 13th Hussars had their headquarters.

In the meantime he showed Cassy the city where her grandmother had been born, and the house where she had lived until she met the handsome young English army officer with whom she fell hopelessly in love. It was a grand mansion, set in gardens filled with roses, marigolds and stands of pink and white oleander growing beneath the shade of banyan trees. 'Does it belong to you now?' Cassy asked as they gazed through the iron railings that surrounded the house and grounds.

Cade shook his head. 'I gave it to my aunts and their families. It seemed only fair as my grandfather had left his fortune to me. I had no wish to live here. It was never my home.'

'But it's beautiful, and it is so different here from London.' Cassy met his eyes with a smile. 'We are part of this, though, you and I. I'm glad you brought me to India, Pa. Whatever happens next, at least I know where my family came from, and I can understand why the beautiful Amira fell in love with your father, even though I never knew him. It's almost like history repeating itself with you and Ma.'

Cade bent down to drop a kiss on her forehead. 'I'm proud to have you for a daughter, Cassy. If your

427

grandfather were alive today he would be enchanted by you too.' He took her by the hand and led her back to the gharry. He handed Cassy into the carriage. 'Victoria station.'

'The station, Pa?'

'I want to book tickets for Lucknow,' Cade said, climbing in to sit beside her as the driver flicked his whip and the horse lurched forward, sending up plumes of dust from the road surface. 'We should leave as soon as possible, providing your mother feels well enough to travel.'

But when they returned to the hotel they found that Belinda was still lying on the sofa by the open window, while the punkah wallah sat outside the door with the cord tied round his big toe as he worked the cloth fan.

'Darling, are you still feeling unwell?' Cade said anxiously. 'We shouldn't have left you for so long.'

Pale but smiling resolutely, Belinda raised herself on her elbow. 'It's the heat, George. You'd think I would be used to it having been born here and spent many years in this country, but at this time of year I would have been in Simla until the cool.'

Cade laid his hand on her brow. 'At least there's no fever, my love. The monsoons will be here any day now and will relieve the heat. Do you think you will be able to travel tomorrow?'

Belinda shook her head. 'I think not, George. I sent a message to my old friend, Eleanor Pilkington, the wife of the British ambassador. She helped me years ago when I came here to give birth to Cassy. Anyway, she visited me today and invited me to stay at Government House until you return.'

Cassy stared at her mother in consternation. 'We can't leave you if you're unwell, Ma.'

Clutching Cade's hand, Belinda gave her a reassuring smile. 'Darling, it's just the heat and exhaustion from the journey. I never was a good sailor and trains make me feel sick too. You and George must go as planned. Eleanor will look after me and I'll enjoy her company. You two must go. I insist.'

Even travelling first class, the train journey was long, slow and uncomfortable, but Cassy was entranced by everything she saw. She was fascinated by the beautiful children with huge brown eyes and blue-black hair not dissimilar to her own. The women were lovely too, like exotic flowers in their brightly coloured saris. Everything she saw filled her with admiration and awe, from the stately elephants carrying howdahs on their backs to donkeys laden with panniers filled with anything from clay pots to bales of straw. She was both spellbound and scared by the snake charmers and it was strange to see cows wandering the streets unhindered and free to roam where they pleased. She was shocked by the poverty in rural areas but she had seen worse in the slums of the East End, and she realised that she had fallen in love with India.

She bore the discomforts of the long hours of travelling without a grumble, even when she discovered that the chai wallah brewed tea in the first class lavatory. She might have refused to drink the clear, slightly bitter brew at home, but thirst was a constant problem during the hot, dusty journey. Each time the train drew to a halt at a station the passengers were besieged by men and boys selling food, and Cassy was eager to try the hot, spicy curry wrapped in a chapatti and boiled rice served in banana leaves. She never forgot the reason for their mission but she relished every second of their journey into the unknown.

After almost two days travelling they reached Lucknow, and Cade hired a gharry to take them to the military headquarters. Cassy waited anxiously outside the Adjutant-General's office while her father went inside to discover whether there was any news of the missing men. He emerged looking tired and drawn. 'Nothing, I'm afraid, Cassy. I've been told to expect the worst.'

'I won't believe that, Pa. Look at what happened to you. You were given up for dead but you survived. If you think I'm going to give up now, you're very much mistaken.'

Cade met her anguished gaze with a nod of his head. 'You're right, my dear. We can't sit back and do nothing. I've made an appointment to see their commanding officer so that I can find out the exact details of their last mission. In the meantime I'm going to take you back to the hotel, and we'll make our plans accordingly.'

The hotel was little more than a guest house, and their rooms were clean but basic with whitewashed walls, bare floorboards relieved by colourful rag rugs, and split cane sun blinds at the windows. Cassy was glad that Ma had decided to stay in the comfort of

Government House in Bombay. The heat was oppressive and the humidity high. She felt as though the air had been sucked from her lungs, but when the rain came it was a shock to see it tumbling from the skies in thick opaque sheets. It drummed on the roof and flooded the gutters, falling in cascades to the ground below which was dried hard by the sun so that the water formed huge pools before it finally drained away leaving a sea of mud.

The rainstorm was over just as suddenly as it had begun and the humidity returned with a vengeance. Cassy paced the floor fanning herself with a palmetto leaf while she waited for her father to return. She had no way of knowing the time and after what seemed like hours she heard quick footsteps on the floorboards outside her room. She ran to open the door. 'Well, Pa? What did he say?'

'We leave for Delhi in the morning. There is a military hospital there. We might find some of their fellow officers who could give us more information.'

'Then let's go now,' Cassy said eagerly.

Cade shook his head. 'There's no train until morning. We'll get a good night's sleep and be on our way first thing.'

Next day they boarded a train which eventually took them to Delhi where they began their enquiries all over again, to no avail. The soldiers in the hospital had no knowledge of either Oliver or Bailey, but a young doctor suggested that they might have better luck in Deolali, which, he said, was situated just a hundred miles north-east of Bombay. 'It's where they send the sick and injured who are waiting to be sent home to England,' he said with a sigh. 'I wouldn't mind going there myself. The rainy season is always the hardest.'

Cade thanked him for his advice and once again they had to wait until next day for a train that would take them on to their next destination. Cassy was disappointed but refused to be downhearted. She was certain now that both Ollie and Bailey were alive. She had nothing but her own conviction and hope to go on, but she was determined to continue searching for them, no matter how long it took. Cade supported her willingly enough, but she knew that he was worried about Ma. He did not say as much but Cassy could tell by his faraway expression that his thoughts were with her mother, and that he was anxious to return to Bombay.

Sitting in yet another railway carriage on a train leaving Delhi, Cassy glanced at her father with a surge of genuine affection. His handsome face was creased with lines of worry and she was certain that there were a few more silver strands of hair at his temples than there had been when they left England. She felt guilty for ever doubting his feelings for Ma. His concern for her was visible for anyone but a fool to see. She had grown close to him in the last few days, and even if their mission proved futile she would always be grateful for the chance to get to know her father a little better. He had stood by her and gone to enormous length to find the two young men she loved, even though they had nothing to do with him and he barely knew them. He did not have to put himself through this and she loved him all the more for being there when she needed him. He was staring out of the window and his sighs were almost imperceptible to any but the most sensitive ears.

She laid her hand on his. 'I'll never forget what you've done for me and the boys, Pa,' she said softly. 'And don't worry about Ma, she's much tougher than she looks.'

Cade turned his head to look at her and his lips parted in a smile. 'I'm proud of both my girls, and I know how much those young men mean to you, Cassy.'

'We will find them alive, Pa. I know we will.'

'As far as I can see, Deolali is our last chance of finding them and it's a slim one to say the least. Don't get your hopes too high, my love.'

Chapter Twenty-three

The adjutant in charge of admissions to the hospital in Deolali leafed through a well-thumbed register. 'I don't recall an officer by the name of Davenport, or a Corporal Moon come to that. We're very particular about keeping our records up to date, as you can see.'

'I can,' Cade said, nodding in agreement. 'Is it possible that some of the men might be unidentified?'

'Unlikely, sir. But feel free to visit the wards and make enquiries. I'd take you myself but I have a mountain of work to get through before I go off duty.'

'Thank you for your help.' Cade beckoned to Cassy who had been hovering in the doorway. 'We won't trouble you any longer.'

'He could be wrong,' Cassy said hopefully as they made their way through corridors lined with stretchers, and queues of walking wounded waiting to be seen by the hard-pressed medical team.

'We won't leave until we're absolutely certain that they aren't here.' Cade signalled to an orderly who had come from one of the wards. 'Could I trouble you for a moment, Corporal? We've travelled halfway across India and back looking for two men who were reported missing. I'm hoping that they might have been brought here.'

The orderly's eyes were red-rimmed with fatigue

and underlined by dark shadows, as if he had not slept for days. 'It's possible, sir. We're full to capacity with cases of cholera and malaria as well as the wounded. You might like to leave the young lady in the anteroom. There are sights that might upset her.'

'Would you rather wait outside in the garden?' Cade said, eyeing Cassy with a worried frown. 'This might prove to be less than pleasant.'

She shook her head. 'I'm not afraid, Pa. I'd recognise Bailey anywhere and you might not. I'm coming with you.'

She was to regret her rash decision as the orderly showed them ward after ward stinking with the vomit and excrement of the unfortunate cholera victims, and, almost worse, the stench of putrefaction from gangrenous wounds. With her handkerchief clutched to her mouth, Cassy fought off nausea and faintness as she made her way from bed to bed. Her heart was wrung with pity for the sick and injured, and some of them were little more than boys, but it was almost a relief to find that neither Bailey nor Oliver was amongst them.

Finally they were back where they started. 'Sorry I couldn't find your men,' the orderly said wearily. 'It's possible they might turn up, though.'

Cassy was not going to give up so easily. She caught him by the sleeve as he was about to walk away. 'Please, wait. Are there any new arrivals who haven't gone through the system yet? We've come such a long way, sir. I can't go without having seen every last man.'

He turned to her with a resigned sigh. 'Honest, miss. I took you everywhere.'

435

'Not quite, mate.'

Cassy turned to the man who had just emerged from a side ward. He was a tough-looking individual with a crooked nose that looked as though it had been broken at some time in the past, and a misshapen left ear that must have taken quite a few punches.

The orderly eyed him with ill-concealed contempt. 'What did you say, Jones?'

'I said not quite, Corporal. There was two blokes brought in last night, dressed like natives but the patrol what found 'em realised they was white men beneath the dirt and walnut dye. No uniforms on 'em so they could be Russian spies. Unconscious and half dead they was, but ain't croaked yet. They could be your men, miss.'

'I want to see them,' Cade said with an air of undeniable authority.

The orderly blinked and cleared his throat. 'I – er – I dunno about that, sir. I'd have to get permission from the adjutant. If they're spies . . .'

'If they are then I'll leave them to your tender mercies.' Cade's tone was jocular but his resolute expression brooked no argument. 'Who is your commanding officer?'

'Colonel Fitzhugh, sir.'

'Barney Fitzhugh? We were at Sandhurst together. Let me see your spies, Corporal, and if there's any trouble I'll speak to my old friend and set matters straight.'

'Very well, sir. Private Jones, take the officer and the lady to see the prisoners, and stay with them. You can't trust them Russians, they're slippery characters.'

With a grunt that might have been assent or disgust, Cassy could not tell which, Jones led them into the side ward. The blinds were partially closed to keep the heat at bay but even so the room was like an oven, and the overpowering smell of carbolic could not quite disguise the all too familiar stench of sickness and sweat. For a dreadful moment Cassy thought that her knees were about to give way beneath her, but making a supreme effort, she steeled herself to approach the nearest bed.

She recognised him instantly, even in such a sorry state. 'Ollie,' she whispered. 'It's me, Cassy.'

'He can't hear you, miss,' Jones said gruffly. 'He's out of his head with fever. They don't call it doolally tap for nothing. Malaria's a real killer round here and probably done for more solders than them Afghans.'

'That's enough, Private,' Cade said sharply.

'Yes, sir.' Jones snapped smartly to attention.

Cassy pushed past them to take a closer look at the man in the next bed, who was tossing about feverishly and mumbling something unintelligible. Even before she reached his side she knew that it was Bailey. A sob of relief broke from her lips as she seized his hand. 'Bailey, I'm here. I've come to take you home.'

'They won't be going nowhere for a while, miss,' Jones said solemnly. 'Both of 'em got malaria. This one here is the worst case though. He's suffered gunshot injuries as well as getting the fever.' He nodded in Oliver's direction. 'Touch and go, I'd say, sir. He's in a very sorry state.'

'All the more reason to get them back to London,'

Cassy said firmly. 'You'll make the arrangements, won't you, Pa?'

But she soon discovered that it was not as simple as that. Neither Oliver nor Bailey had had any means of identification about their persons when they were found. It seemed obvious that they had been involved in some covert mission, but it would take time to verify this fact. In any event they were both dangerously ill and the doctors said that to remove them from the hospital could prove fatal.

Once again, Cade booked them into a hotel and word of their whereabouts was sent to Belinda. Almost by return, he received a message expressing her delight and relief that they had found Oliver and Bailey, and assuring him that she was fully recovered and in the best of spirits. Cassy settled down to write a long letter to her mother, describing their travels and the sights she had seen. She did not mention the overcrowded conditions of the military hospital, or the terrible suffering she had witnessed on a daily basis. She ended on a cheerful note, telling her mother to expect them very soon, although the latter was written more in hope than certainty.

They visited the hospital every morning. Bailey was improving daily and Oliver's condition was stable, so they were informed by the overworked young doctor. Cade had renewed his old acquaintanceship with Colonel Fitzhugh, and as he was able to formally identify Oliver and Bailey, the information had been sent on to their commanding officer in Lucknow. Confirmation of their hitherto secret mission was received and due to his officer status Oliver was moved to a private room, whereas Bailey, who was showing excellent signs of recovery, was sent to a fever ward.

Cassy continued to visit them every day. She was overjoyed one morning to find Bailey sitting up in bed, drinking a cup of tea. His skin was sallow and his eyes sunken in his face but they lit up as she walked into the room, and the sight of his familiar grin brought tears to her eyes.

'Cassy, love. They told me that you'd been here every day. I can't believe that you've come all this way to find me.'

'We almost gave up,' she said, halfway between tears and laughter. 'You wretched boy, Bailey.' She pulled up a stool and sat down beside him. 'We've been travelling round India for over a week, looking for you and Ollie, and this was our last chance. You're looking so much better than when I first saw you.'

'Liar. I look like a death's head on a mopstick. I was allowed to shave myself for the first time this morning and I hardly recognised the face looking back at me from the mirror.'

She put her arms around him and gave him a hug. 'You're alive, that's all that matters.' She would not have admitted it for the world, but his gaunt appearance still shocked her, and the hand that clutched hers was dry and brittle, like a bird's claw. 'You'll soon be up and about, dearest Bailey, and then we'll take you home where you belong.'

He reached up to stroke her hair. 'I've dreamt of this moment for so long,' he murmured, his eyes moist with unshed tears. 'All the time we were out there in the foothills it was blazing hot in the day and freezing at night. The only thing that kept me going was the memory of how you looked when we parted. It seems like years since that day in December.'

'I knew that there was something wrong weeks ago. I had nightmares about bloody battles and I was certain you were in danger.'

'That's the trouble with being in the army,' he said, with a shadow of his old humour. 'The enemy keeps trying to kill you.' His smiled faded and his eyes darkened. 'How is Oliver? They won't tell me a thing.'

'He's still unconscious, Bailey. I don't think it's just the fever, but the doctors don't say very much.'

'He took a bullet in the back, Cass. I carried him as far as I could each day, but then the fever got me and I don't remember very much until the patrol came upon us. I was never so glad to hear a cockney accent, I can tell you.'

A polite cough made Cassy look round to see Jones standing behind her. 'I think that's enough for today, miss. You don't want to tire the lad out now, do you?'

Cassy rose to her feet. 'No, of course not. I'll go and find out how Ollie is.' She turned to him with a smile. 'Perhaps I could have some more time with Corporal Moon later today?'

Jones nodded his head. 'I'm sure the doctors won't object to that, miss.'

'Feel free to visit me any time, miss.' One of the recuperating privates gave her a wink and a smile. 'A beautiful young lady's cool hand on me fevered brow would be just the ticket.'

Bailey raised himself on his elbow. 'Wait until I'm stronger, Figgis. You won't be so full of yourself then.'

Cassy leaned over to drop a kiss on Bailey's forehead. 'I'll be back later, I promise.' She left the ward accompanied by an appreciative whistle from Figgis.

'You'll have to excuse the men if they're too forward, miss,' Jones said apologetically as he escorted her along the corridor towards Oliver's room. 'They don't see too many pretty faces on the ward.'

'I wish I could do more to help,' Cassy said with feeling. 'I'm so sorry for them.'

'You done enough by just coming to visit. Young Moon will get better twice as fast now he's seen his lady love.'

'It's not like that,' Cassy murmured. 'I mean, we were childhood friends.'

'If you say so, miss.' Jones stopped outside Oliver's room and opened the door. He scowled at the punkah wallah, a boy of six or seven, who was sitting cross-legged on the floor, fast asleep. 'Wake up, you lazy little sod.' He poked him with the toe of his boot and the boy opened his eyes with a start. 'What d'you think you're paid for?' Jones demanded. 'Get on with your work.'

The boy began working the cord with renewed vigour and Cassy gave him an encouraging smile. She would have liked to put Private Jones in his place and tell him off for bullying a young child, but she sensed that any intervention might make matters worse for the punkah wallah. She frowned, but Jones seemed oblivious to her feelings, and uninterested in anything

441

other than exercising his authority. He opened the door, standing aside to allow her to enter.

'There you are, miss. Captain Davenport is as well as can be expected today. The doctor says it might be some time afore he comes to, so don't let it upset you. I seen plenty of cases where men have been out for the count for days, even weeks, and then suddenly opened their eyes, sat up and asked for a steak and kidney pudding.'

Cassy tiptoed into the darkened room. The blinds were down and it was almost unbearably hot even though the punkah was now moving the air with its gentle swaying motion. She gazed down at Oliver's immobile features and a shiver ran down her spine. He was deathly pale and his face had the frozen look of a marble effigy. Pa had warned her that the doctors did not hold out much hope of a complete recovery. The attack of fever was comparatively mild, but the injury to his spine was more serious. They had to face the fact that he might never walk again. It had come as a terrible shock. She could not imagine someone like Oliver living life as a cripple, and she had prayed every night for his full recovery.

She took a seat on the chair at his bedside and held his hand. She had felt self-conscious and slightly silly at first when talking to someone who could not hear a word she said. But after a while it had come naturally to her and she chatted to him as if he they were seated opposite each other in the tearoom all those years ago when she was just a child. She had already told him everything that had happened since he left

London, including the exhibition of Jack's paintings, and her plans for opening a shop selling work by the men from the home. She was beginning to run out of things to say, but somehow she managed to keep up her one-sided conversation.

At noon Cade arrived to take her back to the hotel for lunch, and over the meal of curried goat he told her of his plans to have Oliver moved to a hospital in Bombay as soon as he was fit to travel. 'He'll get the best medical attention that money can buy,' he assured her. 'And I've spoken to Colonel Fitzhugh about the possibility of buying Bailey out of the army. After everything he's been though, I think the boy should return to England with us. There's no doubt that he saved Oliver's life, putting his own at risk in the process.'

Cassy stared at him with her fork halfway to her mouth. 'But I'd assumed he would come with us anyway. I didn't think they'd make him return to active service when he's been so ill.'

'He's a soldier, my love. He can't come and go as he pleases, but I'll do everything I can to purchase his release.'

It had never occurred to Cassy that they would go home without Bailey. She could hardly believe that the army would be so rigid in its rules that it would make a sick man return to duty. The prospect of losing him for a second time made her feel quite desperate. She had not realised how her feelings towards him had changed, and how much she loved him, until she thought she might never see him again. How could she have been so blind as to ignore the truth that her heart had been telling her? For a while she had been dazzled by Ollie. He was undeniably exciting and fun to be with, and when he kissed her she had been lost in the thrill of his embrace, but it was only now that she realised the feelings she had for him did not consume her body and soul. She was desperately sad to see him laid low by his injuries and she willed him to recover, but he was not her reason for living. She hoped he would understand.

She continued to spend as much time as possible at the hospital and Bailey's condition gradually improved. He was allowed out of bed, although still very weak. In the mornings, before the sun was high in the sky, they took short walks in the hospital grounds or sat for a while beneath the banyan trees watching the monkeys skittering about amongst the branches. Although he never spoke of love, she was certain that Bailey felt the same as she. Words were unnecessary when two souls were inexorably entwined. The look in his eyes and the touch of his hand told her every-thing she needed to know.

It was still the wet season, and when the skies darkened and the monsoon rains drummed on the roof, sending up sprays of water and clouds of steam as it hit the ground, she sat with Oliver and held his hand. It was over a week since their arrival in Deolali and he had not regained consciousness, but on this particular day he had been restless and Cassy had stayed with him longer than usual. She bathed his brow with a damp flannel and had turned away for a moment to replace it in the bowl of water when she felt a slight movement from the bed. Dropping the cloth she spun round to find Oliver staring at her.

'Ollie,' she whispered. 'You're awake at last. Can you hear me?'

His cracked lips parted in an attempt at a smile. 'Cassy?'

She leaned over to embrace him. 'Oh, Ollie. You've come back to us.'

'What day is it?' he asked faintly. 'Why am I in bed?'

She laid her finger on his lips. 'Don't try to talk, my dear. You've been very ill and you mustn't excite yourself.'

'Where am I?'

'You're in the military hospital in Deolali. Bailey is here too.'

He made an attempt to raise his head and failed. 'I – I can't move.' His lips trembled and his eyes were wide with fear. 'Cassy, I can't move my legs.'

'Don't try, Ollie. You're weak, that's all. I'll go and fetch the doctor.' Rising swiftly to her feet she backed away from the bed. 'Don't worry; everything is going to be fine now.'

It was not, and she knew it, but she must not let him see that she was scared. 'I won't be long.' She hurried from the room and broke into a run as she reached the corridor. She almost barged into the young doctor who attended Ollie as he emerged from a side ward. She grabbed him by the arm. 'Captain Davenport is awake, doctor. He spoke to me, but he can't move. You must go to him right away, please.'

'I will, of course, but it would be best if you weren't

present. I saw Corporal Moon in the dayroom earlier; you might like to wait there.' He strode off, leaving Cassy staring after him.

Her first instinct had been to go with him but her second and more pressing need was to find Bailey. She ran the length of the corridor to the dayroom where she found him playing draughts with one of the other convalescent soldiers. He looked up but his smile faded when he saw her agitated expression, and he rose slowly to his feet. 'Cassy, what's wrong? Is it Ollie?'

She hurled herself into his arms. 'He woke up, Bailey. He spoke to me.' Halfway between tears and laughter, she clung to him as she had when she was a little girl in need of comfort. But the look in his eyes made her draw away and she was conscious of the soldier staring at them with a knowing grin. She felt the blood rush to her face. 'I – I'm sorry. I was just so pleased that he's come round after all this time.' She fumbled in her reticule for a handkerchief to no avail. 'I'm just happy.'

'Of course you are,' Bailey said, taking her by the arm and leading her out onto the veranda. 'I'm glad too. He's a good chap.'

'But he couldn't move,' Cassy said urgently. 'Bailey, I think he's paralysed. He'll end up in a Bath chair just like the men in the home. Poor Ollie.'

He took her by the shoulders, looking deeply into her eyes. 'You don't know that for certain, Cass. You're jumping to conclusions. Wait until the doctors have seen him.'

'Yes,' she said, wiping her eyes on her sleeve. 'You're

right, as usual. We will just have to wait and see what they say.'

The medical men shook their heads and could give no explanation as to why Captain Davenport was paralysed from the waist down. As far as they could tell, the bullet had not shattered any of his vertebrae, but it was impossible to gauge the true extent of the internal damage. They could not say for certain if he would ever walk again, but they were not optimistic. It was left to Cade to break the news to Oliver. Cassy waited in the dayroom with Bailey and she could tell by the tense expression on her father's face that it had been a harrowing time for both of them.

'He took it well enough, all things considered,' Cade said, mopping his brow with a handkerchief. 'I told him that I'm making arrangements to get us all back home. As soon as we get back to Bombay I'm going to book tickets for the voyage.'

Belinda was waiting for them at the railway terminus in Bombay. Cade leapt off the train before it had come to a halt, taking the platform in long strides to sweep her into his arms in an embrace that made the other travellers stop and stare. Cassy watched from the train window and this time she was not embarrassed by her parents' demonstration of their love for each other. She met Bailey's eyes and he smiled. There was no need for words between them.

'What's going on?' Oliver demanded. 'What are you two staring at?'

Cassy turned away from the window. 'I was just thinking how lucky my parents were to find each other again.'

'They make a handsome couple,' Bailey said with a nod of approval as he hefted the Bath chair onto the platform. He climbed back into the carriage. 'Ready, Captain?'

'As ready as I'll ever be. I'm sick of being pushed round like a baby in a perambulator.' Oliver hooked his arm around Bailey's neck. 'The doctors wouldn't give me a straight answer, but I'm determined to walk again. I'll do it, Cassy, I swear to God I will. With you at my side I can do anything.'

Bailey said nothing as he set him down in the chair. Cassy willed him to look at her but he walked away, calling for a coolie to take their luggage.

'You'll do it, Ollie.' Cassy hoped that she sounded convincing. 'You've done wonderfully well so far.'

He caught her by the hand. 'I know I'm a wreck of a fellow but I love you with all my heart, Cassy. What I mean to say is, I don't expect you to stand by me unless you really love me.' He released her with a sigh. 'I'm putting it badly, but I don't want you to stay with me just because I'm a cripple.'

She met his anguished gaze and she knew that to tell him the truth would be the cruellest blow yet. She had allowed him to think that she returned his love, and now she must pay the price for her cowardice. She looked for Bailey amongst the milling crowd of passengers, station officials and coolies, and felt the unmistakeable tug at her heart as she spotted him standing by the entrance with her parents. He seemed to sense her intense gaze, as he looked round and waved to her. Grasping the handle, she wheeled the Bath chair towards the exit. She longed for a quiet chat with her mother, but consoled herself with the fact that there would be plenty of time to talk when they were settled into the hotel where they would stay until Cade had booked their passage to England.

Belinda broke away from Cade as they approached and she took Oliver's hand in hers. 'Ollie, my dear boy. How are you feeling?'

'Never better, Stepmother,' Oliver said, grinning. 'You'll have to forgive me for not rising to greet you.'

Belinda touched his cheek with the tips of her fingers. 'I'm glad to see you haven't lost your sense of humour, my dear.' She turned to Cassy. 'Darling, you look tired. You must be exhausted.' She wrapped her arms around her daughter, holding her close.

'I'm a bit tired, but how are you, Ma? Are you feeling better now?'

'I couldn't be better.' Belinda's eyes sparkled and a delicate flush coloured her cheeks. 'You can't imagine how happy I am to see you, and Bailey too. You're both safe and that's all that matters.' She slipped her hand through Cade's arm. 'I have some very exciting news to share with you all, but it will have to wait until later when you're all settled into the rooms I've booked for you at the hotel.'

'Let Bailey push me, Cassy,' Oliver said, holding up his hand. 'I want you to walk beside me.' He glanced up at Cade with a challenge in his eyes. 'We had an understanding before I left England, sir. When I'm back on my feet I intend to ask you for your daughter's hand in marriage.'

'Ollie, not now, please.' Cassy felt a cold shiver run down her spine as she met Bailey's questioning gaze. She wanted to deny it, but they were standing in the middle of the busy station concourse and her mother was staring at her wide-eyed.

'Is this true, darling?'

'I'll go and find a couple of carriages.' Bailey strode out into the sunlight, leaving Cassy to face her parents.

'I think we should discuss this later,' Cade said, patting Oliver on the shoulder. 'It's early days yet, old man.'

'What do you say, Cassy?' Oliver demanded, twisting his head to look at her. 'Come round here where I can see you properly.'

'Pa's right,' Cassy said in desperation. 'This isn't the time or the place, Ollie. We'll talk about it when we're settled in the hotel.'

That evening at dinner in the grand hotel dining room, the atmosphere was tense even though Belinda kept up a stream of idle chatter. She gave an amusing account of life in Government House illustrated with vignettes of her experiences as a guest at some of the official functions. Cade watched her with an adoring look in his eyes, which made Cassy feel even worse about her relationship with Oliver. He was staring moodily at his plate, pushing the food around and eating very little although the meal was delicious. He had been obliged to put on an ill-fitting suit that the tailor had made for another client who had left it unclaimed with the bill unsettled, but it was the best that could be done at short notice. He was patently unhappy and although Cassy's heart went out to him, she could not seem to shake him out of his depression. She stole covert looks at Bailey who was also looking uncomfortable, although she thought proudly that he looked extremely handsome in the evening suit that her father had insisted on loaning him. They were of a similar height and stature and the garments could have been tailored especially for him.

As if sensing her gaze upon him, he looked up and gave her a smile which made her pulses race. She had not had a chance to speak to him alone since they left Deolali, but he seemed intent on returning to his unit, and she was just as determined that he should come home with them. Pa could arrange it, she was certain. She had absolute faith in him.

At the end of the meal, Bailey suggested that Oliver might like to go outside to take the air, although the heat was still intense. Cade said that he had a box of excellent cigars that they might like to try, and that a fine cognac would accompany the Havana tobacco very well indeed, but Belinda linked her small hand through his arm, smiling sweetly. 'I'm sure that can wait a moment, darling. I think this might be a good time to tell them our news.'

Chapter Twenty-four

A baby brother or sister; the news had come as a complete shock to Cassy. She had never considered that such an event was possible until Ma and Cade made the announcement, but they were so patently delighted and thrilled at the idea of becoming parents again that it would have been a hard-hearted person who could not share their joy. Oliver had congratulated them with obvious sincerity, and Bailey had slipped his hand beneath the tablecloth to give Cassy's fingers a sympathetic squeeze. There had been understanding in his smile with no need for words.

She had done her best to be pleased for them, and she had been sincere when she told them that she was delighted at the prospect of having a brother or a sister, but even so, a small mean voice niggled away in her brain telling her that she was once again an outcast. Nothing would ever completely wipe away the stain of illegitimacy, but her sibling would not have that burden to bear.

She knew that she would not sleep. It was a hot night, and as she looked down from her window at the moonlit hotel garden she had a sudden longing to be out in the silvery cool where the scent of roses and jasmine blotted out the stench of the city. She could see a figure walking beneath a deodar tree, and her heartbeats quickened as she realised that it was Bailey and he was alone. Seizing her lace shawl, she wrapped it around her head and shoulders and crept out of her room, making her way downstairs and out onto the veranda. Sleepy-eyed hotel staff went about their business barely noticing her and she went outside unchallenged. Picking up her skirts she ran lightly down the wide marble steps, across a gravelled terrace and into the rose garden.

Bailey stopped and turned to face her as she ran towards him. 'Cassy, what are you doing out here? It's turned midnight.'

'I had to speak to you,' she said breathlessly. 'We've had so little time to talk since we left Deolali.'

He was silent for a moment, gazing at her with a tender smile curving his lips. They were standing so close together that she could feel the heat of his body and the achingly familiar scent that was his alone, with just a hint of fragrant cigar smoke clinging to his clothes and hair. 'What is it, Cass? What's the matter? Aren't you happy for them?'

'Of course I am. It was a bit of a shock, but they'll be wonderful parents. I just wish . . .'

He wrapped her in his arms, holding her close. 'I know, Cass. Nothing can quite wipe out the memories of old Biddy and Three Herring Court, and it's hard for other people to understand what we went through.'

'But you do, Bailey.' She slid her arms around his neck, looking deeply into his eyes. 'You are part of me, and I can't let you go. Please come home with us. Don't stay here and risk getting killed.'

He stroked her hair back from her forehead with a gentle hand. 'I'm a soldier and I've earned promotion on my own merit. I didn't have a rich father to buy me a commission.'

'And I'm proud of you,' Cassy said earnestly. 'I couldn't be more proud, but I love you, Bailey. I want to be with you always.'

'You're still a child, Cass. I know you love me, and I love you and always will, but you belong to a different world. You were born to higher things and one day you'll realise that.'

She stared at him aghast. Did he really think she was still a little girl, with a child's feelings? How could he be so wrong and so stupid? 'You don't understand,' she said angrily. 'I'm not a baby. I know my feelings and I'm telling you that they're completely grown-up. I love you. Do I have to spell it out?'

He shook his head. 'Oliver loves you, Cass. He wants to marry you and he can give you everything that I can't.' He led her to a stone seat beneath a rose arch and sat down beside her, taking both her hands in his. 'Listen to me, my darling girl. Oliver saved my life. He took the bullet that was meant for me and because of me he's a cripple. When we were lost in that desolate place and before we went out of our heads with fever, all he could talk about was you. He said he was going to buy himself out of the army and return to England. He said that he was going to propose to you on your eighteenth birthday, and he was certain that you'd accept him.'

Aghast, she shook her head. 'No, he was mistaken. I would never have married him because I love you, Bailey. How many times do I have to tell you?'

'But you must have given him some cause to hope, Cass.'

'I may have, but it was unintentional. He kissed me and it was romantic, but I didn't mean to lead him on, you must believe me. I've always loved you and I want to be your wife.'

'I do believe you, but it's not for us, Cassy.' He raised her hands to his lips. 'I love you with all my heart and soul. You're part of me and that's why I have to let you go.'

'Don't I have a choice in all this? You're so busy telling me what to do, Bailey, but I'm a woman now, and I love you.'

'If only you knew how much I've longed to hear those words coming from your lips. How much I've wanted to hold you in my arms and kiss you, but that sort of love isn't for us, Cass. I won't drag you down to my level.' He held her gaze, looking deeply into her eyes. 'Do you honestly see yourself following the drum as a common soldier's wife? You were born for better things and Oliver can give you the sort of life you are entitled to. Even if he never recovers completely, he's an educated man and he has a private income left to him by his grandfather. He'll be able to keep you in style, which is something I could never do.'

She wrenched her hands free. 'Stop saying things like that. I won't listen to you. You're just being stupid.' She leapt to her feet, staring down at him with anger roiling in her stomach. 'Why are men such idiots? What do I have to do to convince you that I mean every word I say?'

'You can't, Cass. I wish it were any other way but I'm eight years your senior, and I've learned a lot since I've been in the army. I know the difference between officers and men, and that goes for their wives too. Can you imagine living alongside women who grew up in the gutter?'

Arms akimbo, Cassy glared at him. 'I grew up in the gutter, and so did you. I don't think anyone could sink much lower than Three Herring Court.'

'But you weren't meant for that sort of life, which is what I keep trying to tell you, my love. I don't know who my parents were. Outside the army I'm a nobody, but in the regiment I have a place and I'm doing something worthwhile for my country.'

She stamped her foot. 'You say you love me, but you don't. You're in love with the rotten blooming army. I hope it makes you very happy.' Turning on her heel she stormed out of the rose garden, pausing at the foot of the steps leading up to the veranda to glance over her shoulder, half hoping that he was following her. But he was still sitting where she had left him, with his shoulders hunched and his head bowed.

Next morning when she joined her parents for breakfast, Oliver was there but Bailey was nowhere to be seen.

'He left first thing this morning, Cassy,' Cade said, following her gaze as she stared at the empty place at table. 'I tried to persuade him to stay on for a while, but Bailey is a very determined young man, and he wanted to return to his regiment in Lucknow.'

Oliver nodded his head. 'He's a good chap; one of the best, and I'll miss him.'

'We all will,' Belinda said, smiling. 'He's been like a brother to you, Cassy, especially in the early days. I'm sure you will miss him most of all.'

Cassy could not answer. If she relaxed for a second she knew she would break down and cry or scream out loud with anger and frustration. How cowardly of Bailey to run away without saying a proper goodbye. He might be a brave soldier but he was not man enough to stand up and fight for the woman he loved. She stared down at her plate and realised that she had broken a bread roll into tiny crumbs.

Cade put his coffee cup down, wiping his lips on a starched white table napkin. 'If you'll excuse me, Belle, I'm going to the Peninsular and Orient office to book us on the next ship bound for London.'

'I say the sooner we get home the better, and I know that Oliver agrees with me.' Belinda's lips twitched and her eyes sparkled. 'I'm sure you do too, Cassy. Oliver told us that you two had an understanding, and last night he asked your father's permission to propose to you. Isn't it time you put us out of our misery and gave him your answer?'

Numb with grief and anger, Cassy turned to Oliver. 'You should have spoken to me first.'

'Perhaps, but I thought we had an understanding, Cassy.'

She met his earnest gaze and was immediately

ashamed of herself. She had not meant to lead him on, and she struggled to find the words to let him down gently, but Oliver seemed to take her silence as confirmation. He reached across the table to cover her hand with his. 'We've wasted enough time. This wretched condition of mine has made me realise that putting things off is never a good idea. I should have asked you to marry me before I embarked for India. We could have had many months together before I was turned into half a man.'

She withdrew her hand, unable to look him in the eyes. 'Don't talk like that, Ollie. You mustn't say those things about yourself.'

'You have our blessing, both of you.' Cade said, rising to his feet. 'We'll get you the best medical treatment that money can buy, old chap. And if you find a quarter of the happiness with my beautiful daughter that I have with her equally beautiful mother, then you'll be a very lucky man no matter what the future holds.'

'Well, Cassy, darling?' Belinda angled her head. 'Are you going to put the poor boy out of his misery? Or is your answer a foregone conclusion?'

She was trapped. Cassy glanced at the expectant faces of the people she loved and she knew that there was no way out. Oliver was watching her closely with hope in his eyes, and she could not bring herself to tell him the truth. She had thought she loved him on that cold winter's afternoon in the parlour at Pedlar's Orchard, and now she was paying for her youthful folly. She had lost the one man she truly loved. Despite her pleas,

Bailey had walked away from her, making it clear that there was no future for them as man and wife. Now she was about to promise herself to the hero who had saved his life. It seemed like a cruel but poetic justice.

'Well, Cassy,' Cade said. 'Don't keep us in suspense.'

Slowly she nodded her head. 'Yes,' she murmured. 'I will marry you, Ollie.'

The passage home took six weeks, giving Cassy time to get used to her new status as a young woman officially engaged to a wounded hero. Oliver had bought her a huge ruby and diamond ring before they left Bombay, but the deep red stone sat on her finger like a drop of blood. Try as she might, that was how she felt. Her heart's blood was being shed to pay for the life of the man she loved, and every nautical mile they travelled drew them further apart. Oliver's condition improved greatly during the sea voyage. Each day Cassy pushed him round the deck in his Bath chair, or else they sat side by side, enjoying the sun and sea air. They saw little of Cade and Belinda, who were absorbed in each other's company like any young couple on their honeymoon.

'We'll be like that once we're married,' Oliver said, taking Cassy's hand in his. 'When I'm cured by those damned clever doctors in London, we'll do the grand tour of Europe.'

'Yes, Ollie,' Cassy said dutifully. 'That will be wonderful.'

It was early November when they arrived back in London and winter had claimed the city in its chilly grip, which made the warm welcome that Mrs Wilkins had prepared for their homecoming even more pleasing. The servants were waiting to greet them, together with Jack and the more able-bodied of the men from the soldiers' home. There were fires in every room and each small detail had been attended to, down to vases of bronze and gold chrysanthemums filling the air with their spicy scent. Word had been sent on ahead and the breakfast parlour on the ground floor had been converted into a bedroom for Oliver.

Within a fortnight of their arrival, he had begun treatment at the National Orthopaedic Hospital in Hatton Garden. He was convinced that he would be cured and able to walk again, and at times he was filled with optimism, but at others he was flung into the depths of despair. Everyone did their best to accommodate his moods, but it was like walking on eggshells. Seeking a means of escape from a difficult situation, Cassy threw herself into preparations for the opening of the shop. During their absence it had been fitted out with a counter, shelves and display stands which were now ready and waiting to be filled with the men's handicrafts and Jack's paintings. She was on the premises one morning, going over the arrangements for the official opening with Jack, when she looked up and saw her father's carriage pull up outside. It was Ollie's day for treatment at the hospital and she hurried to the door, wondering why the coachman had stopped here instead of further along the street in Lemon's Terrace.

The groom climbed down from the box and opened

the door, pulling out the steps and for a wild moment Cassy thought that a miracle had occurred and that Ollie was about to walk down them unaided, but to her surprise it was Lottie who was the first to alight. She stood aside while the groom lifted Oliver from the seat and carried him across the pavement.

Cassy wrenched the door open and ran out to greet them. 'Lottie, what are you doing here?'

'I've had warmer welcomes.' Laughing, Lottie threw her arms around Cassy and gave her a hug.

'Take me inside, man,' Oliver said irritably. 'I don't want the world to see me like this.'

'Yes, sir.' The groom hurried into the shop, followed by Cassy and Lottie.

'Set me down, you fool, and wait outside. I'll call when I need you.' Oliver dismissed him with a wave of his hand.

'What's the matter?' Cassy demanded. 'Why are you so angry?'

He smiled ruefully. 'I'm sorry; I'm being a bear again today, my love. If it hadn't been for Lottie I might have had a serious argument with the doctor.'

'You're a difficult patient,' Lottie said, chuckling. 'We get plenty like you, so don't think you're special, Oliver Davenport.'

'That's right,' Cassy said with mock severity. 'It's time someone stood up to him. We've all been tiptoeing around Ollie, but perhaps he needs a firm hand, like a naughty little boy.'

Oliver pulled a face, turning to Jack who was standing at a respectful distance. 'I suppose you're used to petticoat rule, my man. I don't know how you put up with it.'

'Jack is too polite to answer you.' Cassy suppressed a sigh. Ollie had been particularly difficult for the last day or two, and her patience was almost at an end.

Lottie went to study the paintings one by one. 'These are very good,' she said, turning to Jack with a smile. 'Much better than the ones you showed at the exhibition. I think they'll be snapped up.' She picked up a honey-glazed clay pot in the shape of a top hat. 'This is nice too. I can just see it filled with primroses and violets. You have some lovely things here, and the shop is in a prime position. I hope it does well.'

'I do too,' Cassy said with feeling. 'But how did you come to be with Ollie? Were you visiting someone at the hospital?'

'I've been sent there for six months to study orthopaedics. I think I might specialise in it if I manage to qualify, although of course there is such a lot of opposition from the male members of the profession. It's a real struggle, Cassy.'

'But I'd say you're more than a match for those idiots,' Oliver said stoutly. 'You should have seen her standing up to the doctor who examined me, Cassy. He was talking to me as if I were a two-year-old and Lottie waded in there like a tiny tiger. I'd have her in my regiment any day.'

Cassy looked from one to the other in surprise. In the past their relationship had been fiery. One minute they were laughing and chatting like old friends, and the next they would be sparring like barristers on opposing sides. She met Lottie's amused look with a grateful smile. 'Thank you for taking care of him. As you can see, he's quite a handful.'

'It's not easy for an active man to find himself dependent on others, but what Ollie hasn't told you is that he has recovered a little of the feeling in his feet, which is an excellent sign. We'll have him up and walking yet.'

'You'll come back to the house for luncheon, won't you?' Oliver said urgently. 'I've got a whole list of questions I want answered.'

Lottie shook her head. 'I'm sorry. I'd love to, but I've got to get back to the hospital. I shouldn't really be here but I managed to persuade the consultant that you ought to have someone with you, if only to prevent you from setting about the groom. You really were terribly rude to the poor man, and he was doing his best to help you.'

No one had spoken to Oliver like that for a long time, and Cassy held her breath waiting for him to react angrily, but to her surprise he seemed not to have taken offence. In fact he appeared to be almost chastened. Cassy stared at Lottie in amazement. She had dared to do what everyone else had been too scared to attempt. She had put Oliver in his place.

'I'll apologise to the fellow if that makes you happy, doctor,' he said meekly.

'Not a doctor yet.' Lottie patted him on the shoulder. 'Give me time, though. I'll say goodbye for now, but I really must get back to the hospital.'

'Come and see us again when you get time off,' Cassy

said as she saw her to the door. 'I have so much I want to tell you.'

'I guessed as much, Cass. We never had any secrets from each other, and I can see that you aren't happy.' She glanced at the ring on Cassy's finger. 'That's a splendid gem, but I don't think that ruby-red is your colour.'

Glancing nervously over her shoulder to see if Ollie was listening, Cassy was relieved to see that he was in conversation with Jack. She grasped Lottie's hand. 'I'm in such turmoil. I need to talk to you.'

'I'm off duty tomorrow evening,' Lottie said in a low voice. 'Shall I come to your house?'

'No, I'll come to you. It would be impossible to talk at home.'

Next evening, Cassy found it surprisingly easy to slip away after dinner. Oliver had retired early, having drunk rather too much claret during the meal and had been wheeled away by Maitland, a quiet, dependable manservant who had been taken on to attend to his personal needs. Cassy finished her dessert in silence while her mother and father made plans for an outing to one of the new department stores in order to choose furniture for the nursery. They barely noticed when Cassy made her excuses to leave the table, and she left them discussing when they ought to advertise for a nanny and a nursery maid. She had secreted her bonnet and cloak in the morning parlour, and she waited there until the carriage was brought round to the front entrance.

Feeling like a prisoner escaping from jail, Cassy

slipped out of the house and climbed into the barouche. It was raining. The cobblestones glistened in the gaslight and the muddy water made gushing noises as it ran in rivulets along the gutters to create eddies as it was sucked into the drains. It was cold, and Cassy was shivering by the time she arrived in Spectacle Alley. She told the coachman to return in an hour, and wrapping her cloak tightly against the wind and rain she hurried down the narrow street to hammer on the shop door.

Lottie let her in. 'Good heavens, what a night. Come into the parlour and sit by the fire. Pa sends his apologies but he's got one of his bad chests and he's gone to bed.' She led the way through the dark shop, where the manikins lurked like headless giants in the shadows. When she was a child they had scared Cassy, but she had grown out of such youthful fancies now. Taking off her bonnet and cloak she laid them neatly on a chair.

Lottie went to sit by the fire, motioning Cassy to take a seat opposite her. 'Now then, tell me everything. I could see that there was something terribly wrong. What is it, Cassy?'

It was a relief to pour out her troubles to sympathetic ears. Lottie listened without making any comment until Cassy finished speaking. 'I am so sorry. It is a bit of a pickle, so what will you do?'

'What can I do? I've promised to marry him, and I don't want to hurt him. I do love him, but not in the way he wants. It's Bailey and it was always him, even though I didn't realise it until too late.'

465

'But Cass, you mustn't marry a man you don't love. It will go wrong eventually and then you'll both be unhappy.'

'He'll never know. I mean to make him a good wife, but I just had to tell somebody and who else but my best friend?'

Lottie was silent for a moment, staring into the fire with a thoughtful look on her face. When she raised her head, her expression was serious. 'I wish I had some good advice to give you, but this is something you must work out for yourself, Cassy. I know that your motives are based on loyalty and gratitude, but don't you think Ollie deserves more than that?'

'He trusts me, and I can't let him down.' Cassy reached out to grasp Lottie's hands. 'You've seen the delicate state he's in, and you're a doctor, or soon will be. I want you to promise me that you'll do everything you can to make him well again. He's always been fond of you, Lottie. If anyone can help him, it's you.'

'I don't know about that, Cass. I'll do everything I can, of course, but ...'

'If Ollie could walk again I might be able to tell him how I really feel, but until then I have to keep my promise, to him and to Bailey.'

'And if he never walks again?'

'I'll stand by him, no matter what.'

Cassy returned home feeling relieved to have shared her problem with Lottie, but nagging doubts about the future kept her awake into the small hours. They were not eased when, next morning, Flora arrived at the house in Lemon's Terrace dressed in furs and looking every inch the squire's wife. Cade had accompanied Oliver to the hospital for his appointment with yet another consultant and it was left to Belinda and Cassy to entertain their guest.

'Well, you're a pretty pair,' Flora said, taking a seat close to the fire in the blue and gold drawing room. 'Having a baby at your age, Belle. What were you and Cade thinking of?' She chuckled. 'No, I'll rephrase that question. What on earth were you and Cade thinking of?'

Belinda smiled serenely. 'I can assure you that we're both delighted at the prospect of being parents, and I'm only just thirty-five, Flora.'

'You do look well, I have to admit that.' Flora turned to Cassy with a questioning look. 'And you, miss? I hear that you're engaged to Oliver. What's that all about?'

'Just that, Aunt Flora. We're going to get married.'

'You're taking on a cripple? I've been married five times, and even I would think twice before landing myself with a husband who couldn't walk up the aisle. And this is my nephew we're talking about. Even if Ollie was hale and hearty I wouldn't think it a good match for either of you.'

'Flora, is this really necessary?' Belinda cast an anxious glance at Cassy. 'You don't have to listen to this kind of talk, my love.'

'Ho, you've become very bold,' Flora said, curling her lip. 'I remember the time when you wouldn't say boo to a goose, Belinda. I see that marriage to that renegade has made you into a different woman.'

467

'And one I'm proud to be. No disrespect to poor Geoffrey, who was a good husband, but my true love was always George. I only wish we'd been able to share the joy of bringing up our daughter.' Belinda gave Cassy a rueful smile. 'I regret those wasted years.'

'Yes, well, Geoffrey was a dry old stick, as I've said many a time before, and you're old enough to know your own mind.' Flora turned her fierce gaze on Cassy. 'But I'm not sure that you do, miss. Heaven knows I love my nephew, but I don't think you two are suited. Oliver may think that you are all sweetness, but I've seen a core of steel inside you, Cassy. He may imagine that he can rule you, but I have my doubts. Unless you love him with all your heart, I'd say stop this charade now. Never mind breaking his heart, it will mend. Better to do it before you're married than afterwards. I speak from experience, my dear.'

Cassy bowed her head. She could not meet Flora's knowing gaze. It was as though she saw deep into her soul, and had guessed her guilty secret.

'And how is Mr Mullins?' Belinda said sweetly. 'Are you enjoying life on the farm, Flora?'

'As a matter of fact I'm in my element. I've discovered that he owns land and cottages that bring in rents, when he can be bothered to collect them, as well as the income from dairy farming. I've taken over the business side completely now, and next year I hope to make a substantial profit. To think that all those years I was dependent on my husbands for money, and all the while I've had a perfectly good brain which could have been put to better use than organising parties and making the odd pound or two for charity.'

'You make it all sound so easy,' Belinda said mildly.

Flora pointed a bony finger at Cassy. 'Use your head, girl. I hear you're starting up a shop for the soldiers to sell their handwork, which is splendid news. One day women will earn the right not only to vote but to equal men in the business world. Don't waste your talents on having a baby every year, Cassy. Go out there and fight for women's rights.'

The winter months flew past for Cassy. Setting her own problems aside, she threw herself into organising the day to day running of the shop, although her main aim was for the men to take it over themselves. Business was slow at first but Cade encouraged his friends and acquaintances to visit the premises, and gradually word spread that there were bargains to be had, and works of art to collect which might one day prove to be a good investment. Jack had plenty of ideas for expanding their business by employing one of the men who had been a cobbler by trade. He had lost the use of his legs, but he was more than happy to have his workbench set up close to the window so that passers-by could see him mending boots and shoes. This brought in customers who would never normally have gone into premises such as theirs. Jack also put forward the suggestion that they rent the shop next door where they would sell bread and cakes cooked in the home kitchen. Cassy could envisage the whole row of shops taken over by the ex-soldiers utilising their varied talents and former trades.

As the cold weather was eased away by an early spring, Belinda gave birth to a son. Both mother and baby were doing well and Cade handed out cigars by the boxful. Cassy was delighted with her baby brother, who was to be named George, after his father, and Hubert, after the grandfather Cassy had never known.

Slowly over the months, Oliver's condition had begun to improve. The feeling had come back to his lower limbs and the doctors were now hopeful of a good, if not complete, recovery. Lottie was tireless in her efforts to find new treatments that helped him regain the strength in his wasted muscles, and she was convinced that he would walk again. But Cassy watched his progress with a mixture of hope and trepidation. When he had begun to show signs of recovery, Oliver had decided that they would wait until he could walk down the aisle unaided before they took their wedding vows. She had been glad of the reprieve, but she realised that the time was coming when she must make the final decision that had the power to change the course of both their lives forever.

Baby George's christening was set for a week after Easter Sunday. The guest list was so long that it seemed Cade had invited everyone he had ever known. Dressed in a new gown of pale pink mousseline, Cassy was adjusting her bonnet in the mirror above the mantelshelf in the drawing room when the door opened and Oliver hobbled in with the aid of crutches. She turned to him with a genuine smile of pleasure. 'Ollie, how splendid to see you walking, but are you sure you won't over-tire yourself?'

He made his way to the nearest chair and eased himself into it. 'I'm not going to be wheeled into my stepbrother's christening,' he said, grinning. 'Even if young George isn't my stepbrother now that Belle has remarried, that's how I'll always think of him.'

'I suppose that means I'm still your stepsister, or half-stepsister.' She turned to him, biting her lip. 'I'm sorry; I didn't mean to be flippant.'

'Cassy, there's something I must tell you. I don't know how to begin. It makes me sound like a complete cad.'

'What is it, Ollie? Tell me.'

'I – I can't marry you, Cassy.' His expression was one of anguish as he raised his eyes to meet her gaze. 'I should have told you sooner, but I wasn't certain. It came upon us gradually without either of us realising what was happening.'

The truth hit her like a bolt of lightning. 'It's Lottie, isn't it? You're in love with her. I should have guessed.'

'I hate myself for doing this to you. I'll always love you, but . . .'

She bowed her head, and her shoulders shook.

'Don't cry, Cassy. You'll break my heart if you cry.'

She could no longer control the bubble of laughter that had welled up inside her. 'I'm not crying, darling Ollie. I'm happy for you and for Lottie. You couldn't find a lovelier girl or a better wife. She'll make you far happier than I ever could.'

'I – I don't understand. I thought you'd take it badly.'

'I love you as a brother, Ollie. I couldn't tell you before when you were in such a bad way, but my heart belongs to Bailey. It always has and it always will.'

'Damn me! And yet you were going to marry me? I say, that's not on.'

'And you've been spooning with my best friend, so don't play the martyr, Oliver Davenport.' She bent down to kiss him on the forehead. 'We've both been deluding ourselves, but now everything is going to be all right.'

He blinked, staring at her as if she had gone mad. 'You're not angry with me?'

'Of course not, silly. I wish you and Lottie every happiness, but now I've something I must do. I have to speak to my pa.'

Feeling as though she was walking on air, free at last to follow her heart, she found Cade in the billiard room, smoking a cigar and pacing the floor. He turned with a start as she burst into the room. 'Good grief, what's the matter? Is something wrong with the baby or your mother?'

'Nothing is wrong, Pa. But I'm in desperate need of your help.'

'What is it, my darling? You know I'll do anything for you.'

A week later, standing on the dockside, Cassy shielded her eyes from the sun as she watched the gangway being set in place to allow the passengers to board HMS *Serapis*, a troopship bound for Bombay.

'Are you certain you're doing the right thing?' Belinda asked anxiously. 'You can change your mind, darling. It's not too late.'

'Let her alone, Belle,' Cade said gently. 'Cassy is a woman now. She knows her own heart and mind.'

'I do, Ma,' Cassy said with a watery smile. 'I'll write to you every day while I'm on board, and Mrs Masters will keep an eye on me.'

'It's just fortunate that the Colonel and his wife were at the christening.' Cade slipped his arm around Cassy's shoulders. 'When you told me that it was over between you and Oliver, I couldn't help being glad. He's a fine fellow and I like him well enough, but I've always thought that he wasn't for you, my love. Bailey is a good man, and I trust him to look after my girl.'

'But you'll be leading a very different life, Cassy.' Belinda hugged the baby closer to her as if she were afraid that someone might separate her once again from a beloved child. 'It's not easy being a soldier's wife.'

'You were a soldier's daughter, Ma. I am too, even though I wasn't brought up in the army. I want to share my life with Bailey, and I don't care whether we're living in Duke Street or Deolali. Anyway, I have plans for our future together.'

'I'm sure you have,' Cade said, smiling. 'Would it have anything to do with the children's home that you told me about on our long train journeys across India?'

She nodded emphatically. 'It's what Bailey and I always wanted, Pa. As soon as he's able to leave the army, I'm going to look for suitable premises in the East End. We'll set up a home for unwanted babies and infants where they'll be brought up with love and grow up to be decent citizens, able to earn their own living.'

Taking her in his arms, Cade gave her a hug. 'I'll do everything I can to help financially. I'm proud of you, Cassy.'

'And I am too,' Belinda said hastily. 'But are you certain that Bailey knows you're coming, my love? It's all been arranged with such haste.'

'Colonel Masters has everything in hand, darling.' Cade took George from her, cradling the baby in his arms. 'Give our daughter a kiss and wish her bon voyage. I can see Mrs Masters waving to Cassy from the deck. We'll be waiting to welcome you and your husband when you return, my darling daughter.'

'Thank you, Pa,' Cassy whispered. 'I love you, you know that.'

Wiping the tears from her eyes, Belinda kissed Cassy on both cheeks. 'Goodbye, my dearest. Come home safely, and soon.'

'Be happy for me, Ma.' Choking back tears, Cassy picked up her small valise and made her way to the gangplank. She hesitated, turning to wave to her parents and her baby brother, before taking the first steps that would lead her back to India and the man she loved with every fibre of her being.

Clutched in her hand was the telegram from Bailey. His answer was short and sweet. *Come to me, my love.*

NEATH PORT TALBOT LIBRARY AND INFORMATION SERVICES							
1		25		49		73	
2		26		50		74	
3		27		51		75	
4		28		52		76	
5		29		53		77	
6		30		54		78	
7		31		55		79	
8		32		56		80	
9		33		57		81	
10		34		58		82	
11		35		59		83	
12		36		60		84	
13		37		61		85	
14		38		62		86	
15		39		63		87	
16		40		64		88	
17		41		65		89	
18		42		66		90	
19		43		67		91	
20		44		68		92	
21		45		69		COMMUNITY SERVICES	
22		46		70			
23		47		71		NPT/111	
24		48		72			

Ay. (147)

Neath Port Talbot
Libraries
Llyfrgelloedd
Castell-Nedd
Port Talbot

Books should be returned or renewed by the last date stamped above.

Dylid dychwelyd llyfrau neu eu hadnewyddu erbyn y dyddiad olaf a nodir uchod